Extraordinary Praise for Lori Rader-Day

"Lori Rader-Day's *The Death of Us* is a deftly crafted, winding road of family secrets, unsolved disappearance, murder, betrayal, and complicated lives caught in the crosshairs of suspicion and lies. Masterful. Riveting. What a ride!"

—Tracy Clark, author of the
Cass Raines and Detective Harriet Foster series,
and winner of the 2020 and 2022
Sue Grafton Memorial Award

"One of crime fiction's strongest and most compelling voices."

—Alex Segura, acclaimed author of *Blackout*

"Rader-Day creates deeply believable, empathetic characters and puts the power in the hands of women."

—*Publishers Weekly*

"A master of the sleepless night."

—*Kirkus Reviews*

THE
DEATH
OF US

ALSO BY LORI RADER-DAY

Death at Greenway

The Lucky One

Under a Dark Sky

The Day I Died

Little Pretty Things

The Black Hour

THE
DEATH
OF US

A NOVEL

LORI RADER-DAY

wm

WILLIAM MORROW
An Imprint of HarperCollinsPublishers

This is a work of fiction. Names, characters, places, and incidents are products of the author's imagination or are used fictitiously and are not to be construed as real. Any resemblance to actual events, locales, organizations, or persons, living or dead, is entirely coincidental.

THE DEATH OF US. Copyright © 2023 by Lori Rader-Day. All rights reserved. Printed in the United States of America. No part of this book may be used or reproduced in any manner whatsoever without written permission except in the case of brief quotations embodied in critical articles and reviews. For information, address HarperCollins Publishers, 195 Broadway, New York, NY 10007.

HarperCollins books may be purchased for educational, business, or sales promotional use. For information, please email the Special Markets Department at SPsales@harpercollins.com.

FIRST EDITION

Designed by Diahann Sturge

Library of Congress Cataloging-in-Publication Data

Names: Rader-Day, Lori, 1973- author.
Title: The death of us : a novel / by Lori Rader-Day.
Description: First edition. | New York : William Morrow, an imprint of HarperCollins Publishers, [2023] | Summary: "From the award-winning author of Death at Greenway and The Lucky One comes a chilling suspense novel in which the discovery of a young mother's car submerged for fifteen years reveals betrayals and family secrets that will tear a small town apart"— Provided by publisher.
Identifiers: LCCN 2023012557 (print) | LCCN 2023012558 (ebook) | ISBN 9780063293335 (trade paperback) | ISBN 9780063293373 (hardcover) | ISBN 9780063293342 (ebook)
Subjects: LCSH: Family secrets—Fiction. | LCGFT: Thrillers (Fiction) | Novels.
Classification: LCC PS3618.A3475 D436 2023 (print) | LCC PS3618.A3475 (ebook) | DDC 813/.6—dc23/eng/20230316
LC record available at https://lccn.loc.gov/2023012557
LC ebook record available at https://lccn.loc.gov/2023012558

ISBN 978-0-06-329333-5 (paperback)
ISBN 978-0-06-329337-3 (library edition)

23 24 25 26 27 LBC 5 4 3 2 1

To Ann Cleeves

HERE'S THE THING NOT EVERYONE UNDERSTANDS ABOUT crime in a small town: When it goes down big for the first time in a generation—when some farmer gets out his buck-hunting rifle, say, and turns it on his wife—everybody's asking the same questions: How could it happen? Here, in this quiet town? Their worldview just got yanked to a new angle. They're shocked and outraged, but more than that, they're scared. They didn't see it coming. They couldn't have guessed.

That free-floating unease is good for gossips and business at the diner in town, with everyone stretching out their coffee breaks to chatter and theorize, but it's not good for anyone's sleep.

Not mine. They're down my throat before the blood is dry looking for someone to blame. If they can assign the act to an out-of-towner, a vagrant, even someone from town they never quite took to, the unthinkable can be filed away in its proper drawer. Forgotten.

Then they can get on with things. Bring in the casseroles, send the flowers. Put on a clean shirt and do a pass by the coffin. They can frown their most solemn and serious and think how hot the church is.

We know how to play tragedy.

But uncertainty is another thing. If we don't know who to blame, who to hate and fear, whose company not to keep anymore, that pulls at the threads in the fabric of the community. Pulls strands from the tablecloths under our dinner plates, from our pillowcases, right under our heads.

Now we're all looking askance at people we thought we knew. If I can't one hundred percent believe it wasn't you, what's that say about our supposed friendship? And if we can't trust our neighbors, we don't seek them out, invite them over, keep up with their news, help them out of a jam.

What happens next is an erosion: of fellow feeling, of kindness and attention, and then, finally, of order. That's when someone spots the crack in what's allowed, what a man can get away with.

He can get away with a lot.

He sees his opportunity, grabs what he wants. Grabs all he can take.

Sure. A man just like me.

CHAPTER ONE

Lissette Kehoe's phone gave a loud space-ray zap of a noise, the sound she'd assigned to texts from her son. Her hand shot out to quiet it.

Through the open door of the office at her shoulder, her boss's chair squeaked. Liss quickly closed the window on her computer screen.

"Is that the kid already?" Vera Chan called out from her desk.

Already? When it was nearly six anyway, and almost everyone else in the building—certainly all the support staff in the school's main office—had gone home at the final bell?

Vera was her friend by now, but someone Liss had to read to forecast the kind of day she might have. The weather, as she had come to think of it.

And just as with storm clouds, she couldn't take what came personally. They'd been slammed with student crisis after student crisis since the semester began. Liss only had to schedule them. Vera and Spence, the counselors, did the delicate work of defusing.

But now that the actual weather was turning, days shortening, moods turning sour, they'd hit the skids. Homecoming this week, with all its forced hoopla and dashed expectations, and then midterm exams would claim their victims. The juniors, or their parents, would soon realize the future needed to be planned for, and the seniors applying early decision to their top colleges would haunt the office for reassurances. The next school break hovered out on the horizon like a mirage.

It all made for good reading in the notes Vera and Spence kept in the student database. Of course, Liss wasn't supposed to be reading those notes. But how could she prioritize the students appropriately if she didn't know what they were dealing with?

Instead of snooping in the databases, she should have been getting ahead on her own work. Catching up, really. But she couldn't very well make career fair calls after business hours.

Even as busy as things were, though, she still wouldn't be at her desk this late if not for Callan's football practice. She wasn't Vera. She had a life.

"Last whistle from Coach ten minutes early?" Liss said. "Unheard of."

She reached for her phone. **Mom**, the text said, **don't freak out**

When had that ever worked, on any mom, ever? Practice would run late or he'd forgotten something at his dad's apartment or he needed to build a model of a DNA double helix for biology class, due tomorrow. When Callan was younger, she'd had a total lock on his schedule and assignments. Now he was fifteen. At this age, there was far less need for emergency poster board, but her son was a different kind of challenge. She had to read the weather forecast at home, too.

Mom, Callan had taken the time to type.

Her son's messages to her were usually bare minimum, a handful of characters and shapes she had to parse like messages from behind enemy lines, with the detail she needed buried below code and evasion.

Are you OK? she typed. The phone made a little whoosh as the message went on its way.

Where are you? she typed.

The dots that showed Callan was working on a response danced and paused, danced and paused.

Here came the excuse, the apology instead of having asked for permission, the scurry of excuses. Guess who he'd learned that from?

The dots stopped.

Vera appeared at her doorway. "Everything OK, I hope?"

"He's texting me, so he has most if not all of his fingers," Liss said. "But he says, and I quote, don't freak out."

"Great opening gambit," Vera said. "Sure to inspire confidence."

A new text popped up.

> Tanner had a wreck

"Oh no," Liss murmured. "Tanner Larkin had an accident," she said to Vera.

"Is he OK? That fancy car . . ." Vera said. They couldn't say anything aloud about a student's parents, but a look passed between them.

"This is exactly why Callan's not allowed to ride with just anybody," Liss said.

"Our anyone at all," Vera said.

"His *dad*," Liss said.

"You don't let Callan ride with anyone else because you're a control freak," Vera said. "No offense."

"None taken."

"But," Vera said, "why would *you* freak out about *Tanner* having an accident?"

Because—

"Oh, God." Liss thumbed Callan's image—video call, she had to see his face—"No, no, pick up, pick up." A thousand eventualities rushed through her mind, a thousand things she couldn't live with.

Callan appeared on her screen. He looked annoyed. "I said *not* to—"

"Are you hurt?" Liss said.

"No!" Annoyed was better than injured.

Vera shook her head and went back to her office.

"Is anyone hurt?" Liss said.

A foreign expression rippled across Callan's features. Then it was gone again, and he was so like Link that her breath caught.

Liss always felt a wave of petty relief when Callan reminded her of Link, leaving less room for Ashley Hay to sneak in. Ashley, the incubator who'd birthed and then deserted Callan, who had given up any right to appear on Callan's face or in their lives.

Ashley's *rightful* place was in a dusty frame on a shelf in Callan's room, half hidden behind Star Wars figures and a model car he'd built with his Papa Key, Link's dad, when he was eight. Consigned to the relics.

But sometimes, especially since Link had moved out in the spring, Liss caught the ghost of Ashley, still in their lives. When Liss didn't feel she had a handle on who Callan was, who he might turn out to be. When he had some peevish look to him she didn't recognize, some chippy attitude she couldn't believe he'd come to so quickly. Liss would think, icily, before she could stop herself: *There* she is.

Liss had even caught herself talking to Ashley in her head or under her breath, as though they'd argued and, in the moment, she hadn't been quick enough with the right comeback. Oh, yeah, Ashley? Some moment with Callan gone wrong: How would *you* have handled it, then, Ashley?

Ashley's absence always seemed to have the last word.

"Is anyone *hurt*?" Liss said again.

"I was trying—" Callan said.

"Why were you in Tanner's car? You *know* how I feel about that."

There'd been an accident a few years ago, a car crammed with students from Parkins West, heading into town after dismissal. Every school had a story like it, probably. Liss had attended each funeral, surrounded by young people, teachers, bereft families. Four broken mothers, four holes in the ground. She still woke from nightmares, the image of one of those open graves rushing away from her.

Liss didn't need Vera's fancy college degrees to work out the psychology there, the dreams, the driving. Some part of Liss worried, more than most mothers had to, that she could reach for Callan and he would be gone.

"Tell me you were wearing your seat belt, at least?" Liss said.

Callan huffed impatiently. "Mom, I'm trying to tell you something. There's a car. It must have taken the curve too fast, too. Just like you say—"

"Wait, wait," she said. "*Our* curve?"

Callan's image fumbled away, the sound scratchy as he held the phone to his jacket. He was speaking to someone else.

"Callan? *Callan*."

Vera was in her door again. "Is he all right?"

Liss hadn't found the edges of this story. A car, an accident, no one hurt—oh, God thank you he wasn't hurt—but another car was involved now, and near their house, more than eight miles away from the school when he should have been at practice.

The call with Callan cut out.

"I don't know what's happening," Liss said as she reached for her purse and hit redial. "I need to go. I'll text you."

She didn't wait to see what Vera would say. Liss's footsteps were loud in the empty hall. Callan's phone rang and rang as she passed under the faded red homecoming banner and through the front doors. Outside, it was overcast, already dusk. The wind sliced at her blouse. She'd forgotten her coat, hadn't locked down her computer. She'd have to listen to another lecture from Vera about protecting student privacy.

At the far edge of the parking lot, a pack of cross-country runners passed in and out of her vision.

Callan answered at last, exasperation on his face clear but the audio between them crackling. "Sorry—"

"Stand out of the wind so I can hear you," Liss said. "And start from the beginning. Why aren't you at practice?"

"Brennan got *crunched* on a tackle," Callan said. Someone was laughing on his end, voices in the background. Callan glanced away. "Coach said he had to go to the hospital for X-rays. Practice got canceled."

"And how did you end up out at the curve exactly?" she said.

"I said already," Callan said. On her screen, he hesitated, tilted his head. "He missed the curve."

"I meant—"

One of the boys behind Callan spoke up. "I think he found it, you mean!"

"Who's with you? Tanner and who else?"

"Garza and Ward," he said.

The last name thing, every year the posturing from the field and locker room radiated out to hallways and classrooms.

"I don't understand why you're on our road, though," she said. But she did, to a point. An emergency for the Brennans had wedged open Callan's schedule and given him a window of freedom. An empty house and an unguarded pantry.

He ignored that entirely. "We *missed* the curve and hit the mound and when we got to the top—"

"Callan." Liss gripped her steering wheel. Here was the part she wasn't supposed to freak out about. "Are you kidding me?"

"I know, I know, but I *wasn't* alone."

A Tanner-sized loophole.

The mound was what they called the highest point at the rim of the pond on their property. It wasn't stable. Or it might not be, she couldn't be sure. The low hills between their place and the rise to Link's parents' hilltop house had long ago been hollowed out by a limestone mine, leaving a deep scar to fill with groundwater and rain and a scattering of ten-ton boulders along the edge, like dice thrown by the gods.

Near their house, the road used by trucks to haul rock out of the pit created a patch of shallow water where cattails grew and blue herons waited for fish that would not come. Deer came to drink. But the quarry was a rumored fifty feet to the bed, the drop to the unappealing black-green water sheer, swift. Anyone risking a swim could strike jutting rock on the dive down and, if they survived that, had a tricky climb back to safe ground.

They didn't get too many trespassers or daredevils. Most people in the county would go a long way to avoid a run-in with Link's dad, the former town marshal.

Keeping Callan away from the quarry was another story. A life-long project. "We're going to talk about this," Liss said.

"All right," he said miserably. "But if we hadn't climbed up there, we wouldn't have seen the car."

She'd lost track of the other car. "Was the accident Tanner's fault?" she said.

"No." Of this he sounded very sure. "Mom, the other car is in the *water*."

A pair of headlights ahead were too bright. Liss glanced away, toward the phone screen and Callan, his hair, too long, blowing across his eyes. "Do you mean in the *quarry*? The pond? Did you call nine-one-one?"

"Yeah," he said. "But I think the other car's been there for a while."

Liss concentrated on her knuckles to keep from flying into pieces.

"You can *barely* see it," he said. "Garza says there's no way—"

"What color is it?" Liss said. "Can you see the color of the car?"

"Uh, not really. White, maybe?"

It couldn't be. She reached for the phone and shut off the camera.

"Mom? Are you still there?"

Her stomach hurt, suddenly and violently. She pulled over, untangled herself from her seat belt, and scrambled out of the car to retch into the grass. Gravel cut into her knees.

"Mom?" Callan's voice was otherworldly, wafting from the open door onto the wind.

What had she done?

Liss stood with shaking legs, wiped her mouth. She had come to a stop a few miles from home, in front of the long drive up to a neighbor's place. A light went on in the house, and then the porch. It was too far to call out, to say everything was fine.

Everything was not fine.

"Mom?"

Liss turned back to the car and sank into the driver's seat. "I'm here." Her voice was hoarse, her throat sore. She should be able to think of something to say. What would she say to a student waiting in tears to see Vera or Spence, bringing them one of the insurmountable problems of youth?

All she could think was: Ashley Hay. *There* she is.

CHAPTER TWO

After Liss hung up with Callan, she drove on, the silence now hollow and profound.

The first time she'd laid eyes on Ashley Hay, they were babies themselves, not quite Callan's age. She showed up a new girl mid-year, dressed strangely, like she'd borrowed clothes from her grandpa's closet. Thrift, she would call it when the other kids tried to take her down for it, but Liss caught a whiff of the Goodwill bin, the charity shop.

Ashley had clocked her, too.

They might have been friends. But Liss didn't have the social capital to spare. She was the sort of girl who got by on so-so grades and so-so looks. Who survived in a more literal way on free school lunch and busybody church ladies. She relied on her wits and a few friends, whose mothers sometimes clucked their tongues but sent her home with extra. Her father gone, her mother home only between boyfriends, Liss was a girl whose life seemed determined by other people, their absences, their collapses.

Look, she'd wanted to say to Ashley, I'm barely hanging on as it is.

She didn't have to say a word. They skirted each other, like the ends of two magnets, repelling one another. Liss knew now they would have shown up in the same breath at meetings between school nurses and counselors, on the same lists considered by ladies' societies at Christmas.

Later, Liss didn't have to try so hard to avoid Ashley; the path was well worn, and Liss's social capital had risen sky high. Link Kehoe had looked her way.

In fact, she and Ashley had managed to stay clear of each other until their lives collided, spectacularly.

And now—

Liss drove on, scrounging in her purse for a tissue and a breath mint. Long before the turn onto the quarry road, she could see the curve choked with vehicles. Town patrol cars, a fire engine. But no ambulance. No lights whirling. No emergencies. She'd arrived at the punctuation, as the story ended. At a funeral, and their quarry a yawning grave.

Liss pulled to the side of the road at the edge of the snarl and hurried along on foot, her eyes scraping the scene for Callan.

"Oh, God."

Tanner's car sat against the base of the mound, only a few yards from the drop into the quarry.

Stable or not, the mound had caught them. Saved them.

Liss could imagine the fall anyway, the car careening over the edge, the boys dropped into the water and fighting out of seat belts, to open doors against impossible water pressure as the car sank to the quarry floor.

But there the boys were, milling among the boulders and kicking at the dirt, their oversized kit bags at their feet. One of the boys, Jamie, had climbed atop a stone and sat cross-legged, a small Buddha, with his chin tucked into the neck of his dark jacket against the wind. Callan looked up and came out to meet her.

Her legs shook.

"I'm sorry," he was saying as the distance closed between them. His jogger pants were scratched at the knees and smeared with mud.

She only wanted to get her hands on him. She grasped him into her and made an inventory. He was fine, arms and legs, neck intact. "You're sure you're OK?"

"You think it's her," he said.

She held him tighter.

Over Callan's shoulder, a familiar figure leaned into the open door of Tanner's car. Mercer Alarie, in his town marshal uniform, had removed his hat and was studying something inside the car. As she watched, he folded his long legs into the sportscar's driver's seat with some difficulty and sat among the controls.

Was she relieved or—some other feeling, to know he was here?

"It can't be her, can it?" Callan said. "How can it be?"

"I don't know," Liss said.

Traffic roared along the state road two miles in the distance, but theirs was a quiet patch of country, broken only by the occasional car racing in too fast.

Was that the story? An accident, and everything since just noise? Just pointless and impotent rage directed wherever it could find purchase?

She could barely keep still.

"Jeez, Mom." Callan extracted himself from her. "Are you cold?"

"A little."

"I'm sorry," he mumbled. "About—everything."

"You're safe," she said. "That's all I care about."

"He wants to talk to you," Callan said.

He would be Mercer. Callan had not known what to call him, had tried never to reference him directly at all.

Liss didn't look over. "Why don't you go up to the house? Take your friends, open up some snacks."

The other boys watched them, glum expressions. They'd gone out for a joy ride, kids, and now they were witnesses to something terrible. "I don't think," Callan said. "If it's—if it's—"

"Let's not assume until we know, OK?"

"Gram always said she must have got away but I don't think she did," Callan said.

Got away. Dammit, Patty.

She reached for Callan's shoulder and turned him toward the road and the fields beyond so that anything she said would drift away. Voices carried out here. She also wanted to hold him close for another minute. As long as he would let her. "People will talk," she said finally. "When they don't know anything."

"We should call Dad," Callan said. He tugged away from her. "Shouldn't we? She was his . . . his, um."

Maybe she had protected him too well. "He'll be upset," she said. "But you understand, don't you? Who she is? To you?"

He shuffled a shoe against the grass. "I don't want to call her . . . you know. That."

Liss brushed the hair from his eyes. Link's eyes, thank God. "It might not have anything to do with her, OK?"

"It might, though." He turned back toward his friends and she followed.

It might. It would. Ashley Hay, getting the last word.

CHAPTER THREE

Callan slipped back to his friends. Liss veered toward where Mercer now stood at the quarry's edge. He peered out over the expanse, his dispatch radio to his mouth and a lit-up phone in his palm. His dark hair was clipped a little more closely than the last time she'd seen him, a little too short. He had a sunburn across his nose and forehead, and she couldn't help wondering if he'd had a fun weekend, who might have been with him.

When his radio conversation was over, he held it in his hand, weighing it against the phone. To keep from looking at her, she thought, like one of the kids at school thumbing the toggle on their backpack.

"Lissette," he said, when the silence had stretched between them too long.

Over at the foot of the hill, Callan was keeping watch on her and Mercer with feigned casualness, his hands shoved into his front pockets.

"Do the boys need to stay?" she said.

"Let me get one of my guys to take some info and we can get them away from here," Mercer said. "They've been on their phones so I expect the other parents will be coming out. If they can get through to your house."

"They'll find a way through," she murmured.

"I'll need to talk to you about this," he said. "And Link. It was just the two of you living here then?"

Liss went still. "It's her? You know it's her?"

Mercer looked at her, finally. He had blue eyes, a shade people noticed from a distance and were made uncomfortable by up close. That's how it had gone for her, anyway.

"I won't know for a while," he said. "We'll need confirmation on the vehicle, first step. The license plate isn't readable. I'm hoping for a vehicle ID once the divers get here."

Divers. "Your new guy won't go down for the VIN?" she said. "Pull the car up himself, chain between his teeth?"

The corner of Mercer's lips twitched. "He would if I let him," he said, and turned. As if on cue, the newest of his recruits leapt forward to be of service. "Bowman," Mercer said. "Get the kids' names, parents' phone numbers, all that. I don't want them out here when the hook arrives."

The deputy hurried off. Liss went to follow, but Mercer reached for her, then dropped back. "Just the basics for the paperwork, OK? We don't think kids who were barely born had anything to do with Ashley Hay skidding into your quarry. If it's her."

"Is that what you think happened?"

"What do *you* think happened?" he said.

Ashley had shown up at their door that night, her cheap clothes clinging over baby fat, her canvas shoes squishing as she shifted Callan's carrier from one hand to the other. Well, she'd said, in that sneer she always seemed to have for Liss. Is *Daddy* home? she'd said, like it was some joke.

Liss had had years to work up theories but here was evidence to refute most of them. All but the most damaging.

"I don't know," she said.

"It was dark when she stopped by, wasn't it?" he said. "And raining?"

Liss shivered, nodded. If Ashley had never made it off this road—

She had a lot to answer for.

"OK." Mercer's eyes drifted back to the water. "OK."

Liss's eyes felt gritty. "Cars are always taking the curve at speed," she said. She sounded defensive. "Just like Tanner did."

"Is it possible, though?" Mercer said. "That this car has been here all these years and you've never noticed?"

"It's not like you haven't spent some nights up at this house, yourself," Liss said before she could think better of it.

One of the volunteer firefighters standing nearby in his cartoonish bucket pants coughed to cover a snort of laughter.

Mercer shot him a look and pulled her away. "Look, I'm not making judgments here. I'm just . . . considering scenarios that explain this situation." He had a crescent crease between his eyes, a scar that deepened with worry. Liss remembered lying next to him and reaching to press at it. So *serious*, she'd say, to make him smile.

"Is it possible," Mercer said, "that no one ever looked down at the right angle, from the right outlook? He's got a good eye, your kid. I can barely make the car out myself."

"His grandpa passed down a love of cars," Liss said.

"Sure, you cut teeth on the steering wheel of a Chevy Bel-Air . . ." Mercer shifted uncomfortably. "Look, it could be unrelated. Someone dropped this car in there a long time ago, stolen car, insurance fraud. Getting rid of a junker, to avoid paying Pete Norville to tow it to the scrap yard. Maybe it predates the water. Maybe it was at the bottom of the quarry when it closed and the water filled in around it."

"But you don't think that," Liss said.

"A vehicle left behind by the quarry would be rusted to Swiss cheese by now," he said. "This one still has some structural integrity left to it. But that means we can get it out of there, see what's what."

Her stomach gave a lurch. She risked a glance toward the black water.

"How long have you lived in the house?" he said.

"Fifteen years," she said. "And Key and Patty were here probably twenty before that." She turned her shoulder by instinct, as though to include her in-laws' house in the conversation. From this angle, the house at the top of the hill was only a glow through the trees. Patty would be wondering about the commotion on the road.

"So I'll need to talk to them, too," Mercer said.

"He doesn't speak anymore," Liss said.

The crease in Mercer's brow deepened further. "Hadn't realized he was that far along. I'm sorry."

"Well," she said. "His last word was—I don't want to say it. And he was referring to me."

They shared an awkward glance.

"What's the diagnosis?" he said.

"They can't decide. Something degenerative. And terminal."

"How's Link doing with that?"

"You don't need to pretend to care how Link's doing," she said, more sharply than she meant to. He would have heard about Key. Surely he had the imagination to consider how Link felt, losing his dad by degrees.

"OK," Mercer said. "OK."

She hadn't meant to lose her patience. They should be able to be friends. If she could stay close to *Link*—

But that was the heart of it. The last time she'd talked to Mercer was when she'd broken things off. If there was even a chance of keeping her family together, of reconciling with Link, she had to keep the door open.

"Plenty of doors already open in that relationship," Mercer had said, thinking she could take the joke. Thinking it wouldn't sting. He thought she was too quick to forgive Link. But if she hadn't forgiven Link, if she hadn't been able to accept his apologies and promises, where would she be?

It was a question she'd had a few chances to consider.

She hugged herself and rubbed her arms, wishing again for that coat she'd left at the school. "Sorry. I'm just . . . I saw Tanner's car so close to the edge, and— This could have been really bad."

It still might be.

He looked at her helplessly. "When Curtis has the kids sorted, you can take them up to the house."

"Can they go home?"

"I guess I should hear what they want to tell me before they go put it on TikTok or some shit."

She'd have to text the parents, as she would expect them to text her, but they'd already be on their way. All but the Wards. She didn't expect the Wards. But first she would need to call Link.

"You OK?" Mercer said.

She'd let her eyes close. She opened them now to find Mercer had taken a step forward. He was blocking the wind for her.

"I'm sorry, Liss, if this works out to be her," he said. "But at least it will be closure, right?"

"Closure," she said. "Maybe you and your guys will get a taste for it."

He stepped back and the wind tore at her. Her eyes stung.

"Liss," Mercer said. "I know you're grieving on behalf of a lot of people right now . . ."

On behalf of *other* people, as though she had nothing to lose.

"Boys," she called. "Come up and get warm." She turned to the house, averting her eyes from the quarry. It had a strange new gravity to it, as though the black water itself watched her, had been watching her all along.

CHAPTER FOUR

Up at the house, Liss texted all the mothers reassurances and directions to avoid the blocked road. She ordered enough pizza for everyone who might show up, then went to her bedroom.

Link picked up on the first ring, as he always did. "What's up?"

"I don't know how to tell you," she said.

"Uh-oh. What did he do this time?"

"He spotted a car in the pond," Liss said. "Link, they think it could be Ashley's."

Liss felt more than heard his breath sucked in. "In the pond?" Link said. "Our pond? But . . ."

He'd be thinking of the times he'd been swimming there, the touch of its slick water. "I'm on my way," he said.

Liss hung up and went to her bedroom window. Mercer and some of his men were kicking the tires out at Tanner's car.

What was it about men and cars?

The landline was ringing. Liss picked it up and listened to a few breathless words of a reporter's pitch before hanging up.

Back at the front of the house, the boys sat at the kitchen table with a pile of snack-sized bags of chips, the GimmeGimme brand Link brought home from work by the gross. Tanner's long legs stretched out in leisure.

Liss walked the long way around the table, casting a critical eye over her house before the other mothers arrived and did the same.

There were swatches of yellow on a wall where she'd planned to make the kitchen her own but had never decided on the perfect shade. Across the room, Link still smiled from the family portrait of the three of them, all in blue denim against the white doors of their barn. The frames were all militantly arranged at the same angle upon the shelf, but she saw only the deficiencies, only what the other women would notice. The wall unpainted, the naked hope of Link still on the shelf.

Callan's hair, too long. The boys were uncharacteristically quiet. Shaken, she supposed. She looked among them, from shaggy-haired boy to shaggy-haired boy: Tanner, handsome and glowering. He'd be worried about his car. Mateo, bulky and cherub-cheeked, happily pouring chip crumbs into his mouth. Jamie, narrow-shouldered and twitchy as a mouse's whiskers. And Callan, her lovely boy.

Ashley's lovely boy.

The landline rang again. "Don't answer that," Liss said. "Let it ring."

The doorbell rang, too soon to be Link or the pizza.

"Where is he?" Tanner's mother stood on the deck, her normally smooth Botoxed forehead creased. Kitty Larkin left a cloud of expensive scents behind as she hurried past Liss. "I don't understand what's happening," she said. "Is everyone all right? No one's hurt, right?" She plucked at Tanner, fussed with the hair in his eyes. "Liss? Shouldn't we answer the phone?"

"Hello, Mrs. Larkin," Callan said dutifully.

Liss smiled in his direction. "Let's wait until everyone's here," she said, before any of the boys could jump in. "Including the marshal. Shouldn't be too long. Glass of wine, Kitty?"

Kitty joined her in the kitchen. The proportions of her clothes were high cut and tight, too young for her. All at top expense, of course.

"Should I be calling someone?" Kitty had her phone in hand.

"Like who?" Liss said. Who wasn't already here or on their way? The landline rang again. Liss picked up the handset from the cradle, hung it back up.

Kitty frowned. "I just want to make sure there's someone on Tanner's side here," she said. "Marshal Alarie is obviously already on Callan's."

"We're all on the same side," Liss said. She put a glass of wine on the counter in front of Kitty. "And *you're* here."

"Ennis is coming," Kitty said.

"Good, see?" Liss recognized the voice she sometimes used with students. Meant to be encouraging and helpful but hearing it now, she wasn't sure how students had been taking it all these years. It was cloying.

Liss looked longingly at the bottle of wine, but someone would have to drive Jamie home.

The doorbell rang again. She gladly went to see who it was.

The Garzas stood on the deck. "Is Mateo OK?" Connie said. "No one's hurt? That car is so *close* to the edge!"

"Come in, come in."

Connie Garza rushed in to see for herself. Andrés Garza stepped inside and turned to Liss. "It's the one missing all these years?" he said.

"We don't know yet," she said, already weary of the question. And what did it matter to the Garzas, who, once Mercer had asked a couple of questions of their son, could step away with murmured condolences? Or to the Larkins, other than a scratch to Tanner's car?

Only her family could be destroyed.

Liss poured more wine, watching from the kitchen as the Garzas pulled Mateo in for embraces and a quiet word. Kitty went to stand near Tanner.

Jamie reached for a bag of chips.

"Doesn't your dad *make* those chips, Ward?" Tanner said. Kitty squeezed his shoulder.

"He doesn't *make* them," Callan said.

"Does he get orange snot?" Mateo said. "When he blows his nose?"

"Mateo," Connie said.

"That's what I heard," Mateo said.

"He *sells* them," Liss said. "In the same department as Callan's dad."

Callan's ears had gone red. He and Tanner hadn't touched the chips. Maybe she shouldn't have bothered with the pizza, the boys training so hard for the football season and—

She'd set the wrong tone. A party in place of a vigil.

And what was keeping Link? He needed to be here.

Home, she thought. Though it hadn't been true in months.

The phone started ringing again. Liss felt all eyes upon her as she approached the phone, ended the call, and unplugged the cord. Why did they even keep the landline when it was nothing but robocalls and scams?

The back door opened. Liss rushed to meet Link but instead it was his mother.

"What the devil is going on?" Patty cried. "I could barely get down my driveway. Police cars up and down the road, and not just the one that's usually here."

"Callan's *fine*," Liss said. "The boys had a small accident, that's all. Everyone's fine."

"Then why is there a van in the yard that says 'recovery team' on it? Recovery of what?"

Patty wouldn't have needed to get out of her driveway if she had just stayed home. Now she would never leave, not without Link to jolly her out the door. "Callan and his friends spotted something in the quarry pond," Liss said in a low voice. "Something that shouldn't be there. The police are here to figure things out."

Patty turned her head toward the pond, as though she could see through walls. "What's not supposed to be there? Recovery of what?"

"A car, at least," Liss said. "Would you like a glass of wine?"

"And at *most*?"

Why couldn't Patty be the one losing her sharp edges, instead of her husband? Her mother-in-law could have used some filing down. "At most," Liss said, "they might need to recover a body."

Patty's eyebrow, a thin pencil line, lifted. "You can't mean what I think you mean."

She'd got there faster than Liss had, at least. Liss reached for Patty but the other woman slipped away and turned the corner into the kitchen. She paused in the doorway to survey the crowd that had gathered. "Good*night*," she said. "Was it the team bus that crashed?"

"Hi, Gram," Callan said, in that same hopeful way he always used with his grandmother.

But Patty had seen Kitty Larkin across the room and made her way there, instead. Cheek kisses, old friends.

Connie and Kitty had their boys tucked close to them, but Jamie was small on his own. Liss pulled out the chair next to him and directed Patty to it with a fresh chardonnay plunked down as bait.

"What are you doing with the kitchen, Lissette?" Patty said, glaring at the paint swatches on the wall. "I don't care for it."

The next person to the door would either be Link or the food or Mercer with questions, and Liss felt herself stretching toward that moment, out of the kitchen and out the door, down the road and out to the pond, in all directions at once, not knowing which to hope for.

"Garza," Patty said. "Is that Mexican?"

Liss reached for the wine bottle and then put it down. The delivery man, please God. Give them something for their *mouths*.

"It's Basque," Connie said.

"We're from Cincinnati," Andrés said flatly.

Liss excused herself.

At her bedroom window again, she pressed her face against the glass and wished she could give the house a quarter turn for a better view.

The land had once been a farm, parceled out, the heart of it leased for mining. When the quarry closed, Link's dad had snapped up the pieces. At some cost, he'd always added, telling the story. In his version of the tale, he was reconciling lands, a triumphant ruler, or stitching together a homestead, a pioneer. Key and Patty had raised Link in the old farmhouse below, then built their keep up on the hill. The new house was sharp and modern, befitting the hospital it had become. It had a proud glass face to greet visitors up their long, wooded drive but a cold shoulder turned to the hill above the quarry. The pond, somehow not a feature but a wound.

Out at the rock edge, Mercer stood looking out at the water as one of his men waved in a reversing tow truck. Abruptly, the truck came to a stop. Mercer turned his head to the road just as a figure rushed into view.

She knew it would be Link almost before she could register anyone was there.

He was carrying *flowers*.

"Fuck, Ashley," Liss said against the glass.

The doorbell rang again.

Liss hurried down the hall, putting her face right. She'd lost track of who else could be at the door. Pizza. She'd be sick if she smelled it, she honestly would.

But instead, Ennis Larkin was blowing into her kitchen. He was followed by another man, someone Liss didn't recognize.

"Lissette," Ennis said. "I'd like you to meet—"

The second man stretched out his hand to her. The Larkins' attorney. Their *lawyer*.

Jamie looked as though he might cry. The Garzas turned on her. Yes, in a way, it *was* her fault. All of it.

This would not be a *closure*, no matter what Mercer thought. For Callan, for them, it was the opposite. This was their world cracked wide open.

CHAPTER FIVE

Mercer Alarie stood at the quarry's edge, the wind rushing at his face. "Those boys almost had a hell of a swim," he said to no one in particular.

He leaned out as far as he would dare. A cold swim and a sheer climb to get out.

Could have been bad, Liss had said. Could have been a disaster.

He felt the tug of Liss's absence, toward the house.

She had a fireplace. Funny that he'd be thinking of the *fireplace*, but this gale was really starting to piss him off, now that the sun dipped below the trees on the far side of the quarry and the divers were taking all the time in the world getting suited up to even take a look and tell him there was a chance of a body down there. *Then* maybe they could get this show underway, winch the car out.

The fireplace called to him, though. They'd been together such a short season, a few weeks in June, but he'd already seen the future, that fireplace crackling, mugs of cocoa in their hands. Opening presents at Christmas there in front of it. That fireplace was something promised to him, something denied.

Mercer turned and caught a crack of light at Lissette's bedroom window, then a rush of movement coming in from the road.

"Whoa—"

The press, sniffing blood in the water. Mercer caught the guy by the shoulders and felt his breath on his face before he realized it was Link Kehoe.

"Is it her?" Kehoe said.

"You can't be here, Link," Mercer said.

"Is it *her*?"

Flowers in the guy's fist slapped against their legs.

God damn, Link Kehoe set him off.

Mercer hadn't needed to ask Liss how many years they'd lived in this house. He knew the whole story. Young buck Kehoe getting loose with his morals and his zipper just as he and Liss were on a trajectory, hitting a hole in one, so to speak, that resulted in Callan. Knew all about it, filed it away. Wondered why that hadn't been enough for Liss to end it, right there.

But Lissette Kehoe was not a woman to give up easily on what she wanted. She hadn't taken that free pass and moved on, no. She'd dug in for the long haul. Married this sperm donor, took on the kid—and gave up how many dreams of her own to do it?

Finally, finally, Link had messed up one too many times, which hadn't been all bad news for *him*. He was grateful Link Kehoe was a fuck-up. He'd left the door wide open for Mercer.

It was a door Liss had talked about when she'd ended it, a door still open between her and Link, a door to that perfect family she had in her head. A different door, then, than the one that had closed on Mercer's balls by July.

They said around town that Link Kehoe was a good guy, and his father was who he was, of course. Or had been. Mercer only wished he didn't have to care if he was or not.

Mercer propped Link up at the shoulders. The slice of light at Liss's window was gone. He looked back to Link and quieted his voice until he could have been talking to a stray dog. "You should get up to the house, Link," Mercer said. "Your kid's had a scare, and I bet Liss is looking out for you."

Here she came again, thank Christ, before he had to arrest the guy to get him out of his sight. Mercer watched Liss approach, watched a little too closely, he realized, when Deacon, his right hand, a good one for watching his back, cleared his throat. Yeah, OK.

Liss came right up and transferred the weight of Link to herself like something heavy that had slipped from her hands.

Mercer had to look away. "Give me another half hour," he said. "And I'll come up to the house."

"What choice do we have?" Liss said. She hadn't said it one way or the other, joking or bitter, but he watched her lead the guy away—her soon-to-be, *lingering*, maybe never ex-husband—with a tightness in his chest like she'd scolded him. Again. That quip about getting a taste for closing cases had cut pretty deep, coming from Liss. He got shit from everyone, from the town council on down. A few prehistoric cases had come back to haunt them, bad procedure, bad arrests, that sort of thing, none of *his* doing, but the crime rate was up for no reason he could discern. People had complaints for days.

But—not Liss.

Deak made another noise in his throat but Mercer kept watching until, finally, Liss glanced back. He felt it down to his bones.

OK. OK. He had to do everything right. No room for error, no wedge for them to use on him at the polls, to kneecap his new recruits. Nothing to smear him in the paper. Nothing to let Liss down. It was her place, after all. Her family, her closure.

"Deak," he said. "Get up to the house and take statements from the boys, yeah? Take Bowman."

The new guy lit up like he'd won the lottery, but Deacon stood his ground. "I thought you said the kids couldn't know anything?"

"Just get the timeline, school bell to when they called us," Mercer said. "See if, uh, Mrs. Kehoe will let you use the sunroom or—one of the other rooms, I mean, one family at a time. Deak, you take point. Bowman, you take notes. Good ones, now."

His radio had a lot of chatter for having most of his team here on the ground. He called out a ten-thirty to shut them up and then for Slocum, who was holding down the station, to call his phone. He was thinking of all the radio-heads listening in on their scanners, nothing better to do.

A stretch later Slocum's greasy voice was in his ear. "Chief," he called him.

"What do you have for me?" Mercer said.

"Well, now," Slocum said. He had a long drawl that meant even getting the simplest bits of information out of him was like stepping in chewing gum, and he wouldn't stop hailing Mercer by job titles he didn't have. Was *chief* problematic, too? Racist, probably. Disrespectful, definitely. "Bit of a chore digging that make and model out of the records, Chief," Slocum said.

Everything was hard to find in their records. Everything was a chore for Slocum.

When Mercer finally had what he needed, he hung up and took inventory. His men needed time to clear out the boys and their families and what *he* needed was divers in the water, and by extension for the wind to die down, for Mother Nature to do him a solid and not unload the rain she'd been holding back for months just as he, personally, needed it least. And he needed that Larkin kid's pricey ride off his crime scene before the kid's parents started kicking off.

Which reminded him of another parent. He had a call to make soon if this panned out. No, a visit. You delivered bad news in person. Or was it good news?

He couldn't tell the difference, sometimes.

One thing was certain, though. If this car was Ashley's, new light was sure to shine into dark, forgotten corners.

The problem was some of these cockroaches wouldn't hold up to a spotlight.

CHAPTER SIX

Liss walked Link toward the house, her arm looped in his. She was reminded of their wedding, striding away from the minister and a bower of grocery-store roses, daring anyone to stop them from being happy. This time, Link carried the flowers.

Pink carnations, like a fucking high school dance corsage.

At the house, Callan was relieving the pizza delivery guy of a stack of boxes.

"Hold up," she called out to the driver. She always tried to reward the delivery people for coming this far into the countryside. The last few years had been tough for everyone, but especially service workers. She was just glad not to be one.

The driver was familiar. His face called up memories of a rough patch: visits to the principal's office, calls to his mother. "Jimmy," Liss said, and he flinched. Maybe she should pretend not to recognize them.

"Dad?" Callan jostled the pizza boxes in his arms. "Is it . . ."

"No news yet," Liss said. "Take the pizzas in, OK? Get plates out and I'll be right behind you."

Callan hesitated. Deep in the house, the phone in her bedroom was ringing, ringing.

She went and held the door for Callan. "It'll be OK," she said. That was a promise she'd made to him all along. She would damn well keep it. "Don't answer the phone."

"They *know* it's her," Link said. He put the flowers down gently. "Why won't he say so?"

"They're being cautious." She should be glad the formalities were being observed, a kind of structure that held off the unthinkable. Her mind cycled there, between the impossibility of the car being Ashley's and the dark reality. It wasn't impossible, if only because it would be true. She rubbed at her arms. "Why would that car be in *our* pond?"

"How would I know?"

Liss sat next to him, balling herself up against him out of the wind, knowing his arm would slide around her. He smelled like the new soap he used, now that he shopped for himself, but also just like home, just as she knew he would. It seemed like yesterday and a hundred years ago, both, that they'd set up house here.

Since she had opened the door behind them now and looked out on a drowning woman.

A drowning girl, really.

They'd *all* been kids—

She caught herself. It was no excuse.

Out at the water's edge, the number of people loitering had grown. More police, a county car or two, state vehicles. A big van. The recovery team, she supposed. Would they ever start recovering something? And what would happen when they did?

She said, "You know what this looks like, right?"

"Her car in that pond, on our land, and her out of my hair?" Link said.

Liss sat up and his arm fell away.

"I'm not *stupid*," Link said.

"You've never had to worry about people thinking the worst of you," she said. "And they will, your ex-girlfriend found here—"

"You *know* she was no such thing."

What was the right word for Ashley? Not a girlfriend, not a *lover*, God. A one-night stand. A *complication*.

Liss had always been in love with Link Kehoe from the distance of their social circles and standings. And then during their senior year of high school, Liss had been working another evening shift at the local pizza pub when Link and his crew sat in her section. She'd missed the game, hadn't even realized there was one. Link was on a high from some big play he'd made.

He was a kid used to winning with a smile that made the other waitresses blush. She was on track to be an assistant manager by graduation. The next day at school, though, he came up to her locker, natural as anything. She thought he had a sixth sense for worship but didn't care what brought him to her, only that he was there. Her lack of expectations made her patient and thankful for scraps. They were together and not in those days, the way kids could be as they waited for their real lives to begin.

After some party Liss had missed, working, rumors started up. Later, when Ashley came forward, pregnant and making demands of Link, he'd come straight to Liss with apologies and promises. His plans for college were dashed. Suddenly real lives were beginning.

If she'd thought of stepping back and letting Link's tarnished life go on without her, Liss didn't remember deciding for or against it now. She'd developed a taste for hope, for belonging, and she hadn't wanted to let go.

Maybe Link had panicked. Maybe he hadn't really wanted to go away to college. He stepped up, offered to help Ashley raise the baby, got a job. When he looked up from his new, dire future, Liss was still there.

They got married just before Callan was born, a strange sort of shotgun wedding. The groom, beautiful. The bride's side of the church blessedly empty.

Link kept some of his promises. But he couldn't do anything about Ashley between them. And then came the rainy night when Ashley leaned on their doorbell until Liss answered, and then sneered at her as though she had any right to feel superior. As though she had leverage.

Sure, Liss remembered thinking, people with leverage always show up this late and in a storm.

But she did have leverage. She had Callan, and she barely let Link near him.

"Time is money, cupcake," Ashley had said as Liss stood in the door. Attitude firmly in place, not at all like someone who had come to ask a favor. But it wasn't Liss she'd been planning to ask. "Is *Daddy* home?" Ashley had said, as though Link had somehow already fallen short of the role.

And even if she had died that very night, as it seemed now she had, Ashley's presence between them had outlived the marriage. But don't call her a girlfriend, an ex.

"The mother of your child, then," Liss snapped.

"*You're* the mother of our child."

"You know what I'm trying to say," Liss said.

"So I drowned her in my backyard, then?" Link said. "And my dad the cop covered all my tracks, I suppose. Just to have our kid all to myself? Is that what they'll say?" He rubbed at his face with both hands, groaning.

Inside, the phone started ringing again. They would have said it already.

"I thought she left him," he said with wonder. "All this time I thought she ding-dong-ditched him on us and got the hell out of here, off to, to do whatever she wanted to do. Leaving him like he was some kind of—" His voice grew thick. "I wish I'd been home. Maybe things would be different."

Liss fidgeted the edges of her sleeves. That night and many afterward, she'd had the chance to think terrible things about Ashley Hay, but she wouldn't wish for an alternative universe in which Callan had not been placed in her arms. She still remembered the weight of him in his carrier, both lighter and heavier than she'd expected.

"Something went wrong," she said. "Either by accident or—you know that road, and it was raining. You couldn't have changed anything, even if you'd been here."

"I always wondered what if, if she took him with her when she left?" Link said. "But now—what *if* she hadn't left him?"

The gaping grave of her nightmares appeared to her, Link in his suit at her side. No. She couldn't let herself imagine it, couldn't court the possibility in case fate or bad luck were listening in. In case of portent.

Link in his funeral suit.

She sniffled to silence. Link had last worn that suit for his best friend's funeral.

"Link," she said.

Once she had thought of Robbie, a thousand memories rushed at her. Robbie, their third wheel. Robbie, helping Link build the baby's crib. He'd been buried in the same blue shirt he'd worn as Link's best man. What did it *mean*, all of it, if Ashley had driven from their house right into the water?

"What?" Link said.

If Ashley Hay had wedged between them all these years, Robbie Hubbard had perched on their shoulders.

"Robbie," she said. "If this is Ashley . . ."

Link's chin fell to his chest. The carnations lay between them.

"It might not be her," Liss said.

But it would be. Ashley, gone and not gone, had shoved herself to the front of their life together, all over again.

CHAPTER SEVEN

Liss noticed the shadows crossing the yard first.

Two of Mercer's men were walking in from the pond. Why had Mercer not come himself? She stood.

"Link," Deacon said by way of greeting. They'd been on the same ball team in school, the same Boy Scout troop, something.

"We'll need to talk to the boys," Curtis Bowman said. All business.

"Of course," Liss said.

"Individually," he said, not looking her way.

Like suspects, then.

Inside, the air was thick with garlic. Every pizza box had been opened and ravaged. The boys still slumped around the table, now with greasy plates in front of them. Tanner threw a crumpled paper napkin at Jamie, who didn't even duck.

Link crossed the room, straight to his mother.

To be petted and reassured, Liss thought, as the other parents shot forward at the sight of her.

Andrés started, "I think—"

"I think it's about time for some action," Ennis Larkin cut in.

"These officers have come to talk to the boys," Liss said. "I don't see why Tanner can't be first."

As soon as the Larkins and their lawyer were shut into the sunroom at the front of the house, the Garzas were on her again. Link was escorting his mother out the back door. Leaving Liss to be the grown-up, as always.

"What about Mateo?" Andrés said.

"I'm sure it won't take any time," Liss said. "Mateo can go next."

Connie pursed her lips.

"Why couldn't Mateo have gone *first*?" Andrés said, patting down the lapels of his jacket. "Is he somehow less important than this boy?"

"Of course not," Liss said. The boys left at the table were hanging on every word. "I suppose I was only taking advantage of your patience, Andrés. For which I apologize."

Connie leaned into her husband. "She's getting them out of here faster, Andrés," she said, quietly. "For all our sakes."

"I'd rather Larkin pay an extra hour for that lawyer," he said. But he settled into the sofa. "It would serve him right."

Liss went to the table, shooing the boys into the den to watch TV. She began consolidating uneaten pizza into one box, chewing a crust from Callan's plate. Her cell phone buzzed on the counter, but she ignored it.

Connie came over. "Did you notice? She won't take in a *single* calorie."

"Kitty?" The glass of wine Liss had poured still stood on the counter, untouched.

"Some of the booster moms say they never see her eat a thing."

Liss couldn't say what she knew about some of the booster club moms. She swiped a handful of crumbs off the table into the bin.

"And I suppose the Wards won't even bother," Connie said.

"They didn't mind if I sat in for them for Jamie's interview," Liss said.

"I bet they didn't," Connie said. She looked around. "Callan's taking it well. Did I see Link brought flowers? It can't be easy for you, all the history between that woman and your . . . do you still say 'husband' or—"

"We're all a little heartsick right now," Liss said. "Try to imagine, Connie."

"I—I'm sorry," Connie said, fluttery and unsure.

"She was only asking to be kind," her husband said, rising for a fight.

Liss wasn't so sure. They all stood with crossed arms. In the next room, the boys had the TV up too loud.

"They thought that her other boyfriend must have been involved, didn't they?" Andrés said.

Liss swiped at the table again, though it was already clean. "They who?"

"The police," Connie said.

"Everyone," her husband said at the same time.

Outside they were moving too slow. Inside, they were moving too fast.

"Everyone I ever heard talk about it thought it must have been him," Andrés said. "It's always the boyfriend, right? And this one with a little form, too, from what I've heard? And yet there he was, a free man. Hubbard, wasn't it?"

"Form?" Liss said.

"A record," Andrés said.

"They say he was a bit . . . wild," Connie said, almost apologetically. "Abusive," she added in a whisper.

Liss thought she might be sick again. She needed these people out of her house. "I don't think he ever . . ."

"If he was brown," Andrés said. "If he had a name like ours, you *know* they would have found the evidence against him."

"Andrés," Connie said.

"You know it's true." He sat down again, relaxing back, warming to his topic. "If they could have buried that son of a bitch, they would have."

"You're forgetting something," a voice said from the doorway.

Link had slipped back into the kitchen.

Andrés Garza's head didn't turn. "What's that, Kehoe?"

"You didn't hear?" Link said. "Someone did bury him. Robbie Hubbard was murdered. And I guess you'll all say I did that, too."

CHAPTER EIGHT

The sound of the French doors to the sunroom opening prevented the silence from going on too long. Kitty Larkin bustled through with Tanner in tow, Ennis following at his own pace. "We can't stay," Kitty said, though no one had invited or insisted. "We need to get the car towed out and then Tanner has school . . ."

As though all the boys didn't have school the next day. Tanner broke away, grabbed his backpack from the floor and his jacket from the back of a chair.

The lawyer trailed behind, putting a card into Link's hand. Liss saw them all out. When she came back, Andrés Garza was already escorting his family into the sunroom, leading with his jaw.

The door to the den was left open; the TV boomed.

Link and Liss looked at each other. The long room between them was dotted with discarded glasses of wine.

"They didn't mind a little gossip, did they?" Liss said.

"At my expense?" Link said. He held up the business card the attorney had handed him. "Should I take this as a hint?"

"Give it to me," Liss said.

Their hands brushed in the transfer. Liss took the card to the trash and threw it in. Always the boyfriend, Andrés had said. But the *other* boyfriend had died. "Where's your mother?" she said.

"I sent her home," he said. "She likes to be there for the shift change, anyway." Between the day nurse and night nurse. Normal life. That's what they were trying to do here.

Link went to the sofa and sat. He'd chosen his customary end, muscle memory, habit, the comfort of the familiar. It was his couch, anyway. His house.

If Link ever got around to signing those papers gathering dust in his apartment—

"You said accident *or*," Link said.

"What?"

"Earlier. You said accident *or*," Link said. "Or what? Do you think she drove into the pond on purpose?"

Liss glanced toward the den. That was the question, wasn't it? The same old question, now achingly relevant. Had Ashley meant to leave Callan? Leave it all?

But Ashley couldn't have meant to kill herself. Not the Ashley who had stood on their deck and sneered at her. "I don't believe it," Liss said. But she meant she didn't want to believe it. For Callan's sake, and for her own.

Someone rapped at the door. Liss went to answer it. Mercer stood on the deck, shoulders hunched, uncomfortable. Having him there, again, and Link just behind her—how had her life become so complicated when what she wanted was simple? Callan, safe, and her family, whole.

When she returned to the great room with Mercer, Link's expectant look turned cloudy.

"Uh, an update," Mercer said. "If you're ready."

If they weren't ready now, fifteen years later, when could they ever be?

Liss closed the door to the den and sat next to Link on the couch, side by side, as though nothing had ever come between them.

WHEN THE GARZAS came back through the main room, Liss was sitting alone on the couch.

"I'll call you tomorrow," Connie said but Liss didn't think she would.

Liss showed them out and called into the den for Jamie. She had already sent Link to lie down in their bedroom. Her bedroom.

Jamie, in the doorway, was small and angled.

"Ready?" she said.

"I'm not sure what I'm supposed to do, Mrs. Kehoe."

"Just answer truthfully," she said, tucking him under her arm to lead him through. "It's going to be OK."

At the open doors of the sunroom, they both stopped. The blinds of the sunroom had been pulled open. Out at the quarry, stand lights glared and a state cruiser sat with rolling lights, a beacon. Headlights crept along their road, people slowing down to see what could be seen, getting stuck. Their road had become a parking lot. Their sunroom, with overheads flipped on, would be as watchable as a TV set.

Liss dove for the blind pulls and closed out the view. They wouldn't have had the blinds up for the Larkins, she was sure of that.

When she finally sat next to Jamie, she was almost out of breath. They'd set up two chairs to lord over the low couch. She could feel Jamie shaking through the cushion they shared.

"We just need to hear what happened, Jamie, OK?" Deputy Deacon said, sitting across from them. "And for the record, we have Mrs. Lissette Kehoe here as his support."

Curtis Bowman readied his notes but said nothing. He didn't like her. Because she had dallied with the boss or because she'd ended it, one reason or the other, but now yellow crime scene tape flapped in her yard, placing her among tragedy and ruin. He had the air of someone who'd predicted it.

"Is Jim Ward your dad?" Deacon said. "And Sophie? That's your mom?"

Jamie stared at the floor but mumbled they were.

"Went to school together," Deak said for Bowman, who looked up, bored, from his notebook. He was new to town, probably sick of how everyone was connected. One of the few Black men in the area. Having trouble settling in, Mercer had told her that summer. As though it wasn't also true of himself, and he'd been in town three years.

Deak turned back to Jamie. "OK, can you tell me what time school let out?"

It went like that: What time was football practice? Why did it get canceled? Whose idea was it to take Tanner's car for a ride?

Every question seemed to take Jamie an extra second, as though he was translating from another language.

"I don't know," Jamie said. "Brennan, um, Devin Brennan got hurt today. So Callan needed a ride." Liss must have twitched. Jamie glanced over.

"Tanner just got his license," Liss said.

"It's actually illegal for Tanner Larkin to drive anyone but another *adult* licensed driver as his passenger for another few months," Bowman said.

Jamie jerked alert. "I didn't—"

"You're not in any trouble here," Liss said. "Right, Officers? This is just a formality, isn't it?"

"We need to conduct this interview in a very specific way, Mrs. Kehoe," Bowman said. "If you'd let us."

She could barely sit still, after what Mercer had brought up to them.

Deacon carried on: Who sat where in the car? What was the plan for the afternoon? Liss listened but didn't listen. She was thinking of Link lying in the dark of her room, reeling with the news.

It was Ashley's car. Of course. The divers had been down and the vehicle identification numbers matched. That's all Mercer had been able to tell them.

"We were just riding around, really," Jamie was saying. "Wasting time because . . . Callan said his mom wasn't home yet." He looked guiltily at Liss. "We were going back to the school before the end of practice, the regular time, anyway, because Mateo—his mom was picking him up."

"Your parents were picking you up at school?"

"I walk home," Jamie muttered.

Jamie lived in a badly used little ranch along a busy road in a row of houses just like it. It had small windows and a cracked driveway. Liss knew without having been inside that its air would taste of dust at the corners, of mildew. Of dereliction.

Bowman was flipping back through his notes and said what she'd been thinking. "That's a pretty good walk."

"Yeah," Jamie said, getting smaller.

Deacon leaned over his knees. "You go along the highway?"

Jamie fidgeted nervously and mumbled something about his father picking him up, a bus.

"When you don't go joy riding with all your buddies," Bowman said.

Liss hadn't been listening carefully but caught the tone. "I think we're done," she said.

They were treating these boys like they'd drowned Ashley themselves. It made no sense, but it put her on notice. She was paying more attention later, for Callan's interview. Paying much closer attention, listening to every word, every nuance.

Which was how she was able to spot the moment when Callan lied.

CHAPTER NINE

She could always tell when Callan lied. He'd pause before answering and take on a shifty look far beyond his years, tilting his head a little, like he hadn't quite heard the question put to him. He never looked more like Link.

"Whose idea was it for Tanner to drive you home?" Deputy Deacon had asked, and Callan hesitated.

He was nervous, and who wouldn't be? They'd placed those tall chairs above the couch on purpose, so Bowman was staring down on them, trying to make something of nothing, and Deak good-copping them, as though they needed him to.

"Why'd you boys come all the way out to your house?" Deacon asked.

"Just, you know," Callan said, his left ear tilting toward the ceiling. "Bringing me home."

This time, she knew she wasn't imagining it. He was lying. Jamie had said the boys had been going back to the school, anyway, in time to catch Connie picking up Mateo, so why wouldn't he have gone back with them and caught Liss there, no one the wiser? Only because Tanner had run off the road and got stuck did anyone have to know rules had been broken.

"Are we finished?" Liss said.

She saw the deputies off toward the quarry from the door. Outside, it was dark, cold, windy. She wanted only to tuck Callan into bed, fetch Link some aspirin, watch the proceedings from the sunroom windows and think things through. But Jamie needed a ride home, and Callan would come, too, if only to push off his homework another hour.

"Jamie, where's your jacket?"

"I don't know, Mrs. Kehoe," Jamie said. "It was— I'm sorry."

He'd been wearing it at the quarry. She'd find it later. She had Callan fetch a fleece jacket he'd probably already outgrown and finally they were marching along the road to where her car still sat.

"Seat belts," she said.

"You don't have to say it," Callan muttered.

She drove as though the back seat was stacked with cartons of raw eggs.

She would always call for seat belts. And until she had to face the reality of Callan's learner's permit, she would hold fast to her rule about Callan not driving with anyone else.

It had developed naturally from the earliest days after Ashley disappeared. While everything was in chaos and flux, Liss made Callan her priority, figuring out what to feed him, how often, how to hold him just so, how to settle him to avoid a night of sleeplessness for them all. How to mother him. Liss started to imagine Callan at the center of a series of concentric circles, each ring a layer of people who kept him safe, out and out, a buffer against the harshness of the world.

She was the first circle, the one that surrounded him. She didn't trust anyone else. Not to change him properly, to snap him into his car seat correctly. To take him anywhere safely. Driving, she realized, was an act of trust in other people to follow rules, to pay attention, to have their own sense of self-preservation.

A look passed between other mothers, sometimes, when they thought she wouldn't notice. There would be theories. She was overprotective because she didn't have a kid of her own. Or because her own childhood had been unstable, some would know to suggest.

So she could keep this version of Link on a leash, they might say now.

That look between mothers she wasn't supposed to see told her all she needed to know. Who does she think she is? they were thinking. Trying to be a perfect mother when she wasn't his mother at all. She had an asterisk next to her name, like a hall of famer who'd taken a shortcut.

But she was the only mother Callan knew. And Ashley had handed him to her. A gift. A benediction, like that painting of God touching Adam's finger and giving him life.

Anyway, she was easing up, wasn't she? She had to, now that Link had Callan some weekends, now that he rode with the team to away games. Still, she dreaded next semester when he was eligible for driver's ed and his permit.

Behind her, the boys were quiet but Jamie was restless. He kicked the back of her seat a few times before she spoke up. "You getting comfortable back there, Jamie?"

"Sorry, Mrs. Kehoe."

He was a nervous passenger, she'd noticed. His mother didn't drive at all. Maybe Sophie felt the same way about the rush of cars, about being responsible for another person's life.

"Jamie," she started to ask. But, tonight, mothers and driving were a topic to be avoided. "I'll look for your jacket at home, OK? Are you warm enough? I can turn up the heat."

"I'm OK," he mumbled into the collar of Callan's spare fleece.

They were approaching Jamie's house. Across the road, a light was lit at the end of the long drive up to the Hubbard house. Liss spared a thought for Robbie's mother.

At the Wards', though, the house was dark. "Your mom's home tonight, right?" Liss said.

"Where else would she be?" Jamie said.

He clambered out as soon as the car stopped. Liss waited until Jamie had gone inside and closed the door behind him. She would have left the porch light on, at least.

Liss pulled back onto the road toward home.

No, at the very least she would have come to the door to wave acknowledgment to the mother who'd taken time out of her schedule—out of her *crisis*—to make sure another mother's son was home safe. And she would have come to the door to greet the boy who'd walked away from a car wreck. At the *very* least.

"What?" Callan said.

What scornful noise had she made? "Nothing," she said. "Jamie's OK, isn't he?"

"What do you mean?"

"I don't know." He was so small compared to someone like Tanner. "Does he have enough to eat at lunch?"

"You're being weird, Mom," Callan said.

She sought him out in the rearview, a shadow folded against the door. "How are *you* doing?" she said.

His turn for a scornful noise.

Right. Liss cast out from the car for something to cheer him. "Should we do something nice for Devin? If he broke his leg, he's out for the season, probably."

Even in the dark, she could sense him shift toward curiosity. "Like what? Not *flowers*."

Those pink carnations. They dug at her. By morning, the clerk who'd rung up Link's purchase would be telling the story. "What does he like? Maybe some good snacks?"

"Candy?"

"Great idea," Liss said. "Want to go get Devin some candy?"

"What about my homework?"

And she shouldn't be rewarding him, should she? Breaking rules, lying. He had *form*.

At home, though, would they arrive to Ashley's car dangling like a fish on the line? "Let's forget about homework this one time," she said.

"*Really?*"

He sounded suspicious.

"Really," she said.

"OK," he said, "but I'm going to tell my teachers I was *guidanced* not to do my homework."

When they arrived in town, the grocery store was closed but the gas station at the edge of town was lit up, an alien spaceship docked among cornfields. She sent Callan inside while she filled the tank.

The countryside began abruptly at the edge of the pavement, crackling cornstalks bristling in the wind that would not die down. Was it a storm or just bluster? They needed the rain, desperately, but not tonight, not delaying Mercer and the recovery team.

She gazed into the darkness beyond the bright lights of the station, looking for the cross. Maybe she never would have known precisely where Robbie had been found if his mother hadn't planted that memorial, hadn't kept it neat and his name from fading. Back then the gas station hadn't been here; the town hadn't reached this far. He'd been struck and left to die at the road side, one arm stretched out onto the asphalt, she'd heard. Stretching for help that didn't come.

She would never have let Callan walk home alone along a highway. At any time of day.

Did she have to take on this, too? Ashley and Callan and Robbie *and* Jamie?

The houses at the edge of town showed TV-blue at the windows. Someone was tucked up in comfort when he should be the one to carry the burden of Robbie. Someone who had gone home and wiped their fender clean.

"Mom!" Callan stood at the door of the station.

The gas pump had stopped itself. The tank was full. "Coming," she said.

At the Brennan house, Callan ran up to drop off the bonanza he had selected for Devin. Devin's mother let Callan in and came out to thank her, a nice gesture, she said, you didn't have to.

But Liss did have to.

"His leg's not broken," Devin's mother said, but you know what it's like, she said. These boys, she said, and Liss agreed. These boys will be the death of us.

CHAPTER TEN

Liss stood at the edge of an open grave, toeing loose dirt until it started to fall away under her feet. Someone nearby started screaming.

"Phone," Link mumbled into her neck.

Liss had no idea where she was, or when.

Callan—

She remembered the accident, the car in the pond, and sat up, Link's arm falling away from her. Her alarm clock read an impossible time of morning. Reporters. They'd been at the quarry when she and Callan had come home, but Mercer's men had kept them from the house. Her mistake was plugging the phone cords back in.

She reached for the phone next to the bed. "Hello." She cleared her throat and tried again. "Hello?"

The line went dead.

Liss returned the phone to its cradle. Beside her, Link had turned on his back and fallen asleep again. At some point since the split, he'd started snoring. She shouldn't know that, but she did.

What did it say about her that she'd known when she sent Link back to her room—their old bed—that he would end up spending the night? She had manipulated it as easily as placing Patty next to Jamie at the dinner table that night, as easily as leading a student to apply to the safety school they would absolutely need. She had placed Link in her bed, not wanting to face the night alone.

Liss lay back and caught Link's profile against the early-morning light at the window. There he was, so close, but also so far away. She hadn't meant for it to go this far, into lawyers and paperwork. She'd only asked Link to keep to the promises he'd made after cheating with Ashley—never again, he'd said.

Which had held for fifteen good years. And then—

And then an extra night at the sales conference. Texts from "work" after dinner. Missing hours from his schedule. And when she asked him direct questions, there was that hesitation, that head tilt. Like a dog listening for the voice of its true owner.

She'd forgiven him a lot over the years: money frittered away, time wasted, responsibility forfeited. But even that—her forgiveness—seemed to create an imbalance between them. A new imbalance, pitching the opposite direction, toward Liss. Which was not the bargain Link thought he'd made, she supposed.

Liss had never learned the woman's name. The waitress from their favorite restaurant? Someone she'd met at a GimmeGimme employee-day picnic? Who the woman was hardly mattered. She existed, and Link had broken the foundational promise of their marriage.

Things had gone quickly: an ultimatum, a bluff called. He moved out, put an app on his phone, for God's sake. If he was trying to make a point, then so could she. She'd met Mercer before; he'd come to the school to make awkward prom-season speeches to the student body about drinking and driving. After Link moved out, Mercer came to the school to have a chat with Vera and a student who'd threatened a classmate. "Ma'am," he'd said upon entering the guidance office, his first word to her. A man in uniform and somehow everything Link wasn't. He left that day with her number.

A few weeks, a fling. Not that she hadn't enjoyed it, but her heart wasn't in it. She'd been waiting for something to happen, a reconciliation, a divorce. But neither did.

Link never mentioned the other woman again; Liss put Mercer off. She had the divorce papers drawn up, hoping they wouldn't be needed. He left them unsigned, giving her hope she wasn't sure she deserved.

The phone rang again. Liss reached over and unplugged it.

"Phone," Link said.

"I got it."

He was already asleep again, his hand on her naked thigh. She was wearing one of his old T-shirts, one he probably hadn't realized she'd hung on to. It was too comfortable to let go. But by that same standard, so was he.

The phone started ringing in the kitchen.

Liss slipped out from under Link's hand. In the front room, shadows made the familiar room strange. She hurried through to the kitchen and caught the phone before it rang a third time.

"Hello." Not a question this time, but a dare. The result was the same, the insult of the disconnect tone.

She detached the phone from the wall and put it on the counter.

Normally Liss would have blamed kids. The landline phone number had been the same since Key and Patty had lived here, listed and easy to get. Every fall she fielded a few prank calls from slumber parties and, in the spring, from students itching for summer and freedom. The principal got it worse. Vera was smarter. If she had a landline at home, even Liss didn't know the number.

Four in the morning wasn't a student up late, though. Four a.m.

was insomnia or an early shift, an adult having a coffee and trans-
ferring their first self-loathing thought of the day onto someone
else.

Liss flicked the curtain over the sink. The first pink rays fell
across the hills and fields.

If she positioned herself carefully, she could see the quarry and
mound, all quiet. Tanner's car had been towed home, and she'd
heard the recovery team dragging their trailer out sometime after
midnight. She'd gone to watch from the dark sunroom as the state
vehicles pulled away and the scene was broken down. Then, finally,
the heavy-duty tow and the flatbed truck with Ashley's shrouded
car, the county cars, and Mercer and his men last.

Had they found anything in the car? Proof of life? Of death?
Liss caught her reflection in the gray window, ghoulish.

Coffee. She needed coffee before she allowed self-loathing
thoughts of her own.

She reached for the grounds and scooped them into the machine. And added a little extra. That was how Link liked his.

The gray lady in the window shook her head. Of course he did.
The regular amount of anything was never enough for Link Kehoe.

But how easily she gave it. How easily she slipped into the role
of keeper, fixer. Quieter of phones, heaper of coffee grounds. She
hadn't needed Vera's expertise to source the people-pleasing to
her childhood. She'd always be the one tiptoeing through rooms,
sniffing the air for signs of a bad day. Bringing aspirin and water
to the bedside before it was needed. Spotting the bump in the road
ahead before anyone else.

Liss gripped the counter while the machine started to burble.
She had spotted a bump in the road.

They would have to have a service for Ashley. And she would
have to plan it.

No one else was left to go through the formalities. No one but Callan. It would have to be her.

Something simple, then. Pink carnations, if that was what she'd liked. Liss didn't know. She hadn't known Ashley, not really, but they were in this together, Ashley, she and Link, Callan, little figures in the game of life in the same car.

And Robbie hit by its bumper.

The coffeemaker churned and steamed. Liss milked the first mug before the pot could fill. When shuffling footsteps sounded against the hall floor, she reached for another mug.

Link appeared blinking into the kitchen light, barefoot, shirtless, jeans hanging loose without a belt. "Did I dream the phone ringing?"

"Unfortunately, no."

He took in the T-shirt, her bare legs. Said nothing but accepted the mug she offered. "Always good news, this time of night. Or morning."

"Just some crank," she said.

Link turned the mug around on the table by the handle. "You should mention it to him," he said.

He avoided having Mercer's name in his mouth if he could. He sometimes still referred to his dad as The Marshal, capital letters implied, because, she'd decided, it was too hard to think of him otherwise, diminished.

"I'm sure it's nothing," Liss said.

Link looked toward the spot on the wall where the phone had probably been since before he was born, at the phone lying in the nest of its own cord. "Everything is something right now. Or could be."

Were they both thinking the same thing? Robbie had calls in the night. Harassment of all kinds, all hours. He hadn't been able to sleep, which didn't help his case when he'd come to the house to beg Key to find Ashley. This house, forgetting that Key had already moved up the hill.

Wild-eyed Robbie, storming in, demanding, breaking down. Accusing. Later, he was changed. Unshaven. Unhinged. Was it any wonder people thought he'd had something to do with Ashley's disappearance?

You believe me, don't you? Robbie had asked her. He'd dogged their life until he'd finally got one of his own, only to take up with, of all people, Ashley. What does he think, Liss asked Link after Robbie had come to tell them the happy news, to ask Link's *permission*, good God, like he was Ashley's keeper or something.

What does he think? she'd asked Link. That we'll double date?

She had believed Robbie hadn't had anything to do with Ashley going missing, if only because she thought Ashley had taken herself off. Time is money, cupcake, she'd said, making demands like she held all the cards, like she had some jewel of truth tucked into her back pocket.

But if she never got off their road . . .

The coffee, with the extra scoop, was bitter. Liss drank it like a punishment, watching Link over the rim of her mug.

What would happen if Mercer pulled bones out of that car? If he didn't? No matter what, from now on, people would always wonder if—

A metallic clang sounded somewhere outside.

They looked at one another. Link got up and went to the back door. "Are they still out there?" he said.

"No," she said. "I don't know."

"Stay here." He reached for the baseball bat he'd kept at the back entrance, same as his dad always had, and threw open the door.

"It could be Mercer. Link, wait!" Liss ran to the doorway and hissed at his back. "Wait! Mercer probably just left someone behind."

The wind tugged at her T-shirt, reminding her she wasn't dressed. She ran to the bedroom, pulled on the nearest pair of jeans from the hamper, slipped on shoes, grabbed her cell phone.

At the back door, the motion-triggered light over the deck had flooded the area but Link was already beyond its reach.

"Link?"

Everything is something, Link had said. Or could be.

She dialed Mercer's private number and crept farther out on the deck. Should she yell for Link—or would that only draw trouble toward the house? Callan, upstairs. She stepped back into the open doorway to guard it.

Mercer answered on the first ring. "Liss? What's wrong?" He didn't sound as though she'd woken him.

"Did you leave someone here?"

"What?"

"There's someone out on our property," she said.

"OK, OK, hang on a sec."

The deck light went out while she waited for him to come back. Liss stood in the dark, listening past the hiss of wind in the tall grass near the road. A loose roof panel on the barn moaned and rattled. She had always loved the night sounds of this place, the hush of leaves in the trees once the highway traffic died down, the crickets and other chirruping things in the woods and at the edge of the pond. At certain times of night, she might hear voices from the rest area out on the highway, over-the-road truckers trading notes and laughing. Now she wished desperately for silence.

Was that a footstep? A crunch on gravel? She turned all around, reading the dark for movement.

High in the trees past the pond, a light burned at Key and Patty's house. No sleep for anyone tonight.

She heard a scrape at the other end of the line as Mercer came back. "You there?" he said. "I've called it in. And I'm on my way. Stay inside, lock the door."

"I can't. I—Link is out there."

The quality of the silence between them changed as it stretched and she could tell he was outside, then inside again. Getting into his car, she hoped.

"You called Link?" he said.

"Well," she said. "No."

"Oh," Mercer said. "OK."

As she hung up, a creak sounded out along the road behind her, a car door opening or closing. Liss whipped around, setting off the light again. She might as well be standing in a spotlight.

A car engine roared to life. Headlights glared, then brightened further. Liss winced away. Then the car was reversing and blocked by the barn.

Link came loping back from the pond as the engine faded away along the road. "Did you see anything? Maybe one of the town cars? Mercer keeping watch."

"No, he's on his way now."

"Ah, of course," Link said. "I'd better go then, so the white-hat sheriff can ride in and save the day."

"Don't," she said.

"Don't go or—"

"Don't be like that," Liss said. "Just like your dad used to get called to help people—"

"I can stay until he gets here," he said.

Which was an apology.

She didn't want to be handed from man to man, guardian to guardian, but she'd been reminded how isolated they were out here, how seldom she thought about deadbolts or that baseball bat behind the door for the little lady left behind, a Kehoe family tradition.

She said, "I'll make us breakfast." Which was her apology.

CHAPTER ELEVEN

By seven the morning after Ashley Hay's car had been discovered, Mercer Alarie felt as though he'd been awake for a month. After checking in at Liss's and finding, of course, nothing to do, he'd swung home for a shower and to change into uniform but hadn't had more than a wink by the time he stopped into the Corner Diner for the largest coffee he could carry. The place was jumping.

"There's the war hero," one of the old farmers said as Mercer entered, raising a mug in his direction. "Didn't I see you on my TV this morning?"

The other customers—farmers, retirees, third shifters from the chip factory on their way home—lifted their heads.

Mercer hated election years. He preferred doing the job to securing it, but then he couldn't do the work if they didn't pin the star to his chest.

So: politicking. That's what talking to the press was last night, when it was the last thing he wanted to do. Standing at the site of a tragedy while the divers placed the inflatable lifter bags under that sunken car, while his men interviewed the witnesses, while everyone else did the real work. Standing in the limelight and taking some kind of credit for a discovery he hadn't made.

It was embarrassing. But he'd kept the vultures away from the house and away from the boys, from Liss and her son. Callan had enough to think about, might soon have more.

But not yet. It was too early to think about that yet.

"Coffee, please, Bill," Mercer called down the counter to the owner. The guy wouldn't let him spend his money, but Mercer got out his wallet anyway. People deserved the opportunity to make the gesture, enjoy their own generosity.

"So is it her?" Larry Norville asked. Mercer didn't need to look. Parkins's number one concerned citizen. Around the station they called him Robert's Rules for his calls for procedure from the audience at town council meetings. Or Larry Lawsuit, for all the threats he'd never made good on. Or Petition Patty, for all the threats he had. He sat at the far end of the counter with his son, Pete, who owned the local machine shop and tuned up the cruisers for the town. Probably overcharged, but he was good. And a lot less annoying than his old man.

The room had gone quiet except for the bacon on the back grill.

"The *Hay* girl," Larry Norville said. "Just to be clear, Marshal."

"We don't know yet," Mercer said, getting a few bills out. "It will be some time—"

"You better get it sorted before November," Larry said.

"That's not actually how—" But Mercer didn't want to mention the specter of DNA. The first dive had come back with a report: a skull and bones in the front, the metal base of a baby's car seat in the back. At the thought of that skull, Mercer's stomach rolled over. "Cases have their own schedules," he said.

"This one's schedule is fifteen years, I guess?" someone in the back called out, and that got some laughs.

"Well," Mercer said. "I've only been on the case the last three years, so I suppose we could ask your former marshal why he never dragged that pond."

The bacon sizzled.

The problem—in part—was that Mercer was an impatient man himself. He wanted that DNA, those answers. He wanted to chase down the truth, too. These people had waited a long time. It was against his nature to make them wait any longer, but he would, because that was his job. If he'd stayed a beat cop, skipped the whole small-town experiment, he wouldn't have to be anyone's spokesperson. He could have lived out his career doing the grunt work he liked—not making promises, not kissing town council butt. Not crunching the numbers over and over, trying to figure out where his rising crime rates were coming from, or going on camera and trying to pretend this one solve might save his ass in November, or had anything to do with him at all. He could have stayed in the city, in that hot little studio apartment for the rest of his life. Not solving a single problem for anyone. Not meeting Liss.

His problem was that he wanted to do right by these people.

But mostly the real problem was that the old marshal was incapacitated. Maybe they rode his ass during his tenure, too, or maybe he was held in awe all along as he was now. But the second the old guy lost his grip on his keys, Rockwell Kehoe became untouchable.

The pond was on land the old guy owned, for fuck's sake.

Mercer sighed and worked to even out his tone. "I'll allow that they weren't looking for a *body* back then," he said. "I don't like to assign blame when I don't know the whole story. I imagine you good folks don't, either."

"If you could assign blame at some point, though, for anything at all," Larry said. He had his newspaper rolled up under his bony elbow. No stranger to the op-ed page himself, or to the online chat board. A real hell-raiser in his day, now he spent that energy on Next Door and Facebook, ranting and putting little angry faces on everyone else's posts. "If you could *try* getting some crooks off the street."

How had Kehoe even done it? Mercer had been able to retire out a few of the old guard, so he had a few newbies mixed in with some old bad habits in the rest. They all could have used some additional training in conflict resolution, firearms safety. Maybe some sensitivity training in case they managed to meet up with someone who didn't look exactly like themselves. He'd been laughed down at close range by the town council on that one.

Those twits.

Meanwhile, their call volume outpaced what Kehoe had had to deal with by a factor of almost ten. What was happening to this town?

They hadn't bounced back from the pandemic lockdown a few years back, was his theory. Everyone had streamlined their lives, tightened their circles, narrowed down who they could live without and who they would forgive, and none of it had sprung back. A lot of them thought they were out here all on their own. They'd been let down, certainly, but they couldn't admit who'd done it. They were acting out. Their kids were after killing each other or themselves or both: drink, drugs, dare-deviling. Brawling every step of the way, of course.

He was spread thin, and now this.

"Maybe there was no evidence against Hubbard because he wasn't guilty," Bill said, sliding a big paper cup toward Mercer. Waving his money away. Mercer nodded his thanks and shoved the cash into the tip jar. He appreciated vocal support. He'd try not to take the to-go cup as a request.

"Well, if that's Ashley Hay in that quarry water, I guess he *wasn't* guilty," said a woman sitting against the far wall.

Around the room, Mercer heard murmurs start up. The Kehoes'

name reached him from several points around the room, and he wouldn't mind, except—

"*Someone* put Hubbard on trial."

Mercer looked up, tried to locate the voice among them. The last few murmurs cut out but they wouldn't look at him now, eyes shifting all over the room at empty plates and cold cups and the wide, streaky windows at the front. Everybody looking at their watches and phones, someplace they needed to be.

Vigilante justice instead of the kind they should have had, and some dickhead thought it had all worked itself out. Several dickheads, probably.

"Looks like what you suffered fifteen years ago was two tragedies, instead of one," Mercer said. "If anyone has any information regarding Ashley Hay's disappearance or Robbie Hubbard's death, they know to come see me. Instead of taking matters into their own hands. That's what you pay me for." He gave Norville a look, daring him to say a word. "I'm in office through the end of this term, no matter what happens at the polls."

It was a good parting line, but he still had to walk across the room. Norville had never let a chance to open his mouth slip by, and he wasn't starting today.

"We'll see what happens, *Marshal*."

"That's what I said," Mercer said cheerfully, raising his cup to Bill, then the room generally. "You folks keep safe out there."

In his patrol car, he rubbed at his stinging eyes and wished he'd ordered a biscuit with some of that bacon. He'd refused breakfast at Liss's that morning, a matter of pride to decline when he'd pulled up, lights rolling, and found Link Kehoe sitting at his old table shoveling a plate of pancakes into his smug face.

Mercer sipped at his coffee, thinking about the bones pulled out of the pond. That skull. The long days ahead stretched out in front of him. Maybe he should hope he didn't win the election. He could give this town back, let someone else figure it out.

He should have been a shoo-in in November. His rival had never served a community like theirs and had fewer years of policing under his belt. But he was a tough talker, promising he'd come in guns blazing. A bully, Mercer thought, but some of them would respond to those sorts of promises.

If he lost, to hell with it. He could pull up stakes again, spin out from Liss Kehoe's orbit once and for all. And her ex-husband's. And her ex-father-in-law's.

That skull. *Dam*mit. It didn't make him want to throw in the towel, no. It made him hungry, to get it right. To salvage some shred of justice, even if it was late.

He had decided, without knowing it, where to start.

MERCER FOLLOWED ANOTHER car up the road toward the Kehoes' double property. The compound, as he sometimes thought of it.

A few hundred feet before the curve toward Liss's, a private gravel road led uphill through a stand of trees to the new house. Before turning in, he noted the caution tape still rippling down at the pond and, with some satisfaction he couldn't help, Link's truck gone from Liss's driveway.

The car ahead of him had pulled into Key and Patty's, too, so Mercer trailed behind through the trees, taking the place in as it revealed itself. Key had built himself a modern sort of ranch with wings that wrapped protectively around a conservatory, a dark beast protecting its own glass heart. Behind that central glass was a pool surrounded by potted palms, transplanted from somewhere sunny and now reaching for a white Midwestern sky. The place was wide and sprawling, taking up as much land as it liked and glaring down, superior, Mercer had always thought, on the old house and everything else.

The car ahead of him parked side-by-side with another older sedan already on the drive. Out-of-county plates on both. A dark-skinned woman in light blue scrubs emerged and gave his car a quizzical look. He realized it was far too early for a social call.

He got out but held back, only catching up with the woman when she let herself in at the door to the side of the conservatory and turned her head in his direction.

"Good morning, ma'am," he said, hat in hand.

"Good morning," she said, with a twinkle to her, like everything she would ever say would be at his expense. "Should I let Mrs. Kehoe know you're here?"

"Please, ma'am. Marshal Alarie."

She looked over his uniform and left him standing in the foyer.

After a few minutes, voices approached, and then Patty Kehoe led a second woman in blue into the room. "I assure you the discomfort Mr. Kehoe is experiencing is minimal," the other woman was saying, with a lilting accent he couldn't name. "And offset by the gains we could see. I'm only seeing to it he meets his goals—"

"Let's not put lipstick on the proverbial pig," Patty said. "My husband has no goals. I have ambitions, *for* him, and those are the goals you should concern yourself with. As a home health *aide*, one would think you could *assist* us in this."

"But the therapist said—"

Patty had spotted Mercer. "I'll talk to the physical therapist myself," Patty said. "Now if you'll excuse me, I have a visitor, bright and early."

The aide's eyes flicked over to Mercer and away. "I'll see you this evening, then."

"Siomara, I think we both know I'll be calling the agency as well," Patty said.

The woman hesitated, then walked his way.

"Good morning, ma'am," Mercer said to her.

But she only reached past his shoulder for a jacket on a hook and was gone.

"Sorry you had to witness that," Patty said. "They do a two-week course on the computer and suddenly they're neurologists. Meanwhile he gets weaker and further from . . ." She waved a hand, dusting something unseen away. "From who he used to be."

Patty Kehoe was a well-put-together woman, younger than her husband by a good many years. Had she predicted spending her golden years doing this, wiping an old, drooling man's mouth and commanding legions of nursing staff? Losing her husband—not just once but twice—in a manner that would sap her, then leave her alone?

"You have to advocate for the ones you love," he said. "No one else will."

Patty stopped short. "You sound like you've had your own experiences with our nation's for-profit health—and I hesitate to use this word—*system*."

He should call his mother, Mercer realized. "How's Marshal Kehoe doing?" he said. "If you don't mind me asking, that is."

Patty lifted her chin. She liked hearing her husband's old title.

"I'm sure you've heard the rumors," she said.

"I listen to rumors, ma'am, but—I prefer to collect my own evidence," Mercer said. "Is he up for a visitor?"

"If you mean could you sit next to his wheelchair until you tire of talking to yourself, then, yes. He's in the conservatory. To the left there."

The glass room was warm, too warm. Ferns and glossy leaves

created a bit of privacy from the outside. The woman who'd let him into the house was bent over the old man's chair. She straightened up, that same playful look in her eye. "You're in time for water therapy," she said.

"And me without my trunks," he said. "Hello, again. Didn't catch your name."

"Kellye, with a y-e at the end," she said. "But you probably don't need to memorize it. We're cycling through here pretty quickly, aren't we, Mr. Kehoe?"

The old marshal had aged severely since Mercer had seen him last, his hair thin and greasy across his pate, his face thin and sagging. His hands were gnarled but placed on the arms of his chair as though he might launch himself upward at any moment. An old king on his throne.

"Marshal Kehoe," Mercer said, sitting and leaning into the other man's line of vision. "It's been a while. Mercer Alarie, if you remember me?"

They hadn't gone head-to-head in an election. Mercer had been invited, appointed after Kehoe's retirement and a short, disastrous stint with a town manager that left everyone smarting. But he'd met the guy once or twice before his health had declined. Before the man's son's marriage had split open, and Mercer had wormed his way in. How much gossip did he get up here? How much did Link lay at the old man's wheels? How much did he understand?

Key raised his eyes, blinked.

"Fuckface," the old man said. Plain as anything.

OK then. The health aide was beaming.

"Is that good news?" Mercer said uneasily.

"When he's not said a word for weeks? I'll go let his wife know. You're good company for him."

When Mercer turned his attention back, Key was still staring.

A good steady bead that made Mercer feel bad for things he hadn't done.

"Well, sir," Mercer said. "Thought I'd drop by and say hello." Why *had* he come? He'd known Kehoe wouldn't be available to him. "I don't suppose you're following the goings on down the hill?"

Nothing.

"Has anyone told you we pulled a car out of that deep pond of yours? Ashley Hay's car, turns out."

The guy's eyes widened and his breathing grew rough. He was still in there, then.

"Is there anything you can tell me about that?" Mercer said.

Key shifted in his chair, pitching forward a bit. Excited? Bothered? Worried?

"Easy, now," Mercer said. "The missus won't let me visit again, even if I do get you swearing."

A heavy footfall sounded from somewhere deep in the house. Kehoe's eyes shifted to the side and back.

Mercer leaned in close. "If you could say one word to me right now, what would it be? Other than that last one. Got that one, loud and clear."

Key blinked.

"One word," Mercer said.

The old man stiffened through the shoulders and tensed up, jaw tight and hands dragging across the armrests of his chair to form fists.

"Sir?"

Key's lips were wet with spit and effort to force a sound through them, a sibilant hiss ahead of a click, swallowed. Mercer shook his head and the guy went through it again: hiss, click in his throat.

Just noises? Another insult? Or was he trying to say something real and working too hard? If he gave the old man a stroke, he'd never hear the end of it.

"What's happening?" Patty said, hurrying in. "Rockwell, darling?" She turned to Mercer. "Kellye said he spoke? What did he say?"

"Ah," Mercer said.

Kehoe Senior had gone slack again. Then he tucked his bottom lip in and spoke as easily as if he was ordering a slice of pie off a menu.

"Fuckface," he said.

I'M TRYING TO SAY *SLOCUM*, FUCKFACE.

It's a word I think I might be able to slur through, a sound that could almost swim out on the slick of the drool always gathering at the sides of my mouth.

The skin chaps there, a real bitch. These nurses don't notice. Nurses, I say, as though they were as educated as that. They get certificates from some fly-by-night outfit and then are sent out to wipe my ass. A job they're at least qualified for.

We do go through these women quickly, as the new one pointed out. Always women. Maybe they're stealing from us beyond my sight or back-talking Patty outside my hearing. But they all seem fine to me, if a little sullen. Young, too, not at all hard to look at, and I can't lie, if my flesh was still at all willing, I would have embarrassed myself a couple of times. The new one's the prettiest of the bunch so far but the one with the wide, black eyes, the one who just left. All she has to do is lift the bath sponge—just lift it—and I'm imagining water running down her brown arms and getting that old feeling. Raring to go.

I was a virile man once. Not so many years ago, in fact. I had who and what I wanted, on my terms. My mind is as good as it ever was, a sharp instrument. It's the meat sack around it that's giving out. The road downhill—from being who I was, feared and revered depending on who you asked, to becoming this brain in a jar—has been swift.

I'm a doorstop.

My joys are simple now. Link coming by to chat classic cars and sports scores like I might pop up with a response. Milkshakes, about all I can still swallow. That hand lifting the sponge.

But I'm capable of more than milkshakes. I may be parked here out of the way but I notice things. I see what people wish they could hide. What they say, what they don't say. I knew Link's marriage was over before he did. I know better than he does why he won't sign the papers to make it final, too. I see a man's weaknesses just as well as I ever did. I know who this shithead Alarie is thinking about here in this room.

Sharp as ever in here, folks. Not that it's good for much.

But maybe the gears are starting to slip. My first instinct when Alarie asks me for one word, like he expects me to answer, is to send him to Slocum. He doesn't understand, the numbskull. He's still frowning over what I could be saying when Patty hustles in. Party over. She escorts Alarie out and comes back to make sure I don't call the new aide a name. This new one doesn't seem like she'll put up with nonsense.

But I didn't call the nurse anything. Didn't mean her. Or Alarie, even.

I didn't mean anything, that's the thing. It's been a while since I could get out anything I meant to say. I'm drowning. That might have been my last gasp, who knows? I won't see my last word coming, the last milkshake, the last breath.

Maybe I was slagging Slocum. He could be a *real* fuckface if he wanted to be.

Slocum is the doorstop I used to place and forget about, the eyes and ears that recorded all my sins. Sending Alarie to Slocum is as good as a confession.

And I'm not so far gone as that.

CHAPTER TWELVE

The next morning, after Liss sent a few threats up the stairs, Callan finally shuffled down, still in pajamas, his hair smashed up in the back. "Can I stay home from school today?"

"Do you feel sick, Cowboy?"

"Don't call me that," he said. "Not *sick*."

Liss couldn't stay home from work, and was it a good idea for Callan to be alone? "Do you think it might be better to have the distraction? Until we know for sure?"

He shrugged. "They're going to ask tons of questions."

"The other kids? Who cares? You don't have to answer them."

"Mom."

"You don't have answers, anyway," she said. "Tell them that."

"*Mom*."

"It doesn't matter how long you put them off. Won't they ask you tomorrow instead, or the next day?"

"I just . . ."

She wished she could let him wallow. Grief required a little focused, staggering misery. "I suppose you could go stay with Gram and Papa Key today, if you really don't think you can handle school."

Callan made a face. His grandmother wasn't the sort to make him chicken soup. His grandfather used to be more fun than he was now, a gruff sort of playful, toughening him up, he'd say. Letting him get away with anything, just the way he'd built Link. Gram's house also didn't have a smart TV or a game system. "But you would miss football tonight, too," Liss said.

Callan's eyes roved over the room as he made the calculations. The coaches put a lot of emphasis on commitment to the team and missing a game would drop his stats lower than they already stood, if he wanted to make varsity next year. Also, it was homecoming week, which promised more people in the junior varsity stands. "Will you be at the game? And Dad?"

"Wouldn't miss it," she said, forced brightness.

"I guess I'll go." He slumped down at the table. "Was Dad here this morning? I thought I heard him."

She hesitated. It was one thing for her to hope, but it was another to drag Callan along, too. "He stopped by," she said. "Had some breakfast."

"I wish you'd woken me up."

Somehow the phone calls hadn't. "It was pretty early," she said.

"The table is sticky," he said.

She ran water over a rag and handed it to Callan.

"Why do I have to do it?"

"You live here, don't you?"

The second Link signed those papers, Callan could choose Link over her. But she couldn't let him turn into the same kind of manchild Patty Kehoe had raised.

He moped through it, treating the rag like a biohazard, his mood turning as he scrubbed.

"OK," she said. "Go get ready. It isn't pajama day *or* crazy hair day."

Another day he might have cracked a smile, but not today. He attempted a three-pointer with the rag and missed the sink.

"Callan."

But he was already stomping away and up the stairs.

Well, Ashley, she thought. Could you have handled it better?

WHEN SHE ARRIVED at the office and saw Vera, Liss remembered she'd never texted her.

"I'm so sorry," Liss said. She pulled the phone from her bag to find a long list of missed calls over the last twelve hours and a ridiculous number of texts from neighbors, other team parents. Her old school friend, Sherry. People she hadn't spoken to in a long time and a few from numbers she didn't recognize.

"I wondered what happened to you," Vera said.

Liss put the phone away. "He's fine," she said. "They all are. The night just . . . got away from me."

"That's what I've *heard*." Vera held out a cup of coffee in Liss's favorite mug. The weather was good, today.

When Vera treated her so kindly, like one of the students—like one of the students in *crisis*, someone not quite load-bearing—she didn't know how to accept it without shame. Without recognizing charity and that she was once again in need of it. Today, though, she would take any kindness, gladly.

"Is it all over the school already?" Liss said.

"Well, the teachers' lounge," Vera said. "Apparently some people still watch the eleven o'clock news? And in the newspaper, maybe? And on the radio. I didn't even think of social media." She sipped her coffee. "Callan might have a hard day ahead of him."

Liss groaned. "Maybe I should have let him stay home. But with the career fair bearing down and— What kind of mother am I?"

"A really devoted one," Vera said.

But it was a real question. A million decisions each day, all left to her. She had to get it right, every single thing right. "My poor boy has a broken heart and I dragged him into this lion's den," she said.

"It's her?" Vera said.

"It's her car. That's all Mercer could say. Would say."

"Was that weird, with Mercer?"

Liss drank from her mug for time. "It got weird when he showed up this morning and Link had stayed over."

"What?" Vera crowed. "What is *happening*? That should have been the headline when you walked in the door."

Not her son's safety? Not her old rival's car in the pond? "Nothing happened. Nothing's *happening*."

"I don't understand your life," Vera said with intensity. "But I want it."

This was as close as Vera had ever come to admitting regrets about her own life. That she had never married, never had children. She was several years older than Liss, but wouldn't say exactly how many. She'd come to the area straight from her degree, years ago, but she'd never put down roots. But in this case, her envy was misplaced.

"There was a *recovery* team at my house last night," Liss said. "As in—*corpse* recovery."

"Of course. Of course. That's awful. Did they *find* a body?"

As though they were discussing the chance of rain. Liss set down her cup. "I don't know."

"Poor Callan," Vera said. "It's so hard to be young these days. And he was already in such a strange predicament."

The divorce timeline stretched to screaming, she meant.

The first bell rang, sending students to first period. Liss glanced toward her desk, at the family photo, all three of them in blue. Her cowboy. Then she pictured Callan sitting slumped in his home room, waiting out his sentence. She'd delivered him to the school parking lot after a silent ride in, ears flamed red. Link did the same thing, in the rare instances he could be embarrassed. But Callan was more fragile, more easily wounded . . .

She wasn't supposed to parent him at school, but—

"I'm just going to go check on him," Liss said.

"Good idea," Vera said.

In the halls, students rushed to beat the second bell. A few heads turned in her direction.

"Lissette—"

Callan's English teacher stood in the door of her classroom. Denise had a way of talking about Callan that grated on Liss's nerves, as though they were all raising Callan by committee. There were already too many people in that mix. "Let me get back to you, Denise," she said.

She hurried down the hall and around the corner, sliding to a stop when she spotted Callan walking along with his books at his hip. Jamie hurried to keep up with him. Other students were turning to watch as they passed.

Pink ears, oh her boy.

Then Tanner stepped out from the flow of students going the other direction. He crossed into Callan's path and shouldered into him, hard.

"Hey!" Liss said.

Callan's books had fallen to the ground. He looked up at her voice and then down, quickly, blushing furiously. Jamie fell upon the dropped books, too.

Up and down the hall, students had turned at the shout. A few teachers had popped out of doorways.

Callan gathered his things to him and scrambled into his classroom just as second bell rang.

Liss had lots of rules for Callan but she'd broken the only one he had for her. She'd mothered him at school, in front of his friends.

In front of boys she'd *thought* were his friends. Now she wasn't so sure.

BACK AT HER desk, Liss had a full schedule, mostly students wringing their hands over colleges they wouldn't attend for another two years. She could barely muster the empathy required, not when Callan was slouching through his schedule in another corner of the building.

None of her work could inspire her, today. Not even the career fair, her pet project. Link's company would host a table and supply concessions, a bag of GimmeGimme chips in every hand, but she still needed other local businesses to participate.

The fair was the bone they threw to kids not interested in college. She'd been exactly that sort, dragging along with no plans. She never would have had anything to call a *career*, not if Vera hadn't seen something in her.

Liss had no idea what it was she'd seen, though. She wasn't the sort to glow with undiscovered potential. Not like Link. Not like some of these kids, who had never known a moment of doubt in themselves. She was more like Jamie, trying to make herself small in case someone noticed her. There were people who could be themselves, whatever it was, but she'd never had any confidence, earned or otherwise. Not like Ashley. Like—

Like Robbie.

She opened up the student database and searched for Robbie Hubbard. His record would have been expunged years ago, but it was a habit, a tic, to search the database when a name came to mind. Except for Callan. Not that she was above snooping on her son's record. She wouldn't do it, for her own sanity.

Because she was technically only Callan's stepmother, Link had to provide a letter to the school every year to allow Liss the right to make decisions for him. The letter would have been scanned and placed into Callan's record, where it lived like a stain, a shadow.

It was enough to keep her from digging too deeply into whatever the database had to say about him.

But here was Robert Hubbard. Liss felt oddly comforted to find his name in the records, as though he might have disappeared entirely.

She'd liked Robbie well enough. She'd just wanted Link to herself when they were first dating, yet there was Robbie at every turn, saying remember the time, Link? With every story and inside joke reminding Liss of all the life Link had lived before her. And would live after her. Robbie had only meant to include her. He'd meant to be her friend, too, and offer to her the pieces of Link that he had collected. She'd realized all this much later.

Too late to make it right. To stand up for him.

And now—

Tanner colliding with Callan in the hall. What was that about?

Boys will be boys, some would say. But she didn't think so. Boys were often more.

CHAPTER THIRTEEN

That night, amid crowd noise and the marching band's shaky attempt at a Fleetwood Mac song, Liss climbed the home field risers toward the clutch of team parents, wishing she'd given Callan the day at home and herself a pass on this game.

Or that she could have taken a seat somewhere less prominent. The team parents sat high in the stands, decked in regalia of homecoming pride and team spirit, red and black, jerseys with their sons' numbers.

At her back, Link muttered, "I feel a little underdressed."

Underdressed was an understatement. They were *naked* against this crowd. As she and Link climbed, row after row of familiar faces turned to watch. Students and their parents, people she knew from town, even people she didn't know, all clocking her presence and Link's. The news, Vera had said. Radio, social media. The newspaper, by now.

Connie Garza waved them up and scooted over to make room. "Wasn't sure if we'd see you tonight," she said.

"You haven't missed much," Kitty Larkin said from the row below.

The implication being, of course, that they shouldn't be here, that they *had* missed part of the game. Link sat next to her and handed her the soda they'd decided to split. He'd calmed her down when she'd filled him in on the hallway altercation between

Callan and Tanner. Just kids, he'd said. Now he nodded across her and Connie toward Andrés.

"We thought getting back to normal was the best thing to do for now," Liss said, glaring into the back of Kitty's head.

"I agree with you," Connie said, distracted by something out on the field. "I don't care what other people think. How's Callan?"

"I'm sure the boys are all *fine*," Kitty said quickly.

Now Liss glanced at Link, who had his jaw clenched. What did other people *think*? Should she remind Kitty that one of the boys had far more things on his mind than a road accident?

Out on the sidelines, Callan sat padded shoulder to padded shoulder with Jamie on the home team bench. How *was* Callan? She willed him to turn around, to spot them and wave, but he didn't.

"I don't know about this new coach," Andrés said. "Kehoe, what do you think?"

"Seems to know his stuff," Link said.

"The kids seem devoted," Connie said. "All I hear is Coach says this and Coach says that."

"He's so young," Kitty said.

"He has some great ideas on keeping the boys safe from brain injury," Liss said.

A look passed between Connie and Kitty.

"That's great, as long as they win games," Andrés said, rising to applaud a play.

"Tanner needs to protect his *arm*," Kitty said. "For college."

"He's not going straight to the pros?" Andrés said. "Do not pass go—"

"For varsity first, of course," Kitty said.

Andrés sat back down. Liss had to hand it to him. He really did seem to care about the game, watched every second, supported every success, while she held down the bleacher worrying about concussion and only knew to clap when others did. She attended the games and tried not to watch the tackles through her fingers— that was what she had to offer instead of ardent fandom. Link tried to play down his pride but he'd been thrilled when Callan chose the same jersey number he'd worn during his championship years.

"Varsity," Connie moaned. "Varsity games are every Friday night, ladies and gentlemen."

"College recruiters, babe," Andrés said, digging a handful of popcorn out of the bag between them. "There could be some here now."

Liss leaned back and looked at Link. He shook his head, then stood and went to sit on the other side of Andrés, leaving her in a triangle with the other mothers.

"Nacho, Kitty?" Connie said. She slid the gooey tray under Kitty's nose as she turned to say no. Connie cut a look at Liss.

She was glad to be on this side of the knowing look. She didn't mind sitting with the team parents, really. At least they'd stopped trying to shake her down for a prospectus on their kids' futures because she worked in the guidance office.

Liss craned to search the stands for Jamie's parents and caught a woman across the aisle staring.

Most of their sons' futures would not be decided by a few football games. And that was a good thing. The team wasn't that good. Callan might have gone out for cross country and Liss would have been just as happy to sit in the cold and rain and watch him lope by. Happier, maybe. He would have at least been on the field more often, competing with his own best times instead of risking a knock to the head.

Of course he wasn't risking anything at the minute, sitting on the bench with his legs stretched out. He might have been at home on the couch, watching cartoons. Maybe the Wards had the right idea, staying home.

A whistle blew and Andrés jumped up, clapping. Liss leaned around the Garzas to hand Link their drink. "What happened?"

"Gain of a few yards. You won't be quizzed on it later."

Andrés sat down. "Where's Ennis tonight, Kitty?"

"He had a meeting he couldn't move," Kitty said.

Connie rolled her eyes and shoved a chip into her mouth.

"And how's that Batmobile of Tanner's?" Andrés said. "Not totaled, I gather."

Kitty's spine straightened. "Just a scratch," she said pleasantly. "Things were blown out of proportion, with the police there, only because—" Two team mothers down below them had turned to listen. Kitty lowered her voice. "Because of what they found."

Liss's pulse gave a kick, her heart suddenly hammering in her chest.

She felt that old panic, the long nights with an infant unexpectedly against her chest and the future ahead of her, minutes on the clock passing achingly slowly but also everything rushing at her too quickly so that she could barely catch her breath. She remembered Tanner's car at the edge of the quarry, pointed out toward oblivion. It was not just a football injury she needed to worry about. It was everything.

"They could have been killed," she said.

The mothers below Kitty clucked sympathetically but shared a look.

"Don't be so dramatic," Kitty said. "It was *nothing*. One car, a bad turn, just a fender bender."

"So was *Ashley's*," Liss said.

Link winced.

"Well," Connie said, and then rolled her lips together as though no further word would escape them. What wouldn't she say? Her husband turned back to the field but placed a hand on her knee.

"We'll see, I suppose," Kitty said.

"What does that mean?" Link said.

"Your kid's going in, Kehoe," Andrés said.

Callan had launched from the sidelines into the game. The uniform and padding threw off the proportions of his body, shoulder pads building up his frame into a figure she couldn't immediately recognize. Was he taller than he had been last week? With the helmet firmly in place, he could be anyone's kid. Anyone. A stranger.

Liss stood, applauding. Somewhere behind her, she heard someone say Callan's name but when she glanced back, she couldn't locate the source.

At the next tackle, Callan helped a boy from the other team from the ground. Liss clapped until her palms were pink.

"OK, honey," Link said.

At the edge of her field of vision, Kitty turned her head and she and Connie blinked at one another. Liss sat down. The mysterious nature of her relationship with Link was her thing, then, like how Connie policed every morsel that passed Kitty's lips—or didn't— and how Kitty voiced concern to Liss about Connie's thoughtlessness or Mateo's weight. The way they had worn the Wards smooth, their excuses, their ducked responsibilities.

They wouldn't even be friends, Liss realized, if they hadn't been thrown together by their sons.

She had friends. She did. Liss reached into her coat pocket and grasped her phone with its reassuring number of texts she hadn't yet thumbed through. She had messages from parents from the school, her friend Sherry Harris. Amy, the president of the boosters group! People who cared what happened to her and her family. She turned and surveyed the rows of bleachers, from the top row down to the bottom. Hundreds of people, most of them she had a nodding acquaintance to or better. She had a community here.

But—

When had she and Link ever been able to sit at a school event without people dropping by? Old friends slapping Link's back, neighbors checking in on Key's condition?

Were the texts from friends checking on her family? Or were they from people hungry for an inside track?

A few pairs of eyes slid away as she gazed over the crowd.

That old quarry was suddenly a chasm between her family and everyone else. And who could she say that to? Not Kitty. Not Connie. Link wouldn't know what she meant.

Down at ground level, Vera stood with her arms folded atop the chain-link fence that separated fans from the field. Liss excused herself and bounded down the bleachers.

"I'm flattered you would leave such esteemed company," Vera said.

Liss hooked her fingers into the fence. "I needed a break."

"Team moms are the worst," Vera said, smiling.

"Apparently it's great that we're here, no matter what anyone else says," Liss said.

"Courage in the face of the madding crowd," Vera said.

Out on the field a whistle blew and the announcer called out Callan's name. Liss looked to see what was happening but snagged on a dark uniform on the far side of the fence. Was it—not Mercer, thank God. Slocum was doing the soft job of policing the game tonight.

But then at the deputy marshal's shoulder, in the visiting team's bleachers, Liss saw a face she recognized. Sophie Ward? And Jim, too. Jamie's parents sat in a low corner on the opponents' side, huddled not toward one another but somehow into their own forms, their shoulders hunched.

She didn't have to wonder. Being Callan's parent was the joy of her life, but it came with a lot of expectations. A sort of parallel, exhausting game she'd never signed up for. It would have been far easier to sit among strangers tonight.

Up in the stands, Link was doing fine, talking with Andrés and gesturing animatedly toward the game. Still young, handsome, the same Link Kehoe as ever. Was she worried for nothing? Maybe he would always be fine.

He saw her looking and raised an eyebrow, waved.

It didn't matter who she counted among her friends. She had Link, even now. She pictured the divorce papers sitting on the counter of his apartment, curling with age, collecting coffee cup rings, until one day he swept them into the recycling, the decision made while they were stitching back together what they'd once had.

She waved.

But he was looking away suddenly, standing and frowning out toward the game. In the stands, the team parents rose as one with astonished expressions. On the field, whistles and shouts.

"Oh, no," Vera said.

Liss turned. The benches were clearing and the field flooded, a free-for-all. Boys tussled and tore at one another to get to their teammates while officials tried to hold back the fray and coaches rushed in to peel players from one another.

Liss searched the scene for Callan but couldn't find him. "Where is he?"

When the last of the boys hopped out of the pile or were pulled away, Callan came up red-faced and raging. His helmet had been knocked off, his hair stuck dark to his forehead.

"What's happening? Who—"

The last boy to his feet was Tanner. Callan lurched for him again and only the new coach's grip kept Callan from leaping at him as he walked away.

CHAPTER FOURTEEN

Callan spent the rest of the game twitching and red-eared on the bench. Tanner, also removed from the game, sat on the opposite end.

Liss returned to her cold bleacher seat among the team parents, twitching, too. Link shot her a questioning look. Kitty found a reason to hurry away, her phone to her ear.

"Callan's lucky he's not booted from the game," Andrés said to no one in particular. "Zero tolerance and all that."

"The zero-tolerance policy—" Liss couldn't think of an argument she wanted to make. The policy was for weapons brought to school and drugs found in lockers.

When the home team dragged themselves off the field for halftime, Callan walked with his head down, grim mouth turned toward his dirty cleats.

"Link, let's go . . ." She tried to think of something to suggest that would keep Connie from chirping up to join them. "Um."

"Yep," he said.

She followed him down the stands and through the crowds toward the school.

"Are you going to the locker room?" she said. "Where are you going?"

"I just needed to step away," Link said. "Before I clubbed Garza."

"What did he say?"

"Oh, before he knew it was Callan at the bottom of the scrum, he had a lot to say about how some of Mateo's teammates were raised, bullshit like that."

"It must be nice, having raised the first perfect teenage boy," Liss said. "Except they forget that I work at the school and *know*—"

But she couldn't say. That was the zero-tolerance policy *she* was held to.

"Callan's OK, right?" Link said. "I mean, with everything going on?"

"He wanted to stay home this morning," Liss said. "And I wouldn't let him. I didn't think he should be alone right now."

"Maybe alone is exactly what he needs to be," Link said, nodding toward the field. "He could have gone over to Mom and Dad's for the day."

As though she wouldn't have thought of it. "You're going to have to take this one," Liss said. "I don't know how to tell him not to fight in a game that *rewards* tackling your friends—"

"You don't tackle your own team, Liss."

"My point is . . . He's getting to the age where he really needs you to be there, Link."

As soon as she'd said it, she knew what he would say.

"Well," he said. "You're the one—"

"*You're* the one," she said.

He scuffed his foot at the path. "Yeah," he said.

"Link, you're the one showing him how to be a man," Liss said.

"And a hell of a job I'm making of it," he said.

"But now he's going through something complex and confusing," she said.

"You'd handle complex so much better than I would," Link said.

"He's looking to *you* to show him how to act," she said. "You're his father."

"*You* raised him and we both know it," Link said. "*And* me, isn't that your joke?" A ripple of hurt crossed his face that she almost caught. Then it was gone and he swung his arm around her, pulled her in. "We'll figure it out. We're still a team, OK? Dream team."

"Dream team," she said into his shoulder, comforted by the smell of him, the feel of his arm around her. Not caring, for a moment, who saw, what they would say.

Liss turned her cheek against Link's coat. Down at the gate, someone stared in their direction. The woman turned resolutely away, her profile lit by the bright field lights. "Mim," Liss said.

"Huh?"

"Mim Hubbard," Liss said. "She's over by the gate."

"Should we go say hi? Come on."

Liss stood her ground, suddenly aware of the crowds, of eyes grazing over them and lingering, of double-takes. "Let's not."

"Is that fair? Robbie's an innocent man. The car in our pond proves it, doesn't it?"

"It might prove something else," she said.

"That Ashley had a lead foot," Link said. "Or had, you know, poor kid but . . . instability?"

Liss frowned at the ground. "It doesn't feel like people are finding fault with Ashley or blaming postpartum depression. It feels like they're looking at . . . us."

She loved Callan with all her heart, but once in a while she realized what a small life Ashley had handed them, how Link's big plans being dashed had rolled back on them, crushing them in place. They hadn't built a community, not really. They'd inherited one. They'd never launched their own lives. And now—

Now it was too late. With Key deteriorating, with Callan this close to graduation. This place was home, for better or worse. That house, their sanctuary. Her sanctuary, at least, for now.

Down at the gate, Mim Hubbard gazed back at her, flat-eyed. Something was expected of her, Liss thought. Something was being transferred to her.

She shivered.

"You cold, babe?" Link gathered her under his arm to walk back toward the game.

"You should probably stop calling me that at some point."

"I'll get around to it," he said, with a grin.

He never would. As with most things she'd ever asked of him.

They spent the rest of the game at the perimeter fence instead of in the stands and, afterward, they waited for Callan outside the side exit of the school. Some team parents had gone ahead to the parking lot, but a few waited nearby.

"Hard loss," Link commented. "But they played hard." No one chimed in.

"Good game," Link said to the first group of boys out the door.

"Thanks," a kid said uncertainly. The other two kept moving, their parents stepping up to hustle them away.

What would those families be saying about hers on the way home tonight? she wondered.

"Maybe don't talk to strangers, Link," she said.

"Things are that fucked?"

He'd raised his voice too loud. The chatter among the parents still waiting had cut out. She wouldn't look. "For the time being," she said quietly.

"But they aren't strangers," he said in a small voice.

Jamie shuffled out the door and hesitated at the sight of them. "Callan's talking to Coach," he said.

"Thanks, Jamie."

He wouldn't look at her, but past her, and that's when she realized Sophie Ward and her husband were among the shadows behind them. "Sophie, hi."

Sophie was a small-framed woman in clothes too large for her, as though she were hiding inside them.

"Jim," Link said.

"I haven't been able to find Jamie's jacket out at the house," Liss said. "I'll keep looking."

Jim looked toward Jamie. "What's this about? Whose jacket are you wearing?"

"It's one Callan's outgrown," Liss said. "He's welcome to keep it. In fact, if I go through Callan's things, he's probably got some nice—"

"We don't need charity," Jim Ward said, shedding his jacket.

"It's not *charity*," Liss said.

"Come on, Jim," Link said. "What's this about?"

Jim held out his coat to his son. Jamie removed Callan's fleece and handed it to Liss. "Thanks for lending it to me, Mrs. Kehoe."

"Jamie, let's get a move on," Jim said, and turned on his heel for the parking lot.

"He still has homework," Sophie said to Liss. "You understand."

She did. She'd just been hoping to be wrong.

CHAPTER FIFTEEN

Don't worry about Ward," Link said as Jamie's family swept him away. "He always has some gripe. Especially when it comes to me."

"Is there something going on at work, then?"

"No more than *usual*," Link said.

But things were not usual.

Liss looked back toward the gate for Mim Hubbard. She was gone.

Callan came through the doorway fuming, red-cheeked and moving past them, a train blowing through a station.

"Hey," Link said.

"Let's go," Callan said. "I'm starving."

They chased him to the car, where Callan tried to open the door before she'd unlocked it, thunking at the handle repeatedly. "Hold *on*," she said. The second the locks sounded he threw himself in. It was dark, and he was fast to turn his head, but she'd seen the look on his face before he dove into the shadows of the back seat.

Link stood nearby. He shrugged.

"I think we could do that chat another time," Liss said.

"You sure?" Relieved, jumping at the chance to put it off.

"Maybe you can pick him up from practice tomorrow? Get him some dinner? I'll text you."

She got into the car and sat quietly while Callan sniffled against the door behind her.

"Are we going to *go*, or not?" he said finally. "I have homework."

She started the car. "What happened out there?"

He didn't answer. Fine. She navigated out of the parking lot and toward town, her attention flicking between the road and the back seat.

"What did Tanner do to provoke you?" she said at last.

"He . . . he was being a jerk is all."

"You can't fight every kid who—"

"Never mind!"

"Did he say something about . . . Ashley?"

Callan shifted, sighed.

Maybe she should have insisted on Link having that conversation tonight. Link could be another child in the house, ramping Callan up until she couldn't get either of them to listen or settle down. But if he was Peter Pan, he was also the Pied Piper, even if he didn't know it. Even if he wouldn't take the role seriously.

She sought out Callan in the rearview mirror, could only catch the outline of a cheek against a pair of headlights a few car lengths behind them.

"Did Tanner say something about your dad?" she said.

"*No,*" he said.

That he was willing to answer at all told her she'd hit the vein of truth.

"You don't have to protect your dad from kids at school," Liss said. "Or anyone. Things are . . . well, things are weird right now, and people can be—"

"Assholes."

"Language," she said. "I was going to say insensitive. But yeah."

The headlights behind them had grown bright as the vehicle got closer. Liss flicked her rearview mirror to dim the effect.

"I wish I'd never *seen* that car," Callan mumbled.

"This is not your fault. Or your dad's, or—" She swallowed. "Anyone's."

"Hers."

"We can feel bad that it happened without having to find someone to blame," Liss said. "It was an accident." Liss pictured Ashley standing on their porch. Sodden canvas shoes. God, she hoped it was an accident. "But now we know, don't we? She never would have left you."

"Then why did people ever think she did?" Callan said.

"Well," she said.

She could see him better now, in the too-bright headlights of the truck riding too close behind them. Liss slowed down to let the other driver pass.

"I guess believing she ran away was easier," Liss said. "Easier than thinking she might have been hurt or taken."

"Easier for who?" Callan said.

Liss chewed at her lip. A woman who ran off had *got away*. She was an open-ended story with a chance at a different ending. Some of those happy endings, Liss had never hoped for. If she was completely honest with herself.

The driver behind them hadn't taken the hint. Liss slowed down further.

"The important part is that she loved you," she said.

She didn't actually *know* this was true, but how could she have not? Look at their beautiful boy—

The truck behind them flicked on its high beams.

"What the—"

Callan turned to look. "What are they doing?"

"Being . . ."

"Assholes," Callan said.

"Inconsiderate," Liss said.

The turn to the quarry road had appeared ahead. Should she even drive home, or should she keep to well-lit streets? The truck was already nearly in her trunk—

Liss turned on her signal. The driver laid on his horn.

"Mom?"

"It's going to be OK," she said, trying to sound calm. "Do you have your phone handy?"

"Call Dad?"

"Do you have Mercer's number?"

Callan had his phone out. "Call Mercer?"

"Hold on," she said. "If we turn and he follows—"

She made the turn too quickly under pressure, tires sliding in the gravel. They came to a stop, one tire in grass. The truck blew around them and on toward town, horn blaring.

"Was that someone we know?" Callan said.

"No, of course not. It was just—" She didn't know who to blame. Kids? Drunk drivers?

That truck might just as likely have followed them out of the school parking lot. Someone they knew, someone who knew them.

"Just someone in a hurry," she said, driving on. "This is why I worry about you being on the road."

Callan sagged back against the seat. "I know," he said, miserably, turning his head as they passed his grandparents' driveway.

She crept through the curve, like a show of respect. Would this section of their road always belong to Ashley now?

"He said," Callan started.

"Tanner?"

"Tanner said Dad must have put her into the pond. Must have killed her."

Heat and anger shot through her, like she'd touched a live wire. "Does that sound like your dad to you?"

"But—"

"Tanner doesn't know anything about it." He'd only be repeating something he'd heard, absorbing vile rumor like a sponge. She didn't have to wonder where he'd soaked it up. "People will talk," she said. "Even when they don't know anything. *Especially* when they don't know anything. We're going to have to ignore it until it blows over."

She pulled into their driveway, her headlights swinging from the road, over the mailbox, the ditch, long grass, the barn—

"Mom," Callan said.

The motion-sensor light over the deck flicked on, illuminating the face of the barn. Across the white expanse of the sliding doors, someone had spray-painted a message in red.

KILLER.

"How soon," Callan said, "before it blows over?"

CHAPTER SIXTEEN

It was late—later than he'd have delivered bad news anywhere else—when Mercer's headlights swept over the Kehoe property and caught Liss, wild-eyed, at the doors of her barn.

"Ah, now," he said under his breath.

The two-foot-high red letters had started to fade under her exertions, a ghost of the word now but still there.

She'd startled out of the reach of his headlights but he could still see her there, shading her eyes. A sponge in the other hand, a bucket at her feet.

He killed the lights and got out. "Why didn't you call me?"

She slapped the sponge to the door and scrubbed. "To reach the high bits?"

"To report a crime?" he said.

"What's the point, Mercer?"

He walked across the grass toward her, glancing toward the house. No light on upstairs, Callan in bed. Maybe Kehoe was in there, too. He didn't know the situation anymore. But Kehoe had better not be in there with his feet up while she dealt with this.

"I would think the point to reporting a crime would be to catch who'd done it," he said. "But you don't seem to think we're much good for that sort of work."

"I don't want you spending time on this," she said. "But if you could figure out where the mother of my son went and also . . ."

Her attention refocused on the door.

"And also who killed your husband's best friend?" Mercer said. "When you put the two together like that, makes you wonder."

"It doesn't make *me* wonder." But she wouldn't stop scraping at the door, wouldn't look at him.

He leaned over and peered into the bucket. "How long have you been at that?"

She dropped her hands, defeated. "A while."

"It's not going to come off. Have any paint?"

"Not the right kind."

"Let's see what you have," he said.

She dropped the sponge into the bucket and pushed the doors apart on their rails. A motion-sensor light inside flicked on, but she was already across the room in the dark, off toward a shelf lined with all sorts of chemical hazards, antifreeze and bug spray, weed killer, cleaners, oils. Ammonia and bleach sitting pretty right next to each other. Liss got up on her toes for a rusted can of spray paint, the hem of her shirt pulling up to reveal an expanse of skin, two freckles.

He had to get over this.

She rocked back on her feet and held out the can. "This is the only white paint we have."

We. It was a kick to his gut. "Might do the trick."

They went back out, closed the doors. Mercer slipped off his jacket, rolled up his sleeves.

"You'll probably still want to put a coat of regular paint on top of this," he said.

"I can get some," she said. "I just don't want Link to see it."

He wasn't here, then. That was OK.

Mercer rattled the can. Almost empty. He'd have to economize. He tested the paint over a leg of the *K*. "What do you think?"

"I think it might be enough to keep it from being visible from space," Liss said. "An improvement."

"You're sure you don't want to report it?" he said. "I should at least take some pictures—"

"I'm sure," she said.

Destroying evidence, then, all to keep Link Kehoe from getting uncomfortable.

Mercer began tracing the letters, covering the scrubbed pink with white. "Better?"

"Better," she said, less terse than before. "You don't have to do this. But thanks."

"All part of the service."

That made her smile. "Should have had you out here today working on the lawnmower."

"Today." It occurred to him he was retracing the original vandalism letter for letter, using the same movements the original artist would have. He hoped she didn't notice. "Today I spent some time acquainting myself with some old case files."

They let that sit between them as he obliterated another letter.

"And what did you find?" she said finally.

"That I am grateful for the leaps in technology available to us," he said. "The paper files are dusty and fragile. And the notes on this case in particular are shamefully thin."

He could hear her breathing, *feel* her thinking.

"What will you do, then?" she said.

He looked back. "Investigate."

She nodded, quickly returning her attention to the paint job.

"That's what you wanted me to do," he said. "I thought."

"Of course I did. I do."

"I would have, anyway," he said. "You know that."

"It's your job," she said.

The paint gave out as he touched up the last of the pink. If you knew to look for it, the word was still legible. A middling job until she could get supplies. "Aren't you at all worried about what I might find out?" he said.

"Sounds like you already found out Link's dad wasn't a good file-keeper."

They'd been treading too lightly around what he'd come to say. "I'm not joking anymore, Lissette."

"I never thought you were joking."

He said, "I came to tell you . . ."

Liss tensed. What did she think he would say? What stories had she told herself all these years?

"I came to tell you that we found human remains—"

"Oh, God." Her legs seemed to go out from under her. She folded in half before he could reach for her and crouched there, one hand over her face.

"A skull," he said.

"Mercer." She dropped her hand. "Are you saying—it's Ashley?"

"They're already working on extracting DNA, but that will take some time," he said.

"DNA," she breathed.

"We'd need a sample from Callan," he said. "He's her only living relative or I'd find another way. It's a simple blood draw, nothing too traumatic. And, like I said, we have some time. A few days for the blood draw, anyway." He took his time rolling down his sleeves, buttoning the cuffs. "But there's more."

She went still, all her body gripping time against whatever he would say. She was worried for someone, and he didn't blame her. Someone should be worried.

"More?" she said, in a tone he didn't like pointed in his direction. Maybe she used it on Callan when he came in the house with muddy shoes. Tired, aggrieved. Scolding. "Mercer, how?" she said. "How could there possibly be *more*?"

THE NEXT MORNING Mercer was already at his desk when Slocum rolled into the station. Later than he claimed he always got in, Mercer noticed. He had a waxed paper bag from the grocery store in his fist. Doughnuts, probably, and that made Mercer pricklier than he wanted to be, right off. A man can have a doughnut, but could he get it on his own time, when he wasn't wearing the uniform, like a cartoon?

Slocum stopped in Mercer's doorway. "You're in early, Chief," he said. An accusation.

"Early, late. Time's a little slippery right now with all the goings-on."

Slocum thought that over. "Chance of overtime?"

Slocum didn't want overtime. He was simply like that, poking at anything anyone said. Not as a good detective would, but as though he was testing for weaknesses in the boundaries around himself. He should have retired years ago along with Old Kehoe, but he wasn't married, had no hobbies Mercer had ever heard of. Family somewhere but they didn't like him. Mercer had been able to talk a few of Kehoe's old guard off the roster but not this traffic cone. For better or worse, Slocum was married to his post, and Mercer couldn't force him out without looking like—and feeling like—he'd be sending an old man out to die.

"Let's see what these youngsters can get done in their regular working hours, why don't we?" Mercer said.

"You're the boss," Slocum said. He reached into the bag and pulled out a glazed doughnut. "Of course, you're the one just said you didn't know night from day. What are you working on so hard?"

He rammed half the doughnut into his mouth.

"I'm up to my neck in the Hay case," Mercer said. "I should say up to my *ankles*. Not a lot to go on in this file."

"Hay," Slocum said, his mouth still full. "Confirmed she was in that car, then?"

He'd be down at the diner as soon as he could with anything he learned. "No confirmation yet," Mercer said. "I'm trying to gather up anything relevant. Any reason Kehoe went so light on these interviews?"

"He didn't go light on that Hubbard fella," Slocum said, grinning around the doughball in his mouth. Mercer had to look away before he puked.

"Got the phone book out on him, did he?"

"He—" Slocum caught himself before he dug in further. He wasn't as dumb as he played. "Interviewed him thoroughly."

"What about his own son?" Mercer said. "Did he interview Kehoe Junior? Thoroughly?"

Slocum's jaw slowed down at last. "Link had an alibi, didn't he? How I remember it."

"I haven't come across it. He wasn't home."

"They were having a fight, that's right," Slocum said. "Him and his missus." Slocum gave Mercer a knowing look. "The marshal vouched for him. That's all I know."

"Link should have been a person of interest and his alibi is covered by the investigating officer? That's ugly and you know it." Mercer thought of the old marshal's agitation when he'd gone to visit him. That was a man with concerns, now that the car had been found. "And I suppose Key's alibi was that he was with his son?"

"You can't be serious. Why would the marshal need an alibi?" Slocum shoved the other half of the doughnut into his gob.

"Because the car's been found on his land, maybe? Anyone near the epicenter needs one," Mercer said. "What's yours?"

"I couldn't tell you, it's been that long," Slocum said, sucking glaze off his thumb. "It's always the boy toy, isn't it? The marshal had hers in. For *thorough* questioning. Don't believe what his ma says. Hubbard was no stranger to our lock up."

It would all have to be done up again. Everything collected properly and combed through, and against fifteen years of fading memory. Kehoe gone mute, Hubbard dead. No one pounding on Mercer's door for justice, not even Hubbard's mother, not anymore.

But that skull—

The depression to the skull was at the back, a set of concentric cracks radiating out like a spider's web. Not in a spot the victim could have brained herself on the windshield or steering wheel. Plus, even though the driver's side seat belt had long ago dissolved, the buckle had been found intact, both ends connected, suggesting the driver had been buckled in, not likely to have struck the windshield at all.

The car had sustained no structural damage to speak of. The airbags hadn't even deployed. But the thing that had made the hair on the back of his neck stand up was that the car had been left in neutral. Cars didn't accidentally slide off roads in neutral.

Was the thin file on his desk shoddy work? Or the very careful kind?

The forensics people had to weigh in, first. He had to be patient. Ashley—if the bones were Ashley Hay's—had waited fifteen years already.

But he was an impatient man. That bludgeoned skull was howling murder at him.

Slocum shuffled off to his desk and, Mercer suspected, another doughnut.

You want to talk about a hole at the center of something, Mercer thought wildly.

He pressed the heels of his hands to his eyes. There was a gaping black hole at the center of this. And if he reached his hand in, what would he come up with? There would be more, worse, to discover. More and more and more he didn't necessarily want to know.

CHAPTER SEVENTEEN

Thursday morning, Vera ushered a student out of the office and stopped at Liss's desk. "You OK?" she said cautiously.

Liss froze. "Why wouldn't I be?"

Vera's mouth twisted, as though she'd tasted a new food and was trying to describe it. She pulled one of the student chairs across from Liss's desk closer and leaned in. "I heard about the fight at the game last night."

"Oh," Liss said. "Right."

She'd kept herself busy all morning, trying not to think about the bones Mercer had found, that skull. And *more*, he'd promised, while her heart thundered in her ears.

Not a suicide, he'd said.

She'd had a moment of pure, unearned relief. Ashley hadn't driven away from Liss and Callan directly into the quarry. She hadn't *meant* to do it, anyway.

But the relief was short-lived. Not a suicide. Not an accident, either.

Murder.

Murder, and Mercer was there to ask her a few questions. About Link. Which was ridiculous, truly. Anyone who had ever met Link—

"*Oh?*" Vera said. "You sound pretty casual about it. I heard it was a brawl, and that Callan was the instigator."

"Callan's just wound a little tight right now," Liss said. "And . . . some of the boys on the team might have said something. About his dad."

Vera's expression turned stormy. "Those little . . . Should I send anyone to see Mike?"

The vice principal, who handled student discipline. All that talk about how they'd have to turn the other cheek until things got better—Liss wished she could throw a few punches of her own. "I think he'd prefer to let it go," Liss said.

"You sure you're OK?" Vera said. "Anything you want to . . . talk about?"

Liss hadn't slept well, and her hands were red and raw from scrubbing the barn doors. Someone—multiple people—thought her kid's dad was a murderer, and she probably had a funeral to plan for a woman who'd hated her. Who she had once resented—

Who she *still* resented, for clinging to everything that was good in Liss's life. Tainting it.

Was she so bankrupt as a human being? To resent a woman for being murdered?

Vera studied her.

"I have a new respect for the kids who come in here up to their necks in trouble and won't say a word about it," Liss said weakly.

Vera laughed but let the silence open up, the same trick Vera used to let students rush in with explanations. But Vera was her friend, a real one. And she could use a real friend.

"I have complicated feelings about her," Liss said. "Ashley."

"Of course," Vera murmured. "It would be weird if you didn't."

"She's been a presence in our relationship," Liss said. "All along. Literally, obviously, in the beginning and then . . ."

"An absence that was a presence," Vera said.

She could have walked away when Ashley turned up pregnant.

They were so young, their relationship just kid stuff. No one could have judged her and yet—she didn't. She hadn't wanted to. Link's attention was a prize she had won and she hadn't been willing to relinquish it. She hadn't considered the option, really, hadn't had the sense of herself to know she had the choice.

If she was truly honest, hadn't Link's shame played to her advantage? The apologies, the promises. He was like a bird with a broken wing, now tamed for a household pet.

She couldn't blame Ashley entirely for her small life; it was the life she'd chosen. The one she'd wanted. If it hadn't been enough for Link—

That, she wouldn't take the blame for.

Liss realized she'd been holding every muscle in her body tight and still. Her jaw hurt, her neck. She let out a breath. "She and I are entangled, you know? Like vines that grew too close to one another."

"Fighting each other for the available sunlight," Vera said.

"But then I remember that she's *dead*—"

"They know for sure?"

She wasn't sure what she was allowed to say. "No." A different sort of absence, once they did. "Not for sure. I don't think I'm making sense. But thanks for listening."

Vera reached across the desk and squeezed Liss's wrist. "That's what I'm here for."

Liss watched Vera return to her office. She really did understand student resistance now. Once you'd opened up, you couldn't snatch back what you'd said. She didn't want to talk to someone about what was happening to her family, because talking about it gave it flesh, made it real. She only wanted it all not to happen.

Students passed by the doorway, looking in.

But it was happening. The whispers, the stares.

And it *had*. It had all happened before.

She reached for her phone and typed. You're still picking up Callan?

Always double-check with Link, that was her rule. He was a guy who didn't keep a calendar, who forgot to pay the electric bill.

But he was not a killer, and she had to prove it.

LISS HADN'T ALWAYS appreciated the long driveways of country homes, but now she saw that they served as a lookout for those inside—a first defense against salesmen and intruders.

Which was she?

By the time her tires had stopped crunching against gravel, Robbie's mother already stood on her covered porch with crossed arms. Liss gave the steering wheel a squeeze, then unhooked her seat belt and got out.

Mim Hubbard had been standing with crossed arms for the last fifteen years, waiting for someone to say the proper word to her about her son. Liss thought she understood now why Mim had bothered. When everyone else had abandoned Robbie, who was left to keep his life visible? His death? A grave wasn't enough. A cross at the side of the road.

"Lissette Kehoe," Mim said with irony or wonder. "I wondered who would be the first person to remember we existed. I have to say, I didn't think it would be you."

We, she still said.

And Mercer had not been to see her. "Not the last, I hope," Liss said.

"Hope's the last thing to go, Lissette," Mim said, her arms dropping to her sides.

"I'm sorry," Liss said. "We should have—I don't know."

"You're not apologizing for the whole town?" Mim said. "And

everything they did? You and Link came to his funeral. You stood by him."

Liss looked away.

"And Link," Mim said. "I'll never forget that he helped carry my Robbie."

He'd been the only pallbearer who had known Robbie. The funeral home had been forced to roust up a few sour-faced staff members to help. Liss could picture Link in his suit, creased in odd places, neck pink from a close shave and a complicated sort of shame, she'd always supposed, for having survived whatever had happened to Robbie. For having survived *Ashley*.

"Last night while we were at the school," Liss said. "Someone came and painted a . . . an accusation on our barn."

Mim looked off toward the road as a car went by and shook her head, weary in a way Liss gladly could only guess at.

When she turned to Liss again, her expression had softened. "Those bastards always seem to have a little extra paint, don't they?"

CHAPTER EIGHTEEN

Mim waved her inside. "You might as well come in," she said.

As Liss approached the steps to the porch, a flash of silver caught her eye. Out at the side yard, shiny pinwheels circled in the breeze among overgrown rows of a vegetable garden. She was heartened a bit to think Mim Hubbard could get down on her tired knees to tend tomatoes.

"I don't get visitors, so you'll have to forgive the housekeeping," Mim said.

The front room was fine, if a little stuffy. An old television set blared a game show.

"Didn't mean to interrupt your show," Liss said.

Mim shuffled across the scuffed wood floors and snapped it off. In the sudden silence, a clock ticked.

"I let it play for the noise," Mim said.

Laugh tracks and jangling game shows her only company when Robbie should have been her insurance against an old age planned around *Family Feud*'s airtime. Liss wrapped her arms around herself.

"Cold? I could make a cup of coffee," Mim said. "Might be an old cannister of tea in there somewhere."

Dusty tea, her favorite. "I'm fine."

"Are you?" Mim gestured to a seat and took one opposite on the sagging couch.

"No." Liss took a breath. "No, we're not. I'm worried what's going to happen."

"I would be," Mim said. "If I was you. And I have been."

There was an edge to her voice that Liss couldn't quite read. She couldn't be pleased another family might suffer. Maybe she felt an odd pride in what she'd endured. Maybe she was only glad not to be alone in it anymore.

"Besides the barn, we've had someone out on the property at night," Liss said. "And calls at four in the morning."

"That's how it started for us, the calls," Mim said. "Hang-ups, mostly, just to get me out of bed, but sometimes I could hear them breathing on the other end. Waiting for me to go crazy for them, I guess. Perform." Mim's chin jutted out just as it might have begun to quiver. "Got rid of the whole damn hook-up. Didn't need it anymore, anyway, since no one called but cranks and scammers. And *charities*." Mim swept her arms comically wide to indicate her reduced circumstances.

Liss took the opportunity to look around, spotting photos of Robbie on a side table. Robbie in his graduation cap and gown, Robbie as a boy with his dad. Robbie with Ashley.

"I heard . . . some of what happened to Robbie," Liss said, still looking over the array of photos. Robbie with a dog. Robbie with a baby in his arms. Was that—?

Callan.

A photo of *her* son had grown faded in this house. She'd never even seen that photo before. Who had taken it? Who had placed it in that frame?

Did Mim fashion herself as some sort of *grandparent* to Callan? Did she count Callan among her regrets and losses?

Liss had a peculiar feeling of straddling the known world and a parallel one she hadn't realized existed, and Callan was in both of them, the boy she raised and a stranger, simultaneously. But there would be untold worlds, and versions of Callan in each of them, beyond her grasp. The Callan known to his friends, to his teachers and coach. The Callan known only to Link. The Callan who had lied to the police.

He used to fit in her arms, and now his life folded out like a map to places she could not go.

"I don't think I knew all of what Robbie went through," Mim was saying. "He kept it from me. He *tried*."

Liss dragged her attention away from the photo of Robbie and Callan. "How did you know?"

"I could hear the whispers well enough," she said. "See the looks in the street. Then the paint and knocking about the place at night, just like you said. Some stuff was happening on the computer, I guess. I didn't know anything about that. Until after." Mim's hands lay in her lap, upturned and helpless. "But then he's not going to work anymore," she said. "It's OK, Mama, we'll be fine, Mama. Tires going flat while we're trying to do the shopping. Until the car's gone for the cash, like I'm not supposed to notice he's begging rides wherever he needs to go."

"Link was happy to take him," Liss said.

"Link and a neighbor. The rest all disappeared, you know," Mim said. "His friends. And mine. I used to belong to a ladies' group in town, lunch every third Thursday. Flowers in the planters downtown, that sort of thing. Collecting for the unfortunate."

Liss looked up. Ladies visiting, clucking their tongues, asking her if her mother could come to the door. Women all over this county might have come to her door back then, and they would know her this way, the grubby child, hands reaching for canned goods. The news about Ashley would have put Liss back on their luncheon plates. All their efforts, come to this.

"When Ashley went missing," Mim continued, "those same *ladies* changed the meeting calendar to another day of the week. Forgot to tell me. I showed up on a Thursday to an empty room."

"That must have been hard," Liss said.

Mim dismissed her former friends with a wave of her hand. "The hardest part . . ." Mim said. "The hardest part was how they turned on Robbie. They thought he could harm that girl. They thought he was a *monster*. He was a rambunctious kid, I'll give you that. But that was just *boys*," Mim said. "You know how they do. How they *all* did."

She didn't say Link's name, but Liss heard her meaning. Link and Robbie had both attended the party that the police had broken up for noise and underage drinking. She'd had to work, or she would have been there, too. When the dust settled, Robbie and the others had court appearances, fees to pay, and arrests on their adult records. Some of them were able to get their records scrubbed in time for college and jobs. Link and Ashley had somehow made it out clean. Link's dad would have cleared the way for his son, but how had Ashley escaped the consequences? The rumors started up, then, and were confirmed not much later, Ashley pregnant.

Robbie had trouble with the fees. He wouldn't take Link's help and the fines compounded quickly, trapping him in a cycle he couldn't break, and making him known to the town deputies. After that, they dogged him at every turn. He drove too fast and racked up tickets he couldn't pay. He spent too much time drinking at a dumpy roadside place that would serve a toddler if he crawled to the bar, and from there picked up more trouble, more fees he couldn't pay, more attention.

I guess I'm public enemy number one, he'd said to them, grinning, or trying to, after he'd spent the weekend in jail for failure to pay and Link had gone to bail him out.

"When she disappeared, they sure thought they had their man," Mim said. "The police believed it, and that made it all right to torment us."

Liss wished for the noise of the TV. "It was never all right," she said, weakly.

You believe me, don't you? Robbie had asked her. Begged her. But if she had believed for a minute that Ashley had come to harm, she might have wondered about Robbie, too.

"We came home once to find our mailbox was knocked over," Mim said. "You could say kids done it. You could say it was an accident. But after we'd been through everything else, it was hard to imagine accidents were still possible."

Mim seemed to drift away. Liss sat forward. "And then—"

"Like a dog in the street, Lissette," Mim said. "You can't tell me that was an accident. What would he have been doing out on the road, alone? Your father-in-law didn't bother to figure out what happened, and this new one—" Mim's gaze refocused, on her. She didn't miss much, even without those ladies' lunches. "He hasn't been bothered too much, either."

"The case would still be open, right?" Liss said.

"The case may have its mouth wide open, but no facts are jumping into it on their own, are they?" Mim cried. "They took my *boy*, Liss. My whole, whole heart. They don't tell you about it, do they? What it's like to be a mother? How the second they're born it's like they pried open your chest and ripped out your beating heart, and you're left that way for as long as your child walks the earth? And after, believe me." Her voice caught, but she recovered, licked her lips. "Meanwhile if he turns out rotten? That's your fault. Everything he does tells on you, either way. You're too clingy, you're too cold. You taught him the wrong things about women. Have you heard that yet? You will. All men's faults fall on the women who raised them."

Or the woman who married him, Liss thought.

"They asked me," Mim said. Her voice had grown thin. "They asked me who I thought could hurt him, like they hadn't done it themselves. Like I had to solve that riddle for them, too. But by the time they found Robbie on the road, I couldn't tell friend from foe. I blame them all. Every last one of them."

Liss looked up to find Mim shaking.

"Can I get you a glass of water? I'll get you a glass of water." Liss went to the kitchen and opened cabinets at random. Her hands were shaking, too. This is what they had to look forward to? Blame and torment, open season on mailboxes and barns until—

"Left side," Mim called, her voice hoarse.

The cabinet held cloudy tumblers, a few old souvenir glasses from places Liss was pretty certain Mim had never been. Garage sale bounty, objects discarded by others. On the second shelf sat a conga line of pill bottles. Liss recognized a drug name because some of the students took it for anxiety. The next bottle, for depression. Two she didn't recognize. Blood thinners, maybe. Something for indigestion. Something heavy for sleep. On and on.

Liss couldn't catch her breath.

One way or the other, she thought. One way or the other, someone had killed this family.

CHAPTER NINETEEN

When Liss arrived home, she found Link and Callan posted on opposite ends of the couch in front of the TV for the evening, feet up. As though nothing had changed at all, the separation had never divided them.

Link looked around and grinned at her. "Dream team!"

"Hey, Mom," Callan said.

The heaviness from Mim's crypt of a house had weighed on Liss all the way home, but now she sloughed it off with her coat. "Hey, Cowboy," she said. "How was—"

Link signaled to her with a shake of his head, a no-go.

"How was what?" Callan said.

"Um. That quiz?" she said. "Didn't you have a quiz?"

Callan hadn't looked away from the TV. "What quiz?"

"Never mind," she said. "Must have got it wrong. Link, you want a beer?"

By hand gestures and pulled faces, she got him to kick down the recliner and follow her out to the deck.

"Subtle," he said, hands shoved into the front pockets of his jeans. "He'll never suspect we're talking about him."

"I don't think it's a bad thing that he knows we share information," she said. "So school was bad today, I gather. Did you have that talk?"

"Sure," Link said. "We talked."

That hesitation, that tilt of the head. "Evasive," she said.

"I guess I kind of forgot which talk we were supposed to be having?"

"Link."

"I thought maybe just spending the time, you know? Father-son? I haven't exactly been around as much as I used to be."

"And whose fault is that?" she snapped.

"Hey," he said. "I just mean . . . Look, when I was his age, my dad was barely around, and when he was—we weren't buddies, OK? He was too busy giving the county a hard time to throw a ball with me or take me for pizza—"

"You didn't feed him pizza again?"

Tilt of head. "And if he did find himself saddled with me," Link said, "he didn't spend any time finding out who I was. He was too busy flirting with the waitresses or chatting up someone he knew at the next table."

It was precisely what Link did, had always done, when they were out together, but he couldn't spot it, didn't think of it as flirt-ing, didn't understand why she wouldn't want to eat alone while he caught up with a guy he'd played ball with—or against—in the big game over a decade ago. Didn't see that he himself couldn't be present in his own family because he was skimming faces in every crowd like a politician, looking for adoration. He always found it. Everyone loved Link Kehoe.

Even she did. But not enough, apparently.

Would they all love him now, though? What were the people of Parkins County thinking about Link tonight, their pet, their hometown handsome boy, with the body of his ex-whatever dis-covered on family property, with his son brawling against his own friends? And his wife had already kicked him out, Liss imagined them thinking. What does *she* know? What is she hiding?

"Have you heard from Mercer?" she said.

He turned on her. "Am I *expecting* to hear from him?"

"The night Ashley went missing," Liss said. "Weren't you at work?"

"Whoa, what's this about?" he said. "Are you doing Alarie's job for him?"

"Mercer wouldn't ask for my help," she said. "Even if he needed any."

"He's in over his head," Link said. "He might just lose his election if he can't tamp things down. The crime rate was in the *basement* when my dad was marshal. Criminals moved out of *town* to get out of his reach."

Liss thought the words sounded familiar, something Key might have once said about himself. Key's iron rule had become the stuff of family lore. How people never dared come to the quarry, how only fools would speed down their road. But some of the stories made Liss uneasy. Like the one where Link had bought his first used car and stayed out past curfew. When Link finally arrived home, Key rushed out with the baseball bat from behind the back door to swing at Link's hood. If Key had gone for the windshield—this was Link's winking punchline—it would have grounded Link far longer, until he got the cash together to replace it. But a dent in the hood of the car had been a battle scar, worn proudly. The dent in the bat, even more so. At this point in the story, Link might go fetch the bat, still at the back door of the new house, so that he could roll it in the light to show off the damage.

"You were at *work*, right?" Liss said impatiently.

"Where's this coming from?"

She didn't want to say she was scratching at the story or why. He would say he didn't need protecting. "It's going to come up, you know that."

"Work," Link said. Hesitation, head tilt. "Yeah. To be honest, it's been so long . . ."

The porch light went dark as they let the silence drag on.

"What's going on?" Link said. "Something came through about the car? You're acting—"

"Protective?" She would hold back the onslaught, create an eye in the storm around their child. But Link needed to be there, too. "Finding that car is stirring up all the bad feelings and Robbie's not here to take the brunt. That . . . ill will, whatever you want to call it, it's looking for someone to attach to."

"That's not how it works, come on," Link said. "She muffed that curve. People do it all the time. Hell, Tanner did it the other night, right?"

Liss braced herself to get through it. "Mercer says he pulled up bones."

He crossed his arms and leaned back on the railing. The light came back on, casting shadows across Link's face. "OK. We sorta knew that was coming, though. Didn't we?"

"He can't say if it's Ashley yet but they can tell from the—" She couldn't bring herself to say *skull*. "They can tell it wasn't an accident. She was murdered."

Something shifted in Link's expression, subtle and unbelieving. "That's impossible."

"The car was dumped with her inside, after she died. Or—" She could barely say it. "Or she could have been struck in the head and drowned."

Link leapt from her. "That's just Alarie jumping to wild—what's the word? Conjecture. Right? Murder?"

Liss gestured for him to lower his voice.

"He's just telling horror stories now," Link said. "I don't understand. Why Ashley? She didn't have anything to *steal*."

"What about someone who didn't like her? She—"

"Enough to *kill*?" Link said. "I don't see how anybody could *hate* her except . . ."

Except *you*.

At least he would stop short of saying it. Liss couldn't help but be reminded of how uncertain of Link's loyalty she'd always felt. How uncertain he'd made her feel.

"The point is," Liss said, "people are already looking in your direction—"

"Who?" Link turned on her so quickly, she recoiled. "Who's saying that? Mercer?"

Aren't you at all worried, Mercer had asked. Was she? The light went out.

"Who?" He grabbed her arm, hard, and so quickly, it seemed he'd evaded the motion sensors. She yelped. He let go, and they stood in the dark. "I'm sorry."

She rubbed at her arm, stunned.

As mad as he'd ever been at her, the day she'd called him out for the distraction, the texts turned away from her, the day he'd stormed out of his parents' house and found the apartment, he'd never hurt her physically.

"If you mean what Tanner said," Link said. "Callan told me. You know Tanner's hearing that garbage from his old man."

"It won't be just one kid, though, or one family," Liss said, rubbing at her arm. "Trouble landed on Robbie last time, deserved or not. It could land on you." She looked away. "On us."

"Hey," Link said. He reached out again but she stepped back. The lights flooded the scene, as though they were on stage. He sank his fists into his pockets. "I won't let that happen, OK? And as much as I hate to give him the credit, neither will Mercer. And—you don't need to worry about me."

Hesitation, head tilt. And if she could see through him so easily, Mercer would have Link broken down in no time at all. Whatever truth there was to tell, Mercer would have it.

"Do you want me to stay over again?" Link said.

She did want it, but on terms that felt very distant to her now.

"Well, that answers that," he said.

"You can't stay *every* night," she said.

His jaw shifted. His teeth grinding, a response swallowed, she didn't know. She had only meant that he couldn't keep them safe just by sleeping in their bed.

"That didn't come out the way I meant it," she said.

He was looking toward the door. The door to *his* house and behind it, *his* son. Finally, he said, "It's Callan's weekend with me. Can you make sure he's packed?"

As though she wouldn't have remembered. As though she didn't have it under control.

CHAPTER TWENTY

The next morning, Liss wiped steam from the bathroom mirror and saw that a bruise, violet-angry as a storm cloud and tender to the touch, had appeared on her upper arm. A pinch the size of Link's thumb.

He hadn't meant to. She knew that. But she hadn't slept again, thinking of it, of that head tilt and hesitation when he'd said she didn't need to worry.

She took her coffee to the deck and looked things over before Callan came out. The mailbox still stood. The barn had nothing to tell her, except the roof needed seeing to. She shivered in wet hair. They'd have the first overnight freeze soon, but she couldn't think that far ahead, not when she had no idea what would happen even today.

It had been three days since Ashley's bones had been found, Mercer had his eye on Link for her murder, and Link had lied to her face about . . . something. Liss felt bruised all over.

"Mom?"

"Grab some cereal for breakfast," Liss called, wiping at her eyes with the cuff of her sweater.

She was gut-sick, the kind she might have called in for, but at least she had scheduled a morning away from the office to drop off career fair info packets. She wouldn't have to face Vera's questions and sympathy. She didn't have to pretend to deserve having coffee brought to her in her favorite mug.

At the school, Callan leapt from the car with his overnight bag for Link's.

"Hey," Liss called as the door slammed. She rolled down the passenger-side window and called him back. "I can keep the bag for you until I see you at the game."

"I'm not going to the game," he said.

"You're not? To *homecoming*?" He wouldn't have played, but he could have sat in his uniform on the team bench with the varsity players. Was he off the team? "When did you decide that?"

"I asked Dad last night," he said. "He said he would pick me up."

And Link didn't bother to mention it to her? "Make sure you text him later and remind him," Liss said. "Sometimes he—"

"I *know*," Callan said.

"OK," she said. "I guess I'll see you Sunday."

He turned away, chin to his chest, and trudged toward the school. His pants were too short, his hair too long. He didn't glance back from the door.

She pointed the car toward town, thinking it hadn't been a *minute* since Callan had clung to her at kindergarten drop-off. And now he was acting out, breaking their rules, and lying artlessly to the police. Making his own plans, cutting her out.

He probably blamed her for the separation. He didn't know—and she wouldn't be the one to tell him—how his dad had played around. Her relationship with Mercer had been far more visible to Callan than anything Link had been up to.

Maybe he'd even seen the divorce papers at Link's apartment, with her name at the top, making the petition. Maybe Link had been telling Callan his own version of the story, heavily edited to remain the hero.

She wanted him to stay Callan's hero. Didn't she?

As she drove through the west side of town, she passed Renner

Corp, the factory where Link and Robbie had worked when Ashley disappeared.

Liss struck the steering wheel with the heel of her hand. If he'd been picking up the extra shift, as he'd always claimed, then she wouldn't have to worry. There'd be records, wouldn't there?

Fifteen years later? And Key's files, Mercer was saying, were thin.

On the town square, Liss parked and walked from office to office, handing her career fair packets to perplexed receptionists. A digital marketing firm, a mortgage loan and title company. She skipped the law offices she'd consulted about the divorce. Another storefront proclaimed "business solutions," whatever that meant. Somewhere behind each door was a small-business owner and a staff—people who had chosen a career path or blazed one. She was thinking of the students who couldn't afford college or didn't want to, or needed another year to decide. Kids without anyone telling them they could do more than hire on to make GimmeGimme chips.

Another thing she couldn't say to Link.

In the newspaper office, Liss leaned on the front counter to catch someone's attention. On the counter lay a fresh copy of the latest edition. She had reached for it before she recognized the cover photo.

"Can I help you?"

Liss looked up, then back at the paper. The central image of the front page was the pond—their pond. A clutch of people stood at the edge of the water, out of focus, but she recognized every one of them, including herself. From the angle the photographer had taken, she and Mercer were nearly smashed up together in an embrace.

"No," she said. "I—thank you." She dropped the paper to the counter and dashed for the door.

How had the photographer sneaked onto the scene that night without Mercer chasing them off?

At an insurance company, the receptionist picked up the phone as Liss left. In the real estate office next door, the phone was already ringing.

Was she just paranoid?

At the dance studio, Liss read contempt in what might have only been polite disinterest. By the time she reached the bank at the corner where she'd left her car, Liss had lost her nerve. She threw the rest of the packages into the trunk of her car.

ON THE WAY back toward the school, Liss spotted Renner Corp again and pulled into the parking lot.

Plastics, it said on the sign, but as many shifts that Link had put in there, she had no clear sense of what kind, which of the smallest cogs and whirligigs to make the automated world go round they fashioned here. Astonishing that whole lives could be built around the manufacture of bits and bobs used only to build something else. Whole factories, whole networks, logistics she couldn't imagine.

The office was clearly marked but she had to ring a bell at the side of the door, wire mesh glass in the window. Inside, a few people hunched over their desks. Someone buzzed her in.

"Can I help you?" A woman turned from her ancient computer to make the half-hearted offer.

It was Jamie Ward's mom. "Sophie, hi."

The woman couldn't seem to place her at first, then did. "Is everything OK with Jamie?"

"Of course. I mean, I don't know," Liss said. "I didn't come here to talk about Jamie."

Sophie frowned. "What did you come for?"

Networks, logistics. Those were jobs. "The school's having a career fair in a couple of weeks and I wondered if anyone here might come out and talk to the students about opportunities."

"Opportunities," Sophie said flatly. "To work *here*?"

The room was drab, featureless. A young man at a desk in the back lowered his eyes as Liss's gaze passed over him. "Well, you do," Liss said. "You've worked here how long?"

"But my job is filled," Sophie said, as though tutoring a very slow student.

"What about what Link used to do?" Liss said. "You must hire entry-level positions sometimes."

Sophie seemed uncertain. "If you want to leave a phone number . . . I guess I can have Glen give you a call."

Dismissed. "You don't think this is a good place to work?"

Sophie glanced toward the other workstation and the guy sitting there. "It's fine. Good benefits. But. I wouldn't want Jamie here."

"Jamie's a smart one."

Sophie's spine straightened a bit. "He wants to go to college."

"That's great," Liss said. "Not all kids have university ahead of them, though. They're ready to work and learn on the job. And a job here could be a launching pad. Look at Link."

Sophie moved a piece of paper on her desk. Liss remembered too late that Jim Ward had a chip on his shoulder, reporting to Link.

"But what about people like, uh, like Robbie Hubbard?"

Sophie looked up sharply. "What about him?"

"He would have hated being cooped up at a desk," Liss said. "Right? What did he do here?"

"He was in the plant," Sophie said.

"Exactly," Liss said. "An energetic high school graduate could work in the plant. Being young isn't a drawback there, is it? Robbie was young when he worked here."

"Robbie," Sophie said, sadly. "Robbie was never anything but young."

Liss's breath caught. For some reason, this made her understand the loss of Robbie more than Link's reminiscing, more even than Mim's grief. Robbie was a boy, stunted at a reckless age, before he had become anything he might have been. "Do you ever think about all the things we'll never know?" Liss said. "We could go our whole lives and not know what really happened."

Sophie glanced longingly toward the door. "I think about it all the time," she said. "Did you want to leave a number for Glen or not?"

CHAPTER TWENTY-ONE

Liss left an info packet with Sophie but suspected Glen, whoever he was, would never see it.

Out in the parking lot, Liss sat in her car and looked back at the plant. Plastics. Who knew. Maybe one of the students *could* get hired on.

She was about to turn her key in the ignition when she noticed someone coming her way, quickly, as though she'd left something behind. It was Sophie's officemate. He wore khakis too baggy for his slight frame, a crisp white shirt. A name badge clipped to his belt flapped against his hip. She rolled down the window.

"Did you get your questions answered?" he said.

"Are you Glen?"

"Danesh. You wanted to know about Robbie? You're police?"

"I work at the high school. At Parkins West?" she said. "I was trying to get someone from your workplace to visit our career fair."

He nodded doubtfully. He had very thick, long black eyelashes, the kind any woman would have paid good money for. "But you asked about Robbie Hubbard?"

"I know his mother."

He waited.

"And— OK," she said. "I suppose I was wondering a few things I couldn't bring myself to ask Sophie. Like why Robbie lost his job here before he died?"

"He didn't lose his job," Danesh said. "He left it."

"On his own? With no special invitation?"

Danesh looked away. "See, some of them were making it hard on him. In the plant. And in the office, they might have been looking for a reason."

"Building a case against him?" Liss said. "Was there any reason for it? Was he a good worker?"

"I was only an intern," Danesh said. "New to the place. So I don't really know. But he didn't have any complaints against him before—well. Before."

"What do you make there? Plastics is . . . vague." She should know. She gave Link a lot of crap for not knowing how the household worked, but she'd never paid attention to his job.

"Industrial spools, for wire and that sort of thing," Danesh said. "All sizes."

"I didn't know before now that spools had to be made," she said. "I guess I never thought about them."

"Why would you?" he said. "You don't want me at your career fair, before you ask."

Danesh's ID said he worked in human resources. "Well, you don't seem to like your job."

An SUV had pulled up in the bare shade of a slim tree and sat idling, the driver just a shape, but Liss recognized the Wards' car. It would be Jim, off his shift at the Gimme factory, to collect Sophie. He covered a lot of ground and lost a lot of time driving her around.

Liss had missed something Danesh was saying. "I'm sorry?"

"I hate my job, I said, which is why I'm leaving it soon. And the only reason I'm willing to say . . . See, it's not a great place to be—to stand out." Danesh glanced her way, to see if she understood. "But Robbie was kind to me when he didn't have to be. I never believed what they said about him."

Now he had her full attention. "Which 'they' is this now?"

"Gossip. They said he killed that girlfriend of his, right?" Danesh said. "But he loved her. Would bore you to death if he got started on her. He used to keep a picture of her in his locker, her and the baby. The baby wasn't even his, did you know?"

All these photos of Callan, spread all over the county. "I heard that," she said.

"But he didn't mind," Danesh said. "That's the thing. He had everything he ever wanted." He closed his eyes, longer than a blink, as though he were making a wish, then opened them and looked anywhere but at her. "Until—you know."

"How did he seem once Ashley went missing?"

"Ashley, yeah. They found her car just this—wait." He frowned and looked her over. "Are you a reporter?"

"I work for the school," Liss said. "Honestly, Danesh."

"You can't quote me on anything, OK? I can't be in the paper talking about this."

"I work in the guidance office," she said. "I help kids think about their lives after high school."

Sophie Ward had opened the door of the office and was making her way toward the idling car.

Danesh rattled the change in his pockets, the ID at his hip. He'd be thinking of his own choices, Liss thought.

"See . . ." he said weakly. "I didn't really know him that well."

"So you also worked here when Lincoln Kehoe did?" Liss hurried to ask, before she lost him.

"Oh, yeah." Danesh brightened. "He and Robbie were good friends. You could ask him about Robbie."

"That's a great idea."

He seemed pleased that she thought so.

"How long are you required to keep employment records?" she said.

Danesh's Adam's apple slid down and up his thin neck. "Required? Three years."

"Oh."

"But, see," he said. "They're electronic."

"So you keep them much, much longer," she said.

"Maybe." He was hedging now, glancing toward the office. "The reason I was thinking of Robbie at all is that you're the second person to ask about him today."

Mercer.

"Was he asking about Link Kehoe, too?" Liss said.

"This isn't about any career fair," Danesh said, hands in his pockets finally still. "Is it?"

LISS DROVE BACK toward the school in a daze.

Danesh from Renner had been able to confirm—with more reassurances that she wasn't a reporter—Link's schedule the day Ashley disappeared. He had worked, as he said. But only until three in the afternoon. Only one shift.

There was a gaping hole in Link's alibi. And Mercer would know that by now, too.

You don't have to worry about me, he'd promised her.

But she did.

Back at the school, Liss parked, took a deep breath, and walked toward the doors. A pile of blue fabric lay against the curb, filthy, maybe ruined. She identified a sleeve cuff, plucked it up by her fingertips, and carried it inside.

At her entrance, the three women who worked in the main office stopped talking and stared.

"What *is* that?" the school secretary said primly.

An invisible social structure existed between faculty and staff, probably existed in every high school. Except Liss's low-rung job in the guidance office put her somewhere in the middle, not one thing, not the other. Not a teacher. Not counselor, not administrative assistant precisely. She had no status. In comparison the main office staff formed an impenetrable clique, as though they were still students. As though they could still make the homecoming court, if they circled up and voted each other in.

"Lost and found," Liss said.

"Did you run it over?" the principal's assistant said.

Liss threw the jacket into the bin and got out of there as quickly as she could. At the door to the guidance office, she stopped. A jacket. She tried to picture Jamie Ward sitting on the stone at the quarry, tucked into himself against the wind. Had his jacket been blue? But if he'd been wearing it at the quarry, and hadn't been able to come up with it a few hours later to go home, it must still be in some corner of her house. Liss turned back to the main office to have a closer look.

As she walked in the side door, the admins still out of sight, she heard one of them say, "That's got to be a rock and hard place. Married to a killer . . ."

Liss stopped.

"And sleeping around with a cop," another one finished.

"Worse ways to keep out of jail, I guess," the first said and they were all cackling.

Back in the guidance office, a girl sat sniffling across from her desk, waiting for Vera. Liss offered her a box of tissues but she only rested her head back against a flyer pinned to the bulletin board, tracks of black mascara down her cheeks, a vision of suffering.

Liss had already seen the girl's record in the student database—her plans for graduation were looking dicey—so she didn't bother snooping. She watched as more buoyant students paraded past the doorway as classes changed. Friday of homecoming weekend. A game, royalty crowned from among the beautiful, a dance. All the promise of youth and the future.

For Liss, the long weekend stretched ahead, empty. She pressed at the sore spot on her arm, to make sure it was there. When Vera's door opened, she fixed her face so that one among them, at least, would be hopeful.

CHAPTER TWENTY-TWO

Mim Hubbard came out on her porch before Mercer's car had come to a standstill. He took a deep breath and blew out the air. He was in for a paddling, but he'd faced down tweakers with guns. He could surely face one angry mom.

"Well, at last," she said as he scuffed across the gravel. She stood above him, arms crossed.

"Did I miss an appointment, Mrs. Hubbard?" Mercer said and hated how snide he sounded.

"I thought you'd have the decency to come over here as soon as you found that girl," she said.

"We don't know yet if we've found a girl, Mrs. Hubbard," he said. "I came to tell you we'd found a *car*. Looks like you've heard it already."

"*Her* car."

"Yes. But until we have more information—"

"And a body. That's what I heard."

Only the criminals could keep secrets. He should have known word would be out. "I can't comment on that," he said.

"What's it going to take, Marshal?"

The woman was infuriating. He hitched a boot on the bottom step of her porch. "Well, Mim, I guess if I *had* found a body, it would take a DNA test and match, and then the victim's next of kin would need to be told first, before I could answer your question.

I hope the formalities were observed when it was your time to receive bad news. There's no good way to get terrible news but there sure are some bad ones."

She had a bulge of loose skin at her neck from this angle, wobbling with emotion. "I meant before you'll apologize."

"I'm sorry you lost your son."

"I didn't misplace him, Marshal," she said. "Except when you lot nabbed him off the street."

Thorough questioning, Slocum had said, making a joke of it.

"Did they keep him a long time?" Mercer said, more gently.

She was an old woman, the end of her family coming abruptly and totally. He could dig deeper for kindness, even as she accused him of things he couldn't have done. He hadn't been on the scene.

Old Kehoe, though. In his wheelchair, his lips contorting, wet, around a word he couldn't quite communicate. How much blood did that son of a bitch have on his hands?

Mim's arms dropped. "He came out hollow," she said. "He went in fierce, trying to tell you all something wasn't right, that something bad had happened to her. He came out something else. Hopeless. I used to be so angry about that, whatever happened behind closed doors that day."

"Are you saying he was harmed while in custody? Did he—"

"But now I'm more angry you didn't *arrest* him, proper."

Mercer sighed. He'd come straight from meeting with the HR rep at Renner, who had accounted for Hubbard and Kehoe, both, until three in the afternoon. "Mim, you got me. Your boy was the only one tearing around trying to get someone to take a closer look, and if I can fill in a few more hours, I can clear him once and for all. Isn't that what you want?"

"What good is that, Marshal?" she crowed. "Vindicated but lying in the ground at Prairie Rest. What good God damn would clearing him do now? If you had put him in *jail*, if he'd been in prison all this time, he'd be alive."

Serpentine reasoning, slithery as a snake. Mercer couldn't imagine having to twist around the realities this woman had already known. She did make him want to apologize, if he could think of something he'd done. He took his hat off. "Might I ask you some questions about Robbie's movements around that time?"

"I thought you said . . ."

"It's really Ashley's movements I'm interested in," he said. "Who she spent time with, anyone who might have meant her harm."

"You're doing it," she said, more breath than words. "You're really trying."

He'd have to hear the whole story, everything his predecessor had done and not, as bad as it got.

"Ma'am," he said. "Don't you think it's high time someone did?"

LEAVING THE HUBBARD place, he already regretted the promises he'd made. High time, he'd said. OK, OK, big talk and all he had was a pile of bones. He'd be lucky if he could prove they belonged to Ashley in the first place, never mind figuring out who'd done it.

But Mim's version of her son's interrogation was caught in his teeth now. Come out hollow, blinking away at the daylight. Shit. Robbie pestered and pummeled in town, at work. To death.

He drove straight to Key's place and parked behind the same beat-up box of a car as before.

He'd barely reached the door when it swung open.

"Mercer," Patty said. "He's napping."

"This time I'm here to see you."

"Oh?" She was an elegant sort, her hair a sort of crown of white-blond that couldn't be an accident. She stepped outside. "Forgive me for not inviting you in, but I'm hoping he'll get some rest."

"I won't take much of your time," he said. "I hope you can help me clear up some movements on the day Ashley Hay went missing."

Her eyes fluttered. "Mine?"

"Only incidentally," he said. "Were you home that night?"

"Yes."

"And was Marshal Kehoe with you?"

"Well." Her eyes drifted away, then she closed the door behind her and led him down a neat white-gravel path away from the conservatory to a patch of rose bushes going yellow. The rock crunched under his boots. Stone blasted out from some other hole in the ground. He'd never thought a minute about limestone, but now it was everywhere he looked. He'd done a little research, too, sitting at home at night, what else did he have to do? The stone from quarries like the Kehoes' had been carved into skyscrapers in New York and monuments in Washington, DC—places most people around here would never see. It had been used to build temples to the glory of commerce these folks didn't enjoy, for centers of learning they wouldn't attend, and for places of worship where they would never kneel. Stone from the next county had been crafted into state houses and courthouses across the country, and even sent to fix up the Pentagon after 9/11. The ground beneath them had been chiseled out and carted away for the far-off business of other places.

Close to home, you didn't see the pretty white stone from their hills turned into monuments to beauty or progress. It was the rubble lining your garden path or maybe, at the end of your days, a slab might mark the resting place of your bones.

His late-night internet sleuthing had told him limestone itself was bones. Bones of little sea creatures who'd lived and died over epoch time in what had once been a huge inland sea.

They lived atop a bone pile, all of them. Which was not the sort of thing he had wanted to know.

Patty tended to a rose bush, her long fingers snapping the head off a darkened, withered bloom. Taking her time to consider her options, he thought. Taking her sweet time.

"Mrs. Kehoe?" he said. "Was Key here?"

"No, actually," she said, at last. "He'd gone out."

He'd assumed she would cover for him, either way. "OK. Do you know where he went?"

"You'll find out soon enough if you don't know already that my husband always kept his own counsel," she said, a grim set to her mouth. "But if I had to guess, I suppose I always thought he'd gone to spend time with his mistress."

The lady could land a punch, that was for sure. "Mistress."

"Oh, yes."

"Would you be able to provide me a name?"

"It would only direct you to the local cemetery," she said. "Cancer, I believe, several years back. She was older than I was. Can you imagine?"

He would never understand the mystery of other people, not if he had this job a thousand years. "If she's dead, and I can't question him, why tell me at all?"

"If you're set on scraping up old business," Patty said, "you'll come up with whispers anyway. So you might as well hear it from me."

"No one else could put those two together that day, I suppose."

"I suppose not," Patty said. "They didn't host bingo nights with their time together."

"And what about Lincoln?"

"What about him?" But the bravado had slipped. She was much more sure of a wandering husband than of her son.

"You didn't see him at all that night," Mercer said.

"Why would I see him?" she said. "He was working."

"Were you here alone, then?" he said.

Something about his question had caught her off guard. "And who, exactly, would have been here other than my family?"

Her grandson was her family, wasn't he? "Ashley didn't stop by with the baby while she was in the neighborhood?"

Patty lowered her eyes to the rose bush, snapped off another dead head. "We only saw the baby when Link had him," she said. "Very occasionally. The baby's mother didn't like to share him. And she certainly wouldn't stop by to be social, not with me."

The door opened behind her and the aide he'd met last time popped her head out. "Mrs. Kehoe?" Her eyes darted to Mercer's and away. Kellye—the y-e at the end had helped imprint it into his memory. Or maybe it was that she was a pretty gal. "It's time for his aquatherapy," she said. "You said you wanted to monitor?"

"Thank you," Patty said. "Mercer, I hope this helps?"

"Thank you, Mrs. Kehoe. I hope the marshal's doing OK?"

Her expression softened to something like pity. For *him*. "We cling to the good days," she said. "But they are getting further and further apart."

"I'm truly sorry to hear it," he said. "You take care and if there's anything I can do . . ."

What could *he* do? They were both thinking it, he and Patty both. Well, he could find out who'd killed the mother of her grandchild. But maybe she wouldn't end up thanking him for that.

"Thank you, Mercer." Patty Kehoe turned and went inside, and he felt as though the teacher had dismissed the class.

The aide still held the door.

"You have a good day, Kellye," he said. "With a y-e at the end."

She gave him a smile as she closed the door. Not one of those nothing smiles, which was what he usually got. A something smile. If he could have thought of a reason to ask her a few questions, he would have knocked on the door again.

I'M WATCHING OUT THE CONSERVATORY WINDOWS WHEN A Parkins car comes up the drive. This aide does try to keep me pointed out toward the view, I'll give her credit for that. I paid a lot for that view and it's the least they can do to let me gape at it as I die.

It's Mercer, but he doesn't come into the conservatory this time around. Maybe Patty's sending him off? I don't get so many visitors that she should be turning them down at the door.

Mostly it's Link who comes by, with or without the kid in tow.

I always like to see Link. He comes by and gets out the Bel Air, the pride and joy of 1957 and my garage. He parks it where I can see it and gives it a gentle wash just like I would, careful with the paint job. After, he'll come in and sit a while. He's entertaining as hell, telling me stories about the things he got up to—under my roof, some of them. He's good about pretending that he's talking with me and not at me but sometimes his nerve gives out and he gets quiet. When Link is happy the world is a sunny place, but when he forgets to put on the pretense, it's like a cloud passes over us. He's got something inside him he won't say, even to his mute dad.

I wish I could ask him what's troubling him. But—do I want to know? How much of his old man does he have in him? Quite a bit, that's my guess. Too much.

He comes by every few days. I wish I had known much earlier what good company he is. Maybe this all could have worked out different.

Is this regret?

Am I turning over some new leaf? If I could come clean,

would I? Not for some heavenly reward or some bullshit like that, but to shoulder my share, and his. I'm old. I'm on my way out. I don't worry so much about being hanged for my crimes anymore—but I don't know if I could live with even knowing his.

I hope he never tries to tell me.

"I love you, Dad," he says now when he gets ready to leave. We never used to do that crap but now he leans in to kiss my temple and all I can do is sit here and take it.

I lived a good long life without suffering so much as a twinge of regret, but here we are.

CHAPTER TWENTY-THREE

A t the stroke of the final bell that day, Liss slipped out before Vera could emerge from her office and ask for an accounting of her progress or her plans for the weekend with Callan at Link's.

Any other woman would welcome the *freedom* of a few unscheduled days. Drawing a bubble bath, watching a rom-com without Callan making gagging noises. Feeding herself a bag of microwave popcorn for dinner or trail mix over the sink. Another woman would feel excited at the prospect of an empty house—instead of panicked.

She went to her car and sank into the driver's seat. The strap of her purse had tugged at the tender spot on her arm.

She wouldn't ask Link about the hole in his schedule that day. She couldn't.

How soon, though, before Mercer did?

The morning after Ashley dumped Callan on Liss, Link had come home sheepishly, in rumpled day-old clothing, ready to make excuses.

But she'd been up all night with Callan, doing everything wrong: feeding him the wrong thing, rocking him the wrong way. Ashley hadn't come back. Within a few hours, Robbie would arrive, worried.

Those lost hours in between the end of Link's shift and his

arrival home hadn't been at issue back then. Not to the police. Not to his dad. And not to her. She'd been too sleepless and frayed to notice.

Or was that an excuse? She made a lot of excuses for herself about that night.

Had she only been too afraid to ask questions? To have them asked of her?

In any case, Liss didn't know where Link had spent that time. But she had a guess.

South of the school sat a patch of unincorporated land, more a crossroads than a town. Someone had turned a defunct service station into a roadside speakeasy, an open-air, seasonal bar catering to people with low standards. More a party than a business.

Link Kehoe liked a party. Robbie, too. Robbie had even worked there now and then, for cash under the table.

Liss drove by the place slowly. It hardly seemed like the kind of establishment that needed a bartender. Customers sat hunched at picnic tables on the cracked cement lot where the gas pumps once stood, cans of the cheapest swill lined up in front of them.

She parked along the road and walked back. At the sight of her, a pair of her students stood up and walked away from their drinks.

The bar was a long, warped table inside the old garage, its floor still oil stained.

"We're full up on Tupperware," said the woman at the bar. She had stringy hair striking for blond and missing by a mile. "Whatever you might be selling."

"Shoot, that's that cop's lady friend," said a man sitting in a plastic lawn chair nearby. He was wiry, wearing a dirty ball cap on the back of his head. His eyes darted all around behind her. "Can't be good."

"I'm not selling anything," Liss said. "Buying." She pulled out a ten and laid it on the table. "And I'm not anyone's lady friend at the moment."

"You should try your luck, then, Booth," the bartender said to the man. The guy snickered, scratched his nose, scratched it again. He'd misplaced a few teeth. The woman reached into the fridge at her back and set a can down in front of Liss, a sort of punctuation. Daring her to ask for change.

"They don't keep you in white wine spritzers in town some-where?" the woman said.

"Variety is the spice of life. Or so I've been led to believe." Liss cracked her beer. A shadow fell upon them, but when Liss turned, the potential patron had already started back toward his car.

"Why don't you just get to what you're here for before you ruin my business?" the woman asked in a voice so tired, Liss looked at her in new sympathy.

"I only have a question or two—"

"She sounds just like 'em, Dee," Booth said, his voice gone a note higher.

"They know where to find us any day of the week," Dee said.

"They?" Liss said. She noticed an open door at the back, more plastic chairs.

"The cops. They leave us alone and you should, too, Mary Kay."

"I'm only asking for myself," Liss said. She hadn't planned her approach but plunged ahead. "I want to know about a guy who once worked here."

Dee's face went slack.

"Who's that?" Booth said, eyes darting again. "Me?"

"Robbie Hubbard," Liss said.

"Who said he worked here?" Dee said.

"Someone who knew him well enough to know."

"Why don't you ask that guy your question or two?"

She was sharper than Liss had expected, but then maybe she had to be.

"Because that guy's my ex-husband," Liss said and took a long drink from her beer. "Maybe you know how it is."

Dee looked her over, then sent a dark look down in Booth's direction. "Can't get rid of mine."

"Can we sit down?" Liss said. "In the back?"

Dee sighed, and reached for a puffy jacket off the wall behind her. From the fridge, she grabbed another beer and pointed it at Booth. "I'm counting beers and cash when I get back."

Outside the back door, a man slept slumped against the wall, his legs flung wide.

"Is he OK?" Liss said.

"Generally? No. But he's alive." Dee looked him over. "Probably."

Liss followed her to the chairs. They were set up on a wide concrete pad that ran all the way to the alley, against a cracked cement wall that had no purpose she could think of.

Dee sank into one of the seats with a groan and cracks in both knees. "Well?"

"How well did you know Robbie Hubbard?"

For a long silent moment, Liss thought Dee wouldn't answer. Why should she? But maybe Liss's curiosity was more interesting than a slow afternoon with her ex's elbows on her bar. "Not real well."

"Seems like an employee you didn't know could rob a cash business blind—"

"We don't have *staff*, OK?" Dee popped open her can of beer. "I needed someone trustworthy to cover a few shifts." She looked at Liss. "Had a little court business to see to," she said. "Anyway, Robbie was already here most of the time—until he took up with that chick who went off without telling anyone. You remember that? Guess whose car they found the other day, in a patch of water?"

"I heard that," Liss said.

"You never fucking know, do you?" Dee seemed to find this profound. "Is that why you're here? Because of the car?"

"You said he was here a lot. He drank a lot?"

Dee raised the beer to her lips, winked. "What's a lot? He drank, but not so much I couldn't have him guarding the candy store. You can't leave drunks in charge of an open liquor cabinet." Her gaze drifted over Liss's shoulder to the door, where she might have done just that.

"You said he came here until he started seeing Ashley."

"Ashley, yeah," Dee said. She reached into the pocket of her puffer coat and retrieved a pack of cigarettes. "We're not exactly a date spot," Dee said. "But they came out for a good time once in a while, once they'd dropped off her brat."

The words shot straight up Liss's spine. Everywhere she turned, another version of her kid, *her* kid, not Ashley's, could be found.

"With her car found . . ." Dee said. "Jeesh, the cops will do anything to hang him for it."

"I'm not the police," Liss said. "I'm just trying to learn more about him. His mother—"

But she wouldn't invoke a mother's grief, not to lie.

"Nobody should have to go through what she did," Dee said. "Mim wants you digging up all these old bones?"

But Liss didn't want to talk about bones. "Mim would like Robbie fully exonerated," Liss said. "Publicly acknowledged as innocent."

"And that's what *you're* going to do?" Dee finally lit her cigarette and took a deep drag. Some people smoked like they meant it. "What do you really want to know?" she said.

"Was Robbie here the night Ashley went missing?" Liss said. "Maybe with his friend, Link Kehoe?"

"Link Kehoe," Dee said, looking her over. "Oh, *right*. You checking up on your old man?"

"My former . . . husband."

"Why do you care what your former anything was up to that night?"

"That kid of Ashley's?" Liss said. "We're raising him together, and I would prefer to have what happened to Robbie not happen to my son's dad."

The power of the truth lent her words a keen edge. Dee's smile sagged.

"They ever going to find out who did that?" Dee said. "People around here can't mind their own business until they *can*. OK, look. Yes, Robbie was here that night. He and Link came in too early, drank too much. I made Rob sleep it off back here for a while. Doubt he had enough time or stamina after all that to make someone disappear, but what do I know? He was here until I closed up, three in the morning."

"What about Link?" Liss said.

The woman sucked at her cigarette. "I told his dad all this, years ago."

"Link was drunk, too?" Liss asked impatiently.

"He was drinking, and then he was gone," Dee said. "That was the problem. He was scarce by the time Robbie got sloppy. I had Booth put Robbie out to dry back here about midnight, thinking Link would fetch him."

Link and Robbie had come from work. "Robbie would have had his car, though."

"Not that night," Dee said. "I was out here having a smoke when your man drove up in his truck and Robbie popped out the passenger side to make it all right by me that, they parked here.

And I guess I was in a good mood that night. I let him. Regretted it when I realized Link left Robbie behind. *And* his truck. It sat here all night, for all I know. Until three, at least."

Liss's blood was thrumming in her veins. "But . . ."

"I know that's the opposite of what you wanted to hear," Dee said. "It was certainly bad news to his dad."

CHAPTER TWENTY-FOUR

Liss drove straight to Link's apartment to demand answers.

She remembered only as the door opened that Callan would be there, too.

"What did he forget this time?" Link said.

"Mom?" Callan sat up from the couch. A pizza box sat on the table in front of him. "What are you doing here?"

"I—" All her accusations stuck in her throat.

"Rude, Callan," Link said. "Come on, buddy."

Liss crossed the room and brushed at Callan's hair. "I guess I just wanted to see you, Cowboy. Just for a second." She kissed his cheek.

"Get you a plate?" Link said.

"You smell like beer," Callan said. "And cigarettes?"

Link raised his eyebrows at her. "I could make some coffee."

"No," Liss said. "No, I won't stay. You guys are doing your . . . hang."

"No one says *hang* anymore," Callan said.

"Callan," Link said, a little sharper this time. "Liss? You OK?"

"Can I talk to you for a second?" she said. "In the hallway, maybe?"

"Now you're in trouble," Callan said, turning back to the TV.

The hall was musty. One of Link's neighbors, an older man, skeletal-thin, paused with the key in his door to study her. At the sight of Link, he dodged inside.

"Friend of yours?" Liss asked.

"That guy," Link said. "Larry thinks he's the mayor of the building or something. He's always posting helpful hints for everyone else. On the mailboxes, in the hallways." He looked down at her with apprehension. "Look, this isn't about feeding him pizza again, is it? I would have ordered vegetables on it this time, mushrooms or—"

"Callan hates mushrooms."

"I know that *now*."

"He'll just pick them off," Liss said impatiently.

"That's not the point, is it?" Link said. "How did I not know my kid hates mushrooms? I should know stuff like that. Comes as no surprise to you, does it?"

"I actually came—"

"You tried to tell me."

He looked so miserable, Liss allowed herself to be diverted. "OK," she said. "What are you talking about?"

"You told me I was being a slob and, and *selfish* making you do it all, making you his go-to, relying on you to be the—the *parent*. But I didn't listen. I left it all to you. And I ruined it, didn't I? Us. It wasn't just the—the—" He fell back against the wall.

The texts, the stepping out on the porch to take a call. The missing hours in their lives, for which he had no defense. "Actually, that's why I—"

"It was *everything*," Link said. "It wasn't one thing I did, but all the things I didn't. Now I've got this kid who looks at me like he's disgusted by every single thing I do or say."

He ran his hands up over his face and through his hair, until it was wild.

"Are you kidding me right now?" Liss said. "He's just fifteen, OK? They're all like that, from what I can tell. And Callan loves you. No, he worships you."

"Really?"

And didn't it sting a little? She had put her whole heart into being Callan's mother, far more effort than Link had put into being his dad. Link could do no wrong, even as he *did*. Link simply *was* a parent. She had been forced to turn herself into one, to swallow her self-doubt that she was the right kind. To ignore that she was his mother *and* she wasn't, both at the same time.

"Oh, no," she said.

"What?"

"I just realized," she said. "Callan has to go get blood drawn Monday."

"You got something at work you can't take him or what?"

"They'll need a parent or guardian to sign all the forms, Link," she said.

"You're his . . ." He came off the wall. "We've got that letter we did for the school, don't we?"

Every year. Every year the letter from Link giving her permission to parent their son. It hurt, every year, to turn it over to Vera and watch her check it over. She was thinking of the tricky logistics of getting the letter downloaded: keys for the school, permissions she didn't have. A piece of *paper*—

"We should make it official," Link said.

"What?"

"Let's make it official," Link said. "Let's make you Callan's mom, officially."

They had talked about her adopting Callan before, but the process had always been complicated by Ashley's status, suspended somewhere between dead and absent. Adoption was only a matter of a piece of paper, too, but the one she wanted more than anything.

"We can't get it arranged this *weekend*," Liss said. "And I don't know if I can get the letter by the time he's due Monday morning—"

"I can take him on Monday. This isn't about some blood test." Link reached for her arm, but she flinched away. He blinked at her, then stepped back. "Think about it. We know how this DNA thing is going to come back, right?"

Liss saw it all, everything she had ever wanted. Her family, whole.

Her family was a mirage, shimmering on the horizon, always impossibly out of her reach.

"You still want it, right?" Link said.

"Of course, but . . ." How did it all fit together? In her desire, she saw her own vulnerabilities. She would agree to anything. She would forgive anything.

She would ask nothing else.

"We'll figure it out," Link said, ducking his head to catch her eye.

"It's Callan's decision," she said, finally. "And it's actually not the time, not now. Not while we're still waiting for the ax to fall. We need to get through this first."

"This might take years to get through," Link said. "Mercer might never find the evidence he needs to pin it on me."

He gave her that Kehoe grin, as though all could be well again.

Liss folded her arms across her chest, bumping the bruise again. What had she meant to accuse Link of?

"He won't find anything," she said.

Because it didn't exist. It couldn't.

Callan was everything. Callan was the only thing. She couldn't risk anyone calling Link a murderer, especially herself.

Liss DROVE TOWARD home, averting her eyes as Robbie's wooden cross appeared alongside the white line at the edge of the road.

She was nearly to the quarry road when blue, rolling lights appeared in her rearview mirror.

Was she even over the speed limit? If this was Mercer's method for spending time with her . . .

She pulled over and waited, hands gripping at ten and two. Behind her, the patrol car door swung open and Ronald Slocum leveraged himself out.

Liss sighed and waited.

Slocum prowled toward her, gut first, ticket pad high, and tapped the window. When Liss complied, he leaned down, an arm on her open window. He had a nice watch. Tanner wore the same brand, and yeah, she'd looked it up to get Callan one, too. Too expensive for her blood.

"Well, hello there, Lissette," Slocum said, his breath stale in her face. "I expected Link. This vehicle's registered to a *mister* Lincoln Kehoe. Been a while since I saw you."

It was some sort of weak dig for dropping Mercer, or maybe a little joke at her situation, since he'd missed out on the excitement at the quarry. "We could certainly find a different way to catch up," she said.

"Next time I drop by to see Key," he said, "maybe I should mosey over to see how you're doing."

"I've been meaning to check in on Key," she said. "Maybe I'll see you over there."

"Maybe, maybe," he said. "But I doubt your divorce of convenience is as popular over there as it is in that house you're still living in, so maybe not."

What business was it of his? "Did you have something you wanted to talk about?" she said. "Maybe a five-mile-per-hour discrepancy between the number on the sign and how fast I was driving?"

"Five, huh?" he said. "Now let's not pretend that any ticket I write you would be enforced . . ."

Mercer loathed the guy, she knew that.

"And I like to keep things cordial, though I can't say you're my favorite Kehoe," Slocum said. "Not by far. Consider it a warning."

She'd caught the magic word—warning—but didn't feel as relieved as she should be. Around them, the countryside was dark, the road empty. "That's generous of you," she said.

His jaw was working as though he had something stuck in his back tooth, then he pushed himself off the door. "Yeah, generous," he said. "That's me. Ask anyone."

Liss watched him walk back to his car. Consider it a warning, he'd said.

But about the speed limit? Or about something else entirely?

CHAPTER TWENTY-FIVE

Liss almost expected Slocum to trail her home from the site of the traffic stop but he let her drive away. She eased back onto the dark road with her grip tight on the steering wheel, embarrassed. She knew better. All the lectures about the dangers of the road, and she couldn't even set a good example.

She turned onto the quarry road. Key and Patty's house was a light through the trees. Soon the leaves would fall, and the sight lines between the two houses would clear. She was dreading it, she realized. All summer, she could almost forget that her in-laws glared down on her as she tried to get on with her life.

Divorce of convenience, Slocum had sneered. Except the part where nothing was decided, and no one was happy.

She slowed for the curve and dragged her gaze away from the dark water of the pond—just catching a flicker of light that shouldn't have been at the window of her house.

The sunroom.

The light was gone, just as quickly.

She kept driving past her own driveway and the barn. At the next crossing, Liss pulled to the side of the road and scrabbled in her purse for her phone.

Mercer picked up on the second ring. "Y'ello."

"There's someone in my house."

"Where are *you*?" he said.

"Down the road. I didn't—"

"In the car? Keep driving. Get out of there. Where's Callan?"

She let up on the brake and drove deeper into the countryside. "Is this how it's going to be?" She hated how her voice sounded, high and strangled and helpless.

Mercer's voice was muffled, speaking to someone in the background, another phone line or his radio.

"Mercer?"

"Where's Callan right now, Liss?"

"With Link. Oh, God. What if this weren't Link's weekend? What if we'd gone home straight from the game?"

"But he's safe and you're safe, and Slocum's just down the road—"

"I know," she said.

"—and I'm on my way," he said. "Can you get to somewhere else? Hole up until I call you?"

Houses were sparse out here, and she didn't know anyone well enough to want to involve them. She couldn't come up with the name of anyone who'd be happy to see her just now. All those texts from so-called friends. She hadn't even read them all—and they'd all stopped, anyway. Link, but Callan was with him. Vera. Vera lived on the other side of the school, probably forty minutes away.

"Could you circle back and get up to the other house?" Mercer said.

The light through the trees.

"I— OK," she said.

"Sit tight up there and I'll call you when it's clear," he said.

To circle back without going past her own house again, Liss had to take three right-hand turns on the rigid grid of their county roads. She sailed past the spot where she'd been nabbed by Slocum. This time, she was going terribly fast.

THE DOOR AT the new house opened. Patty wore a robe and had taken off her face.

"I'm sorry to bother—"

"It's late, Lissette," Patty said.

"—but someone's broken into the house," Liss said. "The marshals are on their way. I just need a place to . . . hover nervously for a few minutes."

Patty looked past Liss's shoulder. "Where's Callan?"

"It's Link's weekend."

"And you don't want to involve my son in this," Patty said.

"I don't want to involve either of our sons in this."

Patty turned away, leaving the door open.

They had once been close, having tea out of proper cups and saucers in the kitchen while the men watched a football game in the next room or went out to baby Key's old showpiece of a car with soft rags. Tea poured and gossip spilled, always a few choice words for Ashley, some of which Liss could only agree with. Ashley had *trapped* Link, *saddled* their family. As though Ashley had broken down a thoroughbred for a beast of burden.

Now, of course, Patty would reserve the worst words for her. The woman who would not stand by her son.

Liss had *thought* they'd been close. She'd been, if not another mother to her, then at least a model for motherhood when Liss had needed to borrow one. And if she was an overbearing mother to Link at times, demanding and coddling, Patty had never been an overly involved grandmother, inserting herself or sharing unwanted advice. She had let Liss find her feet.

Patty snapped off the lights in the conservatory and led Liss around the pool to the wall of glass that faced down the hill. No lights showed at the house below, but as they watched, a pair of headlights slid along the road toward the quarry and through the curve.

A town cruiser, with rolling lights switched off? Liss couldn't tell what was happening.

"Tell the truth," Patty said. "You would have called on Link for help if Callan hadn't been with him. It's your son you worry about, not mine."

Liss didn't think Patty wanted to know what she was worried about. "I worry about them both," Liss said. "A lot, lately."

"Because of the trouble your boyfriend is stirring up," Patty spat.

"He's not—" A lot to unpack, refute. She settled for the crux of the problem. "The trouble, as you call it, a *murder*, occurred years ago. He's not stirring anything. He's trying to see justice done. Which is his job, not something I can call off, even if we were still . . . I would have thought you'd have learned the job duties long ago."

Two more pairs of headlights raced along the road in tandem, through the curve. Still no flashing lights.

"The job itself is a duty," Patty said. "A duty to what people *deserve*, reward or punishment, no matter what the dusty books say. That's what I learned."

"Then you had a bad teacher," Liss said.

A light snapped on down the hill at her house. The deck light, responding to movement.

"Something's happening," Liss said, but Patty had left her side.

Liss watched as lights showed the progress being made through the rooms of her house: Downstairs, great room, sunroom. A minute later, the upstairs front, upstairs back. Every window, the skylight. Her house, glowing like a beacon.

"There won't be anyone there," Liss said to herself.

The light of the conservatory snapped on. Liss turned to find Patty at the doorway, arms crossed. "All these years married to my son," Patty said, "and you won't stand up for this family."

Key's law may have folded upon his retirement, but Patty's was still absolute.

If only Patty knew that Liss understood, finally, what it took to protect a family. It took everything, including resources she didn't know if she had.

"Patty, I want to protect Link," Liss said. "But what I want more is for him not to need me to do it."

"If you won't do it, I will," Patty said. "And then he really won't need you. You know, don't you?"

"What?"

"That I still own that house you live in?" Patty said.

Liss dropped her eyes to the pool between them.

"And if anything were to happen to Link, I could seek custody of Callan," Patty said. "Maybe I couldn't win, I don't know. I could ask our lawyers. They do know their business."

Liss could barely breathe.

"Or I could ask our good friend from the classic car club his opinion," she said. "Our friend the circuit court judge."

Liss felt stretched. She was in a tug-of-war, but she was the rope.

"Now, if you'll excuse me, I need to go see to my husband," Patty said. "He needs me, you see. For better and for worse. Maybe you remember saying those words yourself."

Patty waited at the doorway.

As Liss brushed past she caught a glimpse of a slumped shape in the next room. Key, sitting in shadow, like a piece of furniture. He was curled into himself, a tower of a man now collapsing.

Did she imagine a flicker of recognition, a twitch of reaction at the sight of her?

"Key . . ."

Patty shifted to stand between them.

Liss's phone rang in her pocket. It would be Mercer, calling to say all was clear. Calling to say everything was OK. If only it could be.

CHAPTER TWENTY-SIX

At home, Liss parked in a narrow slot next to the barn left by the three police cars in her driveway. The pool of light over the deck showed Slocum kicked back in one of her lounge chairs and Bowman sitting on the railing, legs swinging. They stopped talking as she approached.

Slocum tsked. "Invite us over," he said. "The least you could do is set out some snacks."

Inside, Mercer sat straight-backed at her table in street clothes, jeans and a gray Henley. His notepad sat open in front of him. He stood when she came in, and she could tell that they hadn't found anything. Anyone.

"I didn't imagine it," she said, crossing to the kitchen.

"I didn't say you did."

"There was a flashlight beam—"

"Liss, I believe you," Mercer said.

Outside, Slocum was cracking himself up about something. He had a slick sort of laugh, like a series of dainty, hissing sneezes.

He believed her.

She took down two wineglasses and set them on the counter. "Send them away," Liss said.

Mercer looked from the glasses to her, then went to the door and spoke quietly. She pulled out a bottle of shiraz. Outside, Bowman's boots hit the deck. Slocum's tread was scraping and slow, heavy. Reluctant. While she poured, one car, then two, started, backed up across the gravel, and were gone. Mercer came back into the room, pausing at the doorway. Deciding. Finally he sat at the counter opposite her. It was the closest they'd been in months, except for when they'd had Link sagging between them the night Ashley had been found. The house settled around them, quiet.

He gestured to the phone pulled from the wall sitting in a puddle of its own cord. "What's happening there?"

"I thought you were off duty," she said.

"Even in my time off, I'm a curious man."

"Is this for the notebook?"

"The—? Oh." He showed his empty hands.

"We were getting calls late at night, early morning," she said. "Even during normal hours, it was usually reporters anyway."

"Calls in the night, graffiti on your barn, flashlight beam in your windows," Mercer said. "Anything else?"

"That's plenty."

"It's too much," he said. "Is there anywhere else you can go for a while?"

"I can install better locks on the doors. It's—nothing. If I thought it was anything, I would have called you."

"You did call me," Mercer said. "Twice."

Her face felt hot. Maybe, she thought, he would think it was the wine. "I don't want to talk about it."

"OK," he said.

He took a drink of the wine. He had good hands, fine hairs on his fingers.

"What should we talk about, then?" he said. "Should we talk about the night your husband doesn't actually have an alibi for?"

Across the room, their family portrait stood at a different angle than all the other frames. Had she bumped it? She kept herself from jumping up to straighten it.

"He was drinking with Robbie at that gas station," she said.

"Not after midnight, and you know it, too," he said. "I heard you got there first, which makes me wonder why you'd be worried. After all these stand-by-your-man years."

"I'm not worried." But her voice was tight.

"OK," Mercer said. "Where do you think he went, instead? You already said he didn't come home that night; that's in Key's original notes. One of the few things he wrote down, by the way. So Link wasn't here. He didn't go to the Hubbard place, says Mrs. Hubbard. He didn't go to his parents' place. Says Patty."

Key had come himself to interview her. Alone. He must have known Link wouldn't be there, and she had to wonder why he'd thought it necessary to catch her by herself. Of course she wasn't alone; she had Callan. She hadn't slept more than a few hours in days at that point, could barely get Callan to take a bottle. Key had watched from the corner of his eye as Liss fed the baby, as uncomfortable, she had thought then, as if she'd been breastfeeding. She'd been uncomfortable herself, on display. Proving herself capable before she really was.

What if you don't know him as well as you like to think you do? Key had asked. He must have meant Robbie—but they'd been talking about Link.

"I don't know where he went," she said to Mercer. They stared at one another. "I don't know, OK?"

"He never told you. You never asked. You're afraid to know," he said. "OK. OK. You had a fight, he took an extra shift at the factory to avoid you, went drinking with a buddy to avoid you further, strayed off to parts unknown . . ."

She looked away.

"And ended up missing the moment when the mother of his child showed up on his doorstep," Mercer said. He held his glass for a moment, then put it back down. "What are we hoping for, here? That he was off cheating, I guess, since you've already forgiven him that."

Liss glared into her glass. "He's not a murderer."

"You sound pretty sure," Mercer said. "What were you fighting about?"

"That sounds like the notebook talking," she said. "I didn't ask you to stay to give me the third degree."

"Why did you ask me to stay?"

Because someone had been in her house. Because—

Because she didn't like to be alone.

But she didn't like that answer. She took a swig of the wine and set the glass down carefully so it wouldn't rattle. "Because I wanted to ask you . . . how quickly the DNA results will be back."

He sat back. "What's your hurry?"

"Other than my life being stalled out until they do?" Liss said. "I was thinking there'd need to be a memorial. For Ashley. If it's Ashley."

"I suppose that's something you're getting stuck with."

"I want to," Liss said.

"You should practice that in the mirror," he said.

"I do want to. For Callan," she said.

"DNA will be as rushed as I can request without making enemies," he said, shifting his glass around on the counter. He looked tired. "Probably a while, though, before the, uh, the body could be released. Once we know for sure the DNA matches, you could go ahead. Without the body. If it's about getting it done for Callan. I'm sorry you have to do it."

"I would do anything for Callan," she said.

"I know you would."

And he would do anything for her.

She'd asked him to stay because being with him was easy, when everything else was a mess.

Because she wanted to remember what it was like to be the person he'd believed her to be. Any minute, he might find he'd got her all wrong.

"I've missed you," she said.

His hand stilled at his glass. The silence of the house roared in her ears.

"You know how I feel," he said.

"I've been thinking about you a lot—"

"Don't do this."

"Oh," she said. "OK. OK." She sounded like him.

"I mean. Don't do it if you don't mean it," he said. "If we still have the same chances of getting it right."

"Nobody ever knows their chances," Liss said.

"But you operate, usually, from a chance at a hundred percent, don't you?"

"And we didn't," she said.

She'd kept the door open for Link, long past the moment it should have been closed. She glanced across the room at the framed photo of the three of them that had been knocked askew.

"*I* did," Mercer said. "I went a full one hundred percent."

"Callan comes first for me," she said.

"It's not Callan I wasn't willing to share you with," he said. "And you know that."

"You keep telling me things I know," Liss said. "I don't know anything. Except that I want you to stay."

"That would be a bad idea."

"Nothing has to happen," she said.

But she hadn't practiced lying to him. Neither of them believed it.

"I'm not Link, Lissette," Mercer said. "I'm not going to be your friend."

"OK," she said. "Good."

CHAPTER TWENTY-SEVEN

When Mercer woke, it was to the confusion of a bed that was not his and blinds that let in too much light. The sheets were familiar, but not his own. Softer. He came awake slowly, contentedly, remembering. Not minding the dull headache from the wine. He reached out to find the bed next to him rumpled but cool, empty.

He found his boxers on the floor and started toward the front of the house, then returned to the bedroom for his jeans in case Callan had come home unexpectedly. Kids were unpredictable like that.

He spent a few minutes in the bathroom, where he chewed on an inch of toothpaste, a brand he didn't use. He had once kept a toothbrush next to Liss's in the Ball canning jar on the sink's edge, but it was gone. The missing toothbrush and his haggard face in the mirror made him think for the first time—they'd made a mistake.

He had.

A witness in an active investigation. He'd lost his mind.

In the kitchen she was standing at the stove with bare legs under a long, faded T-shirt. Link's shirt, had to be.

Maybe it was a different kind of mistake he'd made.

"Good morning," she said.

"I don't think you're supposed to cook with that much skin exposed," he said.

"You're not supposed to cook *bacon* with this much skin exposed," she said, turning with a smile that nearly sent him over to her. Repeat offenses of the same mistake only counted as a single mistake. She gestured to his chest with her spatula. "I guess neither of us should be cooking at the moment."

He went to the table and sat in the same chair he'd occupied last night while waiting for her to come home. His notebook lay on the table. He opened the leather cover.

"Did you find what you were looking for?" he said.

Liss brought a plate over. A small hesitation before she slid it in front of him. "What do you mean?"

"I had this pad here turned over to a particular page in my notes," he said.

She turned away.

"And it's not this one," he said. "I just wonder what you were hoping to find."

"I wasn't—" She seemed to reconsider. "I wasn't hoping for anything in particular. Just curious in my off hours, I guess."

"It's not funny, Lissette."

"I'm sorry," she said.

"Was this—*this*? All in the service of getting access to my notes—"

"*No*," she said.

"—to help Link out of a jam?" he said. "At my expense?"

"You can't believe that," Liss said. "Mercer, none of *this* was about Link. I promise you that."

He wasn't so sure.

"I want that to be true," he said. He wanted it more than she realized or understood or—maybe she did understand and didn't want to face it. Didn't give a shit. "Last night was a lot of fun but it shouldn't have happened."

"Because I looked in your *notebook*?"

"Because the notebook has notes about your family, Liss," Mercer said. "Because I had to ask myself just now, ask *you*, if you were trading for time with my investigation. That's no way to go about this, is it? It's not how I want to go about it."

"Oh." Her mouth had a certain set to it.

"I think I just need to do my job for a while. Until—" But he didn't want to put a timeline on it. A timeline that could stretch and stretch away from them.

"Until what?"

"Until things are a little more certain."

"You mean until the election or . . ."

This would never be wrapped up before the election. He didn't want to think beyond it, though. Beyond the holidays and winter spent away from her fireplace and her soft sheets. He had his own place, sure, but he'd never made it a home. The walls were bare, floors hardwood, no rugs. He'd meant to have a different life here than the one he'd scraped together in the city, solitary hours ticked off with routine, years rolling under him while he stood still.

"Tell me you'll figure out another place to go for a while," he said. "Even with better locks—"

"Mercer, you don't get it," she said. "I don't have anywhere else to go."

She did. But he couldn't offer it just now. "I—"

"Don't," she said.

"Here's the thing," he said. "Everybody in the area knows you and Link split, am I right?"

"OK?"

Yeah, they did, and they knew all about Mercer coming up to visit, too. His car parked out back all night would probably be news at the café this morning. He hadn't thought of it. There was hardly a secret left to be had, except the ones he was chasing.

"OK, so why are they painting *your* barn?" he said. "Why are they snooping through your house, calling *your* number?"

"I . . ." She turned her head toward the window.

"I don't know why either, but it worries me," he said. "For you. And Callan. I don't know what's going on, but they know where Link lives. He doesn't have a barn door but he's got a front door, a truck parked on the street at night. A phone number where they could be making accusations if they wanted to blame him."

She set down her spatula. She hadn't thought of it, he could tell.

"Anything you want to tell me?" he said.

Liss pivoted toward him. "You can't think I would *kill* anyone."

"No, I sure don't," he said. "But you're the last person to admit seeing her and you never answered my question last night. What were you and Link fighting about? For the notebook, this time."

She seemed to fold into herself at the shoulders, a paper doll wishing for her clothes. "We argued. That's all, not a fight."

He'd seen a bruise on her arm just about the place someone might grab at her. If Link Kehoe had made a habit of hurting women . . . "Liss, don't make me bring you in for questioning," he said. "What did you argue about?"

"I wanted to talk about . . . the future, all right?" she said. "And he didn't."

"Tell me."

"I wanted to talk about having a baby," she said.

"OK." He sat back from the table. New information. "But he *had* a baby, was that the hold up?"

"We didn't have any custody arrangement," she said. "Ashley would barely let Link see Callan. She would barely let him out of her sight." Liss smiled sadly. "I thought it was because of me. I understand it now. *Now* I do but at the time . . . Callan seemed like something so separate from us," she said. "I wanted to start *our* life. It seemed to me like we would never—"

She'd stopped, looked around her like she'd never seen the place before, hadn't lived there all these years. "We never did."

"You could have . . ."

"But we never did," she said. "Not just kids, any of it. We put it off until . . . until." Her entire being seemed to gesture toward him pointedly. "*Until*, Mercer. Until time passed us by. Until the things I wanted were off the table."

"You're still a young woman, Liss," he said.

She raised her eyebrows at him, like, come *on*. "Not as young as you need to be," she said. "I don't know if I could do it all over again, not this many years later. Because of course, Callan's home was here with us."

"You never resented what didn't happen, though?"

"I never resented Callan," she said.

She didn't want to name it, that's what he thought. "But Link?" he said. "Because you never had children together?"

"We *were* children together," she said. "Except—"

Except only one of them had grown up. And she wouldn't say she resented Ashley, not to him and his notebook.

Liss turned back to the stove, her bare feet planted, a hand on her hip. "Fresh pancakes in a second," she said. "Those are cold. Want some coffee?"

Mercer wouldn't turn down breakfast from her twice in one week. But just as he thought of the time he had, he realized that he was sitting in the same chair Kehoe had been sitting in, that shithead grin on his face. If he did kill Ashley—

If Mercer arrested Link, that would be the end of things. He wouldn't be able to show his face around this house, to this woman, to her kid. The town would lose its collective mind. He'd be out of a job by January.

Link Kehoe stood on this side of everything Mercer wanted for himself, blocking it. He was good and sick of that guy being every direction he turned.

MERCER THOUGHT HE'D be able to get some quiet thinking done at the station among the files on a Saturday morning, but he hadn't been at his desk more than a half hour when a commotion broke out up front.

Bowman had placed himself to keep someone on the civilian side of the front desk. He was trying not to give out as well as he was getting, using the soothing tones they'd discussed in conflict resolution training.

"What's going on?" Mercer said, then saw who it was.

Larry Norville, Parkins's number-one to-whom-it-may-concern letter-smith, stood red-faced, just out of reach of Bowman's long arms.

"Mr. Norville," Mercer said. "What's wrong today, sir?"

"I said I needed to see the man in charge." The guy was a little wet at the lip, more wild-eyed than when he'd been sitting at the café counter throwing insults and dire election predictions at him.

"Who says I'm not the man in charge today?" Bowman said. It was wearing him down, being the one who was different, being held to higher standards.

"I have some information of interest to the case," Norville said, smoothing his hair. He held a file folder to his skinny chest. He had a mustard stain on the cuff of his checked shirt, red faded to nearly pink.

"Which case?" Mercer said.

"*The* case," he said. "At the Kehoes'. You said if we had any information."

"I did say that. Come on back." Mercer shot a look at Bowman then the clock over the front door. Twenty minutes, he mouthed behind the old man's back.

But when the phone on Mercer's desk rang twenty minutes later—Bowman, giving him an out—Mercer ignored it. Norville's propensity for faultfinding had become a joke to them but now, no, Mercer wasn't laughing. Maybe he had got the old guy wrong.

Maybe he had got quite a few people wrong.

CHAPTER TWENTY-EIGHT

On Saturday, Liss drove to the outskirts of the city, forty-five minutes out of her way, to a big box hardware store where she wouldn't know anyone, where no one would know her.

The muscles in her legs ached, a reminder of the evening before. Her pride stung, too. She'd been caught out. And put off. Until, Mercer said. Until when?

Years, Link had said, but wasn't it just as likely they would never see the end of this?

In the big box store, a series of people in fabric vests helped sort out what she needed: a chunky padlock for the barn door, strike plate reinforcements and two hardy deadbolts for the house. Also pin locks for the first-floor windows and two wireless doorbell cameras that sent live video to her phone through an app.

And a gallon of paint, white, to return the barn doors to a nice clean canvas for the next time someone wanted to call Link a name. Or her. Link has a phone number, Mercer had pointed out. Why *weren't* they calling him?

Outside, Connie Garza was coming toward her across the parking lot.

Liss smiled and raised her hand, but Connie hadn't seen her. She'd turned for the far entrance. *Was* it her? "Connie?" Liss called. But the woman, whoever it was, didn't turn around.

Home again, she prowled the house with their baseball bat, then threw her sheets in the wash and went out to put a bright white coat on the barn doors. The afternoon faded behind the woods; her hands went cold. She fixed the padlock in place, added its key to her set. The second key should go to Link, she supposed.

She resisted texting him to check on Callan or start a conversation she didn't want to have.

Inside, she figured out the window locks with a glass of wine within reach, her sheets tumbling in the dryer, her attention drifting to the clock, her phone. Mercer might have called, but he didn't. She resisted texting him, too. She was a grown woman, capable of being alone for an evening. Wasn't she?

And there was her pride—

If she had any. He'd put her off. *Until*, he'd said. Well, then, he'd have to call her. The house could be on fire, and she wouldn't call him now.

Liss picked up a deadbolt package. It was heavy. Possibly overkill.

But that was the thing. Who could know what was enough until it was too late?

Liss sat up in the dark room, gasping. Her legs, twisted in the sheets. Her head, thick.

The clock screamed an unlikely time in red numerals. She'd finished the bottle of wine and most of the reinforcements before finally dropping into her bed. Now the house was quiet.

But something had woken her. A dream? She couldn't remember. A storm?

Liss untangled herself and sat at the edge of the bed, listening.

When the crack came, it was a sound she heard in her chest and tasted at the back of her throat.

Gunfire?

Liss fumbled among her blankets for her cell phone. She pictured the deadbolts, still safe in their packaging on the kitchen counter.

She hesitated only a moment, then dialed Mercer and crept to the window. At the quarry's edge, a light glowed. She caught movement there, a figure in silhouette.

Another crack. Fireworks?

No, not fireworks. The crack of a glass bottle thrown against rock, followed by wild laughter.

A party.

She was only glad Callan was sleeping at Link's.

Mercer's phone was still ringing. Liss hung up and crawled back into bed.

In all the years she'd lived in this house, they'd hardly ever had to discourage anyone from the quarry. Now something had shifted. A new generation alerted, or the thin curtain of protection around the Kehoes torn away?

She listened to the laughter, watching the dark patches of shadow in the corners of her room until they disappeared and the sun was up.

LINK PULLED UP with Callan mid-afternoon while Liss was drilling three-inch screws through the new deadbolt strike plate at the back door.

"What are you doing?" Callan said.

She set down the drill and stood to subject him to a hug. Had he grown over the weekend? "Just a project," she said. "Go put your dirty clothes in the laundry so I can talk to Dad?"

Link hovered near the stairs. "You changing the locks on me?"

The sight of him made her sick. Murderer or serial cheat? These were her choices. "Just some things I've been meaning to get to," she said.

"Things I should have got to but never did, you mean."

"I literally do not have the energy to fight," Liss said.

"He's had dinner already, if that saves your strength for a few punches."

"Not pizza, I hope?"

"As a matter of fact, I took him for Sunday roast at Mom and Dad's," Link said. "Mom said you might have had a party last night?"

"Does this look like a party to you?" she said, gesturing toward the new locks.

"Fuck, Liss," Link said. "How did we get here?"

"I was going to ask you something similar," she said. She was so tired she felt as though she were swimming through the day. "I need you to be honest with me, no matter the answer."

Link bounced his heels from the bottom step. "All right?"

"Where did you wake up the morning after Ashley disappeared?" she said.

His head fell back. "You can't be serious."

"I'm absolutely serious and so is Mercer," she said.

"Well, I didn't wake up with my feet wet or blood on my hands," he said.

"Jesus, Link." Liss went to make sure Callan had gone upstairs and closed the door. "Try to remember that it's his—"

"I'm not the one who forgets," he said.

She might never forgive him that. "You didn't actually answer the question."

Link let out a heavy sigh that turned into a growl. Then his shoulders sank. "I'm sorry."

Her face hurt, her eyes stung. "Yeah, I guess you are."

"What does it matter now?" he said. "We're one signature away from kaput, right? We're through."

"We were barely *started*, back then," she said. "You can't see the difference? We'd been married, what? A couple of months? I meant it when I said those vows, Link, and now I'm finding out you never did. We'd barely got through the thing with Ashley—"

"You'd better be glad about the thing with Ashley," he said, threateningly.

"Or what?" She wanted all the awful truths out now. "Or what? Say it."

"Or nothing," he said. "I just meant we wouldn't have Callan."

"We wouldn't have Callan," she said. "But it's not just that, is it?" If there'd been no Callan, Link would have gone to college. He would have lived the life he'd been promised. "If there'd been no Callan," Liss said. "There'd be no us."

"You can't know how things might have gone," Link said.

"I used to feel special that you chose me," Liss said. "But now I think you chose me because I made *you* feel special. Your beautiful life was skidding right into a ditch, and you needed someone who believed you were still . . . *Link Kehoe*."

"What's that supposed to mean?" he snapped.

"Everything you were meant for. Link Kehoe, the shining star, the hometown hero—"

"Well, we can all see how that turned out," he said.

"You are Callan's hero," Liss said. "You were my shining star. But you were never going to be satisfied with that. I have wasted a lot of time trying not to see that. How many times, Link?"

"Liss," he said.

"How many times over the years did you— You know what?" she said. "I don't want to know. I don't want their names. All I need to know is, will *this* woman confirm you were with her that night and save your fucking neck? And save our son from losing another parent?"

Link stepped backward off the deck. "I'm sorry, OK? I was drinking—it didn't mean anything. It was only one night and I *knew*—"

"At some point, Link, you need to stop giving away your life in single-night increments," Liss said. "Give her name to the police. Let Mercer get this cleared up."

Link looked ready to say something to that but stopped himself.

"Please," she said. She picked up the power drill to have something to look at. It was his, of course. She wanted him to go. But it was his house she was securing, his barn door she'd painted, his child, ultimately, she was protecting with alarm bells and reinforced steel. His future.

When she'd told Mercer she and Link had never started their life, she hadn't realized the truth. Link *had*. He'd started his life. He had everything he needed. He would bounce back smiling, as he always did. And if he needed a little managing, some woman would snap him up and mold her life around whatever he wanted, whatever he needed. And his mother would see to the rest.

Her situation was the precarious one. The stepmother with no claim, living in a house at the whim of the mother-in-law who'd made it clear she was no longer welcome and a husband she didn't trust. Link even had an alibi. She was the one who'd been here, alone, rocking the baby, his cries like a chisel to the back of her head. The last to see the kid's mother alive. The one with something to gain.

As far as anyone knew, she was the one with blood on her hands.

KILLER, in red, dripping letters.

Mercer was right. It was all meant for her.

CHAPTER TWENTY-NINE

Link finally left, and Liss got back to work on barricading her house, fueled by the revelation:

She was the one.

The calls, the looks. The blame for Ashley's death hadn't shifted from Robbie to Link. It had shifted to *her*.

She didn't know what to do about it. Didn't know if anything could be done.

She had just finished with the back door when gravel crunched behind her in the drive and a car she didn't immediately know pulled up. She held the power drill as a weapon, then recognized Sherry Harris, her friend from back in school.

Sherry popped out of her car. "Hey," she said. "You didn't text me back."

"It's been . . ." Liss couldn't think of how to explain. She sagged against the deck railing. "Sorry."

They hadn't been close in years, but she should have known Sherry's text would have been sincere.

"I won't bother you," Sherry said. "I know you're *busy* pulling cars out of the *sinkhole* in your yard. Ex-girlfriends are the *worst*."

It caught her off guard, the black humor. Someone coming at the absurdity of it boldly. "It *has* been taking up a lot of my time," Liss said.

Sherry opened the back door of her car and took out a foil-covered dish. "Now I know you must be drowning in— Oh, shit. I told myself not to say *drowning*."

"Oh, God," Liss gasped. She hoped Callan couldn't hear her. "I'll never be able to say the word again."

Sherry smiled. "Such bad taste, that's me." She lifted the dish in her hand. "So of course I cooked for you."

"You didn't have to do that," Liss said. "But thank you."

"Don't thank me until you've tasted it," Sherry said. "It's lasagna. I figured you'd be getting lots of casseroles."

Liss couldn't bear to puncture the bubble Sherry had created. "We're pro lasagna," Liss said.

"I used far too much cheese," Sherry said. "But in my opinion, cheese fixes a lot of problems."

Another car pulled up, one Liss recognized immediately. Vera.

She could have cried. Cheese fixed a lot of problems, but friends— true friends—fixed everything. "Can you come in for a while?"

"I can stop by another time and stay longer," Sherry said. "How about when you finish the lasagna, you give me a call? I'll bring more cheese and we'll catch up."

"Deal," Liss said.

Vera came up on the deck, watching as Sherry drove away. Vera looked down at the dish in Liss's hands. "I'm just in time for the casseroles of questionable provenance."

Was Vera jealous she had other friends? Or embarrassed to arrive empty-handed? "I'm not questioning a gift lasagna," Liss said. "Hungry?"

"God, no," Vera said. "I just came to check on you. Didn't re-alize I'd be interrupting a packed social schedule."

"You didn't," Liss said. There was hardly anyone left. Her mar-riage, finally over. Mercer, taking time *until*—until some day that may never come. Connie, avoiding her in public. Chatting with

Sherry even for a few minutes had cheered her up. Now her despair was a tide, turning. "Coffee?"

"Maybe something more wine-ish?" Vera said.

"That's what I meant." Liss retrieved the power drill and held the door.

"Have you been watching HGTV or something?" Vera said.

Liss didn't want to talk about it. "I realized nothing was holding me back from my dream of being a Property Brother," she said. She slid the lasagna into the fridge and brought out a bottle for Vera's approval.

Vera grabbed glasses. "Changing the locks? Isn't it still Link's house?"

Liss fussed with the bottle and poured. She had told Vera plenty of stories from her marriage over the years, but the subject was now as tender to her as the bruise still on her arm. She'd shared all her tender spots with Vera, actually. Her childhood, her mother's failings. Her own. "Link didn't seem to mind the upgrade," she said. "He was here earlier."

"Of course he was," Vera said. "And barely missed Mercer leaving, I suppose?"

Liss fumbled the wine, spilled a bit. "How did you hear about that already?"

"What?" Vera said. "Are you *serious*? He stayed over?" She was peering at Liss closely and didn't need to hear the answer. "I'm sure you'll say it was nothing," she said airily.

"It wasn't *nothing*," Liss argued. "It was never *nothing*. Just . . . bad timing. When there was a chance that Link and I might still . . ."

Liss hadn't meant to admit it, but Vera picked up the nuance. "There's no chance now?" she said. "What changed?"

"Nothing," Liss said. "He cheated."

"We knew that," Vera said. She reached over and topped off Liss's glass. "Didn't we?"

"*Thanks*, Vera," Liss said. "I mean that he cheated—from the very beginning, all along."

"Oh," Vera said. She was making little circles in the spilled wine with base of her glass. "Was he naming names or what?"

"I didn't want to know," Liss said. "Look, I know it's denial, OK? You don't have to say it."

"No, I get it. You wouldn't want the picture in your head of your husband—"

"*Vera!*" Liss cried.

"Sorry."

Liss put down her glass, empty again. She'd had too much far too quickly. And to snarl at her boss—

Vera glanced at the bottle's level. "I should go."

"No, don't go," Liss said. "I'm the one who's sorry."

"It's OK, Liss," Vera said, reaching for her. She managed to squeeze Liss arm's just at the spot that was bruised. "It can only go up from here, right?"

CALLAN CAME DOWN while Liss sat at the kitchen table, picking at some lasagna. He slumped heavily across from her and put his head in his arms.

Had he heard her fight with Link? Sherry joking around? The chat with Vera?

"What's wrong, Cowboy?"

"Don't call me that," he said, muffled.

"Are you worried about the blood test? Nobody *likes* needles," she said. "It'll be fast, and Dad would probably drive-through for lunch on your way back to school."

He sat up. "I don't want to eat that garbage," he said. "Coach says..."

Proteins and carbs and something about amino acids, as though Coach had invented it all. But there were worse ways for him to grow away from her.

Like breaking her rules, taking a joy ride, and then pretending he wasn't going to try and get away with it? Like lying to the police.

It pissed her off, actually. Here she was, trying to protect him, even though it was tearing the flesh right off her bones, and he . . . he was playing games. But he'd learned from his father, hadn't he, that a wink and a smile could get him out of trouble. Into trouble and then out again.

But what really bothered her about Callan lying to Mercer's men was how far away he'd seemed from her in that moment. Like someone she didn't know. Couldn't know.

Finally Callan came to the end of what Coach had to say. She could hear a voice somewhere in the house, the TV left on.

"I wanted to talk to you," she said. "About what you said the other day when—"

"Do you want it to match?" he said into the crook of his arm.

"What? Oh, the blood."

There you are again, Ashley.

"I don't know," Liss said, controlling her voice. "It would be sad if it matched."

He pulled his head up. His ears were pink at the tips.

"But it's already sad that she's not here," Liss said. "It's OK to be sad that she's not here."

"I didn't know her," he said.

"But it still feels bad, maybe?"

His eyes shifted up to hers.

"It's not a betrayal of me to be sad Ashley's gone," Liss said. "It's

OK to be sad that you never got the chance to know her. I'm sad about that."

"You are?"

It wrenched her to see him in pain. Wasn't that the same thing? "I am," she said. "I hate that you have to go through this."

He nodded, once, as though he'd come to a decision. He came around the table and let her hug him. Maybe someday he'd become a cheek-kisser like his dad was, to Patty. In this in-between place, he only withstood her affection, like a favor. A favor she would gladly accept, every chance.

CHAPTER THIRTY

Monday morning, Liss opened the door to the teachers' lounge. Conversation at the coffee pot cut out and faces around the room turned in her direction.

"Good morning to you, too," she said.

"Liss," Denise said from the corner table. She taught English, had been Liss's teacher once, and Link's, and now gave Callan encouraging notes on his papers, mostly unwarranted. She wore a bright red Parkins West sweater. She had a closet full of them. "How are we holding up?"

Anything Liss could think to say didn't seem true or like something she'd want repeated by those listening in. She crossed to the coffee station. The two junior high teachers who'd been leaning nearby fell away. "*We* are OK. Thanks for asking," she said.

"I heard Callan's out today?"

Liss gritted her teeth and poured. She wouldn't give anyone the satisfaction of lying. "He'll be back by the beginning of third period," she said. "He's getting blood drawn." Knowing that glances were shooting across the room in every direction behind her back, she raised her voice. "They're hoping for a match to the bones from the pond, as you all must know."

A few of those in the room suddenly realized the first bell would ring soon and started gathering their things.

"I didn't mean to *pry*," Denise said.

But she had. They did. They would pry her open or stand around hoping someone else would empty her out. Even those who meant well.

Liss sighed. There were people who meant well. She needed to remember that. "We really are fine," she said.

The first bell rang, but Denise went back to marking up papers as the others hurried to rinse coffee mugs, laughing and jostling at the sink. Their lives so quietly normal.

"Callan and Tanner have fallen out, I think?" Denise said, once the room had emptied around them. "Thick as thieves until last week. Ah well. Most friendship is feigning, most loving is folly."

Liss had the feeling she was missing something. She often felt that way around the teachers, around Vera and her shiny framed degrees. "Is that . . . what is that?"

"Shakespeare. It's from *As You Like It*," Denise said. "For some reason they only let us teach the tragedies. A shame. I always thought life was too much tragedy for most children already."

Liss turned her coffee mug in her hands. She was never more than a few yards from people who knew too much about her, was she? "I was trying to protect Callan from tragedy," she said. "Any more of it, anyway."

"I wouldn't worry, Lissette," Denise said. "Callan's a good kid. A charmer like his dad, but a good soul. Like his mother."

Liss blinked away. Of course. She'd been Ashley's teacher, too.

"I mean you, Liss," Denise said. "You've passed things down to him, too. Don't forget that."

Liss returned to her desk without any reason to pass the classroom where Callan's first period class would be meeting without him. Most loving is folly. She was no English teacher, but she thought she understood that part. Most love, but not all.

Back at her desk, the framed family portrait she kept there had been nudged to a weird angle, showing the line in dust where it normally sat. Had someone sat at her desk?

She picked up the photo and studied Callan's smile, a side-by-side match for Link's.

Maybe the time had come to replace the photo with one of Callan on his own.

At her computer, she couldn't concentrate on the career fair. Callan would be at the hospital by now. He'd be finding out Ashley's fate. The fate of them all.

Some sniffling was coming from Vera's office. Who was crying at eight in the morning? Liss wondered, calling up Vera's schedule. It was a junior girl who relied on Vera to talk her down weekly. Eating disorder?

Liss opened up the student database and confirmed it. Eating disorder.

Since she was already breaking the rules, she searched for Tanner. Nothing much to see. Boys like Tanner didn't spend much time in the guidance office. They had plenty of guidance at home. But boys like Jamie—

Jamie Ward had been to see Vera or Spence no less than six times since the beginning of school. She hadn't seen him in the office, but then he was an easy kid to overlook.

Spence shifted in his office. Liss clicked away from the database. Maybe six visits wasn't extraordinary.

When she could hear Spence talking again, she went back to the database. Her fingers were tapping out the name before she could talk herself out of it.

Callan Kehoe.

As the results loaded, she realized she had struck through bedrock. She was no longer a person held to the rules. She should have a copy of that letter, anyway. It was easier just to do it herself than explain to Vera why she needed it.

Callan had one entry, a visit with Vera. Liss checked the date. It was long before Ashley's bones had been found.

Here was a kid in *actual crisis* and he would barely grace the doorway to ask for help.

But would he? With her sitting here?

Liss clicked through his record to where scanned documents were kept. His vaccinations, his health forms for football, the letter. She double-clicked on it and sent it to the printer behind her desk.

When she closed that document, she noticed another one saved alongside. She double-clicked to open it. It was a text document with a list of dates and some notations for each. She started reading— "Callan distraught over divorce"—and scrolled—"Custody arrangement in question." What was this? In question by *whom*?

Spence's office opened. Liss rushed to hide the database window behind another application, positioning herself to block Spence's view of her screen.

"Lissette?"

"Yes." She was out of breath, as though she'd been running.

Spence stood in his door, holding it open. "Could you grab a couple of resources for Mr. Brennan, here?"

Devin, still on crutches, emerged behind Spence, hair hanging over an eye. "Hi, Mrs. Kehoe."

"Devin, how are you?" Liss said. "Tell me what you need."

He hoped for a Big Ten school—football, it was a brain fever with these boys. Liss gathered literature from the rack while Devin hobbled behind her. "Thanks for the snacks the other night, Mrs. Kehoe."

Vera had come out of her office. "Liss, are we out of paper clips?"

"I'll get you some."

Devin said, "I told Callan thanks but I'm sure it was your idea."

"Don't be silly," Vera said. "I'll help myself."

Liss watched from the corner of her vision as Vera leaned over her desk.

"You guys totally picked my favorites," Devin was saying.

"Liss," Vera said.

"The paper clips are in the—"

But Vera had the mouse for Liss's computer in her hand and was peering at Liss's computer monitor. Callan's record. She straightened up, then reached for the page on the printer.

It should be forgivable that she'd been using the database to check up on her own son. But she already knew. It wouldn't be.

"Leave of absence?" Liss said, not quite believing what she was hearing. "You can't be serious."

"Just while things are so . . . chaotic," Mike said. The vice principal's primary job was disciplining students, but now Liss understood that his duties were far-ranging. He had a cherry-red tie and the scraped look of a man who shaved too closely and too often.

"Am I not doing a good job?" Liss said. "What about the career fair?"

"It will all be handled," Mike said smoothly. "We'll find a workaround. Or reschedule?" He looked to Vera, who stood at the closed door, eyes down, arms crossed.

"We can reschedule," Vera said.

"I have all these vendors set up—"

"Then we'll work it out with them," Mike said. "The important thing is that you have time for your family right now. For Callan."

But Callan would be at school. Wouldn't he? "Are you expelling Callan?"

Mike pulled at the knot of his tie. Making it tighter. "A few days might be helpful—"

"Suspension?"

"Now we *could* suspend him, for the antics on the football field the other night," Mike said. "Make no mistake. But I understand that he's going through a tough time. Let's call it bereavement leave."

They didn't even know for sure. Almost a week since the car had been spotted, the bones brought up, and they didn't know.

"How many days?"

"As many days as he needs," Mike said.

"I mean for me," Liss said.

He glanced toward Vera. "That can be . . . open-ended," he said. "As many days as *you* need."

Looking for a reason. That's what the human resources guy at Renner had said about what they'd done to Robbie. She didn't need time off. And Callan was doing fine.

Wasn't he? Those notes buried in his student record—who had written them? And were they factual? *Distraught*, she'd read.

Callan would be arriving back to school from the blood draw with a Band-Aid on his arm, a badge of honor—or of shame or of grief or some other emotion she couldn't even predict. He could use a few days. They both could.

"*Paid* leave," she said.

Mike blinked. "Uh, yes."

In the hallway, Vera walked two steps ahead of her, fast, not letting her catch up.

"Vera, stop."

"I have appointments."

"I know you do," Liss said. "I'm the one who put them on your calendar. Do you even know how to do that for yourself?"

"I'll figure it out," Vera said.

"You have a lot to figure out then, learning all the things I do for the office and running the career fair, too. Is it worth all this fuss? Just because I peeked at Callan's record in the student database?"

Vera wheeled on her. "And left it open on your public-facing computer screen."

Her computer screen faced the wall, away from visitors. "What is this about?"

"It's about negligence, Lissette," Vera said. "Mine, for hiring you in the first place. And yours, for being sloppy with student privacy. Any student's privacy. If we're being honest, you've been distracted for a good long while. All the drama with Link . . ."

The drama with *Link*? "You mean the divorce?" she said. "Am I not allowed to get a divorce?"

"A divorce that somehow keeps dragging on and on—"

"It's complicated," Liss said. "We have a kid together."

"No," Vera said. "You don't."

Vera might as well have slapped her. "You don't know a thing about my life," Liss said.

"I know all about your life," Vera said. "You've told me all about your life. But the problem is that you must not see your own life very clearly, or you'd be embarrassed. You should be embarrassed."

Liss felt heat rushing up her neck. "I don't know what you're talking about," Liss said.

"Oh, really?" Vera said. "How many different men have slept in your bed in the last week?"

Far down the hall, a junior high teacher poked his head out of his classroom. "Keep your voice down," Liss said.

"Do you have any idea what that kind of thing will do to a kid?" Vera said. "Oh, right, you *do*. Your childhood was so terrible but you'd inflict it on another generation. Meanwhile the ink on your divorce papers is fading with age. Have you thought about what it does to a man like Link to dangle him along?"

"He—Link is the one—"

"You've created this . . . this psychological *limbo* in which you get to do anything you want," Vera said. "And your husband is *neutered*."

"He's the one," Liss said. "He's the one who . . ."

Up and down the hall, doors had opened and teachers stepped out to see about the noise.

But she didn't need to finish. Vera knew. Liss had given Vera enough information that arguing with her was like fighting with her own self-loathing. All her darkest concerns, stacked up against her.

CHAPTER THIRTY-ONE

Mercer parked in the hospital visitor lot, early, with a cup of coffee and the determination not to have to go inside for a whizz until he got what he'd come for. His dad had tried to teach him to hunt once—it didn't take, not the way the old man had meant for it to, anyway—and now as he lay in wait, he was reminded of that day's lessons: patience, persistence, piss breaks scheduled only on an as-absolutely-needed basis.

Before too long, though, his prey wandered into his sights like a strutting twelve-point buck never had. Mercer watched as Kehoe's truck parked a couple of rows over and he and his kid hopped out.

Mercer caught up with them at registration. Callan looked surprised to see him, but not Kehoe, not a bit.

"Gentlemen," Mercer said, as pleasantly as he could muster. He was surprised himself, to feel real anger coursing through him. He hadn't been sure which one of Callan's guardians he'd run into this morning, but either one would have done. To the receptionist, he said, "I'll take them up."

In the elevator, he sipped his coffee and tried to button himself in a bit. "You doing OK, Callan? Like, school? Football?"

The kid shrugged and Mercer got it. He did. He'd put the kid into a position, hadn't he, with regards to his mother. None of it was Callan's doing. "This will be real quick, I promise," Mercer said. "We're here to get you some answers."

"He can't vote yet, Mercer," Link said.

Callan was looking at him with interest, though. "Me? Get me answers?"

"Yes, sir," Mercer said. "You. You want to know what happened, right?"

Callan licked his lips. "Yeah. Yes."

Mercer glanced in Kehoe's direction. "Me, too."

They had a curtained cube of a room ready for Callan but Link made no move to follow his son into it. "I guess you're here for more than making sure we found the right room," Kehoe said. "A chat?"

"I would appreciate that, since you have the time."

"Let me catch you up," Link said. "I was at work, then I went drinking, then I left with someone who was not my wife."

Mercer tried to keep his feelings off his face, but it must not have worked.

"Look," Link said. "I know, man. I'm a piece of shit."

He didn't need the confirmation, but he had reason to distrust this coming-clean. Kehoe had already fucked up his marriage with a cheat, hadn't he? So what was one more, conveniently timed to cover his ass?

"I guess you're pretty pleased by this turn of events," Link said.

"I'm going to need a name and some contact info," Mercer said.

He didn't trust Link Kehoe and, as it turned out, he wasn't in the mood to give Liss a pass, either.

He'd still had the scent of Liss in his nostrils when Larry Law-suit Norville had come to report an overheard conversation in the hallway outside Link Kehoe's bachelor pad apartment. Link and Liss conferring on knowing the outcome of this DNA test, long before the needle went in, and Liss assuring her shithead husband that Mercer wouldn't find the evidence. Won't find anything, Norville had quoted. He had it written in his little notepad, like a freelance tattletale. The notepad had the contact information of a law office in the city printed at the top in a trustworthy navy blue. Mercer had a feeling whoever answered that number had long regretted the indiscriminate freebie falling into Norville's hands.

So forgive him if he questioned all this remorse out of Link, all these final rites for the Kehoe marriage. If Liss was out making promises in hallways like that—Link's freedom, Mercer's failure—and then plying *him* with her attention for a check-up on his notes, then he wasn't sure of anything, except he might have been played the fool.

He was sick of the whole damn family. Except—

Mercer glanced toward the curtain. "I'm going to sort this out for your kid," he said. "No matter what that blood test says, OK? I'm getting this sorted the fuck out."

"I wish you would," Link said.

Mercer worked to control his voice but underneath his blood was hot-pot roiling. "I wish your old man had, Kehoe."

"I wish that, too," Link said. "Do you think I don't? That day changed everything for us, OK? I can't say ruined—" He looked toward the curtain, lowered his voice. "*Changed*. And this hanging over my head while I need to be there for Callan is . . . is bullshit. I will do anything you need me to do, all right? You want my blood, too?"

"Wouldn't be an awful idea," Mercer said.

Link worked his jaw, trying to figure out if he was being jerked around in some way. "Really?"

"We could rule you out against any other DNA that turns up," Mercer said.

"Fine." Link unbuttoned the cuff of his shirt, plaid like Norville's, but bright. New. Link Kehoe had never had a faded shirt in his life. He was rolling up his sleeve, making the motions as angry as he could, Mercer thought. "Fine," Link said. "Let's rule me out. Let's stop wasting time." He went to join his son behind the curtain, but then turned back. "But I'm telling you, Alarie."

His voice was gruff and low. Threatening. Like a hand on Mercer's neck.

"What's that, Kehoe?"

"Don't break my kid's heart with promises you can't deliver on, OK?" Link said. "Or his mother's."

Mercer knew which mother he meant, but it was the other one he was making promises to from here on out. "I will not."

When Mercer eventually arrived at his desk, Deacon followed him in with a sheaf of papers. "You requested some phone records?"

"Great."

Deacon passed the pages over. "I didn't know we got a warrant on Kehoe's phone already. Or Liss's? You doing a little jealous boyfriend business on the side?"

Mercer shot him a look. He *really* wasn't in the mood. "This is just a little favor among friends, and you don't know a thing about it, OK?"

He *won't* get the evidence? If there was evidence, oh, Liss, you better believe he would get it.

"Those are all recent calls," Deak said. "Is this to do with the bones found?"

The list of calls was longer than he'd imagined, all made to Liss's landline between midnight and five in the morning. "Maybe. No one's going to jail on this. I just want a quiet word with whichever friendly neighbor of Liss's is calling all hours. Did you track any of these numbers?"

"It's only about eight unique numbers," Deak said. "But one or two of them have made a real hobby of it. What's this about? They're just bothering her?"

"It's past that," he said. "That prowler the other night, some light destruction of property. Just looking for a few volunteers for my special attention."

"Well, if sir is looking for some recommendations from the kitchen, I would order the . . ." Deacon raised his arm and draped a piece of notepad paper over it like a napkin.

"Deak, you shithead. Give me that."

"The caller ending in oh-nine-four-four, sir, a little something we like to call the James Ward residence. A real favorite in the list, a daily special, sir."

"Ward? I'll be damned."

"And for dessert," Deak said. "We have the caller ending in . . . six-seven-two-three, a heaping serving of—"

Mercer stood and snatched the page off his arm.

Well, well.

"Friend of Liss's?" Deak said.

"I would say no, wouldn't you?" Mercer studied the list a little longer, noting a couple of numbers he might recognize. The usual cranks making their presence known. "Can you make me a full list of any of these numbers you can trace back? Names, addresses? Might need to make some house calls."

"You want me to do the visits?"

But Mercer knew he wouldn't be able to sit at this desk, anyway. He felt raw and exposed, like he'd been butt-paddled in the town square. And if he had been, then he would need to start cleaning the mess up, himself. "Probably more personal business than should fall to anyone else," Mercer said. "I have a call for you to make to confirm an alibi for a Mr. Lincoln Kehoe, though."

"Oh yeah?"

"And then I have a little project," Mercer said.

"Whatever you need."

"You're the man, Deak," Mercer said. "See if you can find out what *else* was happening around the time Ashley Hay went missing. What other cases were we working? Who was making a bother of themselves around town? How was my predecessor spending his time? And . . ."

Deak must have caught the change in tone. "Sir?"

"Don't involve anyone else," Mercer said. "Not a whisper to Slocum or any of the old guard. You got it?"

"That fancy man is prob'ly getting a manicure. It's his day off."

Slocum, the slob, except he drove into the city every other week for a good haircut.

"Now, Deak," Mercer said. "Let's normalize self-care."

Deak went out laughing, leaving Mercer to stare at the shiny surface of his desk. Personal business, and should he even do it? He was done doing favors for the Kehoe family, painting barn doors and running over on the first ring of his cell phone after hours.

He was done with anything having to do with the Kehoes except figuring out if their brightest boy needed to be sitting in his jail. That and what he would do for a living after he put him there.

CHAPTER THIRTY-TWO

Back in the guidance office, Vera stood in her office door with her arms folded, guarding the valuables, Liss supposed, while she packed her things to leave.

Liss blinked at her desk. Nothing here was hers, just as at home. She'd thought she'd made something of herself. Her family. Her job. But she had nothing to show for it. Only Callan. She reached for the framed photo of her family. Vera made a disdainful noise.

Custody arrangement in question.

"Did you put all those notes about Callan in his record?" Liss said.

"I can't discuss private student information with anyone but the student's parent," Vera said.

"You know perfectly well I am his parent," Liss said. "There's a letter—"

"There's a letter giving a stepparent permission to make medical decisions," Vera said. "A stepparent. But it sounds as though that job is coming to an end, too."

In her car, with shaking hands, Liss texted Link to take Callan home instead of to the school.

He beat her there. As she pulled into the drive, he came out of the house, his keys swinging in his hand.

"What's going on? Why is he not at school?"

"Has he had lunch?" she said.

"Is there news?" Link said. "They can't know anything that fast. Can they?"

"We thought . . . he could benefit from a few days off," she said. "With everything going on."

"We did? I guess we do *always* know what's best for him, don't we?"

"Vera did," Liss said. Those dates in Callan's record. Were they meetings? Phone calls? "Have you been talking to her?"

"*No.*" Link pulled at the back of his neck. "What do you mean?"

"I mean—" Someone had been talking to Vera about the divorce and the custody arrangement, but who? Patty? Was Patty building a case for custody, just in case? "I mean the school *counselor* thought a few days at home might be good medicine for Callan. Just like I said."

"OK," Link said. "But he's going to kick around here with . . . with Nintendo as nanny? I don't have the time to take off."

She was ready for this, at least. "I have some time coming to me—"

"You do?"

"Several days," she said.

"And your boss is OK with this plan?" Link said.

"Vera arranged it," she said.

He looked out across the property, toward the quarry. "You can't cut me out of . . . of the decisions that affect this family," he said.

He was one to talk.

"He had to let us into the house with those new keys you gave him," Link said. "Do you know how that feels?"

"I didn't mean to lock you out," she said. "I need to get some more keys made."

"OK, but big decisions, right?" he said. "That affect Callan? *We* should be you and me. Not Vera. Not . . . *Mercer.* Not my mom. You and me, like we always did. Like we're on the same team."

"Of course," Liss said. "Dream team."

The words had a hollow sound to them. They both recognized it. "Yeah," he said. "Dream team." After a long moment, he shook his head and scuffed across the gravel to his truck.

Inside, Callan looked over from the television. An empty bag of microwave popcorn sat on the coffee table.

"Hey, Cowboy," Liss said.

"Don't call me that."

"Was the blood test OK?" she said.

"My arm hurts." Callan came to the kitchen table, pulled out a chair, and slumped into it. "Just a little, though. Mercer was there."

"To talk to Dad?"

"Why wouldn't he want to talk to me?" Callan said. "I'm the next of kin."

These were words he was trying on, having heard them from some cop drama. To sound grown up, although she wasn't sure that was the effect. She was reminded, instead, of Callan as a little nugget, parroting words he heard Link say, sometimes words they had to talk him out of using. "That's true," she said. "You're Ashley's only family."

And hers.

"Mercer said he would be getting me some answers," Callan said. "He seemed like he really wanted to."

She'd never doubted that Mercer wanted to find the truth. Only that he'd be able to, that he wouldn't ruin their lives in the process. Was it sorted? If Link had given over the woman's name, he'd be out the picture. Wouldn't he? Callan had no idea how close he'd come. He held such faith in Link, he had never considered that he might have lost him, too. "Of course he wants to know what happened. We all do."

"She was murdered," Callan said.

Liss spun around.

"You won't say it," he said. "But . . . she was killed, right? That's what they're saying."

"You're not listening to Tanner—"

"Not Tanner. *Everyone.*" He dug with a fingernail at the edge of the table. "Do they know, already? About . . . about the blood test? Is that why Dad brought me home instead of taking me to school?"

"The test will take some time, probably," she said. "I don't know. But they do think . . . yes, they do think the person they found was murdered."

"They don't think . . . Dad?"

"Your dad would not hurt anyone," she said.

"But do they *think* he did? Does Mercer?"

"No, of course not," she said, but Callan was scowling at her. "He *did*," she said. "But not anymore, OK? Everything will be fine."

Callan's head turned. "Everything?" he said.

"Well, not—"

"Like Ashley will be alive and OK?" Callan said.

"Honey," she said.

"And you guys won't get divorced and Papa Key will remember who I am?"

"Cowboy," she said. "I *meant*—"

"And I'll get a fucking A-plus-plus in geometry—"

"Callan!"

"—and win a million dollars and take a rocket to the *moon*?" he said. His hair hung in his eyes. "Everything won't be fine! Because it wasn't *fine* in the first place, Liss!"

Her hand faltered on the way to him. "What did you just say?"

"Stop saying it's going to be fine when it's not," he said. His ears, already pink. "Stop treating me like a baby."

"*What* did you just call me?"

He dug at the table's edge. A rough spot in the grain of the wood that he had cultivated. "I just thought, you know."

"No, I don't know," she said.

"Because all of this sh—stuff going on." Callan gestured toward the Band-Aid stuck to his arm. "They're trying to figure out, is it Ashley, is it not her, right? She's my mother, right?"

Liss couldn't get a full enough breath.

"And it's just confusing," Callan said. "A little." When he looked up at her now, he had lost the fevered intensity. His eyes, big and worried. "Forget it."

She would never forget it. She had given her life over to this boy, all the hours of her life gone to him—his survival, his comfort, his happiness. All the hours of her life spent protecting him from feeling he'd been an accident, just two selfish people colliding into one another.

"It is your *name*," he said.

His name meant *stone* in some other culture. She'd looked it up years ago. A stone weighed you down. A stone sank. A stone was a burden.

A burden. That's what Ashley had named her son. Fuck you, Ashley, Liss thought.

But had Callan ever had to wonder if he was alone in the world? Had he ever felt small and insignificant a single day in his life? Had he ever had a *moment* of uncertainty?

She had given him sturdy ground. *She* had. Not Ashley. Not Link. Not Key or Patty.

"I'm sorry," Callan said. He got up and hugged her and sobbed into her neck. "Mom, I'm sorry."

But he was uncertain now, and she had done that, too.

Liss remembered how the air would change, how the atmosphere would still and she knew she was out at the edge of her mother's patience, tipping over.

Liss cradled Callan in her arms, surprised at how sturdy he was, her lips pressing apology into the shine of his hair. She thought of Ashley, soaked through on the deck. "I'm the one," she said. "I'm the one who should be sorry."

CHAPTER THIRTY-THREE

On Monday afternoon Mercer held a briefing for the team, but it seemed to him that they were tracing over the same worn grooves of the case. Like painting over that graffiti on Liss's barn door, the same motions, spelling out the same message.

"Have we questioned the homeowner?" Bowman asked.

"Key's nonverbal," Mercer said. "Uh, mostly. But as I said, I also had a chat recently with Patty Kehoe."

Bowman stared at the notes in front of him. "I meant the current homeowner, sir."

"Key and Patty are the home*owners*," Slocum said firmly.

"I've spoken to the *tenants*," Mercer had said just as firmly, ignoring a couple of exchanged looks down the table. "Liss and Callan and—I've spoken to all the Kehoes, as a matter of fact. But we still don't know whose bones we're sitting on, so let's give the lab the time they need to do their job, and then we'll do ours."

It was all talk. He spent the rest of the day making calls up and down his Rolodex, making all kinds of enemies from former friends and looking the fool in a different way, searching for an in at the state lab that would get those DNA results to him even a second faster.

By the next afternoon, he was circling the drain. He couldn't sit at his desk to wait for the call a second longer.

"Coffee," he barked, when Bowman looked up from his desk.

But the diner was closed, already. Mercer jangled the keys at his hip, nodding to those he passed, raising a hand at the windows of the hardware store, checking his watch against the clock outside the bank. Until the results were in, he was dead in the water, so to speak. Until the results were in, his feet were pedaling in a circle like the Road Runner, never getting anywhere.

In the window of the pharmacy was displayed an election poster for his opponent.

"Marshal," said a voice. "Having a *constitutional*?"

Larry Norville was coming along the sidewalk, a tote bag full of library books pulling one shoulder lower than the other.

"Mr. Norville," Mercer said. "I do some of my best thinking, pacing. Thought I'd do it outside and save the taxpayers refinishing my office floor."

Norville grunted. "Didn't mean to interrupt your *best* thinking."

The guy always found a way to put Mercer's back up. "Well, you have a good day, then," Mercer said.

"You're having a good think about what I told you—"

"They say it's coming on cold soon," Mercer said, edging past. "So enjoy this weather while you can."

He wasn't a hundred yards along, Norville in his wake, when his cell phone rang, a number he didn't recognize. "Alarie," he said.

"Marshal Alarie," said a man's voice he almost recognized. "Just how many different people did you send to goose me for your test results?"

Mercer pulled up short, checked up and back along the street. "Terry Bast, you miracle worker, how the hell are you?"

"Save it, Alarie," Bast said. "Science takes the time it takes. Besides, haven't I done you enough favors in my lifetime?"

"I'd be grateful for even a minute saved," Mercer said. "I'd owe you one."

"You owe me about twenty-three at this point, Mercer."

They'd helped each other out. The biggest debt had gone the other way, off the books so to speak, a little clean-up job to scare a meth head nephew straight before he went too far down that drain. But you didn't hear Mercer leaning on that. Anyway, he thought the guy wanted to be important. Otherwise his job was all test tubes and tedium, and all the glory went to the people like his superiors, and Mercer's.

"Make it an even twenty-four, and that's a case of your favorite beverage," Mercer said. "Come on, what do you have for me? Good day or bad?"

Bast let him dangle another stretch. "Is it a good day if it's a match?" he said, finally. "Then you got yourself a good day."

"It's her," Mercer breathed.

"Fifty percent genetic material match between the sample from the bones you fished out of the water to the kid's blood," Terry said. "We found mommy."

Mercer wouldn't even correct him. Callan had found his own mother, the poor kid. "Not a surprise but—fuck me twenty-four different ways, anyway."

"I might have a different kind of thrill for you," Terry said, an unexpected tone creeping in.

Amusement?

"What kind of thrill would that be?" Mercer sounded cautious even to himself.

"You sent up two samples, right?" Terry said. "The kid and . . . his father?"

The state police lab wasn't going to tell him Link Kehoe's DNA had matched the scene, too? Or had lit up the database for some long-forgotten crime? Mercer got a cold feeling in his gut. "The kid," Mercer said slowly. "And then his dad, in case we could rule him out."

"Well, I can rule him out for *something*," Terry said. "Off the record—"

"OK," Mercer said.

"Way the fuck off the record—"

"The whole thing is off-record, Terry." Terry's boss's boss or some statie would call with the news, when they finally decided they could bear to part with it.

"Correct. This is even further—"

"Got it."

The guy must have wanted a drum roll. Finally he said, "Would it be of any interest to you if the test results didn't support that particular familial relationship?"

Mercer looked up and down the street again. "You're telling me . . . what now?"

"The second sample, in regards to the first, shared only approximately seventeen hundred centimorgans."

"You're fucking with me, I can tell," Mercer said.

"In a parent-child comparison, you'd expect a higher percentage—"

"Terry," Mercer said. "Say it."

"That guy's not the kid's father."

A thousand ideas and arguments rushed into Mercer's head simultaneously, unsortable, illogical. Incoherent. Liss. It was all he could think.

Liss.

"Marshal?"

"You're telling me those two thimbles of blood I had sent to you weren't family?" Mercer said.

"I didn't say that," Terry said. "In fact, I said the opposite. They have a familial relationship. Just not the one you told me they had."

Someone was coming along the sidewalk. Mercer ducked around the corner of the hardware store, and put his shoulder against the brick wall, a hand over his eyes. He couldn't take any input, no further information, no sounds, no light, no how-do-ya-dos from passing voters. No other input until he had this. "OK, OK. Try one more time, Terry. Please."

"Those two fellas are likely *brothers*, Mercer. Not father, son. Half-brothers."

"They share a parent," Mercer said, more to himself than the tech.

"Correct," he said. "Just one."

It could only *be* one. The noise in Mercer's mind cleared. Only one ringing note remained. But it wasn't like angels singing truth and hallelujah. It was the blood rushing in his ears.

"Marshal? You there?"

Mercer promised that case of beer as soon as he could—meaning it—and hung up. Around the corner again, the town had a different look to it. Or maybe he had never truly seen it. A used-up place. And who had worn it down? Who had told these people their best days were behind them?

Up ahead was Larry Norville, his tote bag now hanging empty.

"Larry, wait." Mercer jogged to catch him.

Norville turned. "Are we friends now, *Mercer*? I'm still not voting for you."

"One more thing I meant to ask you," Mercer said. "Would you be familiar with rumors about the Kehoes—my predecessor, specifically, Rockwell Kehoe—from the old days?"

Norville blinked behind his glasses. "Rumors, you say?" He glanced past Mercer and along the street. "I've heard a few *tales*.

Nothing I could stand by as fact. I managed to keep out of the grip of the *strong* arm of the law."

Norville used to leave law enforcement to their jobs?

Mercer had an idea, something he'd have to noodle on another time. "Roughing people up?" Mercer said. "That sort of thing?"

"Some men resisting arrest enough to black their own eyes," Norville said.

"OK," Mercer said. "What about stories concerning . . . women?"

Norville made a face. "I don't know anything about that."

"His wife," Mercer said. "She told me Key had someone on the side, offered the information freely. But she seemed insulted by the other gal's age. Older than her, she said."

"*Older?*" Norville spat.

Mercer's breath went shallow. Every centimorg in his DNA or whatever Terry Bast had called it tuned toward what Norville would say.

"You might have noticed, Detective," Norville said, "that the man's *wife* is twenty years younger than he is. Rockwell Kehoe didn't like mutton when he could have lamb."

The thing was, he *had* noticed. He'd noticed just before Patty Kehoe lied to his face.

OF COURSE IT'S ASHLEY.

So they say. So the gossip between the aides at shift change goes. They're the only ones who'll speak of it in front of me.

I worry for how things will go, how much Alarie can unravel. I should have done something about it while I still could. While I could still direct operations and attention. While I could still lift up the rug and sweep it all under. I'm the only individual aboveground who knows how this all started. Even Slocum and all he's collected, that magpie, doesn't know.

Innocent enough, that's how. That little white car of hers—an old Miata, down on its luck by then but still an eye-catcher—blew by my radar one night, late, after everything else for miles had come to a standstill. I stopped it on principle, a taillight out. Now I didn't give a shit about a taillight even though it was an easy hundred-twenty for the town budget, but a stop is a stop is a stop and a fishing expedition to hook bigger game. But more importantly to my mind, I didn't know who was racing that five-speed manual in too high a gear through my patch.

Thought I'd make the acquaintance.

She was already crying by the time I'd run the plates and approached the window. Young ladies always try crying, even though I gave out soggy tickets just as happily as dry.

Something about her, though. She wasn't putting it on, I decided, and she didn't even seem to be crying to me or about me, about our situation at all. She seemed in a hurry to accept whatever punishment I was handing out so she could get back to her sobbing. Like I'd interrupted her.

The car was registered in her name, and I wondered about

that, too. No car borrowed from Daddy? She was Link's age, about. About to finish school. Maybe she'd even been to the house in the packs he ran with.

What're you crying about, I had to ask her. I haven't even writ that ticket yet, and a taillight's not all that much bother or cost to fix. Probably just a bad bulb, I told her.

Some slight among girls at the school, like they do, she told me. If she were still here today, would she even remember what they said? I remember. She told me they were saying around the school that she was boning one of the teachers.

My antenna went up on that one, oh yes it did. Pretty young easy thing with her own car, her own freedom—I paid attention.

Well, are you? I asked her.

And her mouth formed a perfect little pink O. Surprised but sexy, the perfect combination, it seemed to me, of innocence and not-so-much, like somebody'd already got to her long before they should have. She was in and out of county care for a while, I learned later. Maybe one of the foster dads.

I let her off with a verbal warning. That way, she was never in the books. Making plans, even then. I told her I'd fix her taillight for her, and the innocent part of her took the offer at face value and thanked me. She never showed, but things have a way of working out.

I kept an eye out. On patrol and off, I watched for that little white Miata. She'd got under my skin somehow . . . The crying that had nothing to do with me, maybe, like she had a story running before I ever entered the stage. My groin ached to remember that surprised little mouth.

And things might have come to nothing, me putting it to Patty while I thought of sweet, young pursed lips. But then some friends of Link's threw a party, no one old enough to own booze.

They'd got some, anyway, and got rowdy. The neighbors called for noise, and who do you think has to deal with that?

When I got there, Slocum let me peel my kid from the pack before the rest of the boneheads were written up. At the last second, with my hand on Link's neck to let him know we were going to talk about this good and proper, I spotted her, miserable and frantic as a mouse caught in a trap. I'll take that one, too, I said to Slocum, and he said nothing. Just taking notice with his eyes, the way he always did.

She and Link didn't seem to be friends, then. I dropped him off at the house first, told him we'd be chatting in the morning, so think hard on his prayers. Along the way to drop her home, she and I had a different sort of party, in exchange for me lifting the trap and letting little mousie go.

This was before I knew her, knew what she was capable of.

The party's finally over, sounds like.

Except I've been working on a little party trick, a secret. If these gals knew what I was up to, they'd be thrilled. Evidence that I'm still inside this sagging heap of flesh. But I don't need them worried and careful.

Can I make it happen, though, before this all comes crashing down?

CHAPTER THIRTY-FOUR

On Tuesday, the first day of suspension, Liss did all the laundry, cleaned two closets, and sorted out all the clothes that no longer fit Callan to give away. Not to Jamie, and it was too bad. She painted over the color swatches on the kitchen wall, back to the creamy white Patty would have chosen years ago. It felt like retreat.

She left Callan to sulk in his room. She'd told him about the bereavement leave, but he didn't want it, not if he missed football practice, the game that week. So she'd had to come clean about the suspension.

His.

Hers, she kept to herself.

In the afternoon, her new doorbell camera alerted her that Mercer had arrived.

He came in, stiffly, hat in hand, and asked for Callan.

They sat across from one another in the main room, sitting forward on the soft furniture with elbows on their knees. Man to man. Like something she might have wished for, distorted in a fun house mirror.

"Your mother," Mercer said to Callan, looking toward where Liss stood in the kitchen and then away.

His mother had been found, Mercer said to Callan. He was very sorry.

The news that the bones were all that was left of Ashley shouldn't have been a shock, but it was. Liss thought she should be numb to it, the information bouncing off her like a stone skipping across water. Instead, the finality of it seeped deep into her until she wasn't sure what she felt. Pain and also its relief.

Callan looked at the carpet. Ashley's death, confirmed. After all this time, could it even cause him pain? It must feel like a death announced in some faraway place, an assassination in a country he'd never visited.

Mercer leaned over his knees and said to Callan, gently. "It's a lot to take in. Do you have any questions for me?"

Liss expected Callan would shrug and mumble or hurry up to his room. Instead, he stayed, asked questions. What would happen next? Was Mercer any closer to knowing what happened?

Mercer's eyes once again flicked toward her.

"Callan knows his, um, mother didn't die in an accident," Liss said. "That she was killed."

"We have a few leads," Mercer said.

"You do?" Liss said.

Mercer's glance this time was one of annoyance. Liss stood back and was quiet.

"You don't think my *dad* did it," Callan said, his voice cracking. "Right? Because he didn't. He wouldn't."

"Your—uh," Mercer said. "Lincoln Kehoe has been cleared of suspicion."

Liss sank heavily against the kitchen counter, relieved. Nearly sick with it. Mercer was not looking her way now. Pointedly.

The woman. They'd have had to call on the woman Link had gone home with to clear him. That woman existed. Liss didn't care. She couldn't care. If she cared at all, it was more than she should.

"How was she killed, though?" Callan said.

Mercer looked uncomfortable. "Ah, well. She suffered a blunt force trauma," he said. "To the head. Do you know what that means?"

"What did they hit her with?"

"Well," Mercer said. "I'm not sure. Something hard, not too sharp. A rock, maybe? Lots of those lying around."

Callan was thoughtful. "Yeah," he said, his voice thick. "Maybe a rock."

"I'll keep you informed, OK?"

Callan showed Mercer to the door, man of the house. Mercer said not a word to her. Was it only that he'd gone to great pains to center Callan, next of kin, or was there more to his silence?

Callan blasted back through the room and up the stairs. Liss grabbed up the paint can from the kitchen floor and slipped out, catching Mercer just as he started to back out of the drive. He put the car back into park and rolled down his window.

"What now?" he said. "You need help painting your house?"

"Was that it?" she said. "There's something you're not saying."

"I don't think I owe you any more than I've already offered."

His jaw was stiff, his eyes the blue of glacial ice. "Link's cleared," Liss said. "You meant that, right? Are you going to go tell him?"

"I'm sure you still have his number," Mercer said. "You certainly had mine."

"Mercer," she said. "I said I was sorry about looking through your notebook. I couldn't read your handwriting, anyway."

"This is a serious matter, Mrs. Kehoe," he said.

She sucked in a breath.

"I'll want to talk to you about a few things," he said.

"OK," she said. The handle of the paint can was digging into the palm of her hand. She set it down at her feet.

"Not today." He nodded toward the house, toward Callan, she supposed, and his grief. "I'll come another time."

But it was less a promise than a warning. He couldn't think *she*—

Liss watched him drive off, then picked up the paint. At the barn doors, the shine of the new padlock reminded her what they were still up against.

Did it matter that Mercer knew Link hadn't had a hand in Ashley's death, when there were people out there willing to mete out their own kind of justice? Who would inform the person who had marked up their barn that they had done nothing wrong? Who would tell the person who had broken into the house? Who would call off the dogs?

Until Mercer arrested the true culprit, until Ashley's story was told, her family was still in danger.

CALLAN WAS IN the kitchen when she got back from the barn, opening one cabinet after another.

"Are you hungry?"

"Maybe." He opened the fridge and stood gazing inside.

Bored. Angry. Grieving. He wouldn't know what to call the emptiness inside.

"It's just a bunch of *ingredients*," he said despondently.

"Do you want to go into town and get something?"

He looked hopeful. "Tacos?"

Yes, tacos, my God, she thought. If tacos gave him a second of joy, let it be done, amen.

They went to town and drove through at a taco place, then went to the park and perched on opposite sides of a picnic table, making a mess of themselves, not enough paper napkins in the bag for the amount of hot sauce they both used.

Not far off, a group of rowdy preschoolers fought over the swings while their mothers or sitters chatted on a bench.

Liss's hands were cold but the sun was shining and dappled

through the trees in Callan's hair, lighting up individual threads, golden floss. He'd ordered a double portion of tacos and if he wanted ice cream on the way home, what the hell, she was up for that, too. She felt as though they were on the lam from real life.

He had a smear of red sauce at his mouth.

She reached for the bag to search among the wrappers for another napkin and only came up with the receipt. Ten bucks' worth of tacos had purchased this grace. At the bottom of the receipt the cashier had written—

"Mom? What's wrong?"

"Nothing. I—" *RIP Ashley Hay* was scribbled in a round, naive hand, and Liss remembered now the strange, too-familiar smile of the young woman, straw hair, thick eyeliner, who'd pushed their food through the window. "I think they undercharged us."

"Good news for once," Callan said.

She slipped the receipt into her jeans pocket and gazed over her unfinished lunch. "Right," she said. "Good news."

CHAPTER THIRTY-FIVE

At the Kehoes' place up on the hill, Mercer passed the glass room, spotting Key inside. Patty opened the door. "Well, Mercer, it's really beginning to be a habit," she said.

He'd come straight from Liss's, giving Callan the news and fending off Liss's intuition. She was certainly right that he was playing some of his cards close, sitting on the paternity news while he mulled over its implications and gathered information. While he did his damn job, without her nose in his business.

And here was the woman who'd lied to him. How much about her husband's escapades did she know?

Was Patty covering up for her husband out of force of her own habits, to protect him from anything that came his way? Maybe she really did think Key had been dallying around with a woman older than she was—but in his experience, the wife usually knew.

He tried not to think of Liss. Liss, who had already been blind-sided and would be again.

"Would the marshal be game for a friendly visit?" Mercer said.

"He does seem to perk up when you're here," Patty said.

If she meant that her husband would start barking the last slurs left to him . . . Mercer wasn't as charmed by the idea as he might have been on his last visit.

The same good-looking aide as before sat up straight in her chair when he walked into the conservatory.

"Kellye, good day to you," Mercer said. "Could I beg a minute of the marshal's time? Alone? He and I need to chat."

Her smile was uncertain, as if he might be joking. "I could take a break, if you're sure?"

"Thank you," he said. He thought he might get her number before he left. Why the fuck not?

Mercer sat himself in Key's line of vision and listened to Kellye's receding footsteps. He could hear Patty in the kitchen, water running, dishes clattering.

"Key," he said. "We have a problem. And I think you'll understand the predicament that you've put me in."

The old man's eyes slid past him toward the pool. Mercer glanced over. "The deep end, yes, sir. I am not one for metaphor but we're sure in it. I had your son—" He lowered his voice to a whisper that hissed along the slick surfaces of the conservatory. "Your *older* son, now that I know there're two of them, pegged for the murder of Ashley Hay."

Key's eyes widened and his chin wobbled. Mercer paused to see if he'd get a new round of slander out of the guy.

"But it turns out Link was out conveniently cheating on his wife that night. Like father, like son, though, right?" Mercer said. "You must be so proud."

Key's chin lifted, like a kick from a wild horse.

"You've been leaving your seed all over the county, turns out," Mercer said. "And my, didn't it find purchase in the most inconvenient of places. I don't suppose you'd snap out of your medical limitations to talk about sexual assault and murder?"

A dollop of drool pooled at the old man's lip, stretching down the slack corner of his mouth.

"Let me get that for you," Mercer said. He took out a handkerchief, wiped the man's mouth, then pulled out an evidence bag he'd folded into his breast pocket and dropped the hankie into it. On the arm of his wheelchair, Key's left index finger twitched.

"Not admissible, of course, we both know that," Mercer said. "But then I don't think I need it to be. I already have what I need to prove you impregnated that girl. Now I bet that was a quandary when she told you, wasn't it? For a man of your standing? But I can't exactly put you behind bars, can I? The shape you're in."

Mercer stood up and paced along the pool's edge.

"I'm starting to get the sense that there are quite a few crimes I could hang you for, if I could hang you at all. But, as regards to that first revelation, now I'm the one in a pickle. Whose hearts do I break?" Mercer said, leaning with a hand on the window and looking down at Liss's little homestead. "With the information I have, which lives do I absolutely fuck over, knowing what I know?"

My own, he thought.

Every chance of happiness he or Liss, or Callan, or Link, or any of them had, ever again, all gone. The detonation would knock them all off their feet. At the end, he would be lying in the hollow of it, alone.

A whirring noise started up behind him and out of the corner of his eye, Mercer caught movement rushing at him and leapt out of the way. Key's wheelchair.

"Sir!"

But the chair had already listed out of the trajectory to collide into him. No, not listed—directed. Mercer caught the barest flick of Key's finger at the chair's control lever before the chair, the man, zigged sharply toward the pool, sailed over the edge, and plunged like an anvil.

Oaths, epithets, blasphemy.

Later, Mercer would not remember what it was he shouted to bring the others into the conservatory, or that he had shouted anything.

He made noises he was not aware of and dove.

The chemicals in the water stung his eyes and his lungs complained. His boots were far too heavy.

He kicked and fought down to the bottom of the pool where Key's chair had sunk upon its side, the old man folded like a baby with his cheek against the pool floor. His feet floated away from the footplate. The chair—dead weight, total loss. Mercer tugged at Key's arm.

He was buckled in.

Mercer's fingers fumbled and caught at the lap belt and he thought of the young woman, Ashley, sunken in the pond, seat belt holding her corpse in place—please God, a corpse and not just knocked out, left to drown—and then there was a splash and someone was there, pulling him out of the way.

Kellye, pushing him to the side and reaching in to undo the fastener where Mercer was failing, botching it, and his lungs near bursting, and then they were rising, both of them, all three of them, breaking the surface to the shrieks of Patty Kehoe.

Mercer took a gulping breath. He had never tasted air so sweet and fresh, though he knew it was salty from the chlorine and hothouse humid. He imagined them as though from a distance through the glass, this drama unfolding while outside a breeze with a hint of winter in it blew the crinkling leaves off the trees and down the incline, past the fetid water of the quarry pond, where Liss knew nothing of what was happening. Where Liss knew nothing of him, even though he could feel the thread between them tug, even now.

Kellye led them through the water toward the far corner of the pool, where a set of steps descended, and between them, they hoisted Key out of the water and onto the tiled floor.

"Is he breathing?" he said.

He couldn't remember the training. Did they do just breaths or just compressions now?

But Kellye was pushing Patty away from Key's prone body and starting it up, hands crossed and pressing, a rhythm. Her wide eyes sought Mercer out.

"I'll call for help," he said.

He pulled himself out of the water and sloshed out of the conservatory to the kitchen. The phone, the phone, but he couldn't find one, so he ran out the door through the cold air to his car and lurched for his radio.

He called for an ambulance directly but Slocum cut in. "Come again, Chief? Where did you say you were?"

His wet fingers slid off the call button. "Keep the fucking radio clear!" Moron. "Ten-fifty-two, confirm? We need a bus, now."

Back inside, Kellye had brought Key back from the brink. He had a faint pulse and was digging deep for wet, rattling breaths. The wife sniveled against him, smoothing at his hair, and the sopping hero sat back in a daze, legs splayed, hair and makeup ruined.

"What *happened*?" Kellye said.

"That's a thing *I* would like to know," Patty snapped. "What on earth—"

Mercer put his back to the nearest wall and leaned over his knees. "He drove himself off the edge of the pool," he said.

"That's not possible," Patty said.

"I turned and he was coming at me but then he nudged that little lever and—" What did Patty think? That he had pushed the chair into the water himself? So he could jump in after him and fish him out? He looked at Kellye.

"It's possible because that's what happened," Mercer said.

"If he suffers a *second* from this, Mercer," Patty said. "I'll have you in court. For assault. I'll have you facing a firing squad. *And I'll* bankrupt this town for hiring you in the first place."

He had a few things he could reveal about town officials facing consequences for their actions, but now was not the time. He took himself back to the kitchen and out to his car, teeth chattering, soaked to the bone.

I'M SHIVERING ON THE FLOOR BEFORE I REALIZE I DON'T WANT
to die.

This long life and the scope of my existence narrowed down to a piss hole and I want to keep banging against the inside of this skull? Until the ticker gives out? Until the kidneys fail or a stroke finally shoots down like sweet lightning?

Apparently, I do. Fickle fucking biology.

If Patty would stop her screeching, I could remember what it was that Alarie said that triggered go-time. I had it all planned— but I never meant to do it with Alarie around. Walking savior complex, that one. I wouldn't have tried it with any of the broads Patty hires around, all their CPR certificates up to date. I would have done it when Patty was here on her own, distracted, to make good damn sure I couldn't be hauled up again, not while I could still draw breath.

Or maybe that would have been cruel.

And then I remember. I remember what he said.

Alarie thinks *I* killed that girl.

I'm not the villain here. If I was half the man I used to be, I'd shout it in his face. Maybe I *should* have drowned that girl like a kitten when she brought me that pregnancy test. It would have saved me a lot of trouble in the long run, and Link—

Link. My boy.

I lay in stunned wonder on the tile. The time wasted, the effort, the secrets.

For a shining moment I had seen the way through. Alarie, telling me Link had been off tom-catting that night, something he couldn't admit to me at the time. Even to save his own skin, the fool. My kid has a real fear of letting me down. Those divorce papers he won't sign—he thinks I'll think less of him for letting his marriage fail.

And here's Alarie, telling me Link was free of it at last. And then—

And then he'd turned on *me*.

I didn't have a thing to do with it. I was only protecting my family. Protecting Patty from that piece of cheap tail and her claims, and who knew if I was really the one? Who knew, until she turned around and offered Link my sloppy seconds, making sure I paid for her bastard one way or the other. Making sure I could never save Link without coming clean.

Oh, I paid. But Link paid more.

That idiot. He's soft in the head about women, and then he got a notion about being a father, like it was some kind of noble calling.

When the kid was born, it seemed like it might work. Callan was the spit of Link, of course. And me. What man doesn't want another chance? Patty, none the wiser. Link married, reining himself in. I thought. I gave Link some money, fully expecting Ashley to come back and ask for more.

She didn't get the chance. And I thought—

"He's agitated," the aide says to Patty.

Patty is gripping my arm. "You'd be agitated, too, if the police tried to kill you," Patty says.

"You did not just say that to a Black woman," the aide says.

I thought *Link* was the one.

I thought Alarie was making connections that would end in my boy's ruin, his mother's heartbreak. But all this trouble was for nothing. None of us killed the bitch in the first place.

CHAPTER THIRTY-SIX

On the way back from tacos in the park, Liss spotted the rolling blue lights at Key and Patty's from the highway. Her stomach sank. "Oh no."

Callan leaned into the windshield. "Do you think it's Papa?"

"Call your dad and tell him something's going on at Gram's."

Liss pulled into their drive, the gravel pinging the undercarriage of her car as they headed up the hill. An ambulance had come to a stop outside the conservatory. Nearby sat two official town cars, one with lights twirling and a door hanging open.

Callan was unbuckled and out the door almost before she came to a full stop. "Callan, wait!"

She rushed after him.

As she reached the door, Callan was backing out again. EMTs were carrying Key out, strapped to a board. He looked small and frail next to the responders, his thin hair plastered against his skull.

"Papa." Callan reached for Key as he passed, but Key only stared. "Mom, what's going on?"

"Step back," she said, tucking him against her as well as she could.

Patty appeared next, barking orders for the handling of her husband. Behind Patty came a woman in wet scrubs, her dark hair frizzing into curls. And then Mercer, his uniform wet and clinging.

When he saw her, his face passed through a series of expressions, none of which she could have named, all of which burned her feet to the ground where she stood.

Callan pulled away and rushed at Mercer. "Is he OK?"

"Key's pretty feisty," Mercer said, dragging his attention away from her. "They're going to make sure, though, OK?"

"What happened?" Liss said.

"Key decided to take himself for a swim," he said.

The woman in scrubs stopped and looked back.

Mercer said, "A swim still wearing his wheelchair."

"*What?*" Liss said.

A grim EMT helped Patty into the ambulance behind Key.

"What do you mean?" Callan said.

"He rolled into the pool," Mercer said with a meaningful look in Liss's direction.

"Mom, can we go to the hospital?"

"Did you reach your dad? Try him again, Callan. Go get in the car," she said. "Text him to meet us."

The ambulance kicked up a patch of gravel and lit up its siren. The dumpy car at the edge of the driveway drove off after it.

They were suddenly standing on a scene of quiet, of aftermath. Liss turned on Mercer.

"I can't tell you," he said.

She hadn't asked him anything.

"I don't know how he managed it," he said. "But I can tell you he went into the drink on his own steam."

"Key thinks too highly of himself to do something like that," she said. "Did he seem . . . upset?"

Mercer cleared his throat. "I was asking him some questions."

"He can't talk. You remember that, right?"

"I'd given him an, ah, update," he said. "It's possible he found what I had to say distressing."

She knew not to ask, even if he didn't seem as angry with her as he had been earlier in the day. But she'd caught that quiver in the air again, like wind coming from across the quarry. Distance between them, something he wouldn't say.

"Mom!" Callan called from the car. "Dad's on his way."

"OK," she said.

"OK," Mercer said.

But that was what he always said. It was hardly ever true.

THEY ENTERED THE emergency department to find Patty, her blouse still dark with splotches of pool water. "They won't let me in to see him," she said in wretched tones Liss had never heard from her before.

"Let me check," Liss said. "Callan, sit with Gram."

Minutes passed while she tried to get someone's attention and then Link stood at her side, breathless and tousled. "What's going on?" He turned on the woman behind the desk. "My dad?"

Information was suddenly theirs for the asking. The doctor would be out with an update as soon as possible. They should be seated.

Link pulled her by the arm away from the desk. "He fell in the pool? Did he hit his head?"

Link had managed to grab right at the spot where her bruise was finally fading. "He didn't fall," Liss said. "Mercer said he drove himself—"

"*Drove*," Link said, loud.

"In his wheelchair."

"*Himself*," Link said. "What was Mercer doing there while . . . while Dad was supposedly doing laps around the house? When he can barely keep his head up?"

"Sweetheart, please," she said.

"*No*," he said. "Don't do that. Don't call me that."

"I didn't mean—"

"I know," he said. "I know you didn't mean it."

"Well, I *did*," she said. "*I* used to mean it."

"Yeah, blame me," Link said, finally lowering his voice. "Not that you were controlling and patronizing and never missed a chance to point out what a project you'd taken on. Blame me for all of it. And while we're on the subject, you told Callan his mother was *murdered*? Are you insane?"

"I didn't offer it. He *asked* me," Liss said. "And I didn't lie to him."

"God, Liss," Link said. "We've made a mess of this." He ran his hands through his hair until it was wild. Liss thought she sensed the women in the room turning in his direction, like flowers to the sun. "Mostly me, before you say it, but . . . I think it's time we get this untangled. The papers, the house. Callan's living arrangements."

He was still talking but she couldn't take in what he was saying. When she came back to her senses, he was making promises. But what promises had Link Kehoe ever kept?

"We'll work it out," he was saying. "But you said it yourself, he's that age. He needs me. I need to set a better example, I know that—Mom."

He'd seen Patty.

"We'll talk later," he said and rushed to his mother, pulling Callan into a little huddle.

It was happening. If she had never spoken up. If she had never demanded more from him.

Callan was all. Callan was everything.

Without him, she was nothing.

Liss looked frantically around the waiting room. Against the far wall, a woman sat alone with her hands dangling between her knees, stunned eyes staring into middle distance.

She couldn't just sit here. She couldn't just do nothing.

Off beyond the waiting room, a pair of doors expelled a woman in a white jacket.

Liss glanced toward the Kehoes, in their tight little clutch like survivors of a collision.

She edged along the wall toward the pair of doors, watching for attention at the desk to divert. When the doors next swung out, Liss reached in and caught one side.

Behind the barrier, the hall was bright and busy. A woman cried out for another blanket from a gurney. Liss walked over and pulled the thin blanket from the woman's feet over her. A man holding a towel soaked with blood to his head stared at her. Or past her.

What Callan wanted, right now, was to know his grandfather was OK. Surely she could give him that.

None of the faces around the room were Key. She had to look carefully. All the faces were pale, gray. Male, female, she couldn't tell.

Across the room, a patterned green curtain whisked open. She couldn't very well go around peeking into each pod—

Mim. The woman in the bed behind the open curtain was Mim Hubbard.

Liss crossed the room, colliding with someone in a short white coat just as she neared Mim's curtain.

He stood back from her. "I don't think—"

"Is she OK? She's a friend."

"Family only," the guy said.

"She doesn't have any family," Liss said.

He was young. Pliable, she hoped. "I didn't see you," he said, dropping his head to the chart in his hand and hurrying away.

Liss pulled the curtain around Mim a bit and gazed over the lines and graphs on the machine she was hooked to.

What had happened to her? How long would she have lain in that big dusty house before someone missed her?

Liss reached for Mim's hand. When Mim's eyelids fluttered, Liss leaned in. "Mim, it's Lissette."

Mim moaned.

"Is there someone I can call for you?"

"Robbie," Mim murmured.

What had she got herself into? Did Mim have memory issues? Liss took a breath. "Robbie," she started. "Mim, Robbie . . ."

Mim's eyes opened, focused. "No," she said. "Not you. Not you." Each syllable rose toward panic.

"Mim," Liss said gently. The way Link talked to Key, light and clear as though they had only the weather to discuss. "It's Lissette. Lissette Kehoe? Remember we—"

"Where's . . ." Mim seemed to remember, then. Her mouth opened and closed like a fish as her memory unclouded. "Help! Someone help me!"

Footsteps were approaching. She would have to explain. Mim didn't have anyone else. She might need *someone*.

The curtain rods rang out. "Mrs. Hubbard—"

"Get her out," Mim commanded, clear as a bell. "Get her the hell out of my sight."

CHAPTER THIRTY-SEVEN

Watching Liss drive off from Key's, Mercer swiped at the pool water running down his cheek. There was a noise behind him in the house. Who was left?

Slocum. His car still sat in the drive; the door swung wide. The guy sure could put a little pepper on it when his hero was in trouble.

In the conservatory, Slocum stood at the pool's edge, surveying the blue water and the hulk of the wheelchair down at the drain.

"That's going to be a bitch to fish out," Slocum murmured.

As though he would have to do it.

Who *would* do it, though, was a good question, given the status of the home's owner. The presumed status, before today's incident. Key was a source of fascination to him suddenly. What had the man wrought upon this town?

"What kind of fellow was Key, back in his prime?" Mercer said.

Slocum lifted his gaze to study him. "Why do you ask?"

"Because I only know him . . . as he is."

Mercer turned for the door and Slocum followed him into the kitchen, plucking a bright green apple out of a bowl on the counter. "As he is? A colostomy bag in human form?" Slocum said. "He'd be *sick* if he knew what's happened to him. Back in the day, he was a man to reckon with."

Mercer heard in Slocum's voice that he had decided Mercer was no such man. "You don't think he knows what's going on? I think if today's high dive proves anything it's that he's more aware of his situation than you might think."

"Even if he's still rattling around in there somewhere, he can't pilot a friggin' wheelchair," Slocum said. "His finger probably nudged it the wrong way, that's all. He's got muscle spasms." Slocum brought the apple to his mouth and took a bite.

A muscle spasm did not explain what he'd seen. "Let's get out of here," Mercer said. "Before you eat them out of house and home. You really shouldn't snack out of another man's fruit bowl."

"Key gets his food through a tube, Chief," Slocum said. He gave Mercer a narrow look. "And, anyway, you're one to talk."

BY THE TIME he got back to his place, Mercer's ass was lit up, chafing against his damp clothes. It wasn't quite shift change when he arrived at his place, but quitting time, he decided, had come and gone. He needed a fucking drink.

He kicked off his shoes at the door, noticing only now that one of his socks didn't match the other. Perfect. The mismatched socks, one black, one blue and shorter, seemed to him the perfect encapsulation of the day, of himself. A lost cause. He slid them off, then the shirt, undershirt, belt—he'd left his piece in the gun locker that morning, and thank goodness—pants, boxers. His thighs were red and irritated, his shoulders, everywhere the leisure-suit poly of his uniform had touched, and where his boxers had clung he felt puckered, like fingers too long in dishwater. He'd been pickled in the brine of the Kehoe pool.

In the shower, muscle-tired and exhausted as he was, he briefly considered rubbing one out and dug for the memory of that smile the health aide had given him on his last visit.

But what came to mind was her stunned expression over Key's body at the side of the pool as she did chest compressions, then that look she'd given him as she walked away today—as though they'd met at the scene of a crime.

Another lost cause.

Well, he'd saved himself the effort of finding a nice restaurant, of drinking overpriced wine instead of what he really wanted to drink, of putting himself through hours of small talk, of wondering if or when he should make a move. Of trying to read every expression, of trying to read the future. Of trying.

He could drink beer, his own, at home, and that's what he planned to do.

Beer. He'd nearly forgotten he owed Terry from the state police lab that case of beer for the early intel on Callan's DNA results. And when, exactly, would he have the time to get around to paying off that debt? He might have to owe the guy a case plus one next time.

Mercer leaned with both hands against the tiled wall and let the water run down his back. Next time. Next time he received news that would devastate the woman he—

The thing with Kellye was all nonsense. A lost cause from the beginning, and not because of anything *she* felt or didn't. It was just a story he'd told himself.

He loved Liss. *Loved* her. When he was anywhere near her, Mercer knew exactly where she was in the room, could feel something like . . . like energy waves—he knew how it sounded—radiating out. He could probably find her in the dark if he had to. At the bottom of that pool, with his lungs ready to give out, she was all he could think of.

But it didn't matter. Not the way things were looking. He had reached in and now he couldn't come away unscathed. He could throw it all away right now, tank the election, give up the case, let someone else figure out what happened fifteen years ago, or not,

not ever, just walk away from it all. He could do all that and still not claim her, that was the thing. He could do everything exactly right or nothing at all and still lose her. She was already lost.

After his shower, Mercer changed into sweats, put some canned chili on the stove, and posted himself in front of the TV with a deep pour of whiskey. Four or five fingers of it, the whole hand.

Liss wouldn't touch the stuff, hated when his mouth tasted of it. But where was she?

Mercer reached for the remote and turned on the set and caught a quick glance of his own self holding up a backdrop behind a dais and podium. He hoped it would be someone else's bright, shining moment of glory to announce Ashley Hay's death. He would stand off the stage if he could swing it.

"Fuckface," he muttered. Meaning himself.

A man to reckon with, he thought, gulping at the whiskey.

He should be insulted. He should be pissed off. Slocum's damn chomping mouth, always eating something *at* him in a visual assault. Cop with doughnut. Cop plucking another man's fruit from his kitchen.

Mercer's drink was suddenly down to the ice. He rattled the cubes in the glass.

Something was catching at his mind, like a lyric of a song he couldn't quite remember. What was it? Maybe he'd finished the drink too fast, wouldn't be able to snatch it now. He hadn't the fine criminal mind of, say, Rockwell Kehoe.

Who had absolutely driven himself right into that pool to drown. And why? Because Mercer suggested he confess?

But surely the old man had the best defense in the world. He couldn't be expected to confess, couldn't be caught in a lie. Probably couldn't be prosecuted, even with all the damning evidence in the world. Whatever he'd done or not done, he'd got away with it.

Mercer set his glass aside. He hadn't been sleeping well the last few days but now his limbs felt pleasantly weak from the exertion of fetching Key from the pool floor, warmed from the hot shower and now warmed again by the liquor until he was thinking about the fireplace at Liss's. A cold night like this, this house could use a fireplace, like the one they used to have when he was a kid, and his dad would offer help when anyone needed a tree down for a share of the wood. He could have one. They had those electric ones now or he could run a gas line, find someone to run a gas line, ask Deak who did that sort of work. Could he get a woodfire stove set up somewhere? And a chimney to send the smoke—

There was a beeping sound and he was sitting up from somewhere deep down in his chair, coming up from the floorboards, the basement, the earth, six feet under.

The hell?

Smoke. The fire alarm was raging.

He scrambled to his feet.

The chili smoldered in the ruined saucepan. OK, OK. He ran the pan under the tap but it was another lost cause. He threw the whole mess toward the garbage and was only grimly surprised he didn't miss.

CHAPTER THIRTY-EIGHT

L iss had been expelled from the emergency department into the waiting area, where Link and Patty had their heads together. The security officer let go of her elbow, but too late. Callan saw it happen and jumped out of his seat. "Mom?"

"Don't worry about it."

"Did you go back to see Papa Key?"

"I couldn't find him," she said. "We'll just have to wait."

"Gram told Dad to send me home, but I don't want to go," Callan said. "Not until we hear."

Send him home, not take him. Patty would never let Link leave her side, not willingly. Send *her* away is what Patty would have meant, with Callan as the excuse. Liss brushed at Callan's hair and he let her.

"OK, let's see what the doctor says."

They waited as others in the waiting area dragged themselves from their chairs and hobbled away, as worried faces were exchanged for other worried faces. Liss picked up a discarded newspaper and caught a glimpse of Ashley. *Today's* paper, the news about Ashley splashed and rehashed while they had lived a thousand hours in this one day.

She tilted the front page away from Callan. There was another photo of the pond, too, similar to the one she'd seen last week, a wide shot of the action that night, Liss looking up at Mercer as though he hung the moon. So many people were at the quarry that night, but how many could have taken a photo from this vantage point before she left for the house?

The photograph was credited to "provided." Anonymous.

But it could have only been sourced from one of the boys.

Liss got up and shoved the paper into the trash bin. Back at her seat, she looked across at Link. He had lines around his eyes.

"Can I get you anything?" she said. Peace offering. "Water?"

"Why don't you go?" he said. "I can bring him home later."

"I'd like to hear how he is," she said.

"Thank you," he said. "Some water for Mom? If you can find some?"

The vending machine took credit cards, very modern. Liss ignored the rows of Gimme chips and snacks and bought a couple bottles of water. She had turned back to the waiting area when she saw, standing at the information desk, Sophie Ward.

"Sophie," Liss said. "Is Jamie OK?"

Sophie looked over, one brand of confusion falling away for another. "Oh," she said. "What? Yes, he's at the game."

In a different universe, Callan would be sitting on the JV bench. Liss didn't want to admit she'd forgotten the parallel track of normal life that lived on without them. "And is Jim—"

"I'm sorry, Lissette, can I—" Sophie turned back to the desk and leaned over it until she had someone's attention. "They called me about Miriam Hubbard?"

Miriam. What kind of friend was she, really, when she didn't know Mim's full name?

Liss waited at a discreet distance while Sophie received instructions to wait.

"Jim's in the car," Sophie said distractedly when she'd come away from the desk. "We were already in the stands when I got the call. He had to bring me."

She was an inconvenient person for Mim to designate as her emergency contact. But a neighbor. Liss remembered Mim's pretty garden, lovingly tended by *someone*. "What are the pinwheels for?" she said. "In Mim's garden?"

Sophie looked at her directly, then away, craning her neck to see out the door to the parking lot. "To keep the birds from eating the seeds," she said. "I could've taken them out once the plants were established but . . ."

"But they're pretty," Liss said. But Sophie herself could not be prone to sparkle and adornment. Liss had always thought of Jamie's mom, when she did at all, as going through life in a sort of camouflage.

"Mim likes them," Sophie said. "She likes the birds, too. I got her some seed for a feeder in the back."

"*Charitable* of you," Liss said, thinking of the jacket they wouldn't accept.

Sophie blushed. "Bird seed is cheap. And she doesn't have anyone."

Exactly. Mim had no one, and yet she'd screamed for help at the sight of Liss. She'd only spent time with her last week. What had changed? "I could stop by more than I have," Liss said. "Do you think she'd like to see me?"

Sophie looked down at the bottles of water Liss held but didn't ask who they were for, who Liss had come to see. "She can be so unpredictable . . ."

"Maybe some time when you're there, too? I could help with the garden."

"It's mostly weeds this late in the season," Sophie said, her eyes darting around. "The pumpkins are out already. If she'd liked *leeks*—"

"Hubbard?" A nurse held open one of the swinging doors.

"That's me!" Sophie called, all movement.

"Sophie, wait." She'd meant to ask about the photo in the paper. Had Jamie been the one? But what she really needed to know was why Mim had recoiled in fear at the sight of her. "Does Mim think that *Link*—that I—"

But Sophie scurried away without a look back, and Liss was left to wonder that another place was barred to her, another friend turned away.

AT LAST THEY heard that Key was stable but would be held for observation for a day or two. Liss drove them toward home with plans to send Callan straight to bed. It wasn't late, but it had been a hell of a day. A week.

"Have you given any thought to . . . how you'd like to say good-bye to Ashley?" Liss said.

"Like a funeral?" Callan said.

Would anyone attend? Would anyone come to honor and remember Ashley, or would they all be buying a ticket for the carnival? "A funeral or maybe something more private," she said. "A memorial service? You can invite exactly who you want to be there."

He leaned against the passenger window. "I don't know if I . . . Forget it."

"Tell me?"

"I don't know if I'll do it right," Callan said.

"Do what?"

"The . . . service or whatever. I don't know if what I feel is . . . right."

"Whatever you feel is the right way to feel," she said. "And how you feel might change over time."

Her mother's death was more a blow to her now than when it happened, now that she understood life's challenges. Addiction as a disease. Motherhood, almost thankless. The loss could still catch Liss by surprise, a swift punch to her gut when she remembered, when she realized their relationship would always be what it was.

"Can it be just you and me?" Callan said. "And Dad?"

"Of course."

"And maybe Mercer?"

Liss worked to keep her expression neutral. "I'm sure he would be honored to be included."

A police car was parked across from the turn-off to their road—Slocum, keeping an eye on things. She was strangely grateful but when she pulled up to the house, her mailbox had been knocked over.

An accident, hard to imagine.

Inside, Liss pulled the kitchen phone off the wall again.

Callan paused at the bottom step. "Did it ring?"

"I don't want it to," she said, rolling her neck. There was a crick in it that would not be helped by a night's sleep. "And your dad would use the cell phone if he needed me for anything. Good night, Cowboy."

He didn't go up.

"You OK?" she said.

"Thanks for letting me stay," he said.

"I wanted to stay, too," she said.

"I know but Gram . . ." He shrugged.

"You're welcome," she said. "I'm glad Papa Key will be OK."

"He's old, though," Callan said. "And sick."

She didn't know what to say to that. All her instincts had fled her. "Seems like he has a few surprises left in him," she said.

Callan gripped higher on the banister, rocking back and forth as though he would rocket himself up. "Why do some people get to live a long time and others . . ."

Liss didn't want to wish him good night by saying life was unfair. But she couldn't protect him, there. He knew. He already knew that better than almost anyone.

"I don't know," she said.

THE FUCK—

Where am I?

It's bright. Not the conservatory. I'm in a bed, something on my face. Can't—

I'm strapped down. Cords and beeps and someone close the damn blinds, I can't see a thing.

Glad to see you awake, someone says. A woman, but not one of the gals from the home health service.

A hospital—

Then I remember. I remember Mercer's eyes growing wide as I swiped at him in the chair and him flinging himself out of my way and then the flat cool blue of the pool.

More beeps.

Just take a deep breath, Mr. Kehoe, the voice says. Let the machine do the work for you. You're going to be OK.

But I'd hoped not to be OK.

And here I am.

I'd swung big and missed, hadn't I? I'd reached for the bat behind the door and swung for the moon.

I wish I'd gone out on the job, back in the day. Blaze of glory, all the white-glove ceremony of the burial and a corpse still in its prime. Instead, this shell. This pathetic shell, limping over the finish line. There was an ignoble end coming when Mercer put out his theory. Patty, Link. My men, wherever they're scattered, they'd hear about it. They'd hear I killed that girl and they'd believe it. Who wouldn't? Slocum, the last of them, taking just an ounce of pleasure in my comeuppance. Or maybe he'd stand by me, deny. Couldn't be possible, he might say. Not Key. He wouldn't—

I'd hardly had time to wonder, since Mercer had made his allegations.

I'd hardly put a moment into the case back then because I thought I knew the story. But now—

If it wasn't Link, wasn't Hubbard, wasn't me, who the fuck was left? That was the thing now, and it makes my blood boil that I can't go kick some doors in to find out.

Who killed that whore and ruined us all?

Beeps on the machines.

Mr. Kehoe, the voice starts. Mr. Kehoe, just breathe.

CHAPTER THIRTY-NINE

The next morning, Deak put a sheaf of papers on Mercer's desk.

"You shouldn't have," Mercer said. "What is it?"

"You asked for background," Deak said. "The same period of time Ashley Hay went missing?"

"Ah, OK. What did you find? Can you sum it up?"

"Only if you want to take a nap," Deak said.

Mercer had been about half-asleep already, doing the paperwork on yesterday's incident with Key. He still had a headache from last night's whiskey and the smell of burned chili. "Nothing interesting at all?"

"Depends on your definition of interesting, I guess," Deak said. "Couple of deuces, blood alcohol through the roof, crunched bumpers on the interstate. Some stolen liquor at the Shoppe Well. Kids, they figured. Some kind of distress call up at the county line."

"Wouldn't the sheriff's office take a call up that way?"

Deak shrugged. "Busy, maybe? Got bounced to us?"

"Doesn't sound too busy."

"The wreck was a mess," Deak said. "Copied out a few file notes for you on that and the call to County Line Road."

"Thanks." Mercer rubbed his eyes.

"Is there anything helpful in there, though?"

"Context is always helpful. Where was Key during all that?"

"Kept all that fun for himself," Deak said. "He was the IO."

"Every time?" Mercer paged through again, more slowly this time. "He was investigating officer on kids skimming bottles from the liquor store into their backpacks?"

"He had his thumb in every pie, from the looks of it," Deak said. "Pulling over speeders himself. Checking up on noise complaints. Really working for those votes—" He gave Mercer a pointed look. He didn't want a new boss. "Or he didn't think much of his squad, I guess."

"Couldn't be that," Mercer said. "Not with the likes of Slocum carrying his water."

Deak was grinning on his way out.

As MERCER DROVE out to the Ward house later, he realized Key going out on minor calls wasn't all that odd. Here he was doing it himself. But he had his own reasons. He couldn't fix the bigger problems Liss faced—the one she knew about, the one she didn't yet—but he could sweep up a few loose threads.

He caught the Wards just as they were sitting down to dinner—as he had planned.

"Can I get you a plate, Marshal?" the wife said.

Whatever she was slinging smelled better than anything he had to look forward to at his place. "Thank you, Mrs. Ward—"

"Sophie," she said. She was mousy, compact, and plain, with no single feature that would stand out in his mind.

"Thank you, Sophie. No, I don't want to intrude on family time—"

"A bit late for that," Jim Ward said with a wry tone, and then played it straight: "For police work, I mean."

The wife, the son, they looked down at their plates.

Mercer perked up. He enjoyed the sort of idiot Jim Ward seemed to be, the sort who thought himself smarter than everyone around them. What a lucky thing it was to question a fool like that. Like biting into a piece of Mardi Gras king cake and finding that good luck Kewpie doll prize in your teeth. Good luck you hadn't hoped for. Men—it was usually men—who thought they'd mix with him and win were only that: king cake babies.

"Justice never sleeps, Jim," Mercer said in that backslapping way certain dudes-about-town had, though Ward hadn't offered him his first name. "Which brings me to why I'm here, as a matter of fact. I'd like to talk to the member of this handsome family who keeps late hours. Or you may consider them early. Two in the morning, four. Jamie? Are you a night owl?"

The boy moved his fork through the food on his plate and shook his head without looking up. He took after his mom. Small and blank, hardly there.

"What's this about, Alarie?" Jim said.

"Someone at this house has been calling one of their neighbors' phone numbers all hours," Mercer said. "Troubling behavior."

Ward shoved a bite of meatloaf into his mouth and pointed the empty fork at him. "I would've thought you and your boys would be too busy with all the goings-on to track down a few prank calls. Bodies in quarries and all that."

"Oh, we are. But these nuisance calls, well, they're a real pet project for me." He looked around the table but Jamie didn't seem panicked to hear it. Sophie—

She was worried about something, he decided. Nervous. Or guilty? He did tend to make some people nervous at close range.

Yesterday's paper lay on the floor near Jim's feet, the one with the photo that looked like Mercer and Liss were making time while Ashley's bones lay unclaimed in the pond. If the paper kept running photos like that, he'd be lucky if his own ma would vote for him.

"Pet project," Jim said.

Mercer turned his attention back in time to see the twitch of grin at Jim Ward's mouth.

"Is *that* what you call it?" Jim said.

He was just too smart not to let Mercer know he knew *which* neighbor. "Well, no harm done," Mercer said expansively. "If they stop."

"Well, I hope they do, Marshal," Ward said. "That's a real bother—"

"The state actually calls it *harassment*, Jim, a Class A misdemeanor," Mercer said. "Someone found to be guilty of that crime probably wouldn't go to jail. Or maybe even miss a shift." He looked hard at Ward. "But I think the paper would happily publish names. In the case of adults. Phone numbers are awfully easy to come by, this day and age. But you being a parent yourself, Jim, I'm sure you wouldn't want another family harassed."

"Family," Jim muttered, but the king cake baby grin was gone. He had a job to protect, food to put on the table same as anyone. A reputation. "Barely."

The Wards seemed to have lost their appetites.

"Well, that's me on my way, then," Mercer said. "I wonder if young Jamie would see me out?"

Jamie looked up. His dad waved him on.

He followed Mercer to the door and hesitated there. Mercer gestured him out. "Close the door behind you," Mercer said.

The kid swallowed hard but did as he was told.

Dark enough already, it could be midnight. Ahead of them, the long slide into deep winter. The forecasters were calling for a freeze as early as tonight, and then he and his team would be up to their balls in distress calls for cars off the road.

Jamie followed him down the steps.

"You didn't make those calls, did you, son?"

The kid shook his head. "I swear."

"You know who did, though," Mercer said. "Everybody at that table knew, I suspect. Your dad's never missed a chance to make someone's life a little bit harder, has he? You don't have to answer that."

"He doesn't like Callan's dad much," Jamie mumbled.

"Or his mom? Never mind," Mercer said. "What I actually want to ask you about is that accident in Tanner Larkin's race car."

Jamie's hands fidgeted at the long sleeves of his sweatshirt.

"I'm not much of a car afficionado," Mercer said. "But I'm still your average American male around a hot ride like Tanner's. Never sat in one of those before, you know? Had to take my chance. Electric cars. We are living in the future, Jamie."

The boy glanced up from his shoes.

"But here's a thing I noticed when I got behind the wheel," Mercer said. "Well, I say got behind the wheel when I should say I tried. My knees would have been in my neck, the driver's seat was pulled up that far. Almost like someone *small* was driving."

He was getting nothing from this kid.

"Tanner, as I think we can agree, is quite a tall fella?" Mercer said.

Jamie's head dipped, showing Mercer the crown of his home haircut.

"Now, being at the wheel of that car is not a crime unless you're, say, not yet licensed," Mercer said. "But that's not something I would arrest anyone for. OK? OK. I do wonder if there's anything else I might like to know about that accident, from the *driver*."

Jamie mumbled something.

"What, son? Speak up."

"It was an accident," he said.

"Slick spot?" he said. "Deer in your headlights? Or did you just get spooked on that curve?"

"Spooked, I guess," Jamie said.

"You could have just said so," Mercer said. "Did Tanner tell you to keep your lips zipped?"

"He said his dad would kill him."

"Well, I don't have time for another murder case, so he won't hear it from me," Mercer said. "OK? OK. Now get inside before your mom has my ass for keeping you from your dinner."

Jamie didn't need to be invited twice. The kid scurried up the steps and to the door. When it opened, Mercer heard the dad grumble something to his son, in a tone he didn't like the sound of.

Mercer stepped back and took a look at the house. He might drive by here more often, keep an eye out. An eye *on*.

What is harassment? Well, look at that. Maybe he and Key had more in common that he'd thought.

CHAPTER FORTY

Thursday morning, Liss looked across the breakfast table at Callan slopping soggy cereal around in his bowl and decided he had to return to school.

He'd been at that cereal for fifteen minutes, making a performance of his boredom because she wouldn't let him use any screens—not while all the channels were reporting Ashley's identification, with talking-head quotes from this official and that while Mercer stood in the background. Neither of them needed more of that.

The suggestion that she allowed *books*, that he could log in to get his homework assignments and keep up, had been met with appropriate disdain. It was time.

Monday. They would have their memorial for Ashley that weekend and then get back to normal the following week.

She wouldn't even ask the school's permission to bring him in. She'd walk him in and sit him down at his homeroom desk and dare them to say a word.

She wouldn't mention her job. Not yet. The career fair was still two weeks away and they'd said they would move on without her—as clear a timeline as any suggested date would have been. And maybe the writing was on the wall. Vera, regretting giving her a chance. Liss's time would be better spent updating her résumé.

At the thought, her stomach clenched. Not just because she'd

not had to job search for so long, or that a new job would probably require her to commute into the city. Not just that. The truth
was that she loved the job she had. Loved the students. She wasn't
a guidance counselor, but she thought she'd served an important
role, making the office a place where the students felt *known*.

Which was, of course, the source of the trouble.

Liss's thoughts slid naturally to notes she'd found in Callan's
record, the mention of the custody arrangement that would soon
be challenged, whether she was ready for it or not. But who would
have been concerned about it?

Across the table, Callan clinked his spoon against his bowl, chasing a milk-sodden marshmallow.

"You haven't visited the guidance office this year," she said. "Have
you?"

He shook his head.

"You can always talk to me," Liss said. "And Dad, of course. If
there's something you're unhappy about."

"I don't need to *talk*," Callan said with disgust. "I got called
down." He got up and put his bowl in the sink.

She only watched instead of asking him to put it in the dish-
washer. "Who called you down?" she said.

"Ms. Chan."

Vera. "And what did Ms. Chan want to talk to you about?" Liss
said. "Not your grades? Your schedule was set for the year a long
time ago. It hasn't changed, has it?"

"She just wanted to know how I was," Callan said.

Liss couldn't help the pang of insult, but then Vera was only
doing her job. "When was this? Did she call you down last week,
after . . . after the accident?"

"I don't even remember when the first time was," he said. "Can
we please watch a movie or something? I'm so bored."

"Hold on," she said. "The first time?" The notes in Callan's record had been sorted by dates. "How many times have you met with her?"

He slumped back into his chair. "Too many. I don't see why this is so interesting."

"Where did you meet? Her office?"

"The library?" Callan said. "She let me drink a soda in there, which you're totally not supposed to do." He had a smug smile, getting away with breaking a rule. "She said she wanted me to feel like I could come to her if I needed anything."

Without his mother knowing.

Liss felt the ground beneath her hum, her focus narrow. If she'd been standing up, she would have needed to sit down. "Did she— Did any of that make you feel . . . weird? Uncomfortable?"

Callan's attention snapped to her. "What—"

"She didn't ask you anything really personal or *touch*—"

"Yuck, Mom, stop. No, God. That's gross."

Liss took a shaking breath. "OK."

"She just said it might be a lot to have my stepmother the one making the appointments and that I . . ."

He stopped on his own but it was too late. Stepmother.

"She didn't mean anything by it," he said. His ears were already pink. "Just that I might want things to be different now that you and Dad were getting divorced. And it was OK, she said, to want—"

"Did she suggest that you call me Liss?"

He looked miserable. "She said it would show we had an adult relationship now. Like friends. She said you would *like* it. Since you were the one who wanted the divorce."

Like it. Liss tried to keep her voice even. "Neither of us *wanted* a divorce."

"Then why are you *getting* one?"

"And I'm not divorcing *you*," she said.

"I know but . . ."

Neutered Link, had she? "Did Ms. Chan ask about your dad?"

Callan nodded.

"Did she ask if your dad was dating yet?"

"Mom, stop."

"You can go watch a movie," Liss said.

His eyes shifted from side to side. "Really?"

"Make it something with explosions," she said. "Something really loud. Or play one of your games. Blow up some stuff."

When he was in the den with the door closed, she picked up her phone. Texts at odd hours, calls he'd take to the porch. How long had this been going on? She put the phone back down. She hadn't wanted to know, but her *boss*? Callan's *counselor*? She took the phone up again, texted Link.

VERA???

The dots of his reply danced, then stopped. The phone buzzed against the table.

Liss took the phone into her bedroom and closed the door. She let it buzz a few more times while she tried to catch her breath.

She barely had the phone to her ear before he was talking. "I'm so sorry."

"What the fuck, Link?"

"I know," he said. "I know. God, I'm sorry. A huge mistake."

"How in the world is that a good idea?"

"I didn't think you would care so much *who* it was," he said.

"Not care?" Liss said. "She's my *boss*, Link. I mean, for another *minute*, anyway, because she definitely has it out for me."

"Since when? I have to say I didn't think it was a good idea but she's been pretty chill about it—"

"So *chill* that she called our son down for secret conferences to ply him with soda, pester him for details about you, and encourage him to call me something other than 'mom'? You know, just in case he got a *new* one?"

"Wait," he said. "What? When was this?"

"How long have you been dating her?"

"We weren't *dating*," Link said. "Did she say that? Did you confront her about this? Look, I know I should have told you a . . . a long time ago but you can see why I realized it was a bad idea."

They weren't having the same conversation. "A long time ago? How long— Are you just having a— OK, Link? *You* tell *me*." She adopted the tone she used with students. "How would you characterize your relationship with Vera Chan?"

"Uh, I wouldn't use that *word*, relationship, is how I would characterize it," Link said. "I would say it was a . . . a horrible mistake that's been eating at me and I'm relieved—"

He did sound relieved, she realized. He let out a breath that crackled the line between them. "Relieved to have it out there between us," he said.

She was going to throw up. "How long? How long has it been eating at you?"

"I," he said. "I don't understand."

But she did. Fifteen years.

"Vera is the one," she said.

"Liss? I thought we were getting this straight. Look, I'll come over, OK? Let's talk about it if . . . if you want to?"

I didn't think you would care so much *who* it was, he'd said.

"Vera is your alibi," Liss said. "You wouldn't plan the future with me and instead went out, got drunk, and slept with Vera." Just to make sure she'd stated it, put it out there so he could cajole and deny.

Instead he said, "I thought that's what we were—were we not—"

"You didn't think *what* was a good idea?" Liss said.

"None of it, but, well, you working for her," he said. "That seemed like a bad idea. But she was offering you a good job you might not have, uh, have been . . ."

"Qualified for?" she said icily.

A favor she didn't deserve. A friendship she'd poured herself into, even though sometimes conferring with Vera made her feel more anxious, not less. Pumping her son for information—

Pumping *her*. Filling her with doubt and stoking discord in her relationship with Callan. Then the moment Liss had admitted her marriage was finally over, she'd given Vera the perfect opportunity to rid the guidance office of her least favorite Kehoe.

"I'm sure you've proven yourself by now," Link said. "Listen, do you want to talk? About this? I can—we can—"

He was still stuttering through it when she hung up the phone.

WHEN THE DOORBELL rang twenty minutes later, Liss flung it open already yelling. "I didn't agree for you to come—"

Mercer stood on the deck but didn't flinch. "Bad time?"

"It's just one bad time after another," she said.

"OK."

She wasn't sure she could tamp down her anger to have a conversation, with anyone. And how had she and Mercer left things? A mess. "Did you need something?" She sounded short-tempered, even to herself.

"I . . . I don't know if we should do this now."

It was the wariness in his voice more than the words that got her attention. She walked out onto the deck and put her hip against the rail for strength. "Do what?"

It would be the questions he'd wanted to ask her—this time for the notebook. Mercer had finally come to the end of his investigation, and there she stood.

A ride down to the station, a seat behind one of those doors she'd only ever seen propped open, but now the door would be closed and she would have to think of a single person she could call for help. A lawyer. She had a lawyer. A family lawyer. A *divorce* lawyer.

"I didn't do anything," Liss said, her voice rising and panicked. "I didn't do anything to her, or for her. That's the problem. I— There was a moment when—"

"Liss," he said slowly so that her name almost hissed. "What are you talking about?"

Her heart was pounding so hard, it would come up through her throat. She couldn't think, or speak.

"Take a breath," Mercer said. "Tell me."

Silence stretched between them. The wind blew, cold, against her skin, making the loose panel on the barn roof creak like a rusty nail. The long grass at the road rustled. She listened to the sound until she could form thoughts, words. "There was a moment when this all could have been—but I didn't. I didn't help her," she said. "I didn't know. I didn't understand."

"OK . . ." Drawn out, like an invitation.

"She came to the door and the baby was crying and it was raining and I could see that she was exhausted and maybe she could just use—but I didn't invite her in. I didn't *hurt* her." She'd started to cry at some point. "But I didn't help her, either. She was asking for Link and then she was saying something snotty to me, calling me a name even as she's asking me to take Callan for an hour. And—I could see she needed help. I knew. I just didn't want to help her, Mercer. I didn't want to do her any favors—because it would be doing *her* a favor. I didn't offer her even a *minute* of kindness or sympathy."

"But you did take him," Mercer said. "You did do her that favor, even if you didn't want to."

"It was selfish, in the end," Liss said. "I wanted to hold him, even if it was just an hour. And I thought if Link came home . . ."

"He'd see you mothering his kid, see what he's missing?"

"Something like that," she said. "Yes. The funny part is that Callan was colicky, screaming his head off. Not an easy ride, even that first hour. If she'd come and picked him up at that moment, Mercer? I don't think I would have ever had a kid."

"But then she didn't come back," he said.

"And I've been holding him ever since," Liss said. "As close as I can. Too close."

"You're a good mom to that kid," he said. "OK, let's go back. When Ashley came to the door, she was looking for *Link*? She said Link, specifically?"

"She said is *Daddy* home," Liss said, twisting the word as Ashley had, into something like a sneer. "Like that. Is *Daddy* home?"

Mercer sighed, hard. "OK, and she insulted you?" Mercer said. "Try to remember as best you can anything she said."

"Oh, I remember precisely," Liss said. "She called me a cupcake. I know it sounds pathetic to take that as an insult—but you have to know the way she talked. 'Time is money, cupcake.' Which is ridiculous. She didn't even have a job."

"Time is money," Mercer murmured.

"She was like that. She was *always*—but I never would have hurt her. You have to believe me. I would *never*—"

"I believe you," Mercer said. "Liss, OK? I believe you."

"You do? You believe me?"

She held her head in her hands, and then his arms were around her. Why had she ever left them?

"Yeah," he said. "I shouldn't. I think it means I'm bad at my job."

She let out a shuddering breath. He held her until she stopped shaking, then let her go, gently, in stages. She pulled at the neck of her T-shirt and wiped her nose. "Don't tell Callan I'm doing this. Or anyone."

"I don't have a handkerchief to offer," he said. "Proper gentleman that I am."

I'm not going to be your friend, he'd said. But he was.

"Did your father-in-law ever ask you about all this?" he said.

"Of course," she said. "He came down a lot, at first. He and his men were up and down our road asking questions and the whole time— Of course they mostly wanted to talk about Robbie. Robbie was agitating for attention, bothering them at the station and Key at home. And coming by here to see Callan. Even once he sold his car and had to beg a ride. He was starting to lose it."

"Lose . . . what?"

"Well, his job, then his car," she said. "And then his mind, a bit, I think." That photo of Robbie and Callan in Mim's house. He'd lost Ashley and Callan, everything he'd ever wanted. He would have seen it all slipping away. She understood him better, now, too. "People were badgering him and we—you can do a lot of damage by standing by and doing nothing."

Mercer looked away, as though he might be sick.

He was disgusted with her. She didn't need him to say it.

"I think I do still have something I have to tell you," he said. "You probably need to get to work, though?"

"Day off," she said. "Callan's a little under the weather."

If he had caught the lie, he didn't call her on it.

"Ah," Mercer said. "Walk out here with me a bit."

He turned and walked toward his car, leaving her no choice but to follow.

"The paint job looks good," he said.

The paint? Oh. She'd nearly forgotten the barn door, the accusation and who was meant to receive it. But Mercer hadn't. The episode was on his mind, which brought her unease back in a rush. "What's going on?" she said.

"There's no easy way," he said.

Mercer's strides were longer than hers and he wasn't pulling up, wasn't letting her catch up to walk alongside him. Whatever he had to say, he needed to put it into the wind.

CHAPTER FORTY-ONE

When Mercer finally told Liss about the DNA results, she got still. "That's impossible," she said, a reedy whisper. The wind knocked out of her.

He was reminded out of nowhere of when he was a kid and his dad had taught him to hold a long piece of grass to his mouth and blow to make a thin, sharp sound like a horn. A trumpet blast of alarm in every blade.

"Mercer," Liss said. "Come on." Begging him to say he was lying.

"I have no stake in this, Liss," Mercer said. "I wish it weren't so."

"You have no stake? You *hate* Link. You'd rather ruin his life than . . ." But she couldn't seem to think of anything. Too many options. "This will ruin his life," she said.

He had worried it would ruin hers. Maybe he should have kept it buttoned up, zip, zip, nobody ever need know. How many secrets had Key kept, in this job? Plenty, it was starting to seem clear to him.

"I don't know what to do," Liss said. "I don't know what to do."

"You don't have to do anything for now, do you?" he said. "Think on it."

"*Think* on it." She turned to the house, lifted her chin toward Callan's window. "I don't think I'll be able to stop."

He knew exactly what she meant.

"I think I'm going to be sick," she said.

She sat down in the grass instead, her legs splayed like a fallen doll.

"I didn't want to be the one to tell you, but . . . " he said. "But what if you were blindsided by it one day?"

"Instead of . . ."

"Blindsided by it now," he said. "Yeah." When everything *else* was happening. When everything else was just one bad time after another. He was an idiot. "I'm sorry."

"You have nothing to apologize for," she said. Calm as anything. Businesslike, as though they were making a transaction: the information he could have withheld for whatever was left between them. And if he told her now how he felt, how it had felt to hold her again just now, like the familiar front door of home opening after a long trip, how he'd thought only of her at the bottom of that pool as his lungs threatened to burst—it would all be mixed up in this mess, never again be separated from terrible knowledge and Key's perversion and death and misery and confusion.

He hadn't ruined only her life. He'd ruined his own.

MERCER ZOMBIE-WALKED THROUGH greetings and questions at the station, went to his office, closed the door. He slumped into his chair and stared at nothing. He noticed dust motes in the air, then sunlight at the window, then, finally, at the center of his desk, the stack of pages Deak had left with him.

He lifted a page to stare at something, anything, then another. His eyes finally focused, then his attention.

And now he saw a detail he hadn't noted before: Key's own signature, confident and sweeping—cocksure, a word that might've been invented with Key in mind—upon the complaint up on County Line Road. He'd gone himself. Hadn't sent in the county guys, hadn't sent the goons on his payroll. Hadn't missed a chance to squeeze another constituent for a vote.

Mercer shuffled through the pages. Deak had included a printout of that week's blotter, line after line of which officer, what call, times—

Whatever the reason he had gone at all, Key's call to the north end of the county sat solidly within the window of time between Ashley's sayonara to Liss at the old Kehoe house and the first calls, from Robbie, from Liss, to the station, as those closest to Ashley, those who'd been left caring for her kid, began to wonder where she'd gone.

Half the county away, but it would have been a routine call, brief, and then—

Mercer scanned the log. A speeder. Key had made good use of his drive back toward home, stopping someone along the interstate within the hour of that distress call. Wait, *several* highballers, speeders, in a chain all the way south toward home. Cha-ching for the town coffers. He'd prowled all along that heavily trafficked road that night and then picked up a little bonanza when a pair of drunks met, howdy-do, in a pretty big collision out on the expressway. He hadn't called out until that night, late. Mercer dug through the pages, all the way to the bottom. Deak hadn't let him down. Citations for both DUIs from the collision were included.

And Key had processed and signed the paperwork himself.

Key hadn't been anywhere near his house that night, either house, nowhere near that quarry.

Was it too perfect? Was it a carefully constructed timeline to cover his ass? The collision on the freeway . . . he wouldn't have been the only uniform on the scene, but would any of Key's old cronies speak up, if he'd fudged the records? Could they track down the drivers? The speeders, the drunks? He went to his door. Slocum's desk sat greasy, empty. "Deak," he called.

Bowman came running. "Can I—"

He pointed. "Find Deak. I need you both."

Mercer sat back at his desk and went over the known facts again: last-known sighting by Liss, calls that pinged back and forth with rising concern. The window could be larger than they'd thought, given they only had bones to help narrow it down. Ashley might have died a minute after leaving Liss's house, or several hours. She might have died any time between dropping off the kid and that kid, now fifteen, discovering the—

The car.

A girl was a small thing, but a little white roadster would have caught attention wherever it went. No cameras had picked it up, no witnesses could say they'd seen it.

But there were plenty of places to hide a car out in the countryside. Plenty of places to hide a car not far from the quarry. One place, in fact, stood quite near. A roomy little hiding spot now with a freshly painted door.

Without a specific time, without any flesh on those bones for the forensics people to read, he couldn't be sure of anyone.

It was a damn Tilt-a-Whirl, going around and around looking for someone with a little wiggle room in their schedule. Around and around and around and no fucking fun at all.

SCHOOL HAD JUST let out when Mercer arrived, and the students gaped and snickered as he passed them in the hall. Liss had said she had the day off but still Mercer was surprised to see her desk empty as Vera Chan steered him through the guidance office and into her inner chamber. "Now what is this about?" she said. "Not a problem with one of our students, I hope?"

He'd met her before. Trouble with students, that sort of thing. At one of Callan's games early in the season, just off duty. He hadn't sat in the stands with Liss and the team parents, his presence usually having a chilling effect on conversation and everyone's good time, and Kehoe there and all. He had prowled outside the perimeter of the fence—one of them usually did, keeping everything on the up and up with that many kids in one place—but he'd met this woman afterward, Liss making introductions. She had seemed pleased to make the acquaintance, the smile she'd given him a little familiar, a little knowing. A friend of Liss's, he'd been led to believe. Trusted.

She didn't seem pleased to see him now.

"How's your day going, ma'am?" he said, laying on the old harmless deputy dog. He had Deak and Bowman running down the drivers ticketed and arrested for drunk driving that night, and if they came through, that would cut Key out of the mix. Leaving him empty-handed for suspects, again, unless he could loosen up someone's alibi. Like Link's. "Smooth sailing, I hope, even with Liss cutting class today?"

Vera blinked at him. "As smooth as it can be."

"Just a few loose strings need tying up, ma'am," he said. "Can I get you to confirm the details of the evening you spoke to my deputy about?"

"The details? The details of . . ."

Not the *details*, Jesus. He'd come this far without knowing the length of Link Kehoe's dick. He could go his whole life. "Just start from when you arrived at the—do we call it a bar? When you arrived, was Link Kehoe already there?"

"He'd been there a while, Marshal Alarie, by the looks of him."

But that hadn't turned her off, had it? "And you offered to . . . keep him off the road."

"My civic duty," Vera said. With a bit of a twinkle in her eye now that they were such good friends. She was proud of what she'd accomplished, it seemed to him. A little too pleased with herself.

"At risk of perjury, a class three felony, which would preclude you ever working in this profession or in a public school in this state ever again—" His tone was all business now. She buckled a bit under it. "You would swear that you and Link were together and not engaged in disposing of the body of . . . let's just go ahead and say *anyone*? Till about what time the next morning?"

"Seven," she said in a small voice. "No later than eight."

About the time Link woke up with a monster hangover and maybe, if he had a brain in his head, the tiniest inkling of what a fuckup he was. "You're sure of the time?"

"I had an appointment that day," she said. "Had to drive him back to his truck first."

The world's most awkward walk of shame, though he bet she had been only too happy to do it. Or maybe all the beer he'd had on deck would have ruined the sex. Fat chance of that, since nothing had ever gone sideways for that guy.

Not yet.

But that was allowing himself glee over someone else's disaster. Mercer caught his elation like a flyball, right out of the air before it went too far. He would not be that guy. If there was nothing else separating him from men like Rock Kehoe, this was it. He wouldn't stalk the small and broken, step on their necks.

"Now I want to talk to you about something else," he said, stretching back like he had all the time in the world to ruin her afternoon. Vera Chan had inserted herself into the story in more ways than one, and he could see now the direct connection between the two issues. The *link*. He might have laughed if he'd thought of it earlier, on his own.

He looked across the desk, a sad woman. Even now that Kehoe was free to choose her, he wouldn't. "Ms. Chan, I wonder. Do you suffer from insomnia? How often do you pick up the phone early in the morning, just to destroy someone's day?"

CHAPTER FORTY-TWO

L iss had begged Mercer to leave her where she was, on the ground, her heels in the grass. He hadn't wanted to go, had looked at her like a dog she was unleashing and kicking away.

She had listened to the sounds of his tires on the gravel, then along the road, through the curve, and away. Then the twittering of birds and crickets and whatever-elses, the scrape of the loose tin on the barn roof, the whisper of the long grass at the road.

Did she really have to explain to her son that not only had he lost his mother—*his real mother*, her mind supplied—but now he would lose his father? And his grandfather . . .

Old and sick, Callan had said about Key.

A sick *bastard* and—

Callan's *father*.

And now she understood the chess move Ashley had made to snare a father for her baby, to capture the Kehoe family for her own.

Ashley, shivering on the deck that night, had already done this.

"You *bitch*," Liss said.

Liss stood and stalked across the lawn, just to feel the air move against her face, not realizing she was headed toward the quarry, not at first, and then hurrying, as though something there was timed to disappear, a tide shifting.

She came to the stone edge and stopped with her hands on her knees, gasping at her own reflection, down below.

She *had* considered swimming in the pond, once. Only once, Link's idea. He had a way of talking her into things, in stages, so that she might be three yeses into something she didn't want to do before she knew it.

She hadn't been able to go through with it. She'd stood at the edge, her imagination supplying the depths of the quarry, mythic depths that made her feel small and vulnerable. She couldn't jump, even with Link calling to her from the water, promising there was no such thing as monsters—

Liss's knees gave out and she crouched at the edge of the pond, pulling herself in tight and staring out over the dark water. Ashley's grave. She had imagined a chasm between them. She had built one. Now she couldn't find any anger within herself. Not for *Ashley*.

He was the monster. Key. Key had stood in her living room watching her struggle to feed and calm his own child. What if you don't know him as well as you like to think you do? he'd said, giving her that slick look. And all the time, he had wanted her to point a finger toward Robbie.

No more anger for *Ashley*, Liss thought.

It doesn't matter how Callan was conceived or why. It doesn't matter who birthed him, who sired. Link fathered him. *I* am his mother.

Liss remembered Ashley's sodden shoes, her hair hanging limp. She would have been so scared.

Liss reached down and found a stone, pitched it into the pond. The water she had always thought of as tainted and slimy was only water. If she jumped in and sank, screaming violence, what would happen? Barely a bubble would rise, barely a ripple would break. And all around the crickets would sing and the long grasses at the road would wave and hush and the surface of the water would only accept and keep her rage.

———————

WHEN LISS GOT back to the house, Callan was in the den. She grabbed the basket of clean laundry to keep her hands busy. Callan's bright T-shirts in little square piles, everything in its place. Everything—

When Liss's phone rang and it was Connie Garza's number, she almost didn't pick it up. Connie, who'd dodged her in public? That Connie?

Curiosity got the best of her.

"I'm so sorry," Connie said.

It was how everyone greeted Liss these days but she didn't know which part of her life Connie felt the need to apologize for.

"I heard about the accident," Connie said. "Is he doing better?"

"Who—" Key, she must mean. "He's stable," Liss said.

"If there's anything I can do," Connie said.

People said things, Liss thought.

"I'm outside, actually . . ."

Liss went to the door and opened it. Connie emerged from her car with an aluminum tray held aloft. "Ta-da! Tamale pie. I know you have a lot going on and could use a night off."

"You didn't have to do that," Liss said.

There was a tight expression at Connie's eyes, even as she handed over the covered dish. "Now I used the kind of pan you can just throw out, so you don't have to worry about getting anything back to me."

"Thank—"

"But to be honest, I stopped by for another reason," Connie said. "I don't know how to say it but . . . the photo in the paper?"

She knew then what Connie had come to say. "Mateo?"

"I'm so sorry," Connie said. "I've been fielding all these *calls* but someone must have got through . . . I think he thought he was *helping*."

"The reporter," Liss said.

"What?"

"He'd be helping the *reporter*," Liss said. "I can't see a way it would have helped his friend."

"Now—"

"I hope he got paid a lot," Liss said. "Enough to help out with college? Those football scouts might not come through."

"There's no need for that, Lissette."

And Liss could see that Connie held herself high above whatever was happening. They had never been friends. They had been conveniently placed bystanders.

"I was *trying* to apologize," Connie said. "Mateo couldn't know the *harm*—"

"We're fine," Liss said. She thought it might be the thing Connie would least want to hear, the story not worth repeating.

"If you want to point fingers at *children*, Liss," Connie hissed, "you should call up the Wards. Jamie's the reason we're all in this mess and I don't see anyone over there reaching out to make things—"

"Jamie? Hold on, Connie. What do you mean Jamie's the reason?"

"Callan didn't tell you?" she said, with a twitch of pleasure at the side of her mouth.

"Tell me what?"

"*Jamie* was driving the car that night, Tanner's car. He's lucky no one was killed . . ."

Jamie driving. Finally. Finally, the lie she'd spotted that night.

"But," Connie was saying, "I wouldn't put it past Larkin to sue the Wards off the planet, even though they have nothing at all to lose."

Each other. They had each other to lose, and there were people left in the world who didn't understand that. "Jamie doesn't have his license," Liss said.

"*Right.*" Connie drew the word out slowly. "Tanner let him drive and the result is, well, I'm sure you all have suffered the most, no one could argue, but we've all been dragged into this mess and I can't tell you how many people think it is any of *their* business—"

"Why was Jamie driving? Why not Mateo?"

"Because Mateo was raised to know right from wrong, Liss. These boys, I swear."

The death of us, yes. Something would see to it.

Tamale pie dumped in the fridge, Liss went back to the laundry.

Jamie, driving, instead of Tanner. But Jamie didn't *want* to drive. Hated being a passenger.

In Callan's room, Liss put away his boxers, the T-shirts, some of them too tight under his arms at this point. When she opened the bottom drawer, shorts and jeans, something heavy wrapped in a plastic bag shifted, rolled, and thunked against the front of the drawer.

What the—

She should have been afraid to look, she realized, later.

Inside the bag was an aluminum baseball bat, muddy at the grip and—

She didn't hear the footsteps up the stairs, only the door swinging open behind her. "What are you doing?" Callan said.

He came at her quickly and took the bat out of her hands. Along its length, the bat was smeared with mud and something darker, dried and nearly black.

"Is that *blood*?" she said.

CHAPTER FORTY-THREE

On the way back to the station from the school, Mercer passed the quarry road and glanced over.

Habit. Would he ever not turn to look?

Things looked peaceful from this distance, but then they would. From a distance.

He shouldn't have burdened Liss with that paternity bullshit. Well, he'd learned that lesson. He'd keep the identities of the late-night callers to himself, now that he'd had a quiet word with the worst offenders. It wasn't much.

He resisted the urge to turn. He could do Liss the most good by clearing this up.

Could he, though?

What did he *know*? What was bedrock, that he could trust? He drove into town, sliding the players forward and back in his mind.

Link. Link was ironclad nowhere near the pond until the next day, by which point Key's men would have been crawling all over the county looking for Ashley Hay in her little roadster. Wouldn't they have been up and down that road all day?

And Liss: Maybe he shouldn't but he believed her that she'd sent Ashley away and had spent the last fifteen years simmering in something like self-loathing.

And Hubbard.

At the station, Mercer slipped in the back door and into his office, behind his desk. He supposed he understood better why Key had targeted Robbie Hubbard back in the day. He'd seen the list of offenses, so called, the guy had racked up. His major crimes were being poor, unable to pay fees when he got himself into a spot of trouble, and not having the right kind of friends who wouldn't ditch him for an easy fuck.

"Chief?" Slocum at the door.

"Hold on." Something had shimmered, just for a second, like a lantern swinging, shooting him in the eye with brief, brilliant, blinding light. But it was gone. "Fuck."

"Sorry to interrupt greatness at work," Slocum said.

"What do you need, Slocum?"

"Deacon said you wanted to see . . ." His eyes slid across Mercer's desk and caught. "That's Key."

Deak had dug up a photo from the collision Key had been working the night of Ashley's disappearance, a snap from the local rag that had caught Key in distinct profile.

Slocum reached for it. "Is this—when was this?"

"Same night as Ashley Hay went missing," Mercer said. "Were you there?"

Slocum lay the photo down. "There, where?" he said.

Mercer nodded toward the image. "At that accident site."

"I was *here*," Slocum said. "Holding down the shop."

Of course he was. He was a paperweight, overburdening the chairs of the station every shift while the rest of them went about the duties of peace and justice and all the rest. As reliable as an anchor.

"OK," Mercer said. "OK, don't get your panties in a wad, Slocum. I just thought you might have some intel on when Key came and

went, if you were there. I don't suppose you were still here when he
came in later that night?"

He thought it over. "No."

"What time did you clock out?"

"Why?"

Had he never done so much as an afternoon of actual work?
"Because I'm trying to see how late it was that Key might have
come in here after that wreck."

"Why do you care so much where Key was that night?"

He hadn't meant to show his whole hand. "I feel like we've been
over this," Mercer said. "I'm just trying to visualize every piece
on the board. Including the king himself."

Slocum squinted at him. Was he trying to decide if he liked Key
being called a king?

Mercer rubbed a hand down his face. "Never mind. Get back to
work."

"I need to go—"

"OK, go."

He didn't want to be short with the old guy but goddamn could
Slocum jump all over his last nerve. Mercer sat quietly, willing the
flash of understanding to strike again, thinking of himself as a
stopped watch, sitting still and waiting for the time to be correct.

He'd been thinking of . . . Robbie Hubbard. The insight that
had flirted with him stubbornly refused to catch again. He was an
impatient man but he had nothing else in his life, did he? He could
come at the problem from another direction. Every direction. Every one, until they had the truth of it.

Mercer was halfway through the station, back to his car, when
his head cleared. He went back, unlocked the safe under his desk,
and retrieved his sidearm. With the gun in place, his duty belt

was almost twenty-eight pounds. Yeah, he'd weighed it once, and show him the law enforcement officer who hadn't.

MERCER DROVE TO the north end of the county, the sky low and gray. He passed over a creek, noting the twisting white limbs of sycamores along the shore, like spectral arms. Out in the fields, farmers were trying to get ahead of the weather. Everything going along as it always had.

He'd never really burrowed in, somehow. He'd meant to. But even so, Parkins had grown on him. He had only hoped to solve more of their problems, though, instead of creating more. He found himself starting to craft the concession speech, the apologies he wanted to make. The mess he'd be leaving for his successor.

The home Key had been called to the night of Ashley's disappearance was up a long dirt drive. A woman about sixty answered the door, wiping her hands on a worn tea towel. He could pinpoint her near-sightedness by how slowly her expression dropped from curious, maybe expectant, to disappointed, even apprehensive. Mercer stepped back to let the door swing wide of him.

"Ma'am," he said. "I'm Parkins's town marshal—"

"He's out on the fields," she said.

"I . . . couldn't bother you with a question or two?"

"He's the one you'll want to do business with," she said.

He might have guessed the woman of the house could have answered his questions as well as her husband but was intrigued enough about what kind of business he might be offered. He followed the woman's vague nod out to where a combine harvester was cutting a clean swath through a field. It was a monster piece of machinery that chewed through cornstalks as easily as a lawn-mower through grass.

Mercer parked in the lane and waited against the bumper of his car until the guy might have a chance of catching sight of him.

Finally the farmer hauled himself out of the high cab of the tractor and came across the field, head down.

"Sorry to interrupt," Mercer called, friendly. But even this didn't lift the man's head. He trudged toward him as though to the executioner, didn't offer his hand or any kind of greeting. "Mr. Tidewell, isn't it? I'm Parkins's town marshal—"

"I know who you are."

The guy had a face like one of those Easter Island rocks. "This weather pushing you to an early harvest?" Mercer tried.

Tidewell looked at Mercer shrewdly. "I reckon *you're* the one a little early."

It was gone two in the afternoon, but Mercer didn't look at his watch. "Most people complain we drag our feet and are glad when we go," Mercer said.

Tidewell nodded, full agreement, but said nothing. He chewed on a lump packed into his cheek and then spit, not too far from Mercer's left boot.

He was used to people getting a little squirrelly when he showed up, but something felt off. "Were you expecting me, sir?"

"Can't say I was," Tidewell said.

"OK, well. I only wanted to ask you about a visit you had," Mercer said. "Years ago. You might not even remember. The former marshal came out on some kind of distress call. This would have been about fifteen years ago."

"You're joking, right?"

"I take my job pretty serious," Mercer said.

Tidewell looked at him searchingly, then away. "That must've been the night I had a little accident," Tidewell said.

"Sorry to hear that," Mercer said.

The guy glanced up, like a beaten dog looking up from the floor.

"What happened, if you don't mind my asking?"

"My arm," Tidewell said. "I fell off the harvester and broke my arm."

"You fell off that thing?" Mercer said. "You're lucky you weren't killed."

Tidewell chewed and Mercer got ready to jump out of the way. "Who's in charge down there these days?" Tidewell said.

"I am?" Mercer said.

"You don't sound too sure."

"There's an election soon," Mercer said uncertainly.

Tidewell snorted. "And what will that change, exactly?"

As Mercer passed the house again, the wife stood on the porch with a grim face. On the way back toward town, he drove by one of his own election signs stuck at a mailbox. Could nothing change? What good was he to these people?

HOME.

I remember arriving home. All the concerned fluttering, the settling in. Put to bed instead of into the wheelchair, but I suppose the chair is a loss.

Hospital, ambulance, bed . . .

Like counting my teeth with my tongue, I can work through the steps, but there's a gap. A tooth, pulled out, root and all.

Gaps are bad.

I've lived through a lot of gaps already. My speech slurred then stopped, my muscles spasmed and jerked until they gave up the ghost, too, but that was all physical stuff. I'd always had the noggin to fall back on. In here, I am still who the fuck I've always been. Even if I can't shoo off the health aides or tell Patty I hate the show she's left on the TV. Even if I can't tell anyone what I'm thinking, I can *think* it.

Hospital, ambulance, bed.

Gap.

Had I heard Slocum's voice at one point? What's he doing here? Supervising or something, as he does. Helping Patty get me into place? Link came by, a short visit, now I remember. The kid with him. I must have been looking too hard at the kid, putting it all together. This kid. It's all this kid's fault.

Dad? Link said, What's wrong? He sends the kid to wait for him out in the kitchen and asks, like I can answer, You didn't do it on purpose, right?

Why wouldn't I? I went to bat for Link, kept it quiet so he could have that grade B life he was building, white picket fence. I want to roar at him, tell him what a chump he is, accepting anything that's handed him.

And then—

Gap.

Link is gone. Maybe I pulled out one last slimy word. Maybe I sent him away.

Maybe this is the end. The gaps will swell and wring out the last of what's left. The gaps will connect and that's it. The shades will go down. They'll get out the white gloves and shroud their badges. I deserve that much, don't I? They'll call end of watch on the dispatch, and only silence will answer.

CHAPTER FORTY-FOUR

From the Tidewell farm, Mercer crossed the county toward the Hubbard house. Ping-ponging all over the place seeing to things himself. Just like Key, then.

He liked doing his own running around, his own footwork, when he could. Preferred it to town meetings, to the dais and microphone. He liked being out with his neighbors, seeing their faces.

Of course, he didn't go along each place hoping to see his neighbors' faces fall at the sight of him. Had he let them down so badly?

He had an itch between his ears, a little itch of an idea that he might be getting to the bottom of it. Of all of it.

Mim sat on her porch in a ratty chair that had been pulled from among the dusty rooms inside. The chair had a high back, quilted and curved behind her head, a throne. He parked and approached, humble servant, hat in hand, hating the hopeful look he saw, fleeting, upon her face before she caught herself and reined in her expectations.

"Mrs. Hubbard," he said.

"People will talk, Marshal," she said, flatly. "You're here so often, they'll say we're courting."

She was hoping to have it wrong, he thought, hoping he would say that he had it all sorted out for her.

"I don't deserve your attentions, Mrs. Hubbard," he said. "Not yet."

She looked down. "You might as well call me Mim," she said. "I'm old and I don't have the time for all that Mrs. Hubbard this and that."

"Mim, don't give up on me," he said. "One of these days I hope to ride up here and offer you what you've been waiting for. Something better than roses and sweet nothings."

She smiled, but at her hands in her lap. "It's been a long, good while since a man offered me sweet anythings." When she looked up, it was with a sharper eye. "Roses," she scoffed. "It's been a while since you were anyone's sweetheart, I think."

"Now, Mim, I thought we were going to be friends," he said.

"I've given up on friends," Mim said, checking the sky.

Mercer felt his evening slipping away from him. "OK, Mrs.—Mim. Believe it or not I came on business. I came to ask you . . . I'm sorry, but would you go through it with me, through Robbie's last days? Again?"

"Again." But she didn't sound put out or reluctant. "You make it sound like something I ever stop doing."

There was a clang off to the side of the house. Mercer stepped back. "Someone here?"

"Neighbor woman," Mim said. "She's wintering the garden. Cold snap blowing in."

There were birds who cawed ominously at the approach of storms—Mercer didn't know the name for them—and they were at it now, high in the tree behind Mim's house.

"Nice of her."

"She likes to think she's doing me some good works," Mim said.

"But you don't care for vegetables?"

"Oh, I eat what there is. No complaints about the beans and tomatoes. Zucchini to last you the end of days. But it's more for her. I think she needs a break from what goes on, over her side of the street," Mim said, gesturing down the road. "She walks over."

Which explained why he hadn't realized Mim had a visitor, no car in the drive. Sophie Ward.

He was staring out toward the garden, now that he knew it was there. A whirling silver pinwheel made his eyes spin and then his attention and his thoughts were whirling until he had gone off somewhere else and nearly had it, that elusive tip-of-his-tongue he'd had in the office before Slocum had interrupted.

"Don't mention it to her," Mim said.

"Hmm?" The pinwheels still shone in his eyes but whatever he'd almost grasped had slipped away again.

"What I said about what goes on down their house," she said. "I don't really know, to be honest. Only a feeling."

"Something isn't right," he said.

"You've seen it."

Was it the sort of thing he should admit? "I haven't seen it. I've felt it. Is there anything to do? Anything besides letting her tend your crops? Any bruises on her?"

Mim grimaced. "I don't think it's that sort of thing," Mim said. "I hope not."

Mercer pulled up a step and sat with a creak in his knees. He wasn't forty years old and he heard out of his own mouth the sounds his dad used to make when he fell into his recliner after a long day. He had wanted something from this life, something he didn't yet have.

He might only have a few months to clean up behind him in Parkins County. Mop the floors and put away the bucket—

He thought of Liss at her barn door, bucket at her feet.

What did he want that he could *have*?

Mercer rubbed at his eyelids. "All right, Mrs.—Mim. Robbie worked an extra shift that day and Link Kehoe, he picked him up that morning."

Mim didn't answer, and when he turned to see what was happening, she had fixed him with a stony stare. "I thought it was my son's death you was finally working on."

"It is, Mrs.—*Mim*. It is, I promise you," he said. "But it's all tied up together. To be totally honest with you, I'm looking for a loose thread to pull anywhere I can find it. I can't help thinking his death—"

"His murder," she said.

"—began somewhere a few paces back," he continued. "Dominoes falling one into the other. Do you disagree?"

Mim Hubbard had always seemed to him a large woman, fleshy and firm, standing where people didn't want her to be, reminding them as clearly as a bright yellow road sign of things they had failed to do. But she was actually quite small, he realized now, dwarfed by the crown of that threadbare chair.

He had chosen this field as a young man who had no idea what it would ask of him, how much it would cost him to disappoint people like Mim.

"That day does feel like the beginning of the end," she said. When she spoke again, her heart was no longer in it. It was rote recitation. "Link Kehoe picked him up that morning."

"This place is a bit out of Link's way," Mercer said, ignoring the revulsion of giving Kehoe credit.

"They were going to that dive, after," Mim said. "That place they went. It wasn't too long after that Robbie sold his car, anyway, and he got used to borrowing a ride or if he couldn't walk there, he wouldn't go."

"Sounds like—" He nodded toward the garden.

Mim murmured. "She drove, once. She *chose* to give it up."

He gazed out at the corner of the garden, the pinwheels spinning. Mim had said something he missed.

"What was that?" he said.

"I was saying how Robbie wouldn't've given up that car of his for the world," she said. "If he'd not needed the money."

"He liked to drive."

"He liked to be his own man," she said. "He didn't like to be beholden." Mim looked off toward the garden. "That runs in the family, mind."

But she expected what she deserved. It was only that she deserved something he wasn't sure he'd ever be able to give.

CHAPTER FORTY-FIVE

A branch clattered against the window in Callan's room. Liss's gaze slipped past the baseball bat, past her son, silent and glowering in his bedroom doorway, to a clock in the hallway.

"Don't call Mercer," he said.

"I—"

What did it mean? *Whose* blood?

He pushed past her and pulled the plastic bag around the bat.

"Where did you get it?" she said. "You found it?"

Callan threw the thing into the open drawer and kicked it closed. Having it put away cleared some of the noise in Liss's head. But not all.

"OK, let's start somewhere easier," she said. "Why did you lie about Jamie driving Tanner's car that night?"

He grasped the empty clothes basket off his bed, tossed it aside, and threw himself facedown into his pillow.

"Did you think I wouldn't hear it about it, eventually? From *someone*?"

Callan mumbled something, muffled.

"What?"

He sat up. "They all said they wouldn't tell."

"Why? What's the big secret?"

"Tanner said his dad would kill him."

The insurance implications, alone. She hated to think. If anyone had been hurt . . .

She'd been so distracted by the discovery of Ashley's car, the accident itself had almost fallen away from notice. Things could have gone so badly.

"Tanner's dad wouldn't actually kill him," she said. "It's just— We worry about you, that something could happen to you."

Callan rolled to his side.

"Terrible things, if we look away for even a second."

"We, who?"

"Moms," she said. "We don't want anything to happen to you."

"Some things, though." He sat up. "*Some* things should happen, shouldn't they?"

"Like the accident," she said. "How quickly did that go wrong? Jamie doesn't know how to *drive*. He's afraid to be *in* a car."

"He's afraid of everything," Callan said. "Tanner made him."

"Why?"

"I don't know," Callan said. "To be funny, I guess."

"How is that funny? Explain the joke."

He shrugged. "He's just teasing him and stuff. Like he made Jamie put ketchup on his forehead at lunch and he couldn't wipe it off until the teacher noticed. Tanner stole Jamie's jacket and flew it from the antenna of his car."

That explained how it got from her house to the school parking lot. "Tanner's bullying him, then?"

"No, he's—I mean. A lot of the guys pick on Jamie. And other kids."

Kids like Tanner had singled out boys like Jamie since boys had existed. Smaller boys, skinny boys, chubby ones, boys who hadn't struck their growth spurt, whose voices hadn't dropped.

Boys without the right shoes or haircut—or whatever. Boys who were afraid of the world finding out whatever it was they wished they weren't. Boys afraid to drive. Tanner would have dug into that open wound. And girls! Liss knew too well the cruelties of girls.

"What about you?"

"No," Callan said, defensive.

"I mean, do they pick on you, too?"

"Not really." He plucked at a thread in the quilt on his bed. "Sometimes."

"More since the accident?" she said.

He shrugged. She was starting to get the hang of this dialect. A no was clear. A shrug was a reluctant confirmation.

"So that's why Tanner is so mad at Jamie? Because he wrecked his car. And that's it?"

Callan looked up but kept pulling at the bedspread. "Yeah."

If a shrug meant yes, what did an actual yes mean? An evasion? A misdirection, because the real answer was too complicated to explain.

She should know how to speak this language, all these years at the school. But the language swerved their understanding, and they were left behind. They were *meant* to be left behind.

Was Tanner mad at Jamie? She tried to remember Tanner interacting with Jamie the night of the accident. He'd been a shit about the Gimme chips. But what came to mind was Tanner ramming into Callan in the school hallway.

"So why is Tanner mad at *you*?"

He dropped his gaze.

Callan, pulled from the pile of boys in a tackle and coming up swinging, for Tanner. Jamie hadn't even been on the field.

"And why—"

"He's just a dick, OK? And I didn't like how he was treating—

anyone, OK?" Callan was having trouble holding it together, chin tucked to his chest and tears probably brimming.

"OK," she said. "OK." She sounded like Mercer, of all people, when things weren't really OK at all. "He said things about . . . about your dad that absolutely aren't true. We know that, right? Mercer said—"

"I *always* knew Dad didn't do it."

Oh, to have the confidence of a son in his—

Father.

Liss plastered some kind of smile in place. But Callan looked miserable. Oh God—

Had Vera *told* Callan where Link was the night Ashley died? In her little private sessions?

"*How* did you always know?" Liss said cautiously. "Because Dad would never do something like that or . . ."

"Because," Callan said, a hiccup of a sob escaping. He wiped angrily at his eyes but wouldn't look at her. "Because I know Papa Key did it."

Papa. Key had chosen that name for himself, and it struck her cruelly now.

"Papa Key," she said. "How—" How much did he know? How had he come up with it?

"I found it," Callan said. "Near the pond. In the . . . the—"

"The baseball bat?"

"It's the one behind the door."

"Ours is still in the kitchen," she said.

Wait—did she know that?

Yes, Link had grabbed it the night someone had come out to take a look at the pond—the night Ashley had been found. She'd used it herself to make sure the house was secure when she'd come back from the hardware store.

"Their door," Callan said. "It's the bat from Gram's house."

"You think that bat has Ashley's blood on it," she said.

"It was buried in the mound, where the tire got stuck," he said, wiping his nose on his arm. "I hid it in my kit bag."

What would happen to an aluminum baseball bat over fifteen years? Anything? It wouldn't rust. The plastic bag might have kept the blood from breaking down. "Their bat is probably still behind their door, too," she said.

"It's not, though," Callan said. "Dad says they always have one but they don't. I looked the other day when I went to see Papa with Dad." He plucked again at the quilt. "Papa gave me such a weird look—"

"Maybe Gram put it somewhere else. The one you found, someone just left it," she said. The brush and undergrowth around the quarry caught odd bits of plastic and paper as the wind blew over the water and rim. "There's probably all kinds of trash flying around—"

"A baseball bat?" he scoffed. "Wrapped in plastic and buried, like a secret. And it's dented," he said.

"Tanner's bumper . . ."

"Dented just like Dad always says," Callan said. "Remember?"

Link's old car, which Key had beaten to a pulp when Link missed curfew. In the story Link told, the car had more wrong with it every telling, barely road worthy. But it had been. When he bought his first truck, he'd sold the car to Robbie for a song, and even Robbie had sold it on for the cash, relying on rides from Link.

But not always Link, not mornings to the factory, not when he'd come out to see them those nights to rage about Key—

"Mom?"

"I remember," she said. "You should have given it to Mercer. No matter what it is."

"But Papa—"

"If Papa used the bat on Ashley, then he needs to face what he did," she said.

"But," he said.

Key hadn't even been a *loving* grandfather—

And now she knew why.

"But what?" she said.

"But *Dad*," Callan said. "He'll be wrecked."

Which is how Liss realized that Callan had been protecting *them*.

CHAPTER FORTY-SIX

Mercer poked around the corner of the Hubbard house before heading out and startled Sophie Ward.

"Sorry," he said, showing his hands like she was a horse that might bolt.

She was on her knees in the dirt and vegetation, spreading a layer of what looked like mulched, dry leaves. The few stalks still uncovered were brittle yellow, with a bristle cut like they gave for twelve bucks down at the barber's.

"Not your fault," she said. "I wasn't expecting anyone, is all."

Might be more to it than that, but that wouldn't be *her* fault. Maybe he should have Jim in for a chat. "Nice thing you're doing for Mrs. Hubbard here," he said.

Sophie looked back at her work and patted at the mulch, spreading it further. "I like to do it, so she does me the favor of letting me."

"You don't have room for a garden at your place?"

She didn't seem to know how to answer. "Mim has more room, and we get a share from it. And it's nice to be out here by myself." She glanced at him. "It's peaceful. Good place to think."

Mercer let a moment pass. "You know, if there's anything you ever need to tell me . . . I'm all ears."

Sophie's hands stilled. "How do you mean?"

"If there was, I don't know, any trouble at home?"

She stood, lurching to one knee and then both feet. "I don't know what you've heard—"

"I haven't heard anything, Mrs. Ward," Mercer said. "I only want to make sure you're here doing good deeds because you're a woman with a heart of gold, instead of feeling like you can't be at home."

"I don't know about heart of gold," Sophie said. "But my husband is far more supportive than you could possibly know."

"Glad to hear it," he said.

"As long as we're clear," she said to the gray clouds on the horizon. She had freckles, he realized. The only thing about her he'd ever noticed, other than the blankness of her. The emptiness.

"Didn't mean any insult," he said. "Now you be careful when you go, OK? The roads are bound to be dangerous."

"What does that mean?" she said. The freckles were nearly hidden as her cheeks darkened in a blush.

"Only what I said. Storm advisory," Mercer said. "I'd be careful walking along that road."

"Trust me, Marshal," Sophie said, sinking back to her work. "I'm as careful as I know how to be."

MERCER PARKED ON the slab behind the speakeasy and surveyed the scene. A drunk was slumped in a chair at the back door, his head hanging.

Someone stood in shadows at the back door with a cigarette and then ducked away. Patrons would start to dissolve from the front. By the time he'd reach the bar, he'd be as welcome as a rat exterminator arriving under a skull-and-crossbones flag.

A discarded Styrofoam coffee cup blew over the concrete pad. Mercer got out and paced out the distance across the expanse and back before the proprietress came stomping across the grass.

"Is this a bust?" Dee Booth said.

"As long as no one's driving out of here when they shouldn't," he said. "I'm not interested in underage drinkers tonight."

"I think you'll find my clientele is all of age."

They would be, now.

Dee lit a cigarette and sucked at it, her cheeks hollowing into shadow. "Anything I can help you with, Marshal?"

"I'm just working through a few tangles," Mercer said.

She blew out a cloud of smoke and didn't ask which ones.

Mercer looked down at the slab under his boots. "Something used to sit here?"

"Shed," she said. "My dad used to take in mowers and Bobcats to fix. He was no good at it. Old man with old-man dreams, wanting to turn this empire to gold."

The words had the slant of sarcasm, but Mercer thought she was proud of it. "What's to stop you from doing it?"

She looked up sharply. "You kidding?"

"That's the second time this afternoon I've been accused of being a clown," Mercer said. "I'm not a funny man, I don't think. Most people look real unhappy to see me coming, as a matter of fact."

"You expecting a hero's parade every time you show up?"

"Every time," he said. "Mrs. Booth, is there any reason you'd be expecting me? Am I too early for an appointment of some kind?"

She leveled him with a look. "I can't afford a double dip just because the bag man changes, you hear me?"

Realization struck him physically, a dislocated bone snapping painfully into place. Fat envelopes behind every bar, every counter, waiting in how many bread boxes in how many homes? How often?

"Who?" he said. "Who usually comes? How much? How often?"

"If you have to ask," she said.

"What does it pay for?"

"What did it ever pay for? Protection."

"Protection from . . . ?"

"From accidents, of course," she said. "The unexplained kind."

A little accident. Lucky you weren't killed. Mercer moaned. "I'm going to put a stop to it," he said.

"Campaign promises." Dee dropped her cigarette and ground it into the concrete.

"A regular promise," Mercer said. "The kind I make and *keep*."

"I'll let you untangle in peace—"

"Mrs. Booth—"

"—so you can get out of here as soon as humanly possible."

"Generous of you," he shouted at her back.

If he wasn't mistaken—had she flipped him off?

He had to win the election now. Or his promises would be worth nothing and men like Key would keep winning, even long after they'd started losing. No, not men like Key.

Men like *Slocum*. Had to be. Who else straddled Key's reign and his own? Who else couldn't be dislodged?

Men like Slocum were a pestilence. They would keep digging the heart right out of this country, this town, and the weakest among them would follow along because they thought the only way to survive was to shovel everyone else in ahead of themselves.

There wasn't anything in being a decent person anymore? He refused to believe it.

He'd have Slocum out on his ass tomorrow, but to get the trust of the county back, he had to win the election. A good way to ensure a win would be to figure this shit out, once and for all.

Mercer scuffed his boot at the slab below. The story of Ashley Hay's disappearance was like a song he knew all the words to—except his mind kept needle-scratching somewhere near this old gas station.

"OK," he said under his breath, and walked the length of the pad again.

That night, two men had entered the scene together, two suspects, Hubbard and Kehoe arriving in Link's truck, parking on the slab under his feet.

Before the night was through, the woman they had in common was dead.

This is where they'd parted ways, one fellow toward a bad decision that would keep him busy all night and the other, after sleeping off a drunk at the back door as so many had and would, home to mama. If you believed the women in question—and Mercer did—both those boys were in bed, if not asleep, when Ashley arrived at the Kehoe door to make her demands and hand over Callan. What was he missing?

He looked up at the roiling sky. Lightning to the west, heading their way. His stomach had started to rumble, in place of thunder.

But he went through it again. Again, again but there was no crack to wedge the facts of the story apart, no place to grab leverage.

The next morning, Ashley Hay would have been in the water, Key's team roving up and down the quarry road to talk to Liss, retrace steps, and then Link coming home after picking up his truck at this very spot and—

He had it.

Not the answer to everything, but he'd been feeling like a guy with a persistent itch in a phantom limb for a week and now he knew where to scratch.

How had he not seen it before?

Who had driven *Hubbard* home, if Link's truck hadn't left this spot until morning?

"Mrs. Booth," he shouted, and hurried to catch her.

VOICES ALONG THE HALL.

I hear them, know them, swim in them for a while before waking fully.

Patty in hissing whispers. The aides getting theirs, probably. The conservatory bounces noises all around, like a stone cave with a drip-drop of water at the back.

I wake a second time, groggy and my mouth thick. In my dreams I had pressed my cheek against cold rock to sip at a trickle.

My throat hurts like a mother. What did they do to me in that place? I try to form my mouth into a sound that will alert whichever aide's been left on sentry, but there's no one here.

No one?

After that ride into the pool, I would think they'd never leave me alone again.

Patty, louder now, arguing with someone. Someone stupid, I know that tone. I'd been in that position all too many times.

Footsteps are coming along the hall, heavier than Patty's or any of the blue-clad chicks they've sent—

Slocum.

What business that lamppost has in my bedroom, I can't imagine. I guess we're friends now? He's been here enough. He walks around the bed to the window, peeling an orange, checking me out from all angles like I'm a steer on auction.

"You're like one of those creepy paintings, you know?" he says. "Where the eyes follow you around the room?"

When've you ever been near a painting, I want to ask. Should have saved all my last words for this doorknob. Where's Patty?

My wrists are secured down, I realize. Not like I could get away, but they aren't taking chances. I'm not to be trusted.

I will die here. Tethered like a retired horse and having my piss bags changed on a schedule. All of life's pleasures behind me.

"I used to want what you had," Slocum says, shaking his head. He's working the orange peel around in a long coil. Impressive. "But I wouldn't be you now," he says. "Not for all the money, not for this ranch or that lady. Not worth it."

What's he whining about? How would he know what was worth it or not?

Part of the rind of Slocum's orange—my orange, I bet—falls to the floor. He leaves it.

The aide or Patty will get it later but that's hardly the point. I'll have that hard bright stench in the room with me now. In my head. Smells do me in, all of a sudden, including my own, including Patty's perfume and the chlorine in the pool. It starts as a scent, takes up residence, and gives me headaches, like an old lady. Then the internal temperature rises because I can't tell someone to feed me an aspirin. To stop wearing perfume. To take those fucking flowers out and bury them in the yard. It starts as scent and turns to blind rage, and then they stand over me and wonder why the machines are beeping.

There are bright spots in my eyes, now, and I can hope it's my mind, fragmenting as it spins its last.

Maybe this is it. The gentle lights out, at last.

Slocum has come up next to the bed. The machine is beeping, but he's not alarmed. Not paying any attention. And I wonder—

"Your life's not worth the electricity saying you're still among the living, Key," Slocum says. He shoves a big section of orange into his gob. "What happens if I knock the plug out of the wall?" I wonder. There's Slocum, right there. Always right there. I wonder if I'm about to die, and not gently at all.

CHAPTER FORTY-SEVEN

Liss let the stairs lead her down to the great room, into the kitchen. The window was dark. Outside, the wind blew. She opened the fridge door, stood in the escaping coolness, then pulled out the tamale pie. Callan probably would sneer at it, if he came down at all.

He didn't want her to turn the baseball bat over to Mercer but—

Dented. Just like Dad always says.

Liss snapped on the oven and went to the back door. The baseball bat Link had carried into the yard leaned in the corner, as it always did.

The bat at Key and Patty's would be behind their door, too. Shiny and *dented*, a prop for Key lore more than a security device.

But she had no trouble at all believing Key could have turned on Ashley, his too-young—did she have to think the word?—mistress.

Victim?

How long had it gone on? Was Ashley a willing participant? Poor Patty.

In the kitchen, Liss stood over the foil-wrapped casserole dish. Then she turned off the oven and reached for a notepad and pen, then her keys and the pie.

Outside the cold had gone ahead and snapped as the sun fell. She could see her breath in the air. The strip of tin on the barn roof rattled and, as she watched, peeled back, caught, and swept off toward the quarry.

Liss hesitated. She'd have to call someone to fix that, and soon. Link would—

Later. She unlocked the car and got in, wishing she'd grabbed her coat, even for the short trip.

The bat would be behind the door. If not—

Well, she supposed Mercer was already taking a hard look at Key for Ashley's disappearance.

She would have to call him. The bat had *someone's* blood on it. And—

And she missed him. His goofy *OK OK* when he needed a second, just a second, to catch up and get right. That notch between his eyes when something stumped him, when he was taking things seriously.

He'd taken things seriously, with her. Too seriously, too fast. She hadn't had a chance to catch her breath.

She still hadn't. He wanted everything from her, while Liss couldn't imagine a single second into the future. Not a second ahead of where she was on the road.

As SHE PULLED up next to the conservatory windows, the shape of someone moved within. Patty, deciding whether or not she would open the door. Liss rang the bell with an elbow.

Patty finally opened the door. "I told you you weren't welcome here," Patty said. "And it's late, Lissette." She looked down at the tinfoil mound in Liss's hands. "You didn't take up cooking?"

"Not me. Connie Garza sends it—"

"Blech."

"—with her best wishes for Key's recovery."

"You know my husband eats through a tube now, yes?"

Liss thought quickly. "You could serve it to the health aides."

"We're not a coworking facility, Lissette," Patty said. "Or a *teacher's* lounge. Come in, I guess."

"Put it in the fridge?" Liss said.

"Why not directly into the toilet?"

Patty was holding the door open, the better to sweep Liss back out again. If she didn't close the door, Liss couldn't check behind it.

She cast around for ideas. "I could . . ."

Patty's eyebrows, long filled in with pencil, were crooked and grew more so as she raised one.

"I could heat a portion for you, if you haven't eaten," Liss said. "I'm sure you're not taking proper care of *yourself.*"

"What is it? The dish."

"Tamale pie—"

"Sounds *heavy,*" Patty said. But her shoulders sank and she closed the door.

The baseball bat wasn't propped where it should have been.

"I haven't been, you're right," Patty said, her usual sharpness now dull. "With all this going on." She waved her hand generally toward the conservatory.

"Is, uh, is Key on the mend?"

Liss cast around for places the baseball bat could lean.

"There's no such thing for him," Patty said. Her chin trembled. "You must know that."

They would be married forty years soon—if Key could hold on. Forty years, a lifetime. And how cruelly Key had treated her. How deep the betrayal, when the truth about Key came out—

If Key had killed Ashley, Liss couldn't do anything to stop what would happen. She couldn't protect anyone from this. Callan,

Link. Patty would lose her husband in a far different way than she imagined.

There was a noise in the rear of the house. "One of the aides keeping Key out of the pool?"

Patty looked worried. "I should check on him."

"Can I make us a cup of tea?" Liss said.

"It's my kitchen," Patty said. Then sighed. "Sit down. Put that awful thing in the fridge and sit down."

CHAPTER FORTY-EIGHT

The rain kicked in as Mercer drove away from the speakeasy, pissing at first, then really pelting down as the temperature dropped. He called into the station to talk to Slocum, but Bowman was the only one still on duty.

"Can I help with anything, sir?"

Bowman was the future of this place. Bowman and good cops like him. Mercer hesitated. He could have used an ally to keep things proper. But he didn't think taking a second gun along on this particular knife fight would make things any more sociable. "Keep your radio close. The roads are getting slick and we may need you."

Mercer headed back north again. Bing, bing, bing like a pinball all over the county. Just like Slocum on the first of the month, he thought, and was angry all over again. At Slocum, for plundering the county. At himself, for not figuring it out.

At people too afraid to say shit, even when they'd been fed a mouthful. And they had been. They'd been held for ransom for far too long.

Could he find Slocum's place in the dark? He'd never been there. The trees along the shoulder dipped and bent as he drove, warning him about the icy roads to come, as clearly as he'd only recently warned Sophie Ward.

On a turn, his tires slipped a bit, but he was able to right himself in time.

Now he was thinking about the Ward house. Something stank there, too. Nothing wrong with his instincts.

Gardening wouldn't be enough, would it? To shelve away whatever the Wards were going through? *Gardening*. Mercer bought his pickles from the Shoppe Well, same as anyone, didn't care for beets and dirt, which tasted the same. But if it quieted the soul of Sophie Ward—

A deer flashed across the road, through his headlights and out before he had a chance to think. He slammed on the brakes but the road decided otherwise and he went into a slide until the tires caught and the car swung around, his tail-end pointing the wrong way by almost forty-five minutes on the dial and just barely out of the rough, where a barbed-wire fence dripped in the rain. It would have either caught him or tangled him the hell up.

It was all over in an instant, the way these things happened. Mercer had a fleeting thought for those boys, Callan and his friends, just missing the quarry pond, and then, as he peered down the length of the car in the side mirror, another deer darted across the road.

No such thing as just one of those suicidal bastards.

If the surfaces were going to be slippery as all that, they were in for a hell of a night.

Mercer pivoted his car toward Slocum's house again and got moving.

He'd have been *past* Slocum's place. He'd probably been on every road in the county, give or take. He was a restless-leg kind of meat stick at the best of times and in the early days of his tenure in Parkins had driven away the hours he should have been sleeping, socializing, doing anything else at all, getting a feel for the area and the people in it. This was before he met Liss, of course. And since. Television and driving, and a drink, too often, these were his hobbies. Other guys took to hunting or kept up their target practice, he supposed. *Gardening.* Hell, he didn't know what other people did when they had gone their lives without accumulating a kid or two, someone to squeeze, membership in clubs, a golf habit. When they couldn't sit still and Liss wasn't there to put her hand on *their* knee and say enough, enough.

Enough.

So he'd been past Slocum's house, certainly, but it was tucked way up from the road in the trees. His headlights brushed at the bristling limbs either side of the smoothly paved drive, showing him those white arms of sycamores again. Gave him the creeps.

He had time to think how much a driveway like that cost before the last curve opened up. Mercer braked a little quickly.

This couldn't be Slocum's house.

The house wasn't large, exactly, but the two stories of copper-colored logs had a majestic peaked gable jutting off the front, a wraparound balcony sheltered underneath, and windows wide and tall showing off the glow of a cozy interior. Inside somewhere, probably, a nice long bar with good booze. A river-stone fireplace and a cord of wood at the ready on the other side of a red leather couch—that much Mercer could see through a window from where he sat, groaning low, under his breath. If this was Slocum's house—

How often, he'd asked Dee Booth. How much?

How many bags? How many *years*?

Was it only bad timing for Robbie Hubbard that Slocum was picking up Dee's monthly envelope that night, sliding into that speakeasy at closing time just as Hubbard needed to be rolled home? Bad timing for Hubbard and bad timing for Slocum, having to do a favor?

Or lucky timing, to give them someone to bury for Ashley's disappearance before too many questions got asked?

Nothing to do but go ask.

Mercer's cell rang as he was walking up to Slocum's door, shading his face from the stinging rain.

Liss. She was using the landline. At least she'd plugged it back in, a good sign that the harassing calls had stopped. "Liss?"

"It's me," another voice said. A young one.

"Cal? What's going on, buddy?"

Mercer realized too late that they both hated the tone he'd tried on. They both hated this version of *him*.

"My mom," Callan said. "She's been gone a while. She's not with you, is she?"

"She's not." Mercer looked at his watch. It was late. Slocum would be in bed. Any right-living citizen probably would be. He rang the bell, anyway. "She didn't tell you she was going or where?"

"She left a note but it just says to have cereal for dinner and she'd be back soon." Uncertainly, Callan added, "I ate the cereal already."

"Do you know what time you found the note?"

"Um, a while ago? Couple hours?"

Hours. It landed in his gut. The roads, already on their way to treacherous. "Her car's gone?"

"Duh, of course," Callan said. "Or I wouldn't have called you."

"That's all the note says?" Mercer said. "And you tried her cell?"

"She left it. It's sitting right here."

The car but not the phone? "Did you try your grandma's house? I bet she's there. You can't see up there from the sunroom, can you?"

"That's a good idea," the kid said. Begrudgingly.

"It's probably fine, Callan. She'll be along any minute," Mercer said. But his foot was tapping on Slocum's porch. He hit the bell again. Bing bong, like he could expect the butler any minute. "I can stop by as soon as I'm done with what I'm doing here."

"You don't need to," Callan said quickly.

"Half an hour, tops, OK?" Mercer knocked, hard, at Slocum's heavy door, poked at the bell like he meant to raise the dead. "I'll just make sure she's home before I head to bed. At my house," he added quickly. "I meant my house." He shook his head. The things that fell out of his mouth when he was trying to date or not date this kid's mom.

Callan's silence embarrassed him further.

"OK?" Mercer said. "I'll see you soon."

"OK," Callan said. That same reluctance to accept anything from him: friendship, help, his presence over the threshold of his home.

This kid, man. He'd been dealt a bad hand and only knew half of it. The luck of Link Kehoe upon him, though, and the love of Liss Kehoe. He would need every ounce. OK.

CHAPTER FORTY-NINE

As soon as Patty went to the back of the house to check on Key, Liss went over the kitchen. Behind doors, inside cabinets, in among the broom handles in the tall pantry near the back door. No sign of the baseball bat.

She'd paused in the pantry for a second glance at an assortment of pill bottles stacked at eye level. When she heard Patty coming back, she hurried to sit at the kitchen table, a little out of breath.

Patty came in with her mouth twisted with some kind of complaint, seeming to remember that Liss had been staying on only when encountering her again. "Tea," she said, and turned for the kettle.

Liss had just seen the kettle in the pantry during her search, had remembered where the mugs would be, too. Next to the makeshift pharmacy. The multitude, the variety. The bottles reminded Liss of her visit to Mim's and that sinking feeling she'd had as the county's attention had turned in her direction, that the end would come, no matter what she did. For some, more quickly than others.

Patty brought the kettle to the sink and filled it. She looked tired.

"Can I get the mugs for you?" Liss said.

"I can manage cups, Lissette," Patty said, and went back to prove it.

"I thought Key's meds were all intravenous at this point," Liss said.

Patty blinked into the pantry. "These?" she said. "Just supplements, nothing to worry about."

She brought two blue mugs out and placed them on the counter.

But Liss had seen some of the labels, even if briefly, and recognized some of the suffixes: the -zils and -mines of Key's vast regimen, anxiety -pams and -lams. A few names she'd never encountered before—not supplements. All prescribed to Key.

They would be prescriptions whose bottles had outlived Key's ability to swallow pills, but Patty would lie about even this. All to keep Liss out of her business. Out of her family.

Or maybe she was just exhausted, and Liss sat there, giving her more to do, more pretense to keep.

"*I* will be having a nighttime blend," Patty said, looking at the clock. Pointedly.

Liss glanced over. Later than she thought it was. She should have told Callan where she was going. She reached for her phone and realized she'd left it at home. "I'll have the same."

Patty nodded and went back to the pantry. It was as close to pleasing her mother-in-law as she'd come in a long time, and Liss felt an unexpected pang of grief.

"I miss this," she said.

The kettle started to roil on the stove. Patty went to fetch it. "What's that?"

"You were like a second mother to me, Patty," Liss said. "A better mother to me than my own."

Patty dropped tea bags into the mugs and poured water over them. "Your mother was trash."

If only Liss could disagree. Still, the abruptness stung. Pure Patty Kehoe, to rip the bandage off with no thought for the pain. "We could still be friends, you know," Liss said. "If you ever need anyone to talk to."

"Why would *I* need someone to talk to?"

"Key . . ." Liss began helplessly. Patty had never taken to being a public figure's wife, joining clubs, taking up tennis or cards or anything that required friends or attracted them. How would she take to being a public figure's *widow*?

A *disgraced* public figure's widow?

With Key failing, Patty had chosen isolation, superiority. It wouldn't wear well when the news came out. She'd chosen to engage only with her son, to rely on him and make him the central figure of her—

Liss's breath caught. Patty looked over.

The central figure of her entire life.

Was there no way to manage it? To give everything—without emptying out?

"Key being ill," Liss said finally. "It must be difficult for you."

"That's what marriage is, Lissette," Patty said. "Standing by each other even in *difficulty*."

Was there any way to soften the landing for any of them? Patty could cut her losses, place Key in a facility, start proceedings to sell this monstrous house. Go on a cruise. See the world. Surely Patty had wanted something for herself before she'd married into Kehoe's legacy-in-progress, before the roll of the genetic dice transformed her into his nursemaid.

"Difficulty doesn't cover it," Liss said, looking over at the mugs. The tea would be oversteeped and bitter. "For better or worse doesn't cover all the thoughtless ways married people can harm each other."

Patty's eyes lifted from the mugs.

Liss hadn't been thinking of Link, exactly, but now she lifted her chin.

"Are you going to tell me something unspeakable about my

son?" Patty said. "I warn you." But she didn't. She went back to the pantry and dug around one of the shelves. When she came back, she had a packet of cookies, nothing Liss would have chosen, and threw them on the counter between them. She went to the steeping mugs, her back turned to Liss, stiff. "I'm a tired woman, Lissette, so think carefully before you proceed."

Liss took a deep breath and let it out. "He slept with another woman," she said. "Fifteen years ago."

Patty went still, then recovered and reached for a spoon on the counter and pulled out tea bags, thump, thump, tossing them into the sink. "Milk? Lemon?"

Just two ladies at tea.

She knew.

Patty knew all about Link's straying. Liss could tell by the set of her shoulders that she knew and already had a firm position. It would be *Liss's* fault. How could it be any other way?

"*Milk?*" Patty said. "Honey?"

"What?" Liss said. "No, thank you." She didn't even want the tea anymore. She had only meant to reconnect, so that when Patty learned about *her* husband's failings, she had someone to rely on. "I should go—"

"Sit down, Lissette." Patty kept her back to her, stirring.

Liss sat down. She was the one who had started the conversation at—she reached for her phone automatically then looked toward the wall clock—too late o'clock.

The tea had to be tepid now but Patty kept stirring in silence.

Finally she turned and carried the mugs to the table. "Fifteen years ago. When did *you* come by this information?"

"Only recently." Liss took a sip of the tea. As she'd thought—brackish and not hot enough. Cool enough to gulp, at least. She was in a hurry now, in case Callan had noticed she was gone.

"It's not a contest, Lissette," Patty said. "Slow down and tell me how you came to know about it? Who told *you*?"

"The horse's mouth," Liss said.

Patty stared at her. "What do you mean?"

"He fessed up to it," Liss said. She tipped back the tea again. Maybe Callan had gone to bed already. She hoped. "Only after *she* finally did, though, and I guess we all have to be glad she did."

The last sip of tea seemed thick, though she'd asked for no honey.

Patty watched the mug of tea as it traveled between Liss's mouth and the table. "Glad?" Patty said.

"Or he'd still be without an alibi," Liss said. "So, yeah, of course I knew there was some funny business. You have to know the separation wasn't what I *wanted*." What a project you'd taken on, Link had said. And he had been. What a fucking project. Or was she too controlling? She didn't want to be. Other people got to be carefree because they had people to rely on. It was something she had never achieved. "But he'd already broken his promise to me, like, ten minutes into the marriage."

"Fifteen years ago," Patty said.

"But my point—" Her thoughts slipped off track. What had she been saying?

She was exhausted. Maybe she shouldn't have opted for the sleepy tea when she was already tired.

"My point was that you might feel differently," Liss said. Her tongue felt weird. "You might feel differently about the sanctity of marriage being *absolute* if . . . if something similar had happened to you." She could barely get through it.

"Would I? You would know precisely what I should feel?"

Someday soon . . .

Liss felt strange, suddenly, as though she watched the scene from high above, looking down. She was a little nauseated. When had she last eaten? She looked toward the fridge, where the tamale pie had been put away.

"I—"

"*You* would know how I should feel about *my* marriage?" Patty thundered.

Liss reached for the cookies—GimmeGimme brand, of course, past their date—but couldn't seem to get the wrapping open. But now she didn't want them. She was hot and her head swam. "Patty," she said. "I don't feel so well."

Her elbow knocked into her mug. It hit the floor and shattered.

There was a noise at the back of the house. The night nurse would emerge soon to wonder at the noise, and Liss found herself wishing she would hurry.

She'd be sick.

"I'm sorry—I think I'm not—"

She needed air.

Could she make it across the room? Liss stood. The back door wavered. The room—

"You don't know what I've endured," Patty said. "The shit I've swallowed, Lissette. The secrets I've kept. And *you* wouldn't want to know them, let me assure you."

She knew, Liss realized. She hadn't known about Link's transgression, but she knew about Key's, and Callan. She knew—

Liss sank to her knees and the room collapsed toward her.

She knew and—

MY BREATH IS RAGGED, AS SLOCUM LOOMS OVER ME. AN OLD man in his bed. Hardly a man at all.

The threat of Slocum unplugging the machinery still hangs in the air. The truth is, nothing will happen if he does. The room will grow quiet, then something will start to ping or beep, and Patty will come running, but I'll hang on. I'll live.

Starting to think I'll goddamn live forever. That this is my punishment, to sit by as those around me suffer. Mute, tied down, forgotten.

Except by Slocum. "Nah," he says. The rank tang of citrus billows over me. "No need to bother with you, is there? You're getting to the end just fine on your own."

When he backs up, he knocks something off the nightstand, boom, and we both seem to snap out of a shared trance he's taken us to, snake charmer and snake. I fall back, inside, exhausted but more wary than I had been. Slocum—why is he *here*?

There are footsteps coming and then Patty's in the doorway. "Can you keep *quiet*?" she hisses at Slocum. "Hard to explain how a man who can't move is knocking things over."

"What's the harm?" Slocum says. "Tell her I'm back here visiting with Key."

"I'd rather not," she says.

"You'd rather sometimes," he says.

"Ron."

The use of the first name catches me, but I know all Patty's ways, all her tones and expressions and sounds and she'd rather Slocum went to hell. How's that, Ron? The lady would rather you fuck off.

"You'd rather," Slocum says. "Tell me how much you'd rather."

Patty looks my way, in the eye. She's the only one who seems to know I'm still in here. Fully just who I've always been.

"Not in front of Key, Ronald."

"In front of Key is exactly what I want, Patricia. I should have thought of it before now." He presses his fingers down on my bed, testing the mattress.

Did he just suggest—

"I need to get back to the kitchen," Patty says.

"Get rid of her."

"I will," Patty says.

Why's Slocum calling the shots in my house? To my wife?

When she's gone, Slocum paces back and forth at the foot of my bed, scattering orange peel and spitting seeds and shedding impatient noises and his dandruff up and down the room. "You really put me in a spot, Key," he says.

Me? I'm still stuck back at the point where it really and truly seemed like Slocum was suggesting he fuck my wife on my retract-a-sleeper homecare bed, right at my feet.

Like he'd already plowed that ground.

But that can't be. He's disgusting. She's disgusted by him, anyone can see. But she's taking orders like she's on a menu.

He's got something on her, that's all there is to it.

Christ, probably something I did. Some damn thing I did he knows about and she doesn't want it spread to Kingdom Come. Something he knows about—

That he told her.

I sit with that a spell. Something they both know, that puts her in his power.

But it could only be for one thing, one secret, that she would suffer *Slocum's* greasy touch.

One indiscretion, one sly little whore, and I have subjected my wife to this? My family? My career, my legacy?

"Mother," I say. "Fucker." Barely a rasp.

Slocum stops in his tracks, looks my way, and starts laughing. "You in there, Key?" he says. Throws the last of his orange into his maw and chomps. Then he gulps and takes the edge of the blanket from my bed and wipes his mouth.

"Good," he says. "Because I want you to know precisely the wreckage—"

There's a crash and then a heavy thump in the other room and then Patty's calling for Slocum.

"What the hell did she do this time?" he mutters.

He's gone. I'm left with the burning citrus in my nose, in my throat, a headache forming, and white-hot rage. Why doesn't she just let the dominoes fall? Why doesn't she let Slocum go off and try to sell the scandal?

Not to protect the kid. She's doing it for Link. For my legacy, when people probably know more than she suspects. I was always surprised Patty herself didn't somehow catch the scent—

And then I know. I know. I know.

I know how I killed Ashley Hay, even though I didn't. I know.

CHAPTER FIFTY

Mercer couldn't raise Slocum to his door. He stood under the protection of the porch and looked out at the rain. It ran in rivulets down the drive. There would be flooding along the ditches and creeks, across low points in the roads. The air had dropped a good ten degrees since he'd got in the car at the speakeasy.

And here he was, freezing his ass off while Slocum slept in his bed.

If this were his house, Mercer would be on that leather couch sipping something that burned all the way down. He would have that fireplace blazing.

His mind drifted away, to Liss.

Was she out in this? Why was she out in this?

He dodged raindrops back to his car. From the driver's seat, his view of Slocum's house was again overwhelming and nonsensical. Years, he must have been running his scam. But how? Who would be scared of a jelly-filled doughnut like—

"Oh, shit."

Mercer struck the steering wheel and started up the car.

Key was the one who went up to see Tidewell that night. Not answering a call for an accident—creating one.

How had he never wondered where *Key's* money had come

from? The land, the quarry purchased back. That creeper of a ranch they'd built, like Stephen King had a sideline in architecture.

Slocum was no ringleader, no idea man. He was the backup, he was the guy you left for watch out. The bag man, while the real threat lay beyond sight, like the shark until halfway through the damn movie. If you were late on a payment, say, you might get a visit, the distress brought right to your door.

Key was the dirty heart of it, wringing cash out of his constituents for protection against himself.

Mercer took the drive away from Slocum's house a little faster than he should, the back wheels sliding on a curve but righting themselves.

And his cronies would have been learning at his knee to carry on without him. Slocum would have known it all, including what Key got up to after hours. Key would have needed a right-hand slimeball to cover for him if Patty called the station, to nudge him left, right, and center when he was showing his ass, the way Deak watched out for Mercer around Liss.

Holding down the shop, Slocum had said.

And he'd been doing that, all right, but not as a house mouse in the station, the way he let on. He'd been going around and picking up bags, as regular as punching a clock. Or, not regular, not that night. Late, Dee had said. Closing time. He had a few unaccounted hours.

But why? Was he such a frothing adherent to the Church of Kehoe Senior that he would knock a girl in the head for him? Had Kehoe asked him to do this? How would Slocum have had the chance to grab Ashley?

OK. Go over it again.

Ashley would have been tearing up the road in her fast little ride. In a real hurry—

Why did he think that?

Mercer searched his memory. He would need to talk to Liss again. Liss—surely she'd be home by now?

His tires slipped. He slowed down, then sped up again.

He needed his notes. Ashley had said something ridiculous to Liss, some dull knife, jabbing at her. Some sweet word—

Cupcake. Time is money, cupcake.

But was she truly short of time? Or was the operative word *money*?

Ashley wouldn't have been going far at all when she left Liss's house. She would have been going to Key's, for cash.

Is *Daddy* home?

Key would have been waiting for that shoe to drop. But Key wasn't home.

He couldn't quite see how it fit together. Then he did. Saw Slocum strolling through the Kehoes' kitchen with familiarity, plucking a piece of fruit from the bowl like he owned the place.

Maybe he did. Maybe Slocum had seized the moment to be owed.

Maybe he—

It crashed on him all at once, where Slocum would be if not at home, where Liss had gone, expecting to be gone just a minute, the open void of his life if something happened to her and he had to put Slocum in that pond himself and also the white-tailed deer that dashed into the road and put its ten- or twelve-point rack—he noted this almost calmly, a flash of empathy and understanding that his dad would be pleased he'd finally bagged one—right up against his hood and through his windshield.

All his defensive driving flew out the window.

He swerved to avoid the beast and instead drove blind into a patch of ice that lifted all four tires off the ground at once, sending his car spinning across the road and nose down into the drainage culvert that had begun to rage with rainwater. All at once, everything and nothing.

CHAPTER FIFTY-ONE

Liss rose out of nothingness slowly, becoming aware that someone was standing over her. A black boot, planted within her vision.

She closed her eyes.

Mercer. She knew that boot, standard issue and kicked off at the foot of her bed.

Someone was in charge. Not her.

She sank back into oblivion.

When she woke next, her mouth was thick, coated. Next to her face, a puddle of vomit. She had enough sense of herself to be embarrassed, to think of the stories Patty would tell, how Link would hear. Callan would—

Callan.

A footstep behind her. The boot again, probably two of them.

"Merce." She could only manage one sound at a time. "Er."

She could hear someone above, breathing.

Something was wrong.

She tried to remember. The Kehoe kitchen. Patty. She'd been telling Patty about Link's betrayal and then—

No. She'd been trying to tell Patty about Link but the wires were crossed and Patty had thought she meant Key.

Patty knew. She knew about Key and Ashley, about Callan. She *knew*.

And had done nothing?

Had accepted it as fate?

Liss blinked at the mess on the floor. The shit I've swallowed, Patty had said.

But Patty Kehoe did not *accept*.

She didn't play tennis or golf or tic-tac-toe with the child her husband had fathered with another woman.

She played the long game. She played games only when she could win.

The boot had returned. "Mercer," Liss said. Her mouth was so dry.

"Nope," a man said, in a voice shaped by a grin.

"Up you go," Slocum was saying, but Liss was lost between these words and a rushing black velvet, which flew upon her and whisked her away.

". . . GOING TO NEED a younger body man to keep up this hobby," a man's voice was saying. Liss's stomach hurt. Someone's shoulder dug into it.

The rest of her flopped at a back, soft and black and sweaty-damp. Liss bucked violently—

"Fuck it," Slocum said and let her fall to the ground.

Liss curled into herself, mud and hip and pain, and heard sounds she was surprised to realize were her own.

Outlined in the doorway, light, a beacon. Patty.

"Patty," Liss said, reaching through the rain.

"Ron," Patty said.

"I'm trying," Slocum said, puffing. "It's pouring out, if you haven't noticed. She's slippery. Not to mention I'm fifteen years older. And she's far less dead."

"You're the one who insisted the baseball bat be destroyed," Patty said.

Patty. Liss reached across the mud for the gravel.

"It had her blood on it," Slocum said. "And your fingerprints," he added, under his breath. He groped under Liss's arms, copping a handsy feel. "Upsy daisy," he said.

Liss tasted the salt of sweat from his brow and kicked and fought. But he hadn't meant to lift her, only to drag her across the drive. She dug in her heels.

"You're leaving a *mess*," Patty said.

"Get the rake," Slocum gasped. "Something you can surely manage."

"I need to check on Rock," Patty said.

Liss was loose, all joints, a puddle. Slocum had dropped her again.

"He's fine," he said. "Not going anywhere. Except prison, all of us, if you don't hide those drag marks."

Liss reached and pulled at the gravel, clawed over onto her belly.

"As soon as she's gone, then," Patty said.

Gone.

Gone. She was screaming—

Slocum gripped her shoulders, hard, and blew citrus breath into her face, his lips wet. "If you don't shut up," he said, "I'll go down to your house and make sure your kid joins you."

Callan—

"Leave the boy out of it," Patty said, and Liss felt a rush of relief. They wouldn't, they couldn't. This couldn't be happening. It was a mistake. All a mistake.

"Changing your mind about the homemaking arts, huh, Grandma?" Slocum said. "You could make *me* cookies."

"I won't see my son destroyed," Patty sniffed, looking down at Liss. "But he'll bounce back from this tragic, *tragic* loss."

She was rehearsing.

"Patty—"

"But to lose his *son*." Patty cast her gaze down toward the other house. "No, I don't suppose there's any way to make it happen. That little slut strapped that child to me like a terrorist."

Slocum snorted. "Suicide bomber. Except without the suicide."

"Patty, please—"

"Stop dicking around, Ron, and get her in the car."

His hands in her armpits again. "I don't think it's a good idea—"

"I didn't ask your opinion."

Liss got her feet under her and then was off them again, a sack of worthless blood and bones, thrown into the front seat of her own car. "At least a different body of water," he said. "Or let me drop this car somewhere a few counties over—"

"We don't have the time. Cover your tracks."

"*Patty*," Liss pleaded.

"Gee, never would have thought of that," Slocum said, slamming the door.

Liss dove across, but he met her there and closed himself in alongside her. "You should know," he said, hitting the locks as she turned for the door behind her. "As soon as you're tucked away, I'm going down to your house, anyway. Your kid has my insurance policy."

"You stay away from him," she hissed. "I'll . . ."

But there was nothing she could threaten. Over Slocum's shoulder, Patty was gone. The door to the house, closed.

"If you cooperate, I'll just take what I need," Slocum said. "But if you don't . . . Link will still love a son with brain damage, right?"

Liss buried herself into the driver's door. Slocum slid up and spilled over the central console, a mound of flesh but also strength, and turned the key.

"I'd have used Key's Bel Air, nice bench seat," he said. "But what'd'ya gonna do? She wants to keep it for romantic drives."

The car roared to life and only then did Liss realize he'd put her in the driver's seat.

CHAPTER FIFTY-TWO

Mercer was a tangle, trapped in wet bedsheets, swimming among the tentacles of a giant sea creature, twenty thousand leagues under the sea and cold as hell.

He opened his eyes to a headache and a fantasy world, moss and creek and fern.

A white-tail buck's antlers poked like branches of an old growth tree through his vision. He reached up to make sure he wasn't imagining it.

The animal twitched and moaned and started to kick, but it was tangled in with the steering wheel and Mercer. Antlers dug at him—

Mercer's mind dove away.

When he came to, he was surprised all over again. The deer was moaning, or he was. Or both.

He tested out his limbs. His left arm wanted to stay where it was but he was right-handed. The fingers of his right hand grasped, expanded. It took all his strength to exert the effort.

He rested, gathering himself, then tried to bend a knee. He heard the splash of an unexpected body of water.

Past the buck in the windshield, Mercer felt rain still coming down, open air somewhere within reach. OK OK, he hadn't gone into deep water. It was just run-off, a heavy downpour using his patrol car as a byway.

He unbuckled his seat belt but the clasp sat dead in his lap. The electronics of the car were out. The radio, out.

The radio at his belt, if he could reach it, might have battery power.

Mercer focused all his will to dip his head into his chest to find his radio and discovered that the longest point on the buck's rack had punctured his left arm. He stared at it, trying to make sense.

Pinioned by a fucking deer. Somewhere in heaven or hell, his dad was laughing his ass off and there, in the car, in a pickle, Mercer started to laugh, too. They were in the joke together, the old man and him, as the water rose to his knees.

CHAPTER FIFTY-THREE

Insurance policy.

She needed one. Liss's mind scrabbled like a rat in a trap.

"This is not a good idea," Slocum was mumbling to himself. "Going to the same well again."

The same well.

They couldn't think—

They couldn't get away with putting her in the quarry.

But one of them *didn't* think they would get away with it.

"Patty," Liss said, her tongue still thick and clumsy around words. "She's the boss."

"She's the boss," Slocum said. But laughing.

He didn't think so. He thought he was smarter than all of them. Than Patty, than Mercer. Certainly smarter than her, subduing her with promises against Callan. He had an insurance policy and he thought it was in her house.

"You want the bat," she said.

He glanced nervously her way and guided the car around the back of the house. To the woods?

Maybe he wouldn't do what Patty had instructed. Maybe he had something far worse in mind. He was armed, after all.

"Never mind what I want," he said.

"You *need* it."

"Shut up."

"But you didn't find it," she ventured.

Slocum's jaw clenched as he peered through the rain.

"You went to find the bat that night," she said. "You came to look for it at the quarry after everyone finished up."

"I put a lot of effort into keeping that thing dry and exactly where I could get my hands on it," he said.

"Patty thinks you destroyed it," Liss said. "Why didn't you?"

"Because if it came down to it, she's the one who swung the blow, and I had the proof," he said.

Your fingerprints, he'd said.

Patty. Patty had killed Ashley.

"But I wasn't going to store it at my house, was I?" he said.

"You broke into my house looking for it. But you didn't find it."

"I didn't break into your house," he said.

He was right. She'd just seen him at the side of the road when she'd spotted the light where it shouldn't have been. Slocum couldn't have been the one snooping around her house. Who—

"But you're telling me what I need to know," he said. "I bet your kid can lay his hands on it."

"I can get it for you," she said. "Callan doesn't know where it is. You should take Key's car and the bat and get away from her—"

"And what?" he snorted. "Ride off into the sunset and start all over again? At my age? Give up my house and . . . and all the leverage I have?" His breath was coming heavy. "Leverage instead of a life. *Fucking* Kehoes. I was a human being before they got to me. I wanted—"

What he had once wanted was lost, a choke in his throat. He had stopped the car, his foot clumsy in the stretch for the brakes. He set the car's gear in park, turned off the car.

"You don't have to do this," Liss said.

The lull between them stretched until she thought he might agree and then—

"I do, though," Slocum said. "It's slippery."

Liss looked out the rainy windshield. Slippery? Would he let her go?

They sat at the top of a sharp grade from the woods. Down below lay a dark blank that could only be the pond.

Slocum reached for her wrists and began to bind them with long rags. He hadn't meant the ground would be slippery. He'd meant the first compromise, the first mistake. It was a slippery slope and a long way down.

CHAPTER FIFTY-FOUR

Fucking electric-everything cars, Mercer thought. A few drops of water and nothing works.

The seat wouldn't go back, the door wouldn't unlock, the window wouldn't roll down. All that joking around with his dad had cost him too much time, and the car had shifted so that he knew he hadn't yet reached the bottom of the ditch or the worst of his problems.

The deer bucked and jabbed its antler deeper into his arm, and *fuck* that hurt.

OK, OK, there was something he could do about that to end his pain and the deer's. He stretched the agonizing inches to the safety on his sidearm, splashing around in a puddle near his waist that hadn't been there but now, distressingly, was.

He palmed the gun carefully, hands wet. If he dropped it now, he might die here.

The angle was strange and tangled, worse than any quartering-away shot his dad could have tried to prepare him for. But the damned animal probably only needed an excuse to die.

Mercer aimed, worried over it to make sure he couldn't strike himself—he wasn't as far gone as that, Dad—and covered his face against the blood.

The shot was tremendous in close quarters. His ears rang and the air stank of nitro and burn and blood. He dropped his elbow and watched the deer go still.

Mercer closed his eyes. OK.

But he couldn't stay here. Something—

He couldn't remember what he was supposed to be doing, where he had been going in such an infernal hurry.

Liss.

Her face wafted up as though from the water. He'd been going to Liss. Where he belonged.

Mercer looked down at where the buck's antler still stuck into his arm. That? Was going to hurt.

His radio crackled at his hip and a voice sought him out. If he waited much longer, he and that voice would drown together.

He grasped at a sturdy section of antler.

It was like bone. Was it bone?

He gripped, took a deep breath. Beyond the deer, heavy clouds and Liss and life. Beyond the deer was everything.

And pushed.

Beyond pain lay another world he had never been to. He went there, dazzled by stars that were not stars and lights that were not lights but then his eyes were open and they were. They were lights and someone was calling down from the road.

"Officer? Officer?"

All he could do was groan.

"Marshal, is that you?" A man with an umbrella, backlit by the blinding headlights of his car. "I didn't know—I was at home and I thought I heard a gunshot."

The voice at his hip crackled.

That fucking deer had nearly killed him, but it would also save him.

"I need a tourniquet," Mercer said.

"Oh." The man on the road patted at his pockets uncertainly.

Mercer climbed out of his car to the hood, one knee, then on his feet above the water rushing to fill the cavity he had just left behind, boots on either side of his kill—he felt like both a monster and a god.

The man with the umbrella reared back at the sight of the gun in his hand.

"No, I mean," Mercer said. "I *have* a tourniquet." Standard issue. Was he still wearing his duty belt? He was. He holstered his gun, secured it. "*And* I need help putting it on. Pull me up."

CHAPTER FIFTY-FIVE

Wrists and ankles, tight and tethered. The car stank of Slocum's sweat and Liss's animal panic. The windows steamed.

"This isn't going to look like—"

And then a rag, stuffed in her mouth.

An accident, she'd tried to say.

"If they find you," Slocum said. "Took them fifteen years last time and, anyway, I wouldn't worry about it, if I were you. Sure glad I'm not."

The binds were cotton and would decay, dissolve. As would she.

Liss tried to scream and then something flew at her face and struck her in the cheek with such force that she cracked her head against the window.

"That's for sticking your nose in," he panted.

She lay moaning against the door.

"You'd think you'd know all about the weaponry I'm carrying," Slocum said. "Mercer never did nasty things to you with his duty flashlight? Standard issue, always packing. He's not that inventive a guy?"

He was wearing gloves. Her blood had spattered on one of them.

She tried to beg through the gag. Please.

He moved her into place like a side of beef, another fabric tie, this time to the steering column. He pulled out a last cloth and wiped surfaces, muttering to himself. "Faster ways . . ." he said. ". . . like to see *her*."

He paused, looking around. Shook his head.

Please. She begged with her eyes. *He* had not killed anyone before now. He didn't want to. He had the proof. She was able to make a mewling sound.

He slipped the flashlight out again, a fluid movement from his belt and across his body like a backhand serve until—

It slammed across her face. She cried out through the gag and shrank away, but he reared back and flung it at her again and again until she knew only his heavy breathing and the pain, and that he wasn't even thinking of her anymore, only his rage, only the things Patty had made him do. She waited for the final blow, heard the air split as he raised the flashlight a last time and the breeze of it as it flew toward her.

It never landed but slipped past, grazing her cheek and tumbling over her shoulder and somewhere behind her.

Blood was slippery, too.

He swore and reached toward her. She flinched away.

But he was grasping the gear shift, making sure it was set in park. Then he was backing out of the front seat with some effort, leaving her, pulp, eyes blind with blood, in the driver's seat.

Liss caught a whiff of fresh air and freedom through the open door. Out there was life and Callan and every hope.

Liss pried open her eyes.

The flashlight. Standard issue. He would have to retrieve it.

The back door wrenched open with a creak that sliced the night and silenced the noises of the woods. Through blood and the steamy windshield, a lightning strike lit the mound, the boulders left behind like ruins of old. Her house—

The car rocked heavily as Slocum crawled into the back.

The lights of her house veered as the car dipped under Slocum's weight. Callan's window, the deck, the back door wide, everything lit up like a carnival, the brightest hope and direst heartbreak, a horizon she would never reach.

Slocum fumbled in the dark of the back seat. "Where the *fuck* did it go?"

Liss stretched the limits of her binds, reached until blood to her fingers cut off and they were white and complaining and going numb.

And put the car into neutral.

"What was that?" Slocum said from deep behind her seat.

Nothing happened. She fell back, spent, and stared down the slope at the lights of her house. Callan. Blood rushed into her hands. She flexed her fingers, in, out.

Behind her, Slocum mumbled and swore and threw his weight around.

"Aha," Slocum said. The flashlight would be wedged somewhere inconvenient. She could feel him extending, stretching, digging just a little further. His frustration was a scent: salt and sweat and hot fury. He flopped against the back of her seat and kicked the door wide with his boot.

And then they were rolling, just a bit, slowly.

Slocum made a noise of surprise and shifted, then they were moving faster, and he was thrown off balance into the back of her seat, all cursing and limbs. They were bumping along, quickly and inevitably and down toward nothing, the curses turning to cries of alarm behind her and ahead of her only the black water rushing up and accepting her, swallowing her whole.

CHAPTER FIFTY-SIX

The guy with the umbrella hadn't wanted to drive Mercer any-where, and if he had to, if by law he was required to turn over his car or chauffeur Mercer someplace in this disastrous weather, then it was the hospital, not someone's house, surely.

But the Kehoe place was closer than the hospital.

"Well, I don't know," the man said.

Finally, Mercer thought, we're speaking the same language. He didn't know, either.

Mercer's phone made a sad little sound but he couldn't pick up the call. It would need every grain of dry rice in the local Shoppe Well if he had any hope to dry it out, and he guessed even that wouldn't work. He'd been able to radio for help, striking Bowman somehow still at the station, bless that eager shit's heart or the ice storm that had convinced him to spend the night in lockup, answering calls.

But Mercer was still nervous. Was Liss in danger? Maybe she'd come home and tucked Callan into bed.

Mercer tried not to tap his foot as they inched their way over the back channels of gravel. Gravel not likely to slick over like a paved road, he might have gone a *little* faster.

"What *happened*?" the driver said.

Mercer put it to mild shock that his first inclination was to explain what Slocum had done to Ashley Hay and why.

Then he realized what the guy was asking. Mercer was covered in blood, his own and otherwise, and had been fished out of an overflowing drainage ditch. A full day.

"Ah," Mercer said. "Swerved to miss Bambi, rookie error."

"You'll have plenty of paperwork to do."

It was an election year, so he didn't swear. "Sir, could you hurry even just a little bit faster?"

CHAPTER FIFTY-SEVEN

Liss was only aware of confusion, up was down, down was nowhere. She was on the ceiling, she was against the floorboard, Slocum's heft thrown against her seat and away, her wrists straining against the tether to the steering column, her chin smashed against the steering wheel.

Impact.

As things righted themselves, as the nose of the car dipped into the water and drank, she was aware of the cough of her panicked breath through the gag, of Slocum scrambling out of the open door behind—above—and then water, nothing but water.

She took a last breath and then another last breath. Water filled in around her and soaked her through and what was she holding her breath for but the delay of the inevitable?

Last breath.

She felt her body start to lift in the water, the weight and tug easing on the binds on her wrists and then the fabric of the binds giving grace. She scrabbled out of her tangled position into the seat, higher ground.

Last breath.

Last breath.

The binds were wet, her hands, and then her chest and neck and the pocket of air left was thin—

Last breath.

And it was. She was in water, of water, and she hadn't saved Callan at all, only slowed Slocum down a slim minute at best and drenched him, soaked him through, a baptism that could never clean his burnt soul.

She struggled at the binds, her lungs starting to complain.

And she would still die as Ashley had.

Far less dead and she hadn't used it to her advantage, hadn't—

The heel of one of her hands had pulled through the binding.

In the water, the fabric had given—not much.

Enough.

Enough. She pulled until her hands lost feeling.

CHAPTER FIFTY-EIGHT

They crossed the county at a pace that made Mercer crazy, making a full and complete stop for every sign and crossing—even when he promised to God he wouldn't cite the guy with the umbrella for robbing a *bank* at this point. In his car, he would have had the overheads rolling, lit up like Christmastime.

Finally they drew near the Kehoe compound. Mercer calculated the odds. The old house, mom and pop's place, the site of who knew what already? Or Liss's place, where maybe she was safe and sound, amen and good night?

But he didn't have to make the choice because he caught movement out at the pond, just a flash of something dark against the hill. "There," he said. "Go there. Fuck, can you—just stop the car."

Mercer sprang from the car while it was still rolling and slid down the road toward the curve, running, his breath in puffs, the rain in his eyes, just in time to see . . . was it Callan? What was he doing?

Callan Kehoe, soaked to the bone, held a baseball bat high above his head.

"Stop!"

Was it Callan? He seemed bigger than Mercer remembered. Older. Some poor asshole was groveling on the ground at his feet.

"Callan!"

Two faces turned his way, Callan and Slocum, and then Callan was swinging for the bleachers.

No, he was throwing the bat aside and running, but away.

"Callan!"

What was happening?

Slocum was belly-dragging toward the bat when Mercer stepped on it, pressing it into the mud and catching Slocum's fingers at the taper. Just at the sweet spot.

"Ow, hey."

Mercer reached for his cuffs and stepped off the bat to make use of them. "Did that hurt? You have the right not to get your teeth knocked out when that kid comes back, and I'll get to the rest of your rights in just a second."

By the book, that was him.

Slocum was soaked to the bone, but then they both were by now. Mercer stood to look for the kid.

Callan was at the edge of the quarry—no. He was leaping, a flash of movement at the edge of the quarry and then in the air. "Callan!"

Liss would kill them both if that kid hit a sharp edge. Was he not wet enough in this rain? Why would he go into the pond in this weather?

In the dark, Mercer could barely make him out in the water. The kid was slicing across the black expanse in long, stretching strokes, and then—

Gone.

CHAPTER FIFTY-NINE

The binds finally scrape over the heels of her hands.

Her fingers are strangled and dulled and plucking furiously at the ankle restraints and then she is not aware of her fingers or herself, only her lungs bursting. The restraints fall away. Then she is pulling with her arms, weak, weakened, out of the slack door of the car and kicking.

The car, sloughed off like skin, and she is new.

She swims, rises, her arms stretching, pulling, flailing, struggling.

Then they seem to hang and float in front of her until they are strange and foreign.

Her last thought should be—

Callan.

Placed in her arms, dark night, rain. Ashley, I have kept him safe.

A hand dives at her, God reaching down to claim her.

Their arms are entwined, hers and Ashley's, lifting their boy together.

Liss cradles him as she is held, encircled in the arms of the end and the ever after and a stillness and it is all she has ever wanted.

CHAPTER SIXTY

Mercer hesitated at the edge of the quarry, the wind lashing at him. He shaded his eyes from the pelting rain. The rain ran cold inside the neck of his jacket and down his back.

Lightning lit up the sky and—

Callan was really gone. She would never forgive him, never, if he just stood here while her kid drowned.

"What did you do, Slocum?" Mercer shouted back at him. The worm was groveling in the mud, actually crying.

"Nothing I wanted to," Slocum said. "I never wanted it!"

"What did you *do*?"

Then out in the blackness, Callan broke the surface, flailing and fluttering like a drowning man, and that was all Mercer needed. He dropped his duty belt, took a last look at the sharp corners of the stone below, and jumped wide.

People broke their necks jumping into quarries, he had time to think, and then he hit the shocking cold of the water and started fighting to the surface again. He was stroking the pond's surface blindly in the direction he'd last seen Callan and wishing he'd dropped his boots on the rim, too, when he realized Callan's wild side crawl and splash technique wasn't the kid drowning. He was tugboating something behind him.

Someone.

Liss—

"Help!" Callan shouted, half-gagging on a mouthful of water. "Mercer, my mom!"

Mercer's mind went blank and he was a man racing toward the alarm, toward the source of gunfire, into the center of his own heart, oaths made without words and promises, if, if, if only. His arms stretched further. His legs kicked faster. The silence of the water when he dove after each Olympian-sized breath was a lie, a lullaby he would not fall for. He stretched out from himself in every sense, hoping for the sound of her voice.

When he reached them, Liss was not moving, not fighting as drowning people do. He wrenched her from Callan's grip. "Can you swim, son?"

"My mom," Callan sobbed. His mouth dipped below the surface. He came up coughing. "We have to—"

The kid could swim if he'd stop trying to drown.

"I've got her, OK? OK, Callan?"

"OK."

"But you need to swim on your own, buddy." He couldn't leave the kid. Liss would skin him alive. When she woke up. When she opened her eyes. If, if only. "Can you do that? Come on, help me bring your mom in. We'll do it together. That's it."

Mercer towed them both with a one-armed crawl and a long, unbroken prayer of words and encouragement, no idea what he was saying to the kid, nothing but incoherence and the creaking of his pre-broken heart for how limply Liss hung in the water against him. All he could do was keep her head above water.

The wall of the quarry was too high. They'd never make it. She'd never make it.

"Callan, you ever climbed out of this hole before?"

The kid's teeth were chattering.

"I won't tell your mom," Mercer said.

Callan paddled to right and then he was climbing onto a ledge of stone, the water suddenly only up to his shins. Mercer pushed Liss up onto the shelf and crawled up behind.

"OK, buddy, now where?"

Another stone to grip, a foothold. Mercer put Liss on his shoulder and clambered out of the chasm, following Callan's every move to the letter. At the rim, Callan reached back and helped Mercer over.

Mercer lay Liss upon the stone and both of them were on their knees before her. He was shouting at her and pounding at her chest and turning her and whacking at her back, compressing and breathing into her, against current protocols, fuck it, just to have her mouth against his, to have his warmth against her skin.

The seconds ticked by and the rain pelted but he would not say good-bye, not ever again.

Your kid—Mercer had started to say these things aloud—your kid needs you here. Your kid, your son, and me, too.

He had gone all the way down the dark place, so far down that when she gagged and coughed lungs' worth of water and scraped her fingers across the rock and mud, Mercer wondered if he had died, too, and gone where such things were possible but no, there she is. Hacking, wet, and reaching for Callan.

Mercer sat back on his heels and lifted his face to the rain.

WHEN THE SIRENS ARE STILL A FAR-OFF TUNELESS WHISTLE, Patty comes to the room, to the window and away.

I've never seen her this worked up.

She's taken my decline in stride, the aides' mistakes, the visits from people she never wanted to entertain. She's taken it all on the chin but whatever she sees at the window has her worried. She can't sit still, paces the room but in a scurrying way, not like Slocum and his orange peel, not like the mistress of this house. She paces like each corner of the room might hold the answer, then doesn't.

She races from the room at one point.

I doze.

Or maybe I don't, maybe she's back just that quickly and she has a cup, full, sloshing it in her hand. It's dark, like when she used to forget she'd made a cup of tea and I'd find it the next day, a dark rim marking high tide.

Never drank the stuff.

But there's something more settled about her now, at least. Whatever was happening at the window must have been a false alarm.

Except the sirens still keen, whirl, and dip on the wind, under the patter of a hard rain and shitty sleet, against the windows.

Except that Patty's eyes are shining.

Darling, she says. It's time.

We've had our time. My time. I know what she means. She grips the mug with white knuckles.

She moves out of my vision and hits a few buttons on the machine.

Slocum and his threat to unplug me. He didn't know the true damage that could be done was the opposite, to flood my veins with whatever's on tap. Patty hits a few more buttons, up, up, up on this bag, up, up, up on that one. Maybe between the morphine drip and the other, it will be enough. It's no guarantee.

I want to thank her. I want to kiss her and hold her and beg her forgiveness.

She crawls into the bed alongside me. There's barely room. She's not done this since the hospice brought the narrow, retractable bed, a one-man dinghy that would rescue no one. I can't help the gasp of breath she squeezes from me with an accidental elbow.

She nestles in and rests the cup on her chest, settles against me, a second skin.

The machines start to alarm—they aren't built to let so much loose at once, but Patty doesn't rise to quiet them.

There's no single moment when I know that she has taken fistfuls of something in the kitchen, when I know she has left me behind, that she has abandoned me to suffer this, too. The moment comes upon me like the lap of water upon land.

My eyes swim and my breath catches but I can't follow, can't reach for the mug and its dregs. The sirens cry and wail out on the road, the sounds I can't make.

The machines beep and beep their orange, medical emergency. Someone will be along, or not. The mug tips out of Patty's hand and tea pours between us, stains the sheets.

CHAPTER SIXTY-ONE

A hand holds hers.

The first thing she becomes aware of.

The hand is not still. The hand squeezes and rubs. Worries at her skin until she thinks it will wear away and she will be bones. Mercer. He never could sit still.

Enough. Her hand on his knee, bouncing. Enough.

The hand is attached to a body, shifting. Restless.

Callan.

She wants the surface but cannot gain it. Wants to rest her hand on her boy's face. She has been under the water far too long.

The hand twitches. "Liss?"

She is not under water at all, but swimming, heavy, under a bath of white light.

"Liss, can you hear me?"

A face peers at her. Features out of order but sliding into place. Link.

"Hey," he says. "Hold on. I know who you really want to see."

WHEN SHE WAKES again, Callan is lying across her, arms outstretched as though he is diving. Asleep.

"Ah," she manages. She sees through slits. Her face, painful. Throat, sore. Head. Neck. Chin. She remembers flopping around the falling car and makes another noise.

She looks up at a movement across the room. A window, shade pulled. At the edge, a thin bar of white light. Daylight.

Someone stands there.

Mercer smiles. "Good morning," he says.

She had lost him, lost them both, lost them all and the beautiful, terrible world, too. But here they are. Enough, she thinks. More than enough.

CHAPTER SIXTY-TWO

Mercer had his elbows on the counter at the garage, begging, but nothing doing, the guy said. Total loss.

"Come on," Mercer said. "It's just a little water and a new windshield."

"It was a lot of water," Pete Norville said. He blinked away from the TV high in the corner of the workshop. "Not to mention the damage to your radiator, your strut assembly, and your alignment will never be right again. *And* a new windshield. It would cost you more to have me fix that car than it would be to purchase a new one. This is a mercy killing."

How could this guy be Larry Litigation's son? The apple had fallen pretty far from the tree. Pete was as fiercely uninterested in getting involved as Norville was frothing to jump in.

"If I get a new car, you know it's going to be ninety-nine percent computer," Mercer said. "You'll need a floppy disk to fix it, not a screwdriver."

"Look, if I could rescue it, I would," Pete said. "I've brought a lot of cars back from the dead. Yours is scrap metal."

If the election came through in a few weeks, he could put in for a new one. The town coffers might not take the blow, even with the savings he'd made possible, a couple of pensions no one had to pay now, a salary come to a hard stop. They'd have to see how things landed, how many lawsuits the town would be dragged into, with all the stories coming out. His crime rate wasn't likely to drop any time soon, that was for sure. He'd confirmed that little idea he'd had, that crime in Parkins had spiked in the first place because people weren't afraid to report to him the way they had been to Key. Some of them. Those who'd been squeezed for protection money had kept paying, waiting to see what he was made of. It shamed him that Slocum had gone on with business as usual, right under his nose.

"If it makes you feel any better, your cruiser isn't the biggest lost cause I ever dragged to the scrap yard," Pete said, turning back to the TV. "You ever seen a car set on fire?"

"Sure." Mercer came off his elbows. He'd have to use Slocum's car, though it smelled of cologne and old fast food.

"Total toast," Pete said. "Figured it was an insurance scam, you know? Funny thing, though," Pete said. "The windshield had a perfect noggin shape in it, a big ol' spider's web radiating out."

"Ouch," Mercer said. "Someone had a headache."

"No question," Pete said.

"Head injury, probably," Mercer said, thinking Pete was showing some Norville colors at last. The guy had never been this chatty with him. "Head injury, guaranteed, actually. Where'd you pick the burned-up car from?"

"Thought you'd never get around to asking." Pete reached for the TV and nudged it through a few channels. "Jim Ward offered the scrap to me for the tow, as long as I did it some evening, late. When he was there to supervise."

"Jim Ward's big on supervision," Mercer said, thinking. "Driver's side, was it? The bull's-eye in the glass?"

"Passenger," Pete said.

Mercer nodded. They both stared at the TV. "Why didn't you mention it to anyone until now?"

"Marshal, forgive me saying so," Pete said. "But nobody was listening until now."

MERCER DROVE UP to Mim's house with the window rolled down to let the stink out of Slocum's car. He slowed as he passed the Ward house. But it was closed up, no one in the yard.

Up at the Hubbard place, Sophie Ward stood in the garden, flannel and high rubber boots and breath coming in clouds. What was left to do there, he had no idea. He beckoned her over. She stared at him a moment, then dropped her gaze to the ground at her feet. She began to pull at her gloves, a finger at a time.

Mercer ducked back into the car for the flowers. A red petal had fallen to the floor.

Before he could get to the stairs, out she came.

"Mrs. Hubbard," Mercer said.

She had seen the flowers and sat heavily on the top step. She didn't correct him. "Roses."

He placed the bouquet into her arms.

"It was him?" she said. "That Slocum character? What they're saying is true?"

"One moment, please." He stepped back and called to the side of the house. "Mrs. Ward?"

She came around the corner with her head down, hair pulled back, a swipe of dirt at her chin. The gloves off and paired in one hand.

"Mrs. Ward," he said.

"Sophie," she said, barely a word.

"Ma'am, was there anything you'd been meaning to tell me, slipped your mind? Or Mim, here?"

The two women regarded one another.

"Maybe about what made you give up driving?" he said.

"I . . ."

"You used to give Robbie rides, after he sold his car," Mercer said.

"Sophie?" Mim said.

"It was an accident," Sophie whispered.

"You?" Mim said. "*You?*"

"I'm sorry," Sophie said. "I'm so sorry."

The old woman looked around her, bewildered. "And all this time? You thought a few tomatoes would set it right?"

"It's eaten me up," Sophie said. She made a move as though to go to Mim, but the old woman recoiled. "It's torn my family to bits—"

"*Your* family," Mim said. "*Your* family?"

Sophie stood back. It was true, though. Her family was in pieces.

Mercer would have to pull in Jim Ward for the details but he thought his calls to Liss's house had been a matter of throwing stones from glass houses, a distraction.

"You gave Robbie rides all over the place," Mercer said. "To work but also out to the Kehoes' place to bother Key and whoever would listen."

"It was an accident," Sophie said. "He wasn't wearing a seat belt and his head . . ."

Mercer thought Sophie Ward could still see perfectly what had happened to Robbie's head that night. Maybe she saw it in her mind's eye every time she thought about driving. About having the responsibility for another life ever again.

"It was an accident," she whispered.

"But the part where you left him on the road," Mercer said. "That was no accident."

"I'm sorry," Sophie pleaded. "Mim, I'm so sorry."

"Can you get her off my property?" Mim said.

"Yes, ma'am."

"It's not sweet at all, Marshal," Mim said, letting the roses sag in her arms. "What you brought me isn't sweet. Just nothing."

"I know," Mercer said. "I'm sorry you had to wait so long."

He put Sophie into the back of Slocum's car and then went back to help Mim to her feet and inside. She settled into her old, high-backed chair and looked around her, her eyes glassy. "You never know it, do you?" Mim said. "When it's the end."

On a side table sat a photo in a frame, Robbie Hubbard with a baby. Tucked into the corner was Callan Kehoe's most recent school picture.

Mercer said, "Mim, it's not the end until we say it is."

CHAPTER SIXTY-THREE

On the day they were getting ready for the courthouse, a photo on the mantel over the fireplace caught Liss's eye.

"Hurry up, please," she called up the stairs.

The photo stood out, a splash of bright color. Callan, newborn, rested in bright pink cable-knit arms, cozy and small as a bug. She'd found the photo during the move, and realized that she didn't mind the pink sweater anymore, the arms that weren't hers.

Now when Callan started to drive her to the edge of her sanity, Liss would look toward the mantel, local limestone, and find the pink sweater and her son, a tiny button. Remember to take a breath.

She went to the mantel, lifted the frame.

"I still owe you that memorial, Ashley," she said. "I haven't forgotten."

They'd held a service, but for Patty. A private cremation, Key weeping silently, parked in his chair among the flower arrangements, and Link gone mute in shock and misery.

"Why, though?" Link had asked upon learning Patty was the one who had struck the blow when Ashley came to the house on the hill. "I don't understand why she would need to do that."

"She thought she was protecting her family," Liss had said, because it was the truth. They'd had more in common than she liked to admit.

And if Link had really wanted to understand what Liss meant or why Ashley had gone to his parents' house in the first place, he would have kept asking. But he didn't.

He was too busy arranging Key's care and getting the big house ready for the market. The old house, too, of course, now vacant, and all the land around the pond and quarry. No one wanted it now, but they would. Tongues would stop wagging and memories would fade, and someone would see dollar signs. Time would move on, and so would they.

All of them.

Link was taking one of Key's aides on a date, Callan had reported the last time he'd come back from his dad's. And from the way Mercer reacted, Liss was very curious as to which one. But she didn't ask.

They were keeping things on a need-to-know basis. All of it. Mercer had untangled everything and then knotted it back up, just tidy enough for the public record and a deal for Slocum. In exchange for accepting a guilty plea and—nonnegotiable—his silence on certain topics that might hurt people who didn't have to be hurt, Slocum's charges would be dropped down a grade. But his property would be sold and the resulting bonanza split among the many who had funded it.

Mercer promised her Slocum would take the deal. Promised that Callan need never know who his biological father was, that Link's confusion over his mother's actions need never be cleared up.

Liss used the hem of her skirt to polish her fingerprints from the silver frame in her hands and put it back in place on the mantel, just so, matching the angle of those around it. Key, Patty, Link—photos of the Kehoes had been relegated to Callan's room at Link's apartment, but Liss didn't mind having a photo of Ashley in her house, not anymore. Ashley was part of the family.

"Callan," she sang up the stairs. "We need to go."

She'd given Callan the portrait of the three of them from her desk at school for his room, too. A few weeks after things finally settled down, Liss had remembered coming back to her desk one day to find the frame nudged out of its space, dust telling her that someone had come along to take a look. Vera, she supposed, looking at what she couldn't have.

Maybe Vera was the intruder in her house, too, the night Liss had seen a light where it shouldn't have been. Or maybe the intruder had been someone else entirely. The same person who had painted the barn. The one who had knocked down her mailbox. One of the people who had called nonstop for weeks. She would never know exactly who to trust again, but at least with Slocum taking blame for a few crimes, the frenzy had quieted down.

Of course it probably helped that she had upgraded her home security again, this time to a man in the house.

Liss stood at the bottom of the stairs and called up. "Mercer? We still have to pick up Mim."

It also helped that there were good people among the bad, something she had nearly forgotten. She could only try to be one of them.

"OK, OK," Mercer called back. Somewhere upstairs, a door opened and shut. He appeared at the top of the stairs, suit and tie, fresh haircut. He'd taken Callan with him to the barber and now Callan looked so grown up, it hurt. "Link's meeting us there?" Mercer said.

"Looking sharp," she said.

"This is right, right? I shouldn't wear the uniform?"

"No uniform," Liss said. "If you show up in your uniform, someone will say it's a publicity stunt. No election victory laps today, OK? Just family. Is he up there? Where is he?"

"I don't think he's up here," Mercer said, and went to check Callan's room.

Liss crossed to the front door and looked out the window. Out in the driveway, her car was already running, the windows scraped clean of the dusting of snow they'd had that morning, just enough to whiten the hills and fields.

There were fresh footprints leading from the house to the new car. Size twelves and still growing.

"Mercer, he's outside already," she called over her shoulder. "Let's go or we'll be late."

Footsteps on the stairs. Liss grabbed her coat and went to the door. "He thinks he's driving," she said.

"He needs the practice, right?"

"Not today." She was picturing the imposing stone pillars of the courthouse. "I'm already too nervous. Can you drive?"

Mercer squinted out the window. "The roads aren't *so* bad, and we're not actually late. How about he drives to Mim's, I supervise? You sit in the back and chew your nails. Also? You have nothing to be nervous *about*. It's all squared away, right? Today's a done deal."

It was a done deal long ago, no matter how long the paperwork took or what some judge had to say. A done deal from the moment Ashley transferred him to Liss's arms. Callan, crying even before he understood what he was losing.

But she would never stop worrying, that was the thing. Worrying about how he spent his time and who with, worrying about the injuries, body and heart, ahead of him. The new learner's permit was a small thing against the worry that every decision she made from here on out would somehow fold Callan into a smaller pocket of her life, and her, a smaller corner of his. Worrying what he would think of all this change and the changes she was still debating, pros and cons.

She'd have to make the big decision soon. She was still a young-enough woman to do it all again. The door was open, Mercer liked to say. He was smiling crookedly at her now, as though he knew what she was thinking. How much fun it would be. How much joy could be theirs.

And Callan old enough to baby-sit.

"Come on," Mercer said. "How else will he learn if you never let him take the wheel?"

She would worry, always. She was his mother.

"OK," she said. "OK, he can drive."

ACKNOWLEDGMENTS

Thank you to those who shared their expertise with me to get details in this book right: Mark Simison, a former reserve deputy marshal who helped clarify small-town policing procedures and equipment; Todd Thompson from the Indiana Geological and Water Survey, who helped me with quarries and quarry ponds; and Brian Schoon, Illinois State Police, Division of Forensic Services, who gave assistance with forensics. Thank you to Ellen and Tim Chapman for the introduction to Brian.

I am grateful for the time and attention my stories receive from the team at HarperCollins William Morrow, especially Emily Krump, Tessa James, and Liate Stehlik. Thanks also to Virginia Stanley and the Harper Library Marketing team, Chris Connolly for marketing and publicity, copy editor Sarajane Herman, proofreader Amanda Irle, designer Diahann Sturge, and cover designer Mark Robinson.

Sharon Bowers has been on this ride with me for seven books. I appreciate her support for everything I write but I also appreciate—not to be underestimated—texts that make me laugh.

Vera Chan won a Bouchercon Minneapolis charity auction bid to have her name slandered within these pages. Thank you, Vera!

I couldn't begin to thank all the people who have kept me together in the past two years, but I want to mention specifically

Susanna Calkins, Jessica Lourey, Shannon Baker, Erica Ruth Neubauer, Kim Rader, Kristi Brenock-Leduc, Catriona McPherson, Julie Hennrikus, Sandra SG Wong, Tracy Clark, Sara Paretsky, and Ann Cleeves. Also Kellye Garrett and Sherry Harris, and Julia Dahl, Laura McHugh, and Amy Gentry.

Thanks to Tracy Clark again for an early, reassuring read of this book.

Thanks to my entire family, but especially to my mom, Paula Dodson, and my sister, Jill Bryan, whose experiences as mothers have informed this story.

Thanks to Anne Lamott for *Bird by Bird*.

Thank you, as always, to my readers and to booksellers and librarians everywhere for the work they do. Please support those who fight for your right to read whatever you want. (For more information about fighting book bans, visit www.ftrf.org, the Freedom to Read Foundation.)

"Thanks" is hardly enough for Gregory Day, who makes this wild life possible and every day infinitely better. Also, when we're walking our dog, Clementine, he lets me talk out plot points and helps me select the right car to sink into a quarry.

ABOUT THE AUTHOR

Lori Rader-Day is the Edgar Award–nominated and Agatha, Anthony, and Mary Higgins Clark Award–winning author of *The Death of Us*, *Death at Greenway*, *The Lucky One*, *Under a Dark Sky*, *The Day I Died*, *Little Pretty Things*, and *The Black Hour*. She lives in Chicago, where she is cochair of the mystery readers' event Midwest Mystery Conference and teaches creative writing at Northwestern University. She has an MFA in creative writing from Roosevelt University and degrees in journalism from Ball State University. She is a former national president of Sisters in Crime and a member of Mystery of America.

EXPLORE
LORI RADER-DAY'S
OTHER THRILLERS

THE DAY I DIED

Anna Winger can know people better than they know themselves with only a glance—at their handwriting. Hired by companies wanting to land trustworthy employees and by the lovelorn hoping to find happiness, Anna likes to keep the real-life mess of other people at arm's length. But when she is called to use her expertise on a note left behind at a murder scene in the small town she and her son have recently moved to, the crime gets under Anna's skin and rips open her narrow life for all to see. To save her son—and herself—once and for all, Anna will face her every fear, her every mistake, and the past she thought she'd rewritten.

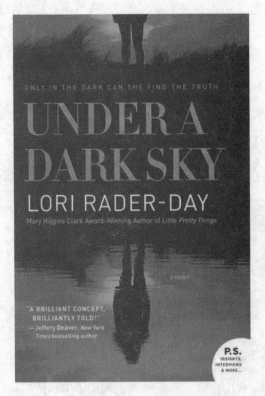

UNDER A DARK SKY

Since her husband died, Eden Wallace's life has diminished to a tiny pinprick, like a far-off star in the night sky. She doesn't work, has given up on her love of photography, and is so plagued by night terrors that she can't sleep without the lights on. Everyone, including her family, has grown weary of her grief. So when she finds paperwork in her husband's effects indicating that he reserved a week at a dark sky park, she goes. She's ready to shed her fear and return to the living, even if it means facing her paralyzing phobia of the dark.

But when she arrives at the park, the guest suite she thought was a private retreat is teeming with a group of twentysomethings, all stuck in the orbit of their old college friendships. Horrified that her get-away has been taken over, Eden decides to head home the next day. But then a scream wakes the house in the middle of the night. One of the friends has been murdered. Now everyone—including Eden—is a suspect.

Everyone is keeping secrets, but only one is a murderer. As mishaps continue to befall the group, Eden must make sense of the chaos and lies to evade a ruthless killer—and she'll have to do it before dark falls...